ADDIE'S HANDS PUSHED WEAKLY AT HIS CHEST, BUT HER FINGERS ALSO CURLED TO BRING HIM BACK.

His body flowed into hers, and she instinctively arched in shock at the intimate contact of his hard, uncompromising strength. Her head swam so fretfully, she didn't know whether to resist the pleasure or give in to it.

"Why?" Zeke said as his lips grazed her cheek and jaw, then moved down to the tight cords of her throat. She didn't flinch or move away, just hung limp against the buckboard.

"I can't breathe." Her words feathered over his cheek and his body tightened to even that mere stimulus.

"You can. You are," he said, feeling the staggered rise and fall of her breasts against his chest. He tried to hide his immediate reaction—a surge of raw lust so powerful it made him tremble—but he couldn't seem to stop himself from reaching for her. His senses were overflowing with the sensual limpness of her body, the innocence of her response. She didn't know herself very well, and the challenge set before him, to help her discover her own passionate nature, surged through him with alarming potency. . . .

LIBBY SYDES

UNTIL SPRING

A Dell Book

Published by
Dell Publishing
a division of
Bantam Doubleday Dell Publishing Group, Inc.
1540 Broadway
New York, New York 10036

The trademark Dell® is registered in the U.S. Patent and Trademark Office.

ISBN: 0-440-21541-2

Printed in the United States of America

Published simultaneously in Canada

November 1993

10 9 8 7 6 5 4 3 2 1

OPM

For Katie, Beau, and Stetson.
You are the best
of all God's blessings
to me.

Prologue

Wyoming Territory, 1875

Anyone under ninety and not half-blind could tell that Mary Adaline Smith was beaten down by life. Not that anyone much cared to notice. When the fine, upstanding citizens of Laramie did bother to look closely, all they saw was a willow-thin frame, nondescript features on a pale face, and lackluster honey-blond hair.

All they felt was pity.

And pity, mingled with the guilt that caused it, was just too hard on their collective consciences. They had all abandoned her; whether outright or unintentionally, all in their own way had managed to turn their backs on her at a time when she had needed them most. It still plagued them like an arthritic joint, a dull pain they tried to ignore to ease their troubled minds.

In a town erected eight years earlier with five hundred structures of canvas, old wagon boxes, and discarded railroad ties to greet the approaching Union Pacific Railroad, there wasn't much room for pity. And in a town whose first newcomers included land sharks, gamblers, harlots, and proprietors of movable shops and saloons, there wasn't much room for anything but keeping the peace.

Still, they couldn't forget that once, four years that stretched like a lifetime ago, Addie had been a sweet, bright fifteen-year-old with an angel's laughter and a teenager's zest for life that had kept her hard-working papa smiling. But it had been a long time since Addie had smiled. These past four years had stripped everything from her but a will to survive—a will that was slowly and painfully crumbling.

There was spirit still, almost buried too deep now to show beneath Addie's thin shoulders, but it showed anyway as she made a quick glance around the deserted graveyard, then defiantly kicked a clump of dirt on the newly turned mound of earth.

Willis Harvey Smith, Addie's husband of four years, had been buried at dawn. She felt no sadness, no remorse, and, more important, no guilt. Nothing but a numbness and emptiness so much safer than the black rage deep inside her. The small outburst was quickly followed by a narrowing of her green eyes and a guarded look, as if she expected a reprimand or punishment. No blow came, no curse rent the air, nothing assailed her but sweet, soft silence.

Willis was well and truly dead. She was free. A tiny flutter of relief formed in her breast and almost burst upon her face in a long-forgotten smile. Like a prisoner released on pardon, she wanted to run and shout and dance like a fairy among the swaying wheat grass, but being in a graveyard demanded a bit of decorum, so she merely turned her face up to the sun and inhaled deeply, as if she could fill her entire body with its warmth. A brisk wind ruffled the curls around her face, sending a chill down her spine. With the cold came reality, intrusive and undermining, stabbing through her with the relentless uncertainty of her situation. Her joy quickly faded, to be replaced by an inkling of rising fear.

What in this god-awful world was she going to do now?

With more energy, she sent another spray of dirt over the mound with the toe of her worn shoe, as if her foot had a will of its own that the deeper, more integral parts of her self were lacking. She almost wished it were her own skinny body lying at eternal rest, but she was either too cowardly or too stubborn to go down in defeat. She was no longer certain which person resided in the heart of her. She'd lost so much herself, she didn't pretend to guess. But with Willis dead, she was determined to get it back.

She darted a glance at the heavens and wondered if God was really there. Addie couldn't think of anything she'd done to deserve her wretched lot in life up to now, but someone had. Some evil ancestor must have done plenty for the "sins of the father" to travel down this many generations and get stuck on her.

She kicked another clump of dirt, sending her faded skirts billowing out to catch the rising breeze. She was barely nineteen, looked a decade older, and felt ancient. She'd been married since she was fifteen because her parents and younger siblings had been killed when a band of renegade Indians had attacked their small farmhouse and burned it to the ground. The bank had gotten the land and what was left of the stock. Willis had gotten Addie.

Scared and lonely and grieving, fifteen-year-old Mary Adaline Wortham had married a man twenty years her senior—and regretted every second of it after. On his good days, Willis had been lazy, unattractive, and mean. On his bad days, he had been viciously insulting, cruelly vindictive, and heavy-handed. After four years of too many bad days, Addie had killed him.

No one accused her; no one blamed her. No one even cared that Willis Harvey Smith had departed this earth in a violent manner. Of course, no one knew exactly what had happened, but the fact still remained that no one cared.

Least of all Addie. Her only regret now was that she hadn't done it sooner.

The sheriff had asked questions—"Beg pardon, Miz Addie, just doin' my job"—and when he was finished he had murmured something about "accidental death" and given Addie his condolences. He had then proceeded, in his easy no-nonsense way, to offer advice about a possible alternative to her lowly circumstance, then tipped his hat in farewell and told her to take some time and think about it.

That well-meaning advice had Addie thinking all right. She bent and picked up the dirt clod, packed it tight in her small palms, then drew her arm back and hurled it at the grave with every ounce of strength she possessed.

What in this god-awful world was she going to do now?

1

Zeke Claiborne stood on the porch of his modest but sturdy home and watched the riders approach. They were mere specks in the distance, dusty black silhouettes against a blazing midday sun, but he knew their destination. He pulled his hat from his head and ran his fingers through his hair in frustration. *This was a very bad idea.*

Pulling his eyes away from the riders, he stared out over the land. Vast, unconquerable, and irredeemable, it was a land formed and shaped by the majesty of a mightier hand beyond mere mortal comprehension. A gentle wind moved over the bluegrass, tufted fescue, and redtops, blending colors with a soft innocence that was deceiving. It was a land impossible to tame. Zeke had learned to partake of the bounty, to live and breathe and become one with it, carefully and constructively. Anything else would have been arrogant and fruitless. The land was as wild as it was majestic, harsh as it was beautiful, and cruel when it chose. It would easily destroy anyone who tried to seize it.

He no longer fought the savage changeable seasons,

but had learned to meld and flow with the violent winter storms and bask in the short sweet summers—the reward for stamina and survival. Cottonwoods and willows bordered the creek that stretched across his acres before winding into the mountains, lending grace to the wild terrain with its crystal-clear water running over slate-gray stones. At times it reflected the deep blue of the sky between snowy white banks; at others it raged stormy from the spring thaw, swelling dangerously from the runoff of melting snow. Summer came green and alive along its borders, pastel wildflowers amid a cushion of sweet grass, a place to rest and reflect. The mountains rose in all directions, like sentries robed in stone and evergreen to guard the fertile valley. Zeke had never seen anything that encompassed more strength and beauty, that commanded more respect.

His gaze shifted, as it so often had in the past months, to the stone marker on the far hill. Pronghorn and antelope grazed there, strong graceful beasts unaware of the price he'd had to pay, the toll the land had demanded. His eyes were bleak and empty, long past angry. *I'm in a fix, Becky. You sure left me in a fix.* But Becky didn't answer. She'd been gently placed in a grave beneath the willow tree nine long, agonizing months ago.

He had given her everything. Every part and particle of himself that the war between the states had not managed to strip clean, he had offered to Becky. It hadn't been enough. Bit by bit, the war had destroyed the southern gentleman who had gone off to fight and recarved him into an adult who saw survival as the greatest challenge, perhaps the only one. Gone was the grand house on rich Mississippi soil flowing with servants, the gardens where ladies gowned in high fashion strolled beneath the moss-draped oaks. Gone was the way of life he and Becky in youth and arrogance had accepted as their due, along with the dreams they had both held for the future. He didn't blame Becky—he bore little resemblance to the young man she'd fallen in love with—but neither could he fully forgive her. She had never learned to become a part of this new land, the new inheritance he was building for their future.

Feeling stricken and helpless, he had listened to and abandoned the circuit rider's words of comfort while watching his neighbors fill the hole. With each shovelful, an emptiness had filled him until there was nothing left inside but the need to get on with living. There had been no time for mourning and no inclination. Grief had been an obstacle he shoved brutally aside in order to get on with his life. Becky was gone, but she had left three sons behind, three young souls counting on him to be everything they needed.

Zeke leaned against the porch rail and closed his eyes briefly against the overwhelming responsibility and burden of being mother, father, teacher, God. "Damn," he said, sounding tired because he was—deep-down tired to his soul.

Eagles soared in the distance, high above the rocky crags where mountain sheep roamed, their thick wool protecting them as the mountain walls did from harsh snowfalls. But elk and mule deer would be moving down to the lower slopes soon, foraging for food to survive another winter. The weather was unpredictable now, portentous, changing daily from icy to balmy. Everywhere the tremor of uncertainty quivered, taut as a stretched wire, for the first real winter storm.

The livestock were restless, their noses sniffing the air more often lately for a hint of what was to come. Mountain lions and lynx, unseen but heard in the higher reaches, cried eerily in agitation while black bears and grizzlies hunted for their holes.

Zeke felt a similar agitation along his own limbs, the restive unease of a man gone too long without certain masculine comforts along with the ever-present weariness of being behind schedule when winter was so close. He squinted into the sun as the riders drew nearer and wondered briefly if he was going senile or merely insane for not taking time to think things through more carefully.

Sheriff Jake Holdman had caught him unawares and vulnerable several days ago, walking into the calamity of early evening when the boys were too hungry and exhausted to be patient while Zeke juggled evening chores, empty bellies, and general discontent. The baby had been sick again and kept him up for two nights crying. Because of the wind, he hadn't been able to take Cole back out to finish chores, and he wouldn't leave him inside with Zeb, who was barely four, or Joshua, who was eight going on eighteen because he'd had to pull the weight of two grown boys. Jake had caught him when his defenses were not only down but annihilated.

Zeke's eyes narrowed resentfully at the riders. The fact that a bunkhouse had to be built and cowhands hired by the spring roundup meant nothing compared to his more immediate needs: the cow needed milking, the other livestock needed tending, three piles of dirty laundry needed washing, and there was no supper on the stove. He didn't have time for a social call.

Dust rose in small clouds beneath the horses' hooves until their pace slowed to the point of inertia. After a brief conversation, one hung back by the gate, obviously wary and unsure. The other continued forward.

This was a very bad idea.

* * *

Sheriff Jake Holdman reined in sharply when he reached Zeke Claiborne's front steps. His friend's eyes were hard, remote, as isolated as the land surrounding them. Jake was used to the look. He'd seen it often during the years they'd spent fighting a losing battle for the South, and more often recently. Zeke had shut himself off and there was nothing Jake could do for now. He turned around in the saddle and tried to smile encouragement at Mary Adaline Smith waiting in the distance, but when he turned back to Zeke his look was speculative.

It didn't matter that they had settled this yesterday, or that time was of the essence. Winter was moving in faster than a cat with his tail on fire and Addie was likely to starve to death in the next few weeks without assistance, while Zeke was working himself into an early grave trying to care for his ranch, his chores, and his three motherless children.

But none of that mattered. When Zeke had that look, there was nothing Jake could do but wait. *Shee-it!*

"Mornin'," he said, just for the hell of it.

Zeke nodded and noticed the lines of fatigue and concern around Jake's eyes. Laramie wasn't the most ideal place to be responsible for law and order. From its inception, the town had tried setting up a temporary government, but outlaws had overrun the streets. Within a month, officials had given up trying to maintain order, and vigilantes had taken over fighting the desperadoes, even lynching and killing several at the Belle of the West Saloon. The federal courts had finally established jurisdiction over the city, but now, almost eight years later, the mentality of those early days still lingered. Jake had his work cut out for him—too much work to be dabbling in this type of nonsense.

Zeke smiled. Though it was spare and sardonic, there were too many years of close friendship between the two men for him not to offer one. He cocked his head toward the gate. "What's she doing?"

Jake shrugged and glanced back over his shoulder. "She wanted me to talk to you again, to make sure."

Zeke offered no response, nothing but a silence and stillness that had been coming more and more easily these past nine months. He was well aware that he had walled off the emptiness in his heart, guarded it like a barricade to keep out any intrusion, but he liked the painless void. The absence of emotion kept him clear-headed and moving forward instead of wallowing in grief. Understanding his shortcomings as well as he did his obligations, he knew that Jake deserved better than his rudeness. But it was beyond him to conjure up useless, idle conversation when they both knew why the sheriff was here.

They had known each other since childhood, boys growing up in Natchez, Mississippi, before the war had ripped family and friendships into tattered rags. There had been three of them then—Zeke, Jake, and Christian—privileged blood brothers of southern aristocracy, young and idealistic, who hadn't known what war meant when they joined the cause, hadn't known how it would rend everything from them but their lives.

The war had gouged out so many chunks of what they had been then—boys of educated, genteel upbringing with notions of honor and dignity toward family and country. They had returned home hardened into callous young men, stripped of everything but an empty future and the vestiges of a background that had not prepared them for the dogged determination needed to start over. They had survived, but not without the internal scars inherent to war. Standing beside the charred remains of Zeke's plantation home, the three men had made a pact to rebuild, but not in the South, where their loss was so new, the memories too keen. Their agreement eventually brought them to a hostile and untamed land that proved as desolate at times as what they had left behind. There wasn't much of those boys left in the men they had become, not in their lifestyles or attitudes or actions. What remained was an understanding and kinship that could never be cut off or ignored.

Zeke shifted his gaze to stare at the young woman in the distance, not because he particularly wanted to acknowledge her, but because at this point in his life he was needy. Not just for a woman, but for the help of one.

She was small and formless, undefinable from this distance. Zeke tried to remember if they had ever met, ever said more than two words to each other. He drew a complete blank. She was nothing to him. He couldn't put a face or voice or any recollection to her at all except to lump her with the citizens he saw regularly in town but had never gotten to know.

The old code of ethics had decayed, but there was enough intrinsic honor left in Zeke to make him feel trapped by the agreement he'd made with Jake as he stared at the nondescript person sitting silently on a borrowed horse. He sent his gaze back to the sheriff with a smile so brittle Jake thought he hadn't seen the like since the battle of Stones River.

"How's Christian doing these days?"

Jake stiffened in the saddle. *Why don't you slap this guilt on him?* was easily translated from Zeke's chilly look. Jake managed to suppress an ugly rejoinder but his tone was gritty. "Christian's fine, I reckon."

Zeke looked away, chagrined by his own nastiness, needing to find an apology that wouldn't surface. He was no longer on speaking terms with the man who had once been as much a part of him as his own flesh, the man whose morals the war had eroded the most. It was water under the bridge, as they say, but stagnant and still reeking of what had passed among them.

At the implacable look on Zeke's face, Jake snatched his hat from his head and slapped it against his thigh, raising a cloud of dust. "Dammit, Zeke. Christian don't need her. You do."

Zeke gripped the porch rail, fighting the urge to deny it. Jake's face had grown as bright as his sandy-red hair, his freckles standing out in prominent relief. His fair coloring had never allowed him to hide his emotions.

"She doesn't seem particularly agreeable to the idea," Zeke said, but knew she probably would be. She had married Willis, after all. He shifted his weight from one lean hip to the other, then curled his fingers into a fist to keep from slamming them into something. "I'm sorry for her, Jake . . . but damn."

The sheriff's voice held neither conviction nor condemnation, just hard, cold truth. "She don't have time for you to decide. If you've changed your mind, tell me now. Sarah and the girls are doing all they can, but Addie's got her pride. She don't like accepting charity any better than the rest of us would. I'm sorta scared she might do something foolish."

Zeke closed his eyes, deepening the frown lines on his forehead, which seemed to be getting more evident by the day. "I can't save her, Jake," he said roughly. "Can't you see I'm too busy trying to save myself?"

Jake saw plenty—a good man gone hard with life's cruelties, a generous man with nothing left to give. His voice carried the intimacy and forgiveness of long-held friendships forged stronger by adversity. "Look, it's not like she won't have any offers. A single woman out here is a rare commodity, ripe for the picking. There'll be cowhands and miners aplenty sniffing around her, but I was hoping it would be you. She's a good girl, Zeke. She deserves better than what she got last time. God knows, you could use the help."

Zeke leaned his forehead against the post and smiled wryly at the irony of Jake's statement. He was hardly the man for any woman at this point in his life. Better for her to take up with a miner who'd greet her at the end of the day with his heart and his pockets full of gold—or a sheriff with noble intentions. "What about you, Jake?"

The sheriff shrugged casually, but a slight flush rose to his cheeks. "My sister-in-law might feel displaced if I brought another woman into the house. It's too soon after Brent's death for her to go looking around for another husband."

And you're half in love with her and won't even admit it to yourself, Zeke thought, but let it go unsaid. Baiting Jake over something so personal wouldn't help matters. He didn't know why he was stretching this out. He had made his mind up the night before last at two in the morning, sitting in a rocking chair that had more miles on it than his ten-year-old mule. The decision had come easily in the predawn hours with the baby on his shoulder making uneven little hiccuping sobs from crying himself back to sleep. Zeke hadn't dared put him down, or all four of them would have been up the rest of the night. But what had been so easy then, now sat like a stone in his gut.

He pulled his head back and chuckled painfully at life's little satires. "Hell of a mess, Jake." The sheriff wanted a woman he couldn't have, and Zeke could have a woman he didn't want. His eyes lifted to the front gate, but his face and voice held no expression at all. "Go on and get her. If I'm going to marry Addie Smith, I guess I'd better meet her."

2

Lord, she's homely.

It was the first thought to enter Zeke Claiborne's head as the young woman dismounted, then walked up the front steps of his house beside Jake. The second was that his first impression had been wrong. He might have lived in this town for close to eight years but he had never really noticed Mary Adaline Smith. He'd seen her in church, but not often. He'd tipped his hat to her in town on shopping days. He was bound to have passed her in the general store. But he'd never really looked at her. He did so now, thoroughly, and saw what most of Laramie saw: thin, unremarkable, life-beaten Addie. And a little something more.

Her hair was a wild mass of curls, honey-blond corkscrews so tightly wound they barely hung past her shoulders. A closer inspection of her face revealed nice, even features and delicate bone structure on a countenance that would have been lovely had it not been so utterly worn out. Lacking any hint of artifice, her face with its gently curved mouth and pastel cheeks held the classic beauty of old money and good breeding, timeless. Yet timeworn, it had been cruelly stripped of innocence. In another time, another place, he would have felt sorry for the gaunt creature carrying herself forward with numb, self-protective fortitude, but his life didn't have room for pity and his needs overrode any emotion beyond getting help for his boys.

Land sakes, he's handsome! Addie paused when she got to the top step, unable to continue under his steady gaze. She knew what he was thinking as his eyes traveled over her; she'd thought the same things herself. Her eyes traveled right back when he turned to say something to the sheriff, but her thoughts weren't at all the same as his must have been.

Zeke Claiborne was an extremely attractive man. Tall, broad shouldered, and golden, his presence commanded light and symmetry, dominating space and throwing everything else around him into shadow. Propped against the porch timber, arms crossed over his trim belly, he had a lean-hipped grace that said he was easygoing, but there was a sternness around his mouth that promised he could be unforgiving. An evening growth of beard shadowed his firm jaw, making him look rough and lawless, perfectly at home in a land of unparalleled beauty and danger.

She had heard the rumors and wondered now if there was any credit to them. It was said that he had been part of a southern dynasty that had crumbled during the war. His family had been wealthy landholders who had lost everything. It was also said that Zeke had ridden with an outlawed vigilante gang for a short time after the South surrendered, trying to help others keep from losing their homes as well to the carpetbaggers. There was that quality about him that hinted at long-ago sophistication, but it was so buried now beneath hard layers that the only thing remaining on the surface was a cool, tempered control—a vengeful golden demigod fallen from his throne. A small shiver of uncertainty moved over her limbs. Stylized in pen and ink, he would have made the perfect portrait of a gunslinger.

He also looked like a man who knew what he wanted, and he didn't want Addie. It was easy to see from the cool reserve in his eyes, the way he intrinsically separated himself without so much as moving back an inch, that he didn't want to go through with this dang-fool plan of the sheriff's any more than she did.

She was grateful, at least, for that.

She fought the urge to duck her head like a scared turtle, and looked him straight in the eyes. His were autumn brown, almost too pretty for a man with their thick fringe of sable lashes, but they were haunted eyes, deep and soulful and hard. A little ripple of foreboding inched up her spine, and she paused to grip the handrail.

With part determination, part desperation, she dared to stare more deeply into his amber eyes and found something worse, a familiar and frightening understanding. The earth tilted beneath her and her stomach lifted, a weightless pause, then settled back in dread. This man had secrets, maybe worse ones than she did. Addie wasn't at all sure that was a good thing. A right risky thing, in fact.

Her gaze shied away. No matter how determined she might have been a second ago, she couldn't hold his stare. Even when he was relaxed, there was energy in this man. It hummed, radiating power and influence. Yet subtle, so deceptively *smooth*, like a candle flame— beautiful, alive, and utterly dangerous when touched.

Wide-eyed, her mouth suddenly dry as cotton, she

glanced over at the sheriff and said softly, "This was a very bad idea." Then she turned on her heel and sprinted back down the steps as fast as her legs would carry her, straight toward the horse. Dust churned beneath her feet as they pounded the ground, but her heart pounded much harder in her chest. She gave no thought to the idiotic picture she must present to the men behind her, just that she get as far away from them as possible. She wouldn't be caught again, encircled in a snare of dominance like a caged animal awaiting the master's scraps.

Jake sent Zeke a startled, accusatory look and took off after her. His hands caught her around the waist just as she started to mount the horse and lifted her away. "Miz Addie, wait," he said, lowering her to the ground. She rounded on him with a panicked look and backed up until he couldn't reach her.

"Don't come any closer, Sheriff!" she demanded, one small hand raised as if she could ward him off. Breathing hard from exertion, she stood poised and ready to abandon the horse and run for the road—and keep on running until she'd outrun the sheriff's insane idea.

It wasn't her unprecedented flight or her panicked, angry eyes that struck Zeke. It was the words she had stolen from his own thoughts. "Yes, wait," he commanded softly.

Mortified by her outrageous behavior, she glanced back up to see that Zeke was still leaning idly against the post, one dark eyebrow lifted over his piercing eyes in scrutiny. He hadn't moved an inch, not one, as if he didn't care a whit whether she ran straight for the hills or collapsed right there in the yard. She tore her eyes away and looked back at the sheriff, her expression fierce yet pleading.

Jake stared back at her with a cross between compassion and pity. "What else are you gonna do, Miz Addie?"

"Something . . ." she said, as if there were. But there was nothing else and they both knew it. The truth was ugly but accurate, and she wouldn't disgrace either of them again by pretending otherwise. Practical even in desperation, she straightened her spine and lifted her small chin a fraction. Taking a deep breath, she marched back to the house and up two of the three steps, then stood as if awaiting sentencing.

Zeke pushed off the post and finished the survey of her scuffed old shoes to her faded dress, then tipped his hat back to study her pale face as if the small drama had never occurred. Her back was rod-straight, prudishly haughty. Her eyes were a curious mixture of light and shadow, green as spring clover or new grass, but without any life now. She presented neither challenge nor capitulation, just a weary intelligence that this had to be faced. And in that instant something passed between them—a tentative understanding, a wary acceptance. A touching of two souls whose lives were unaccountably intertwined with needs unacceptable to both but unalterable.

He touched his hat brim to her the way he'd done countless times on main street. "Miz Addie."

Now as then, it brought an odd flush to her cheeks.

"Mr. Claiborne." She took another breath and stepped fully onto the porch. A long time ago she'd dreamed of a house with a porch.

Jake Holdman hung back, feeling unsettled but right about this. His cheeks grew uncomfortably ruddy as he cleared his throat. "Guess you two have a few things to discuss. I'll just go on out to the barn—"

Addie's head whipped around and the expression on her white face was daunting. As if aware that she had revealed too much, the wildness left her eyes and receded into a self-protective vacancy that stripped all animation from her face. Her gaze darted between the two men, then took refuge in the boards beneath her feet.

Zeke eyed her oddly. A spark of curiosity, long dead and reined in as were all his other emotions, experienced a twinge at the rapid transformation from passionate supplication to blank resignation. Twice now her emotions had swung from one extreme to the other, keeping him from fully assessing the balance of her character. The wind was rising, as it did this time of day, scattering her outrageous curls in sun-drenched spirals. For a brief second he wished he could see her eyes again, then abandoned it as unimportant. Her shifting moods weren't his concern. He slid a glance at the sheriff. "This was your idea, Jake. There's no need for you to go."

Addie only nodded in agreement, feeling hot and tight all over though frigid winds were already blowing strong out of the north. Winter would be here soon, the roads impassable, long cold days spent cooped up inside with this man if they went through with the sheriff's suggestion. Her heart thumped once, twice, heavy with dread before a tiny burst of anger exploded within her at the unfairness of this whole situation and the compromises she was forced to accept. She peered out from underneath her lashes and met dark golden eyes, piercing and knowing, as if they could look right inside her thoughts. Quickly schooling her features, she lifted her chin.

"I imagine you've got some questions," Zeke said.

The comment surprised her, though the deep timbre

of his voice was expected. As distinctly southern as Spanish moss and perfumed magnolias, it held the same qualities as his physical appearance, easygoing yet strong and dominant. Addie wondered just how strong and dominant. She ignored the tug of uneasiness and nodded. She had plenty of questions, tons and tons, but none of the courage it would take to ask them. She pulled a prim and proper countenance around her like a shield and tried for just one.

"I guess, I do, Mr. Claiborne." She clasped her hands together, tight. "I'm sorry about your Becky, she was always real nice to me . . . I know why you're needing a wife. I guess . . . what are you expecting in one?"

Zeke disliked the hesitancy in her voice, though he approved the tone. Soft and clear and cultured, it didn't match her tired looks. "I need a wife to cook and clean and be good to the kids. That's all." His eyes took another cursory run over her. "I don't expect anything else." He avoided glancing over at Jake, wishing the sheriff had gone off to the barn after all. This woman would share his bed like any other wife, but not his heart or his affections or his emotions. Beyond the fact that she was in dire straits, he didn't know her aspirations or expectations for this marriage, but she needed to understand that there would be no hope for emotional intimacy. There was nothing left in him to offer it. "I don't want anything else."

"I see," she said slowly, and hoped to God she did. She dropped her gaze back to the porch, feeling flushed and uncomfortable under his steady regard. "You sure?" She peeked back up to see Zeke give a clipped nod, and let go of the breath she hadn't known she was holding. Her lips puffed out on a bracing sigh. "Well . . . what do I get?"

"I'll provide you with the things a husband usually gives a wife in the way of shelter, food, and clothing, and you would be at liberty to ask for anything I don't think of. I'm not rich, not yet anyway, but I'm not miserly with what I do have. If you don't ask for more than I can provide, we'll get along tolerable."

She contained her immediate reaction: a flare of indignation through the protective layers of numbness set in stony fixity within her. Did he think she was just out to better herself? *I'm not rich.* He had one of the finest spreads she'd seen in these parts, or at least the potential for one, except for the place owned by Liz and Mark Simmons, who everyone knew were too uppity for their own good. He had a huge barn, not just a shed, and it wasn't even falling down. A herd of healthy cattle grazed on pastureland as far as the eye could see, and he also had horses, pigs, and chickens, all of them penned and caged, not roaming loose leaving their droppings everywhere. A good-sized garden had been picked clean and another acre lay ready for spring planting.

She gazed around and thought of her own rough-timbered shanty, her decrepit shed, her strip of poor ground that yielded nothing more during the short growing season than puny vegetables that her two pigs rooted up before she could. Suddenly, a yearning so deep it embarrassed her surged along her veins and escalated the tempo of her heartbeat, causing her cheeks to flush with a false hope that she knew better than to indulge.

Before she could control the impulse, her small chin jutted out even farther. No matter what he thought, she didn't want his money, didn't want him or any other man. But a woman without wealth and not much school-

ing couldn't make it on her own, at least not respect-
ably. It didn't matter that the territorial legislature of
Wyoming had been the first governmental body in the
world to grant women equal voting rights with men, or
that the court had called the first women jurors in
United States history. With no business of her own or
the capital to start one, she'd be reduced to working in a
saloon, and she just couldn't abide that. She needed
food and shelter, a little fabric for patching and a little
extra for a new dress when hers wore out. All that would
be enough. She didn't need riches, especially his.

The firm set of her chin didn't go unnoticed by Zeke.
"What else?" he said suddenly, making her jump. "I
imagine you've got more questions."

Addie took another breath. There were things she
had to know, all right, but she was in no position to
bargain. Starvation was a poor substitute for a warm
cabin this winter, but she wouldn't spend another four
years like the ones past at any cost. She wavered only a
second before her eyes widened and she spoke with a
directness that bordered on defiance. "Do you drink,
Mr. Claiborne?"

Her fierceness wasn't well suited to her pale face and
pole-backed posture. She looked more like a little girl
facing down a bully than a widow at the edge of penury.
"Milk in the morning and about a gallon of water a
day," he drawled.

Addie blinked, then felt the pink climb her cheeks.
Irony dripped from his tone, but it wasn't cruel. She
couldn't recollect that anyone had teased her since her
brothers were alive. "Liquor, Mr. Claiborne. Do you
indulge?"

A sudden hard twinkle lit his eyes at her ruffled look.
She had grit, he'd give her that, but not much humor.

He didn't know what had possessed him to provoke her. Perhaps the jut of her small chin, the stiff and prim pose of her body in the pathetic dress, or the strange desire to see more than resignation in her green eyes. His withdrawal was immediate and evident in his cool voice, but a spark of lazy speculation remained in his eyes. "I have a nip on occasion, parties and town dances and such. Jake here can vouch for me that it's nothing serious."

Jake was nodding, but Addie had never been to a party or town dance, so she wasn't convinced. Still, she could hardly argue against the two of them, so she continued haltingly, "Did . . . did . . ." Her voice petered away with her nerve. This one was much harder but twice as necessary. Gathering her raveling composure, she cleared her throat and blurted out, "Did you ever beat your wife before she died?" *Stupid! That was so stupid, Addie!*

A deafening pause fell around them before he answered drolly, "Only on Sundays before she died."

Addie's eyes went round as saucers. The sheriff slammed his hat against his knee. "Now, look here—"

"Simmer down, Jake," Zeke soothed, regretting whatever insanity had driven him to tease her even the tiniest bit over such a perverse question. It was obvious she hadn't asked it idly. He had to respect the bravery it took to reveal her past, however roundabout, in order to protect her future. But he couldn't tolerate the spark of sympathy it ignited in him, or the picture it conjured of a young girl in the cruel hands of a drifter like Willis. His voice was honest but dispassionate when he spoke. "I'm sorry, Miz Addie, that was tasteless. I assure you, I've never hit a woman in my life."

His eyes narrowed as he looked about the homestead,

and Addie watched a grimness shade his handsome face, as if the world had suddenly grown darker. His voice was emotionless and removed when he spoke.

"I'm not mourning Becky anymore. Nine months isn't long, but there's no time and no inclination with three small sons to raise." He looked straight at her, his eyes forceful yet strangely compelling. "I can't spend the rest of my life grieving; I don't think anyone should."

Neither heard Jake's snort, so intent were they upon one another and their innate need to remain separate yet understood.

"Don't worry about me," Addie said. "The only time I mourned Willis was when he was alive." Zeke's own eyes flared, and Addie felt a bit of satisfaction in that, then a tiny itch of fledgling rebellion. Honesty was as natural to her as breathing, but like so much else in her life it had been drained out of her. Move with care and caution, stay on the perimeters out of notice, out of the line of fire. Still, she couldn't stop the impetus that drove her. "Some say I killed him, you know."

Zeke didn't look at Jake, though the sheriff was staring a hole through him. Neither had liked Willis Smith any better than the rest of the town. "Did you?"

She stared at him in reticence so long, he didn't think she would answer. An emptiness seeped back into her eyes as she slid a quick glance at the sheriff. When she looked back her expression was old and weary and un-committed.

"Might have. Guess no one will ever really know but me and Willis and God."

It wasn't her voice that struck him, but the emotions underneath—tired anguish, abject pain, and the fierce need to control them. Zeke retreated immediately be-hind a barrier of unconcern, far removed from anything that could make him see or feel or recognize the suffering inside her. Her demons were inconsequential to his needs and God knew he had enough of his own. His expression was bland as he lifted one dark eyebrow, but there was a hard glint in his eyes. "You gonna kill me, Miz Addie?"

Her face paled but her chin tilted higher. "You gonna hit me, Mr. Claiborne?"

"Not if you call me Zeke."

"Zeke," she said, and they both succumbed to a strained smile.

Jake let out a loud, self-conscious cough. This was the damnedest conversation he'd ever had to listen to. Stranger still was the silent understanding these two seemed to have reached. "Well," he said, because he couldn't think of anything else.

"Well," they both echoed.

The breeze picked up the scent of evergreen and swirled the dirt in a nearby field until the air tasted like dry mint, both clean and dusty, a strange sort of metaphor for the feelings running through Addie's mind. She stared at her laced fingers to keep from gazing around her with useless longing. There was such abundance here, she could smell it, taste it. If she opened her hand and reached out, she almost felt like she could hold it in her palm. But there was such an awful price connected with it.

Zeke watched the breeze toss the young woman's curls in diverse directions as she wrestled with her thoughts. The air billowed her skirt out briefly, then plastered it against her lower body, revealing the narrow span of her hips, the junction of her thighs, and the long contours of her legs. She wasn't wearing a petticoat. A shiver of restlessness moved through him before it was quickly subdued. He slid a glance at the sheriff and said evenly, "Go on out to the barn, Jake."

At a loss to understand anything going on between these two, Jake turned to Addie for consent. Her face lost color, but she hesitated only a moment before she nodded, figuring she didn't have much to lose. If Zeke Claiborne wanted to talk in private, so be it, but the thought didn't settle well. It made her anxious and uncertain. Beyond the fact that the suggestion was highly improper, she never, *never,* liked being alone with a man. It had been more than difficult just riding out here with the sheriff.

"If you're sure, Miz Addie," Jake said.

She wasn't sure about anything but nodded just the same, ready to get this over with.

Jake collected the horses and headed for the barn, feeling as though he'd either done a good thing or a terribly wrong one.

There was a mellow silence after he was gone. Neither had much to say, but it wasn't exactly awkward. It was just . . . silent. Zeke shoved his hands in his pockets and leaned against the porch rail. Addie followed the movement with her eyes, wishing she had pockets for her own hands. She didn't, so she ran them down her skirt to rub off the clamminess, then clasped them together again.

"Mr. Claiborne," she said, feeling too awkward to use his first name.

There was a lot more she wanted to say, wanted to ask, but part of her was fearful. Not afraid exactly; after Willis she wasn't too much afraid of anything. She just wasn't certain she wanted to hear his answers. Best ask them anyway, she reasoned, and get them behind her. Never at rest, the breeze whipped up again, lifting a curl by her face, and she shoved it behind her ear. It wouldn't stay and sprang free to bounce against her cheek.

"I want to say that I know you don't want to do this . . ." She paused; she had her pride after all. "I mean if it's pity—"

"It's not," Zeke said, but that was all.

"Well . . ." Addie clenched her hands so tight they began to hurt worse than her misbegotten pride and she looked at him fully. There was a hint of curiosity and uncertainty in her eyes, but more blatant was the frank, almost accusatory look. "Why are you considering me, then? There are several pretty girls in town who would have you."

Zeke only stared back at her. Looks were immaterial. He needed a wife, and she needed a husband.

As his silence lengthened, Addie blushed scarlet to the roots of her undisciplined hair at being so forward and looked away. Her throat closed up, refusing her leave to say more even if she'd wanted to, which she most certainly did not. The wind picked at her dress, sending cold chills prickling up her bare legs, and she slapped her skirt down with an unstable hand. The sound seemed unnaturally loud in the quiet, drawing Zeke's eyes to her lower torso. Embarrassment flooded her at the attention and unfathomable appraisal in his eyes.

"Let's go inside," he said. "We'll talk in there."

Her gaze narrowed in apprehension. She didn't think that was such a fine idea, going into a man's house unchaperoned, but it wasn't like she had any reputation to protect. Who was gonna know, and who in all the Wyoming Territory would care if Mary Adaline Smith went into a man's house alone? There wasn't much to hold your head up about after living with Willis.

Steadying herself, she looked at the door Zeke held open and forced herself to move forward. She inched past him cautiously and stepped into his home, prepared to despise it as much as she suddenly despised its owner. Not hatred for the man himself—she didn't know him well enough for that yet—but hatred for what he represented: the only solution to her problem.

And hatred for herself for being in the exact same situation she'd been in four years ago, as if she were somehow responsible, as if had she just been stronger or smarter she could have avoided this.

Trouble started when she took that first step inside and felt a sort of sweetness creep up on her unawares, subtly at first, then with a burning sting. His house was warm and cozy, the kind of house a person should have. It had known a woman's touch in the curtains that draped the windows, the braided rugs on the floors, and the stitchery on the walls. A huge stone fireplace gave it the sturdy beauty of the land, but the feminine touches gave it the beauty of a home. The warm clutter everywhere gave it the beauty of a family.

Toys were scattered about, well worn, well loved. A set of tin soldiers was tumbled in a heap, the war put to rest but not put away. A small fishing pole leaned like a tired old man in the corner, its line tangled around a bent hook. A tiny scuffed shoe peeked out beneath a chair, its laces irreparably knotted.

Addie's eyes wandered aimlessly, absorbing and self-protectively abandoning old, familiar pictures from a lost childhood. A band tightened around a heart she'd thought long dead as she spied a stuffed ball atop two tiny knitted socks, then squeezed tighter at an open picture book, its pages grimy from hands too eager to wash. She squeezed her eyes shut, unable to look closer, deeper, into the private life of this man and his family.

There had been pain before—loss, loneliness, isolation—but nothing like this. This pain was new and unbearable, a twist in her heart for what could have been, what truly was, and for all the desecrated hopes and dreams she had held for the future.

Zeke watched her eyes fill briefly with misery, then dim before she shut them completely. He knew anguish, knew how the hurt rips and shreds the insides until there's nothing left but a hollow, gutless feeling—a nothingness so much easier to endure. The torment he kept locked safely away threatened to edge to the surface at seeing Addie's small inflexible frame standing in the home he had shared with Becky, the home where she had welcomed him in the evenings with a smile and later in the bedroom with more. Damp and sated, their bodies still merged, they had laughed and loved and planned a lifetime.

He tore his eyes away, safeguarding himself against the emotions rushing at him—ire, resentment, and dread. This small pitiable woman didn't belong in his house, in his life. She had no right to his children. He curled his fingers into a hard fist to crush the intolerable bitterness and the fact that he was feeling anything at all. She was a victim, too, blameless; he needed to remember that.

Addie knew she could hardly stand like a wooden Indian in this man's home with her eyes closed, so she forced them open and searched for a safe place to look. She found it on a pile of dishes in the sink. Lord help her, there was a pump! Right inside the house. She'd never have dirty dishes with an inside pump. After lug-

ging water from a well all her life, she couldn't even
imagine the luxury.

Zeke watched her eyes widen on the mound of
grease-caked dishes and figured she'd either turn tail
and run or be convinced of his need. After a moment he
noticed she hadn't run, but then she hadn't seen the
mountain of filthy clothes yet. Or the boys. He had sent
them over to the Parkers' so he could meet her alone.

"You like children?" he asked.

Addie dragged her gaze from the pump. "I think so."
That brought a darkening to his eyes, and she mentally
flinched and backed up a step, then hated herself for
cowering. "I don't have any."

"I have three," he said, in warning.

She knew. It was the only reason she had allowed
Jake to bring her here, that and the impending threat of
starvation. Nothing else on earth could have made her
even consider remarrying. She pulled her gaze from his
and stared again at the tiny socks, the small toys, the old
but achingly familiar memories from her own childhood. To have that again, the noise and clutter and
chaos of family life . . .

"I do like children," she said softly.

"Liking them and raising them are two different
things," he said, then added carefully, "You and Willis
never had any."

It wasn't a question, didn't pretend to be one, but it
held that certain note of conjecture that such sentences
do when one person wants another to elaborate. Addie
wasn't about to discuss it—not now, not ever.

"You've got a pump," she said.

If Zeke was jarred slightly by the switch in topics, he
covered it smoothly. "Yes."

"It's . . . it's a nice pump."

"Yes."

"I imagine it works real well."

"It works fine."

"Brings water right inside the house."

"Right inside."

"I've never used an inside pump . . ."

Her faint amazement was undisguised for the barest second, a hint of wonder and longing for nothing more than a stupid pump. Zeke crossed his arms and leaned back against the door. "I've got an icebox and a stove too," he said dryly.

Addie missed the mild sarcasm in his tone and continued to look at the numerous conveniences in an otherwise simple home until she realized that her mind had strayed. The silence had stretched to the point of awkwardness. She turned to find Zeke staring at her with a lazy, appraising look.

Flustered, she nevertheless returned his scrutiny with a wary and assessing look of her own, and Zeke glimpsed a hint of what she might have been at fifteen in the dainty, patrician bone structure forming a face that had grown too thin, the skin pale and pulled too tightly over the sharp angles, making her eyes appear overlarge. Her lips were full and shapely but wind chapped; her hair looked like it had never met up with a comb. There was something about her that alternately encompassed and rejected vulnerability. Irritated and not knowing why, he said, "The pump is great, perfect. But there are a few more important things we need to clarify."

Addie nodded and looked away. He must have thought she was an idiot to go on that way about the pump, a simpleminded fool without the sense God gave a groundhog. Tension invaded her shoulders and back, support against too much prying. "All right," she said in a slightly mulish tone, when she really wanted to crawl off in a hole and hide. "I . . . I've just never had an inside pump, that's all."

Zeke didn't think talk of pumps was what had her so riled, but he sensed she'd pucker up like curdled milk if pushed any further. "Sit down, Addie," he said, and pulled out a chair.

Startled by the courtesy and the use of her given name, she moved forward and sat down gingerly on the edge. Zeke spun his own chair around, straddled it, and tipped forward toward her. Addie shrank back a bit, intimidated by his size and handsomeness and direct gaze. Color stole up her cheeks but she paid it no mind and stared back at him. There was freedom even in that, at being able to stare at a man with impunity. It felt heady and scary and even a little indecent.

Zeke noted several things in her guarded expression —resentment, resistance, and maybe a little something else. "You afraid of me, Miz Addie?"

"No." She was more afraid of starving.

"Sure look like you are."

"Just thinking," she hedged, though she was no good at pretense. Reality lashed at her daily, leaving no room to learn or practice even the mildest deception. She shrugged. "Maybe I look scared when I'm thinking. I never looked at myself when I was . . ."

Bemused by her nervous rambling, Zeke let her carry on for a moment before he interrupted. "Your knuckles are white as flour where they're gripping your dress. You must be thinking mighty hard."

Her honey-blond head jerked downward to contemplate the hands fisted in her skirt, then she flashed him a look that was halfway to being a glower, as if she didn't appreciate having *that* pointed out to her. Just as quickly her expression changed and her hands relaxed to rest limply on her lap. Her eyes, so dismal and straightforward, bore into his. "Truth is, Mr. Claiborne, I think you're getting the bad end of the deal."

"Really?" he asked coolly. "I'd say you're not coming out any better."

Addie's eyes darted around the cabin. "You didn't live with Willis."

"Can't say as I regret that."

"I can say for certain that I did. Still do."

Zeke could see that she instantly regretted the forthright statement. Her hands were fisted again, her cheeks losing color. "That bad, huh?"

Her silence was more eloquent than anything she could have said aloud. She grew solemn, glancing anywhere but at him. "I'm not aiming to change you; I know better than anyone that I'm not in a position to make demands, but there's things I can't . . . *won't* live with again."

"You have rights, Miz Addie, just as I do."

She shook her head, trying to keep the bitterness from her voice, but the core of numbness inside her battered heart cracked slightly beneath the weight of helpless anger, and her words came out clipped and decisive. "No. I don't." She heaved a deep, heartfelt sigh that shimmied clear through Zeke's body, startling him. "From the way Sheriff Holdman makes it sound, you don't have many choices either. But I'm not completely stupid. I'd like to know why you'd have me when there are other girls to choose from. I know what I am, Mr. Claiborne. I'm not pretty. I'm not overly smart. I don't even have much experience with kids." She started to keep going but figured she'd debased herself enough.

Whether or not she was pretty was debatable, depending upon one's perspective. She might consider herself intellectually deficient, but she was intuitive, and Zeke knew experience was gained only through practice. "You need me," he said simply, then raised his hand when she started to protest. "We need each other. Neither one of us wants to be in the position we're in. Neither one of us wants another spouse. If I married one of the girls in town, she'd expect me to be the kind of husband she's dreaming of. I can't do that, not again. What we have is something that's convenient to both of us." He paused to let his next words sink in. It wasn't his intent to be cruel, but neither would he be evasive about the truth.

"If I lived closer to town, I'd offer to hire you to come out and care for the kids on a daily basis—" Her eyes lit up with so much hope at the suggestion, the irises became crystal-clear green around dilated black centers without a speck of gold or brown to mar their clarity. Zeke felt almost criminal when he had to continue. "That option is closed to us. It's too far to make the trip twice a day."

"But I'm widowed now," she said, her expression painfully open at the fruitless prospect. "Couldn't I stay here like a nanny or governess?"

"You're only nineteen," he said. "There would be talk."

Addie's expression faded into a self-protective blankness. Measuring it against the alternative, she didn't give a tinker's damn about talk, but apparently Zeke did. She felt ignorant for making the suggestion, as if she needed to apologize or dissemble. *Oh, I knew that. I was just testing you, Mr. Claiborne, to see if you were an upright, honest man.* But most of all she felt stupid for allowing herself a little hope.

"I guess marriage is the only respectable solution," she murmured, to exonerate herself.

Zeke felt the coolness of her acceptance settle like a chill in his gut, a forewarning he didn't quite understand. He abandoned any attempt to cloak the truth in niceties and offered a warning of his own. "You better be sure, Miz Addie. You better be damn sure this is what you want. You're still young enough to make a good marriage with someone who wants the same things young women want."

He paused and leveled her with a hard, intense look that made her insides squirm. "Your position here will be little better than an employee, but with no way out. I have three boys who take up every ounce of energy I can conjure. I don't want any more. I won't blame you if you want to wait for someone who'll give you a full marriage and children of your own body."

Addie swallowed thickly at his boldness. She didn't feel young, certainly didn't want to do that thing with a man that was necessary to make babies, and she had no dreams left where marriage was concerned. They were gone, smothered by the harsh, cruel existence of the past four years.

"I'm sure as I'll ever be about this," she said tonelessly. With winter coming on, it made a body mighty sure about such, even if it didn't make a body happy. Then again, happiness was something Addie had given up on a long, long time ago, so it really didn't matter. Safe, warm, and fed went a long way toward replacing happiness.

The air around them grew heavy and oppressive with unspoken thoughts and feelings abandoned in favor of the severe reality they needed to face. Zeke watched her stare at her hands—tiny, chafed red hands that had known plenty of toil. She was only average height and yards too thin. He wondered if she could hold up under the added work his boys would impose. His stomach rumbled, and he wondered if she could cook. It wouldn't be right to saddle his sons with someone who couldn't fry up a decent side of bacon.

Hell, Claiborne! You can't cook either. You're just thinking up excuses not to take her.

A lock of her hair fell forward, and she absently pushed it behind her ear. It sprang free and she gave up and blew it out of her eyes. The gesture struck Zeke as childlike. A woman her age should have her hair put up, but Addie's curls spiraled wild and unkempt to her shoulders without even a bonnet to secure them or protect her face from the wind. Her dress was as drab as the rest of her, styleless, showing too much wear.

You buy the boys' clothes, Claiborne; she'll have to dress them in whatever you purchase. You'll be buying her clothes, too. Maybe then she won't look so shabby. He was ashamed of his uncharitable thoughts. He had no cause to disapprove of her poverty, but if she was going to be his wife, he would need to see that she didn't want for decent clothes.

Addie sighed, her skinny shoulders lifting beneath the frayed fabric of her dress, her spine curved as if the weight of the world sat on the back of her neck in one big, burdensome lump. She knew he was looking at her, but didn't care. He'd take her or he wouldn't. Best he knew beforehand what he was getting.

If there was one thing she could say about Willis, it was the fact that he had wanted her. He might have been shifty and mean as a rattlesnake, but he had wanted her. What would this man, who didn't even pretend to want her, be like? She shivered, not liking to think about it. She could see by his place that he wasn't lazy like Willis. His clothes were clean, if a bit wrinkled, and he seemed honest enough, not that she dared trust her own judgment anymore. Maybe he wasn't like Willis in any of those other ways, either. Or maybe she just wanted to think so.

But she remembered too well that Willis hadn't been nasty until after they were married, when it was too late. Her mama had always claimed it took years to get to know a person. *Well, Mama, it sure didn't take me long to find out that Willis Harvey Smith was the scourge of the earth.* In any case, it still didn't matter. There was no way to tell Zeke's—or any other man's—true nature on such short acquaintance. And all she had was a short time to decide. She'd just have to go on what she already knew about him and what Sheriff Holdman had said. And the fact that winter was moving in. Zeke Claiborne would be whatever he was once they were married, and there wouldn't be a darn thing she could do about it.

Her stomach felt queasy as she glanced up at him, but her voice was steady. "You made up your mind yet?"

"I'm not fickle," he replied, regretting the fact that the starchiness had gone out of her. "I had a long sleepless night to think this over. I try not to make decisions lightly, so I don't have to go back and regret them later. Understand?"

"I reckon," she said. Reckoned he at least had choices to make, unlike her, who had no choice at all. There was something vastly unfair in that, something lonely and sad and—she figured she was waltzing herself right into a fine pity-party with such thoughts and determined to stop them. She wasn't the only one hurting here, the only one thrust into an unjustifiable situation by necessity. She recalled the dark, undefinable shadows lurking in his deep amber eyes, the lines of exhaustion fanning tiny grooves at the outer corners. As badly as she felt for herself, she almost felt worse for him.

She gathered the remnants of whatever courage remained inside her and faced Zeke squarely. Her expression softened just a bit, making her look younger and shy as she unconsciously tilted her head to the side in inquiry. "You . . . think I could see your boys?"

Zeke exhaled slowly, but it came out more as a resigned sigh. "That'll be fine."

3

Zeke sat at Beatrice Parker's long wooden table, his hands wrapped around a steaming mug of coffee, and savored the homey and inviting smells of fresh yeasty bread, apples baking in cinnamon and sugar, vegetables seasoned with bacon drippings simmering on the stove —things he didn't associate with common life anymore except when he came here. He wondered again if Addie could cook. She was upstairs with two of his three boys getting acquainted. He'd thought it best to let them have some time to themselves.

With a pithiness well suited to her disposition, Beatrice looked sternly across the table at the troubled man. "You sought the Lord on this, Zeke?"

"Me and the Lord haven't spoken in a while," he admitted, because Beatrice wouldn't judge him even if she did feel it her bounden duty to offer advice. And because she was a master at getting to the truth, anyway. She had eight kids to practice on, eight kids who would rather bite their own tongues off than get caught lying.

"I'm glad you offered for her," Beatrice said, "but I

don't s'pect she's too eager to get married again after Willis."

"She doesn't have much choice."

"Nope." Beatrice sniffed, as if an offensive odor permeated the air. "Darn shame that. She's a sweet little thing who's had more than her share of trouble." She rubbed her work-roughened fingers together around her cup and shifted her considerable bulk around in the ladder-back chair, making it groan. "Guess I never have gotten over the guilt of letting her go to that mealy-mouthed drifter without putting up more of a fuss. Willis hadn't been in town long and nobody knew what his real nature was like."

"I was told it was her decision."

"Yep," Beatrice snapped in the same pointed way she did most things. "Same as now. No decision worth making." She looked up to see that none of her children were within hearing range. "I'm not one of those high-minded females, Zeke. A woman's got her place just like everything else in God's creation, but I can't help thinking she should have some options in life."

"So should a man," he countered, sounding bitter though his feelings had long since gone numb. "Becky left me without any, and Willis left her the same way. Maybe the best thing for us to do is to take up together."

"Can't say as either of you will be happy with that."

"Can't say as we won't."

"Nope, can't say that neither. But this is Bea you're talking to, boy. No need to tippytoe around what's troubling you."

Zeke smiled sardonically. Beatrice was as "high-minded" as they came with a blunt, outspoken personality that matched her square, stocky shape. She might be brash, but she was also realistic. She'd seen a lot in fifty years and not more than half of it had been good, but she'd learned to make the best of whatever life threw her way and tip the odds in her favor. She was a woman who wasn't well liked in the community, but oddly enough, she was well loved.

"God knows, I don't want to remarry, Bea."

"God don't have nothing to do with it if you haven't consulted him," she said imperiously, then softened, "but I can't say as I blame you."

He had known, of course, that she wouldn't. Zeke just stared into his coffee, not bothering to indulge the profitless wish that things weren't the way they were. "Marriage is so . . . damned hard." He glanced up at her. "It takes work, self-sacrifice, self-denial. I don't know if I can offer that anymore."

She sent him a pinched look. "Don't reckon you can offer less, if it's to work."

Zeke nodded. He knew. "I guess I feel guilty, too. There won't be any more kids out of this marriage. There'll be a hundred men ready to court Addie when word spreads that she's available. She's young yet. I figure she has the right to have a normal marriage and kids of her own."

Beatrice's eyebrows shot up. There wasn't much that could shock her at this stage of life, but Zeke had made a good start on it. "Something wrong with your workings, boy?"

Zeke didn't bat an eyelash. "I don't reckon."

"Something wrong with hers? She tell you something that makes you think she can't conceive?"

"She didn't much want to talk about it."

"Well, I should think not!" Beatrice scoffed. "She wasn't married to Willis all that long, and she was so young when they started out . . . well, she can't be certain."

Zeke just shook his head, not wanting to go into it, but having said too much to back down now. "There won't be any more children, because I don't want any. I've got more than I can handle right now. I'm not about to start over."

Beatrice sent him a level look down the blade of her nose. "There's not a whole lot you can do about it."

Zeke returned the look. "The marriage will be more like a business arrangement, without emotional attachments."

The knee-slapping loud guffaws following his statement blasted his eardrums, showing just what Bea thought of his declaration. " 'Business arrangement' my foot!" she hooted. "I'd like to see that." Her laughter faded as abruptly as it started and her eyes narrowed dubiously on the healthy, handsome young man. "What you're saying is, you're not gonna bed her."

Zeke felt a flush of heat rise beneath his collar and bit back a grimace at the adolescent reaction. "That's none of your business—"

"I'm making it mine," she snapped. "Are you?"

Zeke's eyes narrowed in warning, though he knew Beatrice couldn't be beaten back with a look. "I'm not a fool," he said slowly. "I'm just saying when it comes to that, I'll be careful, use precautions."

"Well, I never heard such vulgar talk!" she huffed. "Have mercy, Zeke, I can't imagine what possessed you to speak to Addie about such, instead of letting nature take its course."

"It wouldn't be fair to deceive her," he said, but the words rang hollow even in his own ears. Fairness didn't enter into this situation on any rational level. "Besides, she seemed perfectly agreeable."

Beatrice's eyes grew watchful. She'd seen enough of life to have collected a pretty accurate understanding of human nature. She and Sam didn't have eight kids of their own by choice, but lack of restraint. Both widowed, they'd come together with two children each, then added four more. She loved each and every one of her offspring but couldn't say she'd planned them.

Zeke was young and hale. In eight years, he had fathered three boys and several others Becky had lost early in pregnancy. His feelings might have changed with Becky's death, but his needs wouldn't be all that different once they bypassed his emotional turmoil. And a man's needs had a tendency to override his judgment no matter how sound.

"You can deny it, but I know you're still mourning Becky," Beatrice said bluntly. "But time will take care of that. As far as Addie is concerned, she didn't have it too good with Willis. He stayed up at the saloon more than he was home. I can't figure where he got the money, 'cause I don't recollect that he ever did an honest day's work." She fidgeted with her coffee cup, her eyes taking on a snooty ingenuousness. "I've heard rumors—not that I listen to gossip, mind you, nor repeat it—but it's been whispered that Willis was pretty rough with some of Ruby's girls. Maybe it was even worse at home. Maybe that's why Addie's so agreeable, or maybe she's just too scared of you to do anything else."

Zeke said nothing. Whatever Willis may or may not have done would have no bearing on what went on in his house. His biggest problem was getting help with his boys, and she seemed the best solution.

Thwarted by his silence, Beatrice pursed her lips in a

stubborn look. "She's young, you said it yourself! She doesn't know what she wants yet, but she's got a right to have a decent marriage and everything that goes along with it, including kids of her own." Though her voice had risen, her look turned worried. "Lord, Zeke, you can't expect that girl to go through life barren. It's not natural."

"She doesn't have to accept," he said coolly.

"And if she's smart, she won't!" Beatrice retaliated. Zeke was a good man and handsome enough to turn every unmarried female head in Laramie, along with a few too many married ones as well. Addie could do worse. But going into this arrangement with only partial intimacy was about as stupid as a cow wandering into a butcher shop. There wouldn't be anything but hurt and aggravation before long. Addie might be agreeable now, but she'd feel cheated later.

Men had needs and women had to oblige them. But women had needs too, and an empty womb wasn't one of them. If the woman was smart enough to listen to her own feminine instincts, she made demands of her own. Sure as heck couldn't leave it up to a bullheaded man to know what a woman needed.

Beatrice's look was a mixture of shrewd intellect and sly speculation as she regarded Zeke. "Winters get awful long out here . . . close quarters get even closer. A man could get right . . . jittery."

Zeke knew the word intimately. "Not enough to forget himself," he said, and threw her a biting look, which had about as much effect at plugging her up as trying to fill the Grand Canyon with a teaspoon.

Bea continued with dogged determination. "You know yourself those contraptions to keep women from conceiving don't always work."

Zeke knew. Becky had suffered the consequences too many times. He also knew her case hadn't been normal, and the devices were usually reliable. With no children of her own, he assumed Addie already knew how to use them. He damn sure hoped so.

At his silence, a look of satisfaction entered Bea's eyes, and she reached over to pat Zeke's hand. "Just be good to her, and the rest is liable to take care of itself."

Zeke nodded, glad they'd reached the end of the conversation. He didn't like the expression on Beatrice's perceptive face and wouldn't offend her further. He was going into this out of desperation, with his eyes open, his heart uninvolved, and the rest of him as tame as he could keep it.

There was such a sweetness in watching a baby sleep. Addie crept closer to the crib where eleven-month-old Cole lay scrunched up like a roly-poly bug, his bottom sky-high, his fist in his mouth, his pink cheeks turned into the sheet. If there was a God, he'd done right well making this one.

Like a thief who had no right to be there, Addie stole closer on tiptoe and peered over the rail. It wouldn't take much. She wouldn't have to love him or even like him to do her duty, just feed and dress and keep him clean. Caught in the netherworld between dreams and wakefulness, Cole's eyelids fluttered and his small mouth turned up at the corners in a cherub's smile. Addie felt the reaction in her chest, a heady warmth, a breathless flutter that beat against her rib cage. *Oh, Lord.* He was so small, so innocent, so unaware of the meanness and cruelty just waiting to snare him in the outside world.

Tentatively, she reached down and touched the top of

his head, feeling the softer-than-soft down of his blond hair and inhaling the powdery scent of talc. With his plump pinkness and angelic features, he would have fit perfectly in *The Nativity* by Grünewald. For a fleeting instant she wished she could sketch him, could capture the soft rounded edges of innocence on paper. Of their own volition, her fingers softly stroked his pale blond curls, feeling the cottony, infant-only textures sensitize her fingertips to an acute awareness of things so transient. Childhood passed so quickly, its innocence forgotten in the rigors of growing up.

At Addie's touch, Cole stirred and began sucking fretfully on his fist. She snatched her hand away and pressed her fists against her middle, then stumbled back a step, feeling guilty for disturbing him.

To think that this child, along with two others, could be hers was just too much to hope for someone who'd given up on anything that resembled optimism. But the truth rested there, just beneath her fisted hands in the anxious pounding of her heart. She closed her eyes briefly, unable to escape or deny it. *Just a little while, God, just give me a little piece of time to hold and nurture and pretend he's mine.* She didn't dare ask for more and backed farther from the crib, feeling shaky and scared that it was all somehow going to start caving in and she'd be the reason for it.

She turned suddenly at a sound from the pine bed along the wall. Four-year-old Zeb sat up, rubbing sleepy eyes and grumbling under his breath at being tricked into taking a nap. A cap of dark hair covered his head, curling softly at the ends. With his brown locks and blue eyes, he favored Becky. Addie thought it must be wonderfully difficult for Zeke to look at his son day after day and see so much of his late wife. The child blinked when he saw a strange woman staring at him as though one of them had done wrong.

"Where's Pa?"

"Downstairs," she said, apprehensive at facing one of Zeke Claiborne's kids awake.

"Who're you?"

"Addie Smith."

"I'm Zeb," he answered, and began to recite by rote. "Zebulun Taylor Claiborne. I got my middle name from my grandma, but it's not a girl's name. It's a *family* name. I'm bigger than Cole. He's just a baby. Where's Josh and how come he didn't have to take a nap? I want my pa."

Addie's head reeled at the rapid succession of questions, and she didn't know which one, if any, to answer first. She disregarded them all and said carefully. "You want me to help you with your shoes so you can go find your pa?"

Zeb looked down at his stockinged feet, perplexed, then his face screwed up in comical disgust. "Gracie was just gonna read me a story. You know Gracie?"

Addie nodded. Margaret Grace was Beatrice and Sam's fourteen-year-old daughter and must have read Zeb to sleep. Having lost younger brothers and a sister, Addie wasn't a stranger to the many contrivances a teenager employed to get a child down for a nap.

"Gracie is nice," she offered lamely.

"Gracie is sneaky," Zeb mumbled, then perked up. "I can tie."

Out of practice, it took Addie a moment to gather her wits but she managed it admirably. "I heard you could," she said with a hint of forgotten impishness, "but I didn't know whether or not to believe such a tale. Want to show me?" She picked up his shoes and offered them to him. A small spark of exhilaration quickened her heartbeat when he nodded eagerly and took them from her hands.

There was no suspicion in his eyes, no cold calculation, just the easy acceptance of a child. It felt odd to be the object of such absolute trust. Her world seemed to pause, then catch a rhythm she was unaccustomed to, a steady gentle rocking that warmed her from the inside out. She was torn between the impulse to cry or smile, truly smile for the first time in more years than she could remember. If not exactly fearless facing Zebulun Taylor Claiborne, she found herself filled with a fledgling sense of liberation in simply being able to talk to him, in having him converse back without censure or disapproval.

It took the child forty times as long to get his shoes on and the laces tied as it would have if Addie had helped, and they ended up so knotted it would take twice the effort to get them back off, but her patience was rewarded when he stuck both legs out board-straight and sent her a beaming smile. Feeling off-balance but heartened, Addie smiled back and offered to help him off the bed.

Zeb put his small hand in hers and scooted to the edge, then paused. As if a lamp had suddenly lit up inside his young mind, he tilted his head to the side and peered up at her closely.

The Impressionists, she thought, then *no.* Not all of them, with their lack of realism, plain textures, and flat design, but maybe Renoir with his warm colors for the surface qualities and flesh tints, and cooler tones for Zeb's grave, dark eyes and hair.

"Are you the lady Pa told us about?" he inquired, head still tilted in that way children have about them that is both curious and demanding. "You gonna be our new ma?"

Oh, Lord. Addie's breath lodged in her throat. "I hope so," she said cautiously.

Zeb's brow puckered in a frown. "You don't look like my ma. She's in heaven." Addie didn't know what to say, just waited in silence while he swung his legs back and forth in deep thought for a moment before he eyed her astutely and said in a furtive whisper, "Don't tell."

Addie shook her head, her pulse suspended. "I won't."

"My pa cried. Josh says only sissy babies cry, but Pa did. He's not a sissy baby." He eyed her suspiciously. "You gonna make my pa cry?"

"No," she whispered, her heart crumbling.

Zeb looked back at his shoelaces, as if the answer to all life's perplexities were waiting just there for someone to untangle. "I can't 'member her all the time now. Josh can, but sometimes I forget." His head snapped up, his blue eyes dancing suddenly as he latched on to the only thing nice in an unconscionable situation. "She's an angel now."

Addie figured he'd been told that and nodded. She remembered her own parents' death, the awful desolation and the absolute necessity of finding something good and bright and soothing to keep from perishing as well. She wasn't certain she'd ever found it for herself, but she'd do everything in her power to help Zeb keep the faith. Her hand tightened on his small one, and she smiled over the tightness in her throat. "My parents are angels too."

Zeb's small mouth rounded in an *O* of wonder. "Right up there with my ma?"

Addie nodded. "So they'll never be lonely. Bet they

can fly too, higher than the clouds and faster than the wind."

"Yep." Beaming with satisfaction, Zeb scooted off the bed and hit the floor running, almost colliding with Zeke, who was standing in the doorway.

"Pa!" he squealed. "This is Addie Smif. I showed her I can tie."

"Good," Zeke said affectionately.

Addie watched as Zeke hoisted the child high and settled Zeb securely in the crook of his strong arm. The gesture was easy and natural, something they had done a thousand times, and now took for granted. Zeke's face and voice were different as he talked to his son, less severe and more open, though there remained a distance in his eyes, a reserve that was painful for Addie to watch given the child's innate enthusiasm. *He's holding back,* she thought. *He loves his son but he's keeping part of himself inviolate.* She wondered why.

Zeke turned to find Addie standing self-consciously in the middle of the room, looking as though she didn't know what to do with herself now that he was here. He'd been watching her with Zeb and hadn't found anything to criticize, then felt disgusted with himself for looking for some reason to back out of a decision already made.

But his children were everything to him, the only thing he had left of Becky to build a future, the only remaining legacies of his father and grandfather. It was imperative that he be able to trust the woman who would become their mother, and that she be able to offer the boys everything he himself had seemed incapable of giving these past nine months—time, tenderness, reassurance.

He was surprised to find that the washed-out young

woman had a gentle hand, a soothing voice that bespoke patience, and a keen awareness of childhood fantasies. Her voice had been filled with expression and her eyes had held a youthful effervescence when she and Zeb talked of flying higher than the clouds. He didn't know what he had expected but it wasn't this many-faceted personality with the ability to adapt and change to suit the needs of a young boy.

She was vastly different here than at his home, though the transformation was more subtle than definitive. Nothing he could really put his finger on—a softening, a natural ease, a warmth and sensitivity that he would have thought stripped away by her past. He was relieved to find her more comfortable with Zeb than she had been with him.

"Miz Parker's got fresh cookies," he said, and put his son down. Zeb was gone the second his feet touched the floor. Zeke stepped into the room and noticed that Addie inadvertently took a step back, seemed to collect herself, then turned quickly to watch the baby sleep.

"He's sure pretty," she whispered.

"He's teething," Zeke said, as if that negated everything otherwise precious about a child.

Addie smiled, remembering, and looked back over her shoulder. "He must be fussy."

"That's too nice a word," Zeke said. Her smile was wistful yet rusty, as if her facial muscles were unused to the task. There was a youthful innocence in the gesture totally at odds with her tired looks. He walked closer to the crib, and noted that Addie again tensed up slightly, then seemed to force herself to relax. With one eyebrow arched slightly, he gave her a reflective stare, but said nothing. He didn't need to mention that things were going to get a lot more awkward than this if they carried through with their plans. "Gracie's gone outside to fetch Joshua. I'd like you to meet him before you make a final decision."

Addie couldn't think what meeting the oldest Claiborne child had to do with anything, but she agreed and followed Zeke out. When they reached the kitchen, she discovered there was a whole lot to consider as soon as the eight-year-old raced through the door.

Rosy-cheeked and laughing from hard play, Joshua looked like any vivacious boy as he bounded into the room. But as soon as his gaze found his father standing next to a strange woman all youthful similarities ended. His face fell into a sort of closed-off belligerence before he turned rudely away and ran back outside.

"Josh!" Zeke called sharply.

Addie flinched at the command, but her eyes stayed fixed on the empty doorway. *Chiaroscuro,* light and dark. Only Ruisdael or El Greco or Tintoretto could have portrayed the hueless dimensions of anguish in the child's eyes. There had been much more than sullen rebellion or jealousy; there had been fear.

Her heart sank sickeningly to her toes at seeing her own expression for the past four years mirrored back at her. She swallowed and lifted her eyes to Zeke's but couldn't think of one appropriate thing to say. Even with Cole's innocent sweetness and Zeb's lively acceptance, it was the misery in Josh's eyes that touched her in a way the others couldn't, cried out for everything she needed for herself. "Please . . . give him time," she whispered.

Zeke stared back at her but he was miles away, at a spot beneath a shady willow tree where a child had watched his mother laid to rest and had seemingly buried the joy of childhood with her.

With brisk efficiency, Beatrice Parker glossed over the strained moment by ordering everyone to the table for hot coffee. She sent one of her children out with a cup for Sam, who was too busy to come inside, and seated herself to study the young woman sitting—so pale and prim and self-conscious—in a kitchen that had been built around the noisy laughter, good-natured teasing, and ferocious arguments of eight lively children. Proper manners were an incontestable rule in Beatrice's house, but they were never formal. Her eyes went to Zeke. "You best go check on Joshua. No telling what that boy's got himself into by now."

Zeke nodded and rose, glad for the excuse to escape. Before long he wouldn't be able to just walk away from Addie and the stillness of her spiritless countenance. He glanced back at her bent head just as he reached the door and honestly didn't know how he was going to get through the rest of his life.

Beatrice waited until Zeke was gone, then slapped her palm down on the table, causing Addie to jump. "He's a good man," she said sharply, "the kind your pa would have wanted for you."

Addie nodded, but kept her eyes averted. Beatrice Parker was the single most intimidating woman she had ever met. Loud, outspoken, and brassy, Beatrice said what she thought and dared anyone to disagree. In many ways Addie admired the woman's daring effrontery, but she couldn't say she'd ever gotten used to her.

"No, now listen, girl," Beatrice continued. "I'm not trying to pretty things up. Zeke's got his good days and bad like all of us, but his good is worth exercising a bit of patience now and again to get through the other. He's still hurting—oh, I know he says different—and I don't s'pect that's gonna change today or even tomorrow, but someday the healing will come, and I think you just might be the one to help it along."

Addie's head shot up and her lungs swelled, as if they were filling up with too much air. How in the world could Beatrice think that she, Addie Wortham Smith, the consummate collector of bad luck, would be able to help a full-grown man when she'd never even been able to help herself? She let out a pent-up breath and gave Beatrice a look that questioned the older woman's sanity.

Beatrice laughed outright and patted Addie's hand. "You'll do, girl. You'll do just fine." Her eyes narrowed and scanned the kitchen for keen-eared kids before she whispered, "Zeke is right handsome, if you take stock in such."

At the absurdity of the statement, Addie's eyes widened and she felt the knot in her stomach ease up for the first time in days, maybe years. *Handsome?* Yes, he was that and more with his wheat-gold hair streaked with coppery highlights, eyes the color of sun-shot whiskey, and his bronze skin and expansive shoulders. Out of nowhere, faster than she could see it coming or do anything to stop it, tears prickled behind her eyelids. Everything past, present, and future welled up inside her in one huge, painful suffocating knot. She dropped her forehead to the table, and her voice broke on a helpless moan. "Oh, Bea. What am I gonna *do*?"

Beatrice blinked back the unthinkable moisture in her own eyes and said brusquely, "Git by the best you can, honey, like always. Nothing else you *can* do." She cupped the young woman's chin and forced her to look up. "I was such a fool to let you get hitched to Willis without knowing more about him, but you had so much pride, girl! Wouldn't listen to any of us, wouldn't take handouts."

"Don't—" Addie began, but Beatrice cut her off.

"Horse dung! If I weren't a God-fearing woman, I'd say something stronger. I do blame myself and a few other so-called fine citizens, too, but it's different this time, Addie. You've got a choice, such as it is. You just say the word and I'll fix you up a bed here, right now. It's not like it was four years ago. We've got plenty of room in this new house, and you don't have to go anywhere or marry anybody."

But to Addie it was exactly the same as it had been four years ago. Maybe not as painful or heart-wrenching, but every bit the same. Nowhere to go, nothing to do but marry some horrid man who didn't want her. Her jaw clenched until it hurt, and she felt the sting of useless defiance and rage dwindle until she couldn't feel anything but blessed numbness.

Beatrice noted the young woman's retreat and glanced around again for eavesdroppers, then whispered fiercely. "You listen to me real good, Addie Smith. What I'm about to say might not hold with Bible teaching such as we get blasted with regularly, but you can't prove it by me. Fact is there's a shortage of single women on the frontier, always has been. Bad as it sounds, you're a valuable article right now, and that gives you power.

"Men are so busy collecting riches, they don't have time to enforce the old laws that have always kept us females subservient and under the same civil codes as infants, idiots, and criminals. A smart woman knows this, and knows how to use it."

Plucky and intrepid, Beatrice chuckled slyly, but she was brutally adamant that Addie understand. "That's how Esther Morris got us the vote when she still lived in South Pass City. She was made a judge, Addie, a *judge*. No other woman in this country can claim that honor. Women don't even have the right to vote in other places yet, nor are they likely to for some time. Esther used her worth as a woman in a man's land and played the Democrats against the Republicans. She had them men so tangled up in worrying about politics, that we women got exactly what we wanted.

"Nothing bars a woman from doing whatever she pleases out here except her own conscience. A woman pampered and petted and put on a pedestal will die in this land right alongside any man who tries to live by the old ways. We've had to work beside our men at jobs that never knew a woman's touch, and we've equaled or bettered them at the tasks too. Some men are shamed by this, but the others—the smart ones, and there are precious few—take it as long overdue. We've got women in professions that never saw a petticoat before—politics, business, and even outlawry—and we've done it with such tender deftness that the high-and-mighty males were barely aware of what was happening to them."

Beatrice squeezed the younger woman's hand firmly. "But there's a price also, Addie. Too much independence and a woman can end up with nothing left in life but a lonely, childless existence. Independence is a fine thing, but it's no substitute for the love and companionship of a good man." Her eyes grew passionate with her convictions. "You can stay here and try to make a life for yourself, or you can accept Zeke's offer. He needs you something awful, Addie. And I think you need him too."

"I . . ." Addie's throat felt thick, her eyes dry now from staring unblinking at Beatrice's earnest face. The stirring words had tossed out a line of hope that Addie was afraid to grab yet also afraid not to. To take control of her own life, her destiny, seemed so farfetched she could hardly consider it. But to do anything else right now seemed absurdly foolish. Guilty with her own conflicting thoughts, she dropped her eyes to the table. "I don't have any money to start a business. I'd be living here on charity, and I just can't tolerate that."

But there was something more beneath the words, and Beatrice knew it. She waited.

Addie's heart was in her eyes when they lifted. "He's got kids, Bea," she whispered with profound, unabashed longing. "We'd be a real family. I want those kids so bad I ache with it, but I'm scared."

"The kids come with a pa," Beatrice warned. "You best remember that."

Addie remembered it all the way back to town as she rode beside Zeke, holding the baby tight to her chest. Young Zeb kept up a steady stream of chatter that eased the sharper awkwardness between them all, and also deepened the yearning inside her. He was a cheerful child, excitable over the smallest thing in ways she could barely remember.

The scamper of a sage hen through the brush set him to giggling. The flight of an eagle high above the towering cliffs had him exclaiming in wonder. His childish amazement was like a balm to her soul, soothing and renewing a spirit broken by four years of lack. She wished she could be that free again, carried by nothing but the wind and her imagination to float among the clouds.

Joshua was just the opposite, sullen and brooding . . . and scared. It was there in his belligerent eyes and mumbled answers. Where Zeb's enthusiasm allowed her flight, Josh's moroseness grounded her. Addie could hardly bear the pain of looking at him.

She hated the uncertainty that lay before them as much as he did, as much as he must hate the idea of someone taking his mother's place. She understood what he was going through but was powerless to change the inevitable—adjusting to a new family, new ways of doing things, the idiosyncrasies of strangers trying to make a place together.

The wagon rolled through the middle of town, the creek and grind of the wheels and jingling of the harness sounding unforgivably loud to Addie's ears, drawing unwanted attention. They noticed; every last shopkeeper and saloon owner who stood on the dusty street or boarded walk noticed her passage and would speak of it. Nothing passed through a town this size without escaping focus. Addie kept her attention on Cole and ignored the curious glances and belated waves from people she'd known half her life. Most had offered to take her in when her parents died; none had really meant it.

Even now she remembered the Jamisons hesitantly eyeing their two sons, fifteen and seventeen, when they'd offered to find her a spot. Addie didn't claim an overabundance of smarts but it hadn't taken much to know what was going through their heads. Henrietta Pickens, with her pinched expression and prayer book righteous posture, had looked askance at her husband Josiah and offered "out of the Christian goodness of their hearts" to take her in exchange for work if she didn't prove to be a nuisance. Liz Simmons, heavy with her first pregnancy, had wept softly into her lace-trimmed hanky as her husband Mark explained with just the right touch of suffering in his politician's smile that

he just couldn't see overburdening his wife at this delicate time.

There had been other well-meaning families with
well-meaning excuses, but the only ones who had really
seemed genuine in their offer were the Parkers. But at
that time they still lived with eight kids in only two
rooms over the general store. Addie had turned Sam
and Beatrice down when Willis Smith had stepped forward, smooth-tongued, his hat in his hands. She didn't
recall the lies he'd spoken or the false promises he'd
made, just that she had buried her family one day and
married him the next. Her hell had begun within a
week.

Addie stared harder at the road leading out of town,
as if she could hurry the wagon along. She'd tried to
leave Willis once. She couldn't remember now where
she was headed, just the terrible desperation that she
get away. He'd caught her before she reached town and
beaten her beyond recognition. She had learned two
very important things that day. She couldn't escape, so
she'd have to be smarter than Willis to survive.

The physical abuse had been infrequent after the first
year, though there had never been a cessation of the
mental anguish. Slowly and painfully, she had learned
what she needed to get through the days—move carefully, anticipate his moods. She had become a substanceless shadow with quick reflexes and the uncanny
ability to hide within herself while outwardly attending
his needs. By the second year, she had unknowingly and
unwillingly become an asset to him. He had found a
talent in her he could exploit, one he wasn't willing to
destroy with his fists, though he threatened often
enough to keep the terror real. Since his death, she had

tried to cast Willis and the things she'd been forced to do from her mind. But she couldn't forget.

Viciously, she turned the thoughts aside. The hatred and bitterness drained her, left her limp and cowering inside. She knew she would need whatever strength she could muster to get through the coming days. When the wagon reached the outskirts of town, where the false-fronted stores dwindled and homesteads began to dot the landscape, she turned to Zeke and asked him to let her off so she could walk the rest of the way home, too embarrassed for him to see where she lived.

Zeke slowed the horses but didn't stop. Instead, he looked over at her with a cautious expression. "Your place is a good mile from here. No reason why I shouldn't take you the whole way. If you need something in town first, I'll wait."

She played with Cole's curls, while the baby chewed on his fist contentedly. "Just thought I'd walk," she murmured. "I like this time of day."

"It'll be dark before you get there," Zeke said, slightly agitated for no reason he could name. She was a perplexing woman, hard to read, harder still to understand. "The cowhands will be flocking into town as soon as the sun sets; it's not safe for a woman to be out alone."

For four years Willis hadn't cared that she'd trudged back and forth, as long as she wasn't in town when he was. "I just . . ." She shrugged, pleating the baby's gown into small creases to avoid Zeke's eyes. "The place is a mess."

Zeke knew; he had seen it. He clicked his tongue to get the horses moving faster again. "You won't be there much longer."

Addie felt her stomach turn over. "When?"

"The circuit rider will be through here Sunday. It'll be another month before he gets back, longer if bad weather hits."

With a leaden heart, Addie watched the landscape amble by, as if it were moving instead of the wagon she traveled in. Her life felt too stagnant to have any motion of its own, time going on without her yet ironically repeating itself, circling back on a continuous track of wretched monotony that only seemed to be getting deeper and more rutted by the day, harder to break free from.

Eyes fixed on the road ahead, she murmured, "Do you think he'll stay over an extra day? I don't want to get married on Sunday." She didn't want the entire town present for the wedding like last time.

"We could drag it out to Tuesday or Wednesday . . . or next year."

Addie's head swung toward him at the inane words to find his golden eyes sharp and knowing above a wry smile. She couldn't help but smile back a little at the unspoken but bald-faced truth. Drawing it out wouldn't help things one iota. "Monday will be fine."

4

Zeke stood in the small clapboard church and listened with only half an ear to the circuit rider expound on his latest journey, then roll without pausing for breath into a lengthy diatribe on the problems of "heathen savages" facing men of the cloth. Zeke nodded absently but kept most of his attention focused on the boys to make sure they weren't getting too rowdy. He was ready to be done with the ceremony and get back to the chores awaiting him, but Addie hadn't shown up yet. He was beginning to wonder if she would.

An old part of him, something from his youth and long severed, had hinted that he should have called over the past week or sent flowers or at least offered her a ring. But time away from work was precious, and it was beyond him to play the suitor in this forced marriage. He recognized the slip immediately and almost smiled in self-derision. It wasn't like Addie had held a gun to his head and demanded, "Marry me or else!" No, she wanted this even less than he did. Yet part of him felt that way—trapped, forced, without options.

He watched as Zeb darted between the pews and

Cole tried to follow. Josh tagged the baby by the wrist before he tumbled head over heels, but Cole had no appreciation whatsoever for being saved and set up an ear-splitting yowl. The preacher sent the boys a snooty, disapproving look, but Zeke didn't have the heart to reprimand them. He'd had enough trouble getting Josh to the church peaceably. The fact that his son was resigned and willing to help with the baby deserved a bit of indulgence. They had been sitting still for the past thirty minutes, and their patience was exhausted. Zeke's was getting there. If Addie didn't show up soon, he was going to pack his boys up and head home to continue on the way he had been—overworked, overtired, and perpetually behind schedule.

A movement caught his eye at the church entrance and he thought *finally* and turned toward the door just as Jake entered followed by his sister-in-law, Sarah, her two little girls, and . . . Addie? It took Zeke a stunned moment to reconcile the girl paused in the doorway with the washed-out woman he had agreed to take as wife.

Someone had done her hair. Haloed by the sun, it was shiny clean and streaked with buttery highlights. Drawn back away from her face, it fell in a cloud of tight, silky ringlets to her shoulders. There was no complete taming of the unruly curls; a lock still fell across her forehead as if to defy the effort, but the rest had been coaxed into a reasonable style that lent a roundness to her normally sharp cheekbones, softening and filling the gaunt hollows, and giving her a prettiness that he hadn't thought probable even though he'd recognized the possibilities.

Her gown did the same for her spare figure. It was neither a child's nor a woman's, but one designed to mark that interim passage between the two when girlish things are put aside. It had been created to catch a young man's eye without being too bold or obvious, leaving innocence intact but with promise.

It was that promise that held his gaze longer than was decent, even for a bridegroom, bringing home with crude efficiency how long it had been since he'd enjoyed the comfort of a woman. A flush spread up his throat, antagonizingly juvenile, but he didn't turn his gaze away. She stood paused and uncertain, a tangible arresting stillness, as if one more step would send her hurtling over the edge of a precipice. Then Zeb rushed forward in welcome and the invisible barriers that held her seemed to give. She smiled and bent toward him, hands braced on her knees in a gesture so artlessly childlike it made Zeke's pulse respond for an unstable second.

Her smile was as warm as the sunlight streaming through the open door as she spoke to Zeb, and Zeke's eyes strayed to the peachy flesh rising above the low, scooped-necked white cotton, then traveled slowly over the tight bodice to the skirt flowing out daintily to her toes. The hem was scalloped and embroidered with blush-pink rosebuds that matched the sash at her trim waist. The baby toddled up and gave her a hug, pressing her skirts against her legs. The turn of a delicate ankle peeking beneath her hem sent an unexpected kick to Zeke's gut. *Hell.*

Backlit by a morning sun, she looked fey and ethereal, the persona of youth and springtime and wistful imaginings. Things he had long forgotten and didn't want anymore. A time, he suspected, she had never fully known. He felt unbalanced a moment, as if he'd been tricked into accepting one thing when he was actually getting another.

His eyes narrowed in resentment for the brief instant

it took him to realize how irrational his thoughts were, but he couldn't deny that he felt somehow betrayed or duped. He had steeled himself to bring a wife home after the ceremony, a shadowy figurehead who would meet the needs of his household, not this young woman whose brightness outshone her surroundings. She lifted her head and their gazes met and locked. Her smile vanished. A trace of panic entered her eyes before she quickly lowered her lashes to conceal it.

Addie scooped up Cole, then took Zeb's hand and forced herself to cross the short distance separating her from Zeke, though it was difficult to make her limbs move in any direction other than back out the door. She stopped three feet away and offered him a strained smile, feeling about as bad for him at having to be here as she did for herself. Worse, maybe.

He was as handsome as any man she'd ever seen, tall and important looking in a black morning coat and striped trousers that contrasted nicely with his dark blond hair. Michelangelo's *David* flitted through her mind, then was abandoned. Zeke was much too rugged and severe looking for the comparison, yet there was the same grace and strength in the sculptured lines of his face, the same masculine beauty. With his looks and money and good standing in town, he could have had any girl he chose. She fixed her smile tighter. It was his own darn fault for choosing her.

"Addie." He nodded formally in greeting.

"Zeke," she returned shyly. In the past week, she had thought of this moment a thousand times, and a thousand times she had pushed the thoughts aside. The meeting, the greeting, the roles they would have to play offered at least the pretense of normality for the boys' sake, for their own. But the images had brought indecision and discord, so she had concentrated instead on the ranch and the house and the boys, and how wonderful it could all be if it hadn't been for the man who went with the package.

"Such nice weather," she said inanely, then blushed when Zeke gave her a dubious smile.

Zeb skipped in a circle around her to garner attention, then stopped and grinned self-importantly. "We're gittin' married today! You and me and Pa and Josh and Cole."

Addie's gaze softened and her smile turned genuine. "How about that?" she said.

But at the words, the realization, her palms grew clammy and she absently smoothed them down her dress. She hadn't worn the gown for her first marriage, though it had been her Sunday best at the time. Four years ago she'd worn a black mourning gown borrowed from a neighbor out of respect for her deceased family. She refused to wear black now on account of Willis. It was a small rebellion but sufficient enough to make her smile.

Zeke gave her an odd look and she sobered up immediately and stopped fidgeting with her dress, hoping she hadn't offended him by not wearing a traditional wedding gown with a neat high neckline and long sleeves for discretion and modesty. Not that she had any choice. She'd worn the only thing she owned that was halfway suitable, a debutante creation designed to grace a young woman's coming-out into society. In hopeful anticipation of her young daughter's future, her mother had copied the pattern from a dress she had seen once in Chattanooga before the family had left Lookout Mountain, Tennessee.

Like so many other Tennesseans, the Worthams had

been neither slaveholders nor anxious for secession. They'd had no vested interest in the sometimes worthy, oftentimes foolish, bickering between states and had bided their time when talk of war began, thinking surely the ruckus would die down and a nation would not rise up against itself. They weren't ignorant but naive, simple mountain folk with a dedication to family rather than politics. When Yankee and Confederate soldiers had stormed their mountain haven like some sweeping human plague, they had packed their few belongings and made ready to seek a new place to live in peace, far from the ravages of a war that made no sense.

Peace had not come. Shamed by Confederate uncles, cousins, and friends, the oldest Wortham son, Tommy, had joined southern forces to fight for a cause he didn't believe in, but for a people he did. And the family had postponed their trek west to wait in anxiety for the return of a son they would never see alive again.

The dress Addie wore this day and one other were the only things she had left of the family who had moved to escape the South's destruction and the cruel death of their firstborn, only to have their own lives stolen. She had taken the garments into town to buy ribbon and thread that fateful day their farm had been attacked.

The whole thing had been unprecedented and unprovoked. Most of the Indian trouble was in the northern part of the territory, the southeastern area being more secure. Because of the large amount of overland travel that passed through on the Oregon Trail, there were more than ordinary amounts of U.S. Army units centered not only at Fort Laramie to the north but also at Fort Fetterman, Fort D. A. Russell, and Fort Bridger. The presence of the roving cavalry and a good many veteran army units had a sobering effect on the Indians in this area, but apparently not enough.

Addie felt herself growing tense and let the embittering thoughts go. It was useless to speculate on fate and its virulent nature, useless to wonder how anything so cruel and hostile could happen in a land so supremely breathtaking it overtook the soul.

The baby, having again escaped his older brother, toddled toward her on chubby legs that pumped faster than his coordination would allow. Josh was hot on his trail and scooped Cole up before he landed on his bottom, which set the baby to squirming and fussing again. Addie caught the minister's stern look out of the corner of her eye and forced a cordial smile as she turned and extended her hand, relieved that he wasn't the one who had performed her marriage to Willis.

"I don't believe I've had the pleasure."

Reverend Hinkle introduced himself, and Addie was further relieved when Gracie Parker slipped up behind her and took the boys off so the minister would cease sending them censorious frowns. She listened silently to his gushy felicitations on the "upcoming, blessed event and the sanctity of marriage" but she felt like a sham deceiving a man of the cloth. She hadn't had to endure such with Willis. The minister who had performed her first marriage had also presided over the burial of her parents. The ceremony had been as somber as the occasion warranted.

She bore Reverend Hinkle's enthusiasm stoically, knowing she could hardly blurt out that a fast-approaching Wyoming winter provided more impetus than any deep affection or personal aspiration of hers for a husband. When at length the man seemed inclined to go into an endless discourse on the merits of "God's holy union," Addie decided he just liked the sound of his own voice, since she hadn't offered one word to keep the conversation going.

She dared a glance at Zeke while the minister worked up a good head of steam, and found his expression fixed, his eyes vague. But there was just the tiniest hint of a sardonic smile at the corner of his mouth, and she felt her heart give a funny little lurch and a spark of answering humor. She wanted to pinch him for not interrupting the oration, but the familiarity of even thinking such a thing made the blood rush hotly to her cheeks. She pulled her gaze away and searched the church, dismayed to find half a dozen people trickling through the door.

There were no guests invited except Jake Holdman and the Parkers. Most of the town, wearing strained and guilty smiles, had turned out for Addie's last wedding, and she wanted no repeat of the same solicitous mockery. But Addie's wants were of little concern in a town the size of Laramie. People knew their duty in keeping with occasions such as birthings, weddings, and funerals —stitch those pillowcases, bake those pies, offer condolences or congratulations as the situation dictated, and keep that advice coming—with or without an invitation.

Marcus Bennet, a cagey old land attorney and real estate agent, moved toward the front followed by the elderly Barrett sisters, Lucile and Annie. The two ladies had traveled west on the same wagon train with Addie's family and were waving snowy linen hankies at her, as if this were the social occasion of the decade. She couldn't help but smile at the two irascible women.

"We're old," Annie had been fond of saying over the long dusty days, "but we're not dead yet. What we need is adventure!" Adventure had dropped Lucile off the side of her horse. A broken hip had kept her convalescing in Laramie so long, the sisters had decided to settle there. If Addie had been of sound mind four years ago, she would have moved in with the two ladies, but they struggled on a meager pension left to Lucile by her late husband, and the added mouth to feed would have been a terrible burden.

Christian Lafleur, the town's only physician at present, slipped in to sit indolently on the back pew. He was "heart-stopping handsome," as Beatrice would say, but his piercing black eyes and cold manner made Addie uncomfortable. She assumed he must be here for Zeke, because the doctor was staring straight at her future husband. She herself had very little acquaintance with the physician. The only time she'd personally had call for his services was a little over a year ago, a matter so private she hadn't been able to look him in the eye since without turning beet red and feeling a devastating mortification.

She watched Jake Holdman take his seat near the middle with Sarah, along with a smattering of busybodies who never missed a thing in town. One by one they ambled in, as if it were their right. Ian MacAlister and Nathaniel Pickens, traveling as a pair, trailed the gregarious Widow Clarkson. She, in turn, pretended to pay them no mind as she took her seat, but Addie saw her cut a glance behind her to make sure the two men were still in attendance. Mark and Liz Simmons swept in like a king and queen smiling benevolently at their subjects.

Animosity kindled inside Addie. She felt small and manipulated and mocked. Things were awkward enough without a portion of the town's population around to speculate on her fortune or woe. She was neither blind nor stupid and knew Zeke Claiborne was considered a good catch. If she hadn't already been caught once in the matrimonial snare, she might have thought so too, but there were few delusions left in her mind now about life with a man.

She tore her gaze away and tried to ignore their presence, but she couldn't fully ignore the last person to walk through the church doors on the arm of her oldest son and editor of the weekly newspaper. Esther Morris. *Judge* Esther Morris. Six feet tall and 180 pounds, she was a woman whose mere presence commanded attention, but it was the person she was, the deeds she had accomplished, that commanded Addie's respect. Esther Morris, despite disgrace and scandal, had had the bravery to issue an arrest warrant against her abusive husband, then had left him and moved to Laramie.

Addie felt the sting of self-disgust burn behind her eyelids. *Go away,* she wanted to shout, *I don't have your stature or stamina. I can't make it on my own, and I don't want you here to witness it.*

As if divining her thoughts, Esther nodded gravely and stared right back at Addie without one ounce of censure or disapproval. Esther had seen similar looks from a hundred different women in a hundred different towns. Esther knew; she *knew* how it was for a woman. Upbringing, attitudes, and poverty handicapped them. She might have been the first woman judge in history but she didn't have the education or speaking skills to become the leader they all wanted. She had been called mannish and outspoken, but the truth was she wasn't militant enough to fulfill the role she had been thrust into.

She might have had the gall to thumb her nose at propriety and leave her husband, but she'd been virtually penniless and had to move in with her son, who could offer her little more than room and board. Esther was tired of being held up before women young and old as some sort of avenging heroine. Though she had held office proudly, she knew better than anyone that women's suffrage had progressed beyond people's wildest imagination in the Wyoming Territory only because *men* had allowed it. With a sober look, she nodded encouragement and broke eye contact first to allow the pale young woman to get on with her own life.

Zeke touched Addie's arm, and she turned slowly. As much as she dreaded what lay ahead, she wanted this part over with. With more determination than desire, she followed him to the front of the church, thinking again how handsome and dignified Zeke looked in his tailored clothes. She was glad she had washed her old dress and put up her hair. It hadn't mattered with Willis, but for some reason she hadn't even tried to define, she had needed to look presentable for Zeke.

"Shall we?" Reverend Hinkle, with grave reserve and upright posture, cleared his throat and began the wedding ritual both Zeke and Addie had heard years ago—he in joy and expectation with the sweetheart of his youth, she in numb grief with a stranger.

"Join hands, please."

Trembling suddenly and mad at herself for it, Addie placed her hand in Zeke's to keep from running headlong out the door and found his large palm warm and sturdy, somehow comforting.

"Dearly beloved . . ."

She let the words roll past her, as if they might not be real if she didn't listen too closely. It was better this time than it had been before when she'd been so numb and grief stricken she couldn't even hear the preacher's words. If her emotions were tangled, her choices just as scarce, at least this time her mind was clear. She knew what she was doing even if she didn't want to do it.

It was disheartening to know she would leave the church as Zeke's wife, but she would also leave as a mother. That more than anything else gave her the will-power to stand erect and endure the minister as he repeated words committed to memory in a singsong voice that lulled the listeners into a somnolent state of well-being.

The smell of polished wood and warm bodies permeated the air, along with the scents of hair tonic, starch, and soap. Sunbeams streamed through the windows, trailing dust motes and golden light across the smooth floor. As the minister extolled the virtues of marriage, someone wept softly in remembrance, another shifted restlessly in his seat. The thump, thump, thump of bored young feet tapped the bottom of a pew. The ruffling of pages whispered along the air before the prayer book hit the floor with a dull thud and a whispered reprimand followed. At a muffled snore, Addie smiled secretly, knowing Ian MacAlister must have nodded off.

Too ashamed of her circumstances, she hadn't attended a church service in years, but she remembered the sounds and smells from childhood, the inner peace that an hour of worship among friends and family could bring. She had believed in God then, believed in goodness and mercy and hope. She wasn't so sure now.

Sunday mornings had been cool on the Tennessee mountain where she and her family had dressed in their crisply ironed best and hurried off to church to sit shoulder to shoulder on the family pew. She could see them now so clearly, memories held dear and close to her heart in an inner circle of warmth kept safe from intrusion by the outside world. Ma and Pa had always divided the little ones between them as best they could to keep order.

The memories swirled like a kaleidoscope in her mind. Tommy, his hair slicked down and his cowlick sticking straight up, singing the hymns off-key to make her giggle. Willie and Ben elbowing each other for breathing space and catching the blunt end of their father's displeasure for wrestling in church. The baby cooing sweetly and making small milk bubbles. Always, it seemed, there had been an infant in her mother's arms.

Peace drifted through her, seeking a place to dwell. Reassurance, like a forgotten melody, tinkled in her mind as she remembered a hard wooden bench in a Sunday-school room and the memory verse from Joel, a promise. *"And I will restore to you the years that the locust hath eaten." Restore the years . . . restore the years.* The words were so strong, so clear, so definite. It could not have been her own childish voice in recitation that had spoken them. Her heartbeat quickened at the possibility of a new beginning, but after the past four years she didn't dare let herself believe.

A fly buzzed past her nose and landed on her hand, causing her to twitch. She felt Zeke's fingers tighten reflexively for an instant, then resume a casual grip. She eyed him askance and wondered if he was thinking of Becky, remembering years past as she was, regretting being here as she did. There was no expression on his face. His eyes were fixed, his attention focused on Reverend Hinkle as the words continued to pour out by rote.

"If there be any man to show just cause why these two should not be—"

"I have just cause!"

The words boomed through the small church, shatter-

ing the stillness. Addie went rigid and cold at the familiar voice. Sick dread moved through her in waves, rolling and ebbing with the shocked gasps and murmurs
beginning to hum behind her like a swarm of disturbed
bees. *No, no. Please, God.*

Her hand tightened spontaneously in Zeke's, her
nails biting into his palm. She couldn't find her place,
her reason; the scales had been tipped sickeningly off-
balance and she felt as if she were falling. Her feet were
leaden; she didn't know how she managed to turn, except that she wouldn't be caught undefended from behind. Frowning severely, Zeke turned also to face the
intruder, while the congregation stirred to crane their
necks as well.

Grady Smith, a slightly more appealing replica of his
younger brother, stood at the church entrance looking
cocky and belligerent. "I have just cause, preacher
man!"

He strolled forward, his oily smile causing Addie inadvertently to step back into Zeke. Her fingers became
a death grip on his hand. Sensing her fear, Zeke's arm
went around her shoulders, instinctively sheltering her
as he would one of his sons when danger threatened.

"This is highly irregular," the preacher croaked in a
thin voice, but no one paid him any mind. Their attention was riveted on the scandalous events unfolding.

Zeke felt a wave of sullen irritation move through
him as Grady continued forward. An irate brother-in-
law, for God's sake! He didn't need this thespian-styled
drama in his life. "What are you doing here, Grady?" he
asked with cool civility.

Grady's eyes roamed intimately, insultingly, over Addie. "I've come to see my brother's widow get hitched

not two weeks after he's been laid in the ground. You reckon he's got cold yet, Addie?"

She didn't deign to answer, just stared back at Willis's brother and pressed farther into Zeke, unknowingly accepting the lesser of two evils.

Grady noted the gesture with a sneer. "You been carrying on with Claiborne all along or just since my poor brother lost his life?"

Zeke lunged forward but Addie's frantically whispered "No!" checked his progress. Sam Parker came to his feet in the first pew, Jake Holdman in the center, while the murmur of shocked gasps escalated among the townsfolk. Beatrice's face flamed as if she had swallowed a fireball.

A strangled whine caught in Addie's throat, even as her heart threw up the numbing barriers to protect herself and keep anyone from seeing her shame and fear. But still the ugly question pierced through her defenses because there were innocent children present who didn't deserve to have to listen to Grady's unfounded accusations. He drew closer and her knees trembled violently. She felt weak and insignificant and afraid, all the things she had sworn she would never feel again.

Zeke's arm slid from her stiff shoulder and he took a slow but lethal step forward. Whether in warning or challenge, Addie didn't know, and realized she couldn't stop him this time. As his hand slipped from her, she felt as though she had been abandoned, left to flounder in thick, suffocating quicksand. Her arm fell limp to her side, useless, but she wanted desperately to reach out and cry for him to come back.

Please, God. She couldn't abide a scene, not here with half the town present to witness her shame. Her brother-in-law was capable of any vile or despicable thing to gain his own end. If he chose, he could destroy her.

The knowledge moved her forward, only one small step, but the physical action provided the impetus she needed to speak. "You didn't show up for the funeral, Grady," she said in a tremulous effort to turn the nasty tide back. "We waited an extra day, but you never showed."

Annoyance fleeted across Grady's face, then his expression changed with patent fabrication to a pained, compassionate look. If it had been offered as a coin, Addie would have bitten down hard to test it.

"I just couldn't make it," he said, looking sufficiently pained before his voice grew syrupy. "But I'm here now, Addie, come to take care of my brother's grieving widow. It's what Willis would have wanted."

Panic shot through her and her nerveless limbs shuddered uncontrollably. Zeke stood just ahead of her, his back broad and shielding in an assertive stance. She wanted to touch his strength, to absorb it into her, or hide behind him until the nightmare was over. But she couldn't move, couldn't speak. She just stood, bereft of all feelings save despair. She might not want to marry Zeke, but she'd burn in hell before she'd be turned over to Grady.

Noting her pale cheeks and bloodless lips from hooded eyes, Zeke stepped back and put his arm around her shoulders, then slid his hand down to her waist and pulled her securely against his side. Her muscles contracted at the force. There was nothing at all comforting in the hard grasp of his fingers. Addie looked up, then cringed at the implacable look on his face. The move wasn't protective but blatantly proprietary and subtly challenging. She closed her eyes briefly, wondering which manner of hell was worse. The one in front of her that she understood too well, or the one beside her that she didn't know at all?

Zeke splayed his fingers wide over Addie's rib cage and felt her muscles retract. He didn't need to sense her fear and revulsion to form his own opinions. Grady Smith was a successful gambler with a shady reputation. He'd never been called a cheat outright, but his consistent good luck was a little too sterling for comfort.

Grady reminded him of the carpetbaggers who had scoured the South after the war, reaping the benefits of other people's misery. He thought Grady cunning enough to capitalize on Addie's misfortune, and his presence here meant he was manipulative, but the looks he was giving Addie also meant he could be dangerous. What Zeke didn't know was what the scum wanted with his brother's penniless widow.

Another shiver coursed through Addie's slight frame and his hand tightened instinctively on her waist in a protective gesture. Anger and self-mockery flooded him at the sudden realization that he might not want her, but he'd be damned if he'd let someone like Grady have her.

His eyes narrowed lazily. "I'm sure Addie appreciates you getting here as soon as you could, Grady."

Only Jake recognized the hard glint in Zeke's eyes, evidence that he was keeping the peace for the sake of everyone present, but his words sent a streak of fear through Addie. She wanted to beg him not to change his mind now that someone else had stepped forward to take responsibility for her, wanted to remind him how much he needed help with his children. But she wouldn't do either. She'd never grovel before another man.

"Well," Grady said, satisfaction in his eyes, "I appreciate your intentions, Claiborne, a right neighborly thing you've done in offering for her. But I feel it's my duty to see to Addie now, being the only family she's got left."

Addie's gaze flew to Zeke, but his expression was unreadable. She felt ill and adrift, and knew any second she was going to disgrace herself by fainting or being sick. Her pleading eyes searched the room desperately for help, but it was Zeke's firm hand that kept her on her feet, along with his words.

"Addie and I have decided to marry. I'm glad to know she has a family to care about her. Now, she'll have two."

Oh, Lord! She wanted to weep with relief or dissolve, her legs felt so weak, but Grady's hate-filled gaze stabbed straight through her, his threat barely hidden.

"Like I said, right neighborly of you, Claiborne. But that won't be necessary. She'll be better off with me—"

"No." Addie's voice came out pitifully weak but determined. She dared another glance at Zeke, then forced her gaze back to her brother-in-law. "I can't go with you, Grady. I've made my promise." Her stomach churned while she waited for his reaction, then went dead cold when he grinned. It was so controlling, that terrible smile, so familiar. The room seemed to dim, and the air felt as if it had been sucked out into a lethal, fathomless void. *Please don't do this, please.*

His smile grew wider, sweeter, and the sickness of its power seeped into her bloodstream. If she didn't do something now, this second, the shame and terror of the past four years would never end. Her heart slowed its frantic beating, and a numb calm invaded every pore of her body. She could feel Zeke beside her, supporting her, but for the first time in her adult life she felt it was she herself who actually had command of something. The notion of power almost made her light-headed.

She took a small, seemingly insignificant step forward. "I won't go with you, Grady," she said quietly. "You can't make me."

It was a grievous mistake. The moment the defiant words left her mouth, she knew the foolishness of baiting him. Blood thrummed in her ears as his smile vanished and his eyes went flat.

"Can't I?" Grady asked softly. With cunning, he began to walk forward, one slow step at a time to heighten the intimidation. When he stood less than two feet from her, he stopped and grinned again, knowingly. His voice held the sibilant whisper of a snake, a terrible warning that her display of courage would be her downfall. "I'll tell, Addie. I'll tell Claiborne all about you and me and Willis."

All color drained from her face. Her entire body went limp, and she would have collapsed had Zeke not tightened his hold, a forceful demand for her to stay on her feet. He heard the trapped moan in her throat and felt her try to pull away, to isolate herself as if contaminated, but she didn't have the strength. The air grew stale with the cheap repugnance of Grady's words.

"There's no need," Zeke said with a dangerously congenial smile. "Addie's told me everything. It doesn't make a bit of difference to me." His eyes speared straight into the other man with deadly accuracy. "Now, get the hell out of here."

Grady's eyes widened in shocked disbelief for a brief second, then narrowed slyly. "You're either a liar or a fool, Claiborne," he sneered. His spiteful gaze went to Addie, but she knew it was over, at least for now. Grady couldn't ruin her without ruining himself as well. "We're not done, *sister,* understand? Willis took my chest, and I want it back. You give me the chest and we'll be square."

"I don't have it," she whispered dully, dying inside, every hope she had held for the future shriveling to dust.

"Find it," Grady said softly. "I'll be in touch."

He turned and strolled casually from the church, tipping his hat to Beatrice on his way out. She wanted to scream "horse dung" at him, but clasped Sam's hand instead and turned her gaze back to Addie, who looked as near to fainting as a woman could look without actually toppling over. "Get on with it, preacher!" she said in the raised tone she used to cower the town council or make her children obey without question. "A visit from the devil don't have no consequence in God's house."

Too humiliated to face the small congregation staring at her in stunned confusion, Addie turned back to face the minister. Her voice was quavery but sure. "Mr. Claiborne might want to rethink things before . . . before—"

"We'll talk later," Zeke said, a hard-bitten edge to his voice. He despised men like Grady, who were manipulators and opportunists always ready to prey on the weaker. He wouldn't let Grady accomplish whatever the man had intended by coming here, but to say he was unconcerned would have been a lie. He had three small, impressionable sons to consider. The woman beside him would have a tremendous influence on their upbringing, ideals, and morals from this day forward.

Addie watched his expression harden but saw more than stubbornness surface in his deep amber eyes. He was confused and concerned, trying to do right by her, but needing more to do right by his boys. It was that depth of honesty that gave her the strength to rise up against him on tiptoe. "Now," she whispered. "I think we should talk now."

Zeke gave a brusque nod. "If you'll excuse us a moment?" he said to the minister, then threaded his fingers through Addie's and tugged her along behind him out the side door.

Confused whispers erupted inside the church, then mercifully faded as Addie stepped into the sunlight. A bird fluttered past her, indignant at being disturbed from pecking at the crusty remains of Sunday's picnic. The air was redolent of the scent of pine, fir, and juniper growing on the lower mountain slopes, but the breeze promised crisp days soon, and worse—freezing temperatures and high, keening winds that turned dry snow into ground blizzards. Sick at heart, Addie stirred the dirt with her toe, needing to face Zeke but unable to.

"You lied to Grady," she said, eyes fixed on the ground. "Why?"

Zeke didn't know why, except that she had looked so vulnerable against Grady's filthy insinuations. Maybe Beatrice or Sam or even Jake would have come to her defense if he hadn't spoken up, but it had seemed his place to do so, his responsibility.

"Talk," he said to her bent head. "If there's something I need to know, Addie, go ahead and say it. We have people waiting."

She lifted her head, determined to be honest, but found she couldn't speak. Zeke's eyes were remote, looking straight through her. He was obviously braced for the worst. If he refused to take her, no one would blame him, and his hard, closed expression proved he was capable of it. She watched him rake his fingers through his hair and shift his tense gaze to the mountains, then reluctantly back to her. It was then that she saw what was hidden beneath the isolated surface of his eyes.

Honor. There were miles and miles of trampled honor in this man. His innate integrity had been crushed at some time in his life, but it was still so much a part of him that he could consider her feelings while knowing he must protect his boys. *He wants to do the right thing,* she thought. Oh, Lord, how long had it been since she'd been around a man who wanted to do right? Guilt flooded her at being the source of his frustration, and she wanted to weep at causing him the burden of having to choose between standing by her or refusing.

His face was set, his eyes distant as he waited for her to speak. Though the sour taste of his conflict was almost palpable on her own tongue, there was no possible way Addie could defend herself against what Grady had said, or voice the sick humiliation she felt when she thought of the times he had visited his brother.

She tore her gaze from Zeke's, bargaining for time she couldn't afford, a future that was quickly slipping out of her grasp before she'd even had a chance to take hold of it. "I can't explain," she whispered, shaken. "I thought maybe . . . I just can't."

Zeke suddenly felt as ill as she looked. He was no stranger to the desolation in her eyes or the haunted vestiges of wrath and shame. Once, in the latter days of the war, he had come upon a small plantation, needing supplies. He and his men had thought the place safe. The Yankees were still many miles to the north and hadn't gotten that far yet, but something worse had—deserters. When his regiment had entered the house they found two women huddled in a corner, clutching each other like children. Their clothing was torn and stained with their own blood.

Their eyes looked like Addie's.

Zeke reeled with the memory but kept his voice steady. "Did he touch you, Addie? Did that bastard put his hands on you—"

"No!" Her head jerked up, all color leached from her cheeks. She had cried the word too quickly.

Zeke's eyes went hard and alert as if they could see right inside her soul. "Addie?"

"Oh, please," she whispered desperately, and averted her face.

"Son of a bitch," Zeke rasped, clenching his fists at his sides. A vein throbbed in his temple as he fought for calm, a way to deal rationally with the urge to take off after Grady and smash the man's head against a wall. "Where the hell was Willis—"

"No!" she cried to stop the flow of words, the underlying accusations. "It's not what you think." Her throat worked in spasms as she tried to crush the memories and hold the panic at bay, to contain it in the hard, hurting knot in her stomach, but it was coming at her like a gale, consuming and overwhelming.

"Tell me what to think, Addie," he said quietly, but she was shaking her head in frantic snatches, and Zeke knew whatever had happened was still too vivid and humiliating for her to discuss. Her arms were wrapped around her middle, crushing the pretty satin sash.

Her eyes were stark and growing desperate, so huge in her pale face. Zeke had seen the look before. "Breathe," he commanded evenly to calm her. "It's all right, Addie, take a deep breath." He reached out to take her hand, but she shied away so quickly, she backed into the church wall. Her palms flew down to brace against the wood, as if he were stalking her instead of her memories.

"I . . ." Her heart beat too fast, overtaking her. Hands, groping and seeking in a dark shanty, touched her even now. Lascivious eyes roving over her in daylight. She pulled her arms more tightly around her and held her breath until her lungs burned, needing composure, escape. She tried to wet her lips but her mouth was too dry, her tongue thick. "I swear . . . I *swear* I would never do anything to hurt your boys."

"I know," Zeke said carefully. The faces of young frightened soldiers swam before him, tender inconsolable boys barely loosed from their mother's apron strings. Surrounded by the wounded and dying, they teetered on the edge of panic. Now as then, he grew deadly calm and in complete command of the chaos, removed and separate, to keep from being consumed by it. "I know, Addie. That's all I need to know."

His words barely penetrated her mind, but his implied meaning screamed at her. *"For now at least"* lay loudly and profanely unspoken between them, as intangible but prevailing as the wind fluttering her skirts. The evidence of it was there in his eyes and set jaw; he wouldn't let it alone.

"No . . . oh, damn," she whispered brokenly, then cried it. "Dammit, no!"

Zeke lurched forward and put his hand over her mouth to hush her before the preacher and the others heard. She'd suffered enough humiliation from Grady this morning without adding profanity to the gossip that would circulate faster than a brushfire.

She felt the press of his fingers, the smothering domination, and made trapped little sounds behind his hand. "Ummm . . . ummm . . . ummm." But there was no fury or meanness in his eyes, just grave concern and bewilderment. Addie shrugged his palm off and buried her face in her hands. Everything in her seemed to diffuse, to come apart slowly until the fabric that knit her bones together tore asunder and she slowly slid down the wall to her heels.

Shadowed under the eaves of the church, huddled against the wall, she looked like a small, broken doll thoughtlessly discarded. Zeke felt his insides contract and crouched down in front of her, his eyes aware and searching. "Addie, what does Grady want from you? What's in the chest?"

Her life, her death. Heaven and hell a handsbreadth apart. She shook her head, her muffled voice strident from the depths of her palms. "Don't ask me about it. When Willis died, I thought I was free. Don't ask me."

"No, I won't. Not now."

Her hands flew down to brace against the wall. "Not ever!"

Zeke couldn't promise that, not even in the face of her desperate pleading. Whatever had been done to her might have no bearing on how she raised his children, but it was eating her alive. He was certain that it also had plenty to do with her obvious mistrust of him, the unease she showed every time he drew near. She hadn't been more than fifteen when she married Willis, when she met Grady. What had the sons of bitches done to her?

It all came back to him in a brutal rush, his words when he stated the provisions of the marriage and the despondent look on her face coupled with the unbelief in the tone of her voice.

I don't want anything else.

You sure?

Such hopeful words. It made him ill now to think her relief had not been based solely on the mutual agreement that neither of them wanted a personal relationship, but had come instead from his releasing her from something she thought profoundly distasteful, even frightening.

The realization staggered him. It also changed things somehow, challenged him in ways he didn't want, or need, to find out what horrors she had suffered at the hands of Willis and his brother.

Zeke tried to tear his gaze from the sight of her huddled in the dirt, but a lock of hair had slipped loose from its pins and hung in messy spirals over one cheek, beckoning him to push it back. He didn't want those feelings or any other emotional attachment to the young woman he was marrying for selfish reasons, the young woman crouched against a church wall as if she had folded in upon herself. He'd invested a lifetime of feelings in Becky, and it had all come to nothing but a profound sense of abandonment and abject loneliness. He couldn't do that again, wouldn't.

He wanted the two of them to remain polite strangers working for a common goal, brought together by their needs, but unattached and unaffected, distanced from any emotional entanglement. The breeze whipped her hair across her wan face, scattering gilded curls across her eyes and lips, but she wouldn't let go of the wood to brush it behind her ear.

Touch it, he wanted to shout. *Get it out of your eyes. Tell me what's going on here!* When she didn't move, Zeke had the terrible urge to do it for her but clenched his fist instead and took a step back.

He'd been raised to honor and revere women, to pro-

vide for and protect them. But so much of that upbringing had been cauterized by four years of bloody senseless battles, then castrated completely with Becky's
death. He didn't want to feel that benevolence again for
any female, didn't want to be her champion or defender,
her helper or healer. He needed a mother for his sons, a
keeper for his home, a bedmate for lonely nights. He
didn't want anything else.

You sure?

He swallowed back an oath. "It's over, Addie. Grady
won't get near you again."

She looked up at him with eyes as bleak as a winter
sea, as if to test his words or his intentions. The boards
were rough against her back and palms but she couldn't
accept Zeke's proffered hand. Instead she pushed away
from the church wall and rose to her feet on legs that
trembled. She stood braced a moment and stared at
him, hardly breathing.

"Not ever. I don't want to talk about Willis or Grady
ever."

Zeke only stared back at her. "Or what?"

"Or . . ." She didn't know. She had nothing to bargain with. She needed this marriage worse than he did,
especially now. With Grady back in town she needed
protection. "Just don't," she whispered, biting down on
her lower lip to keep it from trembling.

Something inside Zeke went cold and barricaded. He
gave a clipped nod, and once again offered his hand.
She flinched slightly, then shook her head and took a
difficult step forward under her own power, as if she
badly needed the isolation and self-jurisdiction.

"Wait." His hands fell on her shoulders and she went
violently rigid for a split second, then spun out from

under his touch. Zeke's eyes flared, then narrowed; his voice was flat. "Fix your hair."

Confusion clouded her eyes. She reached up and touched the dangling locks as if they were something foreign and unknown to her.

Zeke made an impatient sound as he stepped forward and swept her hand aside. "Here, let me." She closed her eyes and waited, dwindling inside, willing herself to remain still as his fingers gently put things to right. Once done, he dropped his hands and stepped away. "Let's go back in."

Addie nodded, her eyes searching his for an answer to the question she wouldn't ask. To what purpose did they return? To take vows, or gracefully decline?

"Let's get it over with," he said. "We need to get home before dark."

Relief flooded her like a soft spring rain and pooled in her eyes and throat until she couldn't see or speak, could only follow.

When they entered the side door, Addie noted the relieved look on Sam and Beatrice's faces, the confusion on the older children. Baby Cole, innocently unaware of the thick tension in the air, bounced on Gracie's lap, while Zeb leaned forward in the pew, swinging his legs to ease the monotony of waiting for his pa and Addie to return. Joshua was slumped back, disgruntled, not yet old enough to show any dignity in his rebellion.

It was Joshua's eyes that held Addie. She wanted to promise she would never hurt him, that he need not betray his mother's memory by liking her. She only wanted, needed, his acceptance and to erase the fear in his eyes—the painful reflection of her own.

She offered no apology to the people seated before her, though she felt solely responsible for their anxiety.

Instead she turned to face the minister, hoping for the first time since accepting Zeke's offer that she was doing the right thing by him, not just the only thing possible for herself.

5

Beatrice had prepared a wedding reception of sorts. The Parker farm lay along the trail to Zeke's and provided a convenient stopping place that would help pass the day for two strangers who were much too uncomfortable to be newly wedded. Beatrice had always believed that doing a little something was better than doing a whole lot of nothing.

"Those two got a rough road ahead of them," she murmured to her husband, Sam.

But Sam was a man of few words and only mumbled, "Yep," as he steered the wagon to the front of their two-story frame home.

Two years earlier, dwelling number twenty-seven had been ordered from the Bridges' Ready Made Houses catalog at a cost of $1,850 and shipped west by boxcar. The railed porch stretching across the front and side had been added later at Beatrice's insistence. It offered cozy elegance to an otherwise sturdy, accommodating house.

To Sam's despair, it was in constant need of whitewashing, but Beatrice had wanted more for this house than the cramped two rooms they had started out in above their general store. She didn't regret one second of their progression from the store to this large roomy house, but neither would she go back. She had paid her dues and now accepted the fruits of her hard work as her just reward.

Zeke pulled his wagon up beside the Parkers' and set the brake. He stepped down and offered to help Addie, but she was already climbing off out of reach. He caught Zeb under the arms and swung him to the ground, then checked on Joshua and Cole, who had ridden with the Parkers. Gracie was striding toward the house with the baby on her hip, and Josh was begging a piggyback ride from seventeen-year-old Luke. When Zeb darted off to join the crowd, Zeke turned back to see Addie still waiting by the wagon, looking lost, as if she didn't quite know what to do. Or, he suspected, prolonging the moment before she had to do what everyone else expected. He wasn't too anxious himself to go inside and pretend the role of happy bridegroom for the sake of everyone present.

"Would you like to take a walk?"

Her head snapped up. "What for?"

Her eyes were so leery, so guarded. "Just to give things time to simmer down. You ever walked into Beatrice's house behind a herd of hungry children? A body could get trampled flat and no one would find you till after coffee."

Addie smiled slightly, and the worry faded from her face to reveal a hint of lost youthfulness. "I imagine it could get right dangerous."

Zeke strolled around the wagon until he stood just inches from her, feeling as ill at ease as she must, out of kilter with the roles they must play. He leaned against the wagon and took tobacco and paper from his pocket. "Does this bother you?"

Addie shook her head, surprised that he had asked, pleased a little by the courtesy. "My father smoked a pipe." Her mother had always made him take it out back except in winter. On cold evenings the smell of his tobacco would fill the house and mingle with the scent of supper cooking on the warm stove. Addie had liked it.

She tipped her face up. She could hardly ignore Zeke, but she felt so uncomfortable in his presence, drained from her outburst behind the church and deeply embarrassed. She suppressed a nervous shudder and pulled her shawl more tightly around her shoulders. She had felt almost protected earlier by his strength in the face of calamity, but that same quality now unsettled her.

He was her husband with all the rights and privileges that went with the paper they had signed. Even in this enlightened age, women were little more than chattel. Anyone who denied it was either blind or stupid. She sensed Zeke wasn't a bad man, nor one who shirked his duties, but she knew little else. What would he be like when angry? What would he do if he didn't like her cooking or cleaning?

She thought she could be a good mother to his sons because she wanted it so badly, but she didn't know if she would make a good wife. She stared out over the pasture and wondered why it had never mattered that she be good enough for Willis. Some flaw in her character perhaps, or just the intrinsic knowledge that no matter what she did or how hard she tried she could never have pleased him. Would Zeke be any different? She had barely endured the four years with Willis, but after the episode at the church she believed Zeke deserved more than her ambivalence. In spite of everything he must have thought or felt or wondered, he had stood by her.

She remembered the remote look in his eyes, the tense lines at the corners of his mouth. Somewhere in his past he had suffered, in ways different from her maybe, but pain was pain. She recognized his every time she looked into his golden eyes, and didn't want to be responsible for causing him more.

She needed to say something, anything, but found simple words helpless in bridging the gap between them. They might as well have been separated by centuries instead of inches, so complete was the silence. The light was glaring behind him, creating an aura that cast his face and shoulders in shadow but glinted off the ends of his dark blond hair. He stood so near she felt diminished in his presence, small and towered over, like a sapling beneath an oak. His eyes were striking, sun-struck amber, but distant and unreadable as he regarded her. With a strange flutter in her chest, she swung away and began walking briskly toward the corral, pointing to the stallion cropping grass along the wooden fence.

"He's nice. Good lines," she called over her shoulder, searching for small talk, a way to remove his direct attention.

Zeke wondered at her sudden need for escape and followed at a sedate pace, studying the sway of her hips as she hurried off, the way the pink ribbon bounced gently against the slender curves of her buttocks, the way her heels kicked up just the edges of her skirt. When he reached her side, he crushed the cigarette beneath his heel and leaned idly against the fence post.

"His name is Champion. Sam finally saved up enough to buy him last month from Mark Simmons."

Addie curled her fingers around the wooden rail and leaned into it, studying the beast with an approving eye. "Mark's got the best stock, all right, at least around here." She watched the stallion swing his head back to bite at a horsefly, then kick his heels and charge off around the pen with a strength and economy of movement she admired. "Sam's gonna have a time with that one, though. He's frisky."

Zeke nodded, listening to her words but watching her face with even more interest. There was a bit of color in her cheeks now and her eyes had lost their dullness. "You seem to know a bit about horses."

She shrugged. "Pa knew a man in Chattanooga who raised them. We used to go there sometimes."

Zeke leaned closer to point out the new mare in another pen, and Addie unconsciously scooted away. He recognized the protective gesture immediately; she employed it anytime he got near, except when her brother-in-law had entered the church. There was something downright provoking about the fact that she was only a little less afraid of him than someone as disreputable as Grady Smith.

Eyeing her to see what she would do, Zeke stepped even closer and watched her inadvertently sidle over another inch. He wasn't in the mood to play chase, so he took one bold step and let his hands fall on the top rung of the fence on either side of her, knowing even as he trapped her that there must be an unscrupulous streak of adolescent meanness inside him, like pulling a puppy's tail just to watch it squirm. He watched her stiffen from head to toe but kept his hands planted, wondering if she'd tell him to move or just duck underneath his arms.

She did neither, just stood dead still and stared at the stallion as if it were the only thing of importance left on earth. But Zeke noted that her elbows locked as if to fortify her, and her knuckles grew white from gripping the rail. He leaned forward, careful not to touch her but crowding her just the same, and watched the fine curls at her nape stir under the flow of his breath.

"Sam's got a nice strong mare. With Champion he'll breed a good line."

Gooseflesh shivered across her skin and a faint blush stained the back of her neck. Zeke leaned even closer, the insides of his upper arms just touching her shoulders. A clean, soapy scent teased his nostrils and heat seemed to radiate within the circle of his arms. Had they been anyone other than who they were, lovers instead of strangers fresh from a marriage ceremony, he would have leaned into her, his chest against her slender back, his hips against her buttocks, his lips finding the fine soft skin of her neck.

But they were strangers, needy and damaged goods from their flawed pasts. "Why don't you tell me to stop, Addie?" he asked, his voice causing another rush of shivers to course through her. "This bothers you something fierce. Why don't you just move away or tell me to stop?"

She swung around suddenly, her back digging into the fence, her eyes defiant. "What would you do?"

He shrugged. "Move. Or maybe stay here until you explain why it bothers you so much." He held her gaze by sheer willpower, feeling the suppressed energy build and expand within her, as if she wanted to run and run and keep on running until she was too far away for him to touch her. The space between his arms grew charged with a volatile, electrifying intensity. He could almost smell her fear. "Addie, I would never do anything to hurt you."

As if a coiled spring inside her suddenly snapped, she swung her hands up blindly and shoved hard against his chest, clipping him on the chin in the process. She lurched to the side when he stumbled back, and stood frozen, her heart pounding furiously in her breast. Her bonnet slipped from her head and tumbled to the ground, forgotten. When Zeke didn't retaliate or even move, her spine went rigid and her body flooded with shame. Her eyes were too bright in her pale face, but her chin remained mulish even when it threatened to quiver.

Zeke fingered the sore spot on his chin and looked straight at her for tense, endless seconds, then shook his head. "You've got a mean left hook, *Miz Claiborne.* Remind me never to make you real mad."

Addie felt the ground sink beneath her, as if it were falling away. Her stomach lifted, and she blushed to the roots of her hair. "I'm sorry. I—" She swallowed, not knowing what else she could say.

Zeke's gaze lowered to the small hands fisted at her sides, then lifted back to meet her eyes. "If I make a suggestion," he asked dryly, "are you gonna hit me again?"

She almost strangled on the air lodged in her throat. God's sake! How could she have struck this man who had just rescued her from Grady? She was about to spend the rest of her life with him; trying to knock him senseless was some fine way to start things off. She squeezed her eyes shut, wanting to laugh and cry and groan all at the same time.

"I . . . no, I won't hit you again."

"You sure?"

Her lips parted on a pained smile and her chest heated up something terrible. "I'm sure."

"Well . . ." His expression was one of utmost seriousness. "We're going to walk down the path just a little ways. All right? I don't want to have to explain a bloody nose to the boys."

Addie's eyes widened before she turned her burning face away. The man was teasing her. It felt so strange and good at the same time, she didn't know what to make of it. She peeked back at him. "Why?"

A smug, very masculine look crossed his face. "Blood scares them."

She lowered her eyes on a smile and spied her bonnet. She bent to retrieve it and held it to her stomach as she straightened and looked back at him. "No, why are you joshing me?"

She made it sound like an accusation. Zeke just shook his head, then pried one of her hands loose and laced his fingers through it. "Come on, Addie."

After only a slight jerk of hesitancy, she walked beside him, feeling unwieldy and wondering how she could disengage her fingers with little notice. She tugged once on the pretense of pointing at a grouse, but his hand only lifted with hers, his amber eyes much too keen not to realize what she was doing. She snatched her attention back to the path, feeling dreary at being so transparent.

They strolled several yards into the sparse woods bordering the creek until a canopy of willows and cottonwoods shaded their passage. Addie remembered similar walks with her brother Tommy, when they were young, high atop Lookout Mountain. The woods had been thicker there, the fecund smell of moist earth and crushed greenery rising beneath their feet.

Scampering barefoot through the foliage like wild things, they had been free, young, and full of heart. The Tennessee River had been far below, winding like a sparkling ribbon that beckoned them to chance the boundaries of imagination. Unencumbered by such adult things as reality, they had made wings of thin branches and leaves and chicken feathers, determined to fly right off the mountain and soar like hawks above the river.

But the war had taken all that. Flights of fancy and dreamy-eyed adolescence had been stolen in one brutal second on a battlefield. Addie searched the path for wildflowers, for something bright and pleasing to ease her discomfort, but there were so few left now that winter was near. The stream gurgled nearby, a pleasant backdrop for the call of an eagle circling the tall pines and the chirp of a starling in the branches of a cottonwood. She swung the bonnet at her side and tried to ignore the lack of human voice in the sound-filled surroundings but the air around them seemed to grow unaccountably heavy and unnatural. She tilted her face up to regard Zeke.

"Were you in the war?"

He frowned slightly, then nodded. "Your pa?"

"No, my brother." Her eyes dimmed. "He was killed at the Battle of Stones River."

Hell's Half Acre. An invisible shudder passed through Zeke and he looked away, lest she see the reflection of the bloody debacle mirrored in his eyes. Cold fog had cloaked the Stones River and surrounding farmland that gray morning in December of '62. The normally fordable river was swelled with rain, dividing the field of battle. Dense cedar thickets, marshy glades, and ground broken by limestone outcroppings had complicated the prospect for troop movement as he and Jake and Christian had rolled up their soggy bedrolls and wished for a better day to fight. But both sides had smelled victory, and there was no stopping men when bloodlust was their only bedmate.

Jake's grandfather had been a staunch Confederate from Nashville. At his request, the three had been sent to give medical aid to the Confederate Army of Tennessee, which was blocking the main road and rail routes to Chattanooga. With more resignation than heart, they had mounted their horses and stuffed cotton in their ears as the cannons wheeled into position for what would prove to be one of Tennessee's bloodiest days of the Civil War. When the smoke cleared, twenty-three thousand Confederate and Union soldiers lay dead.

Locked into silence by the memories, Zeke was unwilling to elaborate on the horrors he'd spent years trying to forget. The battle had proved to be a physical defeat but even worse—an emotional one without dignity or honor. By January 2, the gory fiasco was over, his division decimated by losses, demoralized, their confidence in General Bragg at its lowest ebb. The Confederates should have won that day, but instead they had retreated because of an elaborate scheme of deception played out by Rosecrans, the Federal forces' general, who had duped them into believing he had seventy thousand men and was receiving reinforcements, when he actually had fewer than forty-seven thousand.

The Southern troops had retired from the field at Murfreesboro because of nothing more than stentorian voices heard in the night giving orders for imaginary regiments to take their respective camping grounds, and fictitious companies to stack arms and break ranks. They had fled at the growing number of campfires being built in front of supposed reinforcements. Rosecrans had achieved success in his first big-scale command by employing a ghost army.

Zeke's hand tightened on Addie's at the internal embarrassment of being tricked along with the senseless waste of young lives. He'd taken a bullet himself in that battle but he had survived. Too many had not. He had never, in all the years he served, become accustomed to burying boys his own age and younger. And in the ensuing months, he'd grown cold and callous as a soldier, as mechanical at witnessing death as he was at healing, but he'd never grown immune to the pain or guilt, or the fear that he or someone he knew would be next.

Addie sensed his dark musings in the hurtful grip of his fingers and tried to pull her hand away. His hold only tightened as he turned to her, his look hooded.

"What was your brother's name?" he asked.

Her throat went dry, but she managed to rasp out hesitantly, "T . . . Tommy."

There had been a million Tommys. "I'm sorry. I don't remember him."

"You don't . . ." She paused, puzzled, then realization dawned. "You were there?" Something desperate and grasping stirred within her at his brusque nod. She wasn't even aware that her fingers had curled tightly through his. "Maybe you met him. Maybe you just didn't know his name." She could hear the breathless pleading in her own voice but couldn't stop it. Just one word, one recollection, about the brother she had lost would be enough to salvage years of disappointment and grief.

Addie blinked to clear the yearning from her eyes.

She had learned long ago not to appear too eager and give a man a weapon to use against her. Yet, as hard as she tried, she couldn't disguise the hopeful longing in her voice. "James Thomas Wortham."

Zeke closed his eyes briefly. *Hillbilly.* Hair darker than his sister's, eyes just as green. A bony-framed boy with a thick backwoods Tennessee drawl that had kept him on the teasing end of conversation. He'd been a freckle-faced child in a man's uniform, who had blushed at the risqué playing cards passed around and cried at night when he thought no one heard. Weeks of dysentery had weakened the boy into a thin, wasted shell. A minié ball had finished him.

Zeke's expression closed over and his voice grew chilly and dismissive. "Like I said, there were so many."

He watched Addie's expression fade to disappointment, felt her palm grow lax in his, and tried to harden himself to it. *Dammit, girl, you don't want to know how he wasted away, how he grew so skinny he could barely keep his pants up, how he shivered so we could hardly keep him still . . . how he had cried out a girl's name that everyone thought must be a sweetheart.*

Zeke felt his gut twist, but he couldn't bring himself to simply ignore Addie like he had the glory seekers, those out for a retelling to keep the hatred alive. She just wanted word of a lost loved one, but he couldn't give her the uncolored truth.

He pulled her hand up and traced the fine bones with his thumb but didn't meet her eyes. "We called him Hillbilly. He had more red in his hair than you; it was rusty looking by campfire. He took a lot of teasing but gave as good as he got. The men respected him for it." His eyes met hers, but there was no expression there.

"He was a proud boy, Addie, who died like a man. That's all I remember, I'm sorry."

It was enough just now to know that Tommy was remembered at all by the hard, enigmatic man standing before her. She sensed what the memory had cost Zeke by the shadows lurking in his eyes, the grim set of his mouth. "Thank you," she whispered. "I . . . thank you." Ill at ease, she kicked at a loose stone and watched it roll under a clump of dry brush, wishing she could hide that easily.

He tugged on her hand and they continued walking under the shelter of the trees. Sunlight speckled the ground in muted shades of grayish green and brown and spilled through Addie's curls with shimmering radiance. Her skin was pale but utterly flawless, her eyes subdued but so perfectly green. She was slender to the point of being thin but round enough in the right places for him to realize what a month of hearty meals would yield.

A rabbit darted for cover across the path, causing Addie to flinch and pause. The lone cry of a distant mountain lion raised chills along her arms, and she hugged herself against the reaction. Zeke sighed, then pulled her around to face him, grasping her upper arms firmly. He watched her eyes flare and felt her body tense. She was so easily startled, always on guard. He knew the destructive power of fear. It could totally immobilize a man or cause him to act rashly. It apparently made a woman cower at the slightest, most natural thing.

His thumbs stroked her arms, but Addie felt the flutter of it deep in her belly. There was no expression in the eyes that bored into hers, but his voice was laced with determination.

"You don't have to be afraid of me, Addie. Whatever

Willis was to you, whatever Grady did, you don't have to be afraid of me."

She grew stubbornly mute and tried to pull away, but he wouldn't release her. "I don't want to talk about them," she said sharply.

Back off, Claiborne, he warned himself. *Let the lady fight her own demons.* But he couldn't seem to stop himself from intruding. No matter how she denied it, her skittish nature would have an effect on him and the boys. He didn't want to walk on eggshells for the rest of his life.

"We don't have to discuss this right now, but I think we need to later." She shook her head with dogged obstinacy, but Zeke was just as headstrong. "I don't want Willis's ghost haunting my house."

"It won't," she said through set teeth, so icy and stubborn and sure. She'd forget quicker than she could blink if possible, if everyone would just let her.

"You resurrect him every time I get near you."

She shook her head, trying to deny it, but there was no escaping the truth. "You loved Becky," she said defensively, "but I loathed Willis, despised him! I know that sounds sinful but it's true. I won't talk about him now or ever."

She pressed her lips together as if to prove it, but she didn't expect him to understand. How could he? She remembered seeing Zeke and Becky in town on shopping days, laughing and exchanging pleasantries with others along the street. They had made such a fine pair, a perfect contrast with Zeke's sun-streaked hair and Becky's dark locks.

And she remembered other things as well, the forbidden yearning she'd felt every time she chanced upon them. Deeply embarrassed by her own duplicity but unable to help herself, she'd even taken to looking for them, shy and furtive glances that made her feel like a voyeur. Within the shadowed confines of a store window, she'd clutch her purchases to her chest and watch them stroll through town, Zeke's hand at Becky's elbow, his smile so handsome and attentive. And for the briefest moments she would indulge her silly, childish imagination. Inevitably, guilt would intrude and she would slip away feeling evil and covetous, because those fantasies stirred within her a longing for things she had never had or wanted with Willis.

She felt Zeke's fingers idly moving down her arms until his palms lay beneath hers. His hands were callused and warm, frightening for their strength. The tendons in her elbows flexed as she tried to pull away, but his hold only tightened. Overtly, he presented no threat, not here within screaming distance of the Parkers'. But what about later, when she was alone at his house with nothing but three small children for protection? He had always been so solicitous of his first wife in public, but she knew better than anyone what could happen in private.

"Let me go," she said, tugging more forcefully, her voice both obstinate and anxious. He released her hands, and she laced them behind her back, out of sight, out of reach. She dropped her chin and stared at the fallen leaves along the path and scattered clumps of sweet cactus, wishing she could go back to Beatrice's and play with his boys, the only bright spots in this untenable situation.

She heard the rustle of a foraging raccoon or fox and looked for the source to avoid looking at Zeke. The sun slid behind a cloud and the forest seemed to close around them, a secret room, encasing them in the scents and sounds of nature while blocking out the rest of the world.

"Addie."

She didn't answer. She had nothing to say and wouldn't allow him to question her further. When he said nothing else, she looked up to find him gazing off into the distance, his expression impossible to read, perhaps remembering another woman, one he had freely chosen. His profile was fine and strong, the beauty of generations carved into each feature. She had never thought to find herself married to anyone so handsome. But looks weren't the measure of a man, as she knew only too well.

There were only the two of them in the secluded forest, but a host of memories crowded in beside them to view a man grieving for what he'd lost, she supposed, and a woman sickened by what she'd had.

The sameness and the difference together formed a bond somehow, one that seemed much more validated surrounded by the scent of evergreen and the simplicity of their quiet musings than by the vows spoken earlier before a minister. The silence seemed important now, a tacit permission for peace. Neutral ground had been established and recognized. Addie didn't know what it meant, but something akin to comfort flowed through her, relaxing and renewing, and she felt a sense of ease for the first time in weeks.

She turned to look where Zeke did, at the clear stream trickling over rocks worn smooth and rounded by the constant flow of water. The land was enduring, not always stable or fair, but enduring. Time shaped it and changed it, but its existence was constant. The sun beat down upon her neck and shoulders, warm against the cool breeze. Had she been bolder or more frolicsome, she might have slipped off her shoes and wandered over to the stream to wade along its shallow bottom. She thought wistfully of the refreshing picture a moment longer, then looked up to find Zeke staring not at the water but at her.

His next words suddenly shattered the solitude. "What about tonight, Addie?"

Her expression changed instantly from peaceful to pensive, and confusion dimmed her eyes. "What . . . about it?"

"You skitter off like a scared rabbit whenever I get close," he said. "I was thinking how . . . awkward tonight will be for both of us if we don't settle this."

His words set off a violent reaction. She swung away so fast she almost tripped on her own feet, and his hands reached out to steady her. It was a simple and nonthreatening gesture, meant to help her regain her footing, but every contact with a man screamed a warning to Addie.

"Don't," she cried, straining so against his grip that he had to tighten his arms to hold her in place. Her horrified expression said if he let go now she'd be tearing off through the woods so quick he'd be all day hunting her.

"Wait," he attempted reasonably, "it was just an observation . . ."

But Addie didn't hear the rest. He was staring at her with eyes as golden as an eagle's and just as predatory. His hands felt like iron shackles on her arms. She murmured an oath and twisted violently. Startled, Zeke pulled her rigid body closer and slipped his arms around her back, her stony resistance making her feel bony beneath his fingers.

"Addie, wait—" She twisted again, cleaving his words.

His expression darkened as he tried to restrain her from hurting herself or him in her ridiculous struggles. "Dammit, wait!"

But she was beyond hearing or heeding the command, so he wrapped his arms around her more securely while formulating words she would understand, held her mere inches from a body he would have thought immune to sexual enticement at a time like this. But when she jerked again, their bodies brushed—thigh against thigh, hipbone against groin. His responded in a timeless, predictable way. *Oh, hell.*

There was nothing at all appealing in her frightened eyes, wan cheeks, or bloodless lips, but she appealed to him still on some level that he couldn't name or understand, something less basic than the carnality of flesh. The inborn, protective instincts of a man for a woman, he thought, then disregarded the analysis in favor of cynical realism. He'd been too damned long without a woman.

He wondered if she realized it as well as her body swung back and forth in his hold, grazing him repeatedly, maddeningly. With a silent curse at the treachery of his own body, he released her suddenly and she stumbled back a step, almost falling. His hand lashed out and caught her arm to steady her before she landed on her backside.

"Don't," she rasped, poised for flight, her breathing fast and troubled. "You said . . . you promised!" The woods grew darker, no longer cozy but suffocating, like the man. "You promised!" she cried again as her hands flew up to push against his chest.

Promised? What did I promise? His hold was purposefully unbreakable now, his voice strained but quiet. "Addie, I would never hurt you."

She shook her head, not believing him. She was trapped within the circle of his fingers, her heart beating a crazy rhythm as his own pounded against her palms. She could feel the corded strength in his muscles, the corresponding weakness in her own. Panic hit her like a wave. It was too late. The words had been spoken, the paper signed. Half the town had witnessed the marriage. She pushed again, hard, but his chest was unyielding beneath her hands. She twisted wildly to get away, shocking him anew with the degree of her fury and fear. He hauled her up more tightly against him.

"Listen, Addie. No, listen! I'm not going to let you go until you hear me out."

She went deathly still in his arms; she knew well how to obey a husband.

But she couldn't hear him for the roaring in her head. She squeezed her eyes shut, as if that would make him disappear, and tried to carry her mind off to some other place that was warm and sunny and safe.

His hold relaxed, but his body was so close his breath whispered across her forehead. "Addie, if I let you go will you stand still and listen to me?"

She nodded numbly, feeling battered by his betrayal, insanely furious at herself for thinking he might be different. *Stupid, ignorant Addie. Will you never learn?*

His arms released her and he stepped back, wondering if she'd bolt. She didn't move an inch, just stood stiff and silent and so self-contained he knew she wasn't getting enough oxygen. "Breathe."

Air filled her lungs, and her eyes lifted to his, dull green at first glance, but deep down where she thought it was hidden lay a raging fire of defiance.

"You've got plenty of spirit," Zeke said. "I'm sorry Willis tried to beat it out of you."

Shame flooded her that he knew, but she couldn't react, not even when his hands reached up to touch her face. Not by the flicker of an eyelash did she twitch, but her eyes flared with loathing.

"I'm not him," he ground out softly, distinctly. "Get it through your head that I'll never hurt or humiliate you."

The back of his knuckles brushed her cheek, and she jerked her head back, her eyes stark and revealing. Something deep inside Zeke shifted and his eyes narrowed, seeing much more than he wanted to, bringing everything he had only suspected earlier into clear, undeniable focus now. His indrawn breath hissed between his teeth. "You don't want to be touched at all."

She didn't speak or nod; she didn't have to for him to see the truth plainly written on her face. His hands slid to her upper arms and he moved back a fraction, trying to keep his voice calm and composed, but a trace of antagonism colored his words.

"Addie, this won't work. We can't pass the rest of our lives without contact." He heard the muted groan in her throat, rising panic, and continued in a firmer voice, "The boys need it, too. They need to be touched and hugged, to know that it's normal. They can't see you flinch every time I get near."

"I won't. I promise," she said, bargaining and bartering, anything not to make him angry.

"Yes, you will," he said. "At least until you get used to me." His face lowered and she didn't budge, but her entire body radiated defensiveness. His lips touched hers so lightly she might have imagined it, then were gone. "Was that so bad?"

No. Her mouth formed the word obediently, but she had no voice. Tears stung her eyes, making them appear glassy. His hands opened on her arms but one finger trailed down to her wrist, and she felt textures this time —softness, warmth, the slight abrasion of his callused skin. Her heart did a stutter-step, and her lips parted slightly on small distressed sounds that ricocheted through Zeke like riflefire.

It had been so long since a woman had moaned beneath his touch, he couldn't tell at first if there was anxiety or submission in the muted cry. He pulled his hands away completely and watched her sag with relief, and knew it had not been submission but rising desperation. He stepped back slowly and gazed off into the distance, seeing nothing emotionally, feeling too much physically. His hands found his pockets, safe, confining.

His expression grew reserved, mirroring his internal withdrawal. He couldn't spend the rest of his life beside a woman without touching her; it was ludicrous even to imagine it. His eyes bored into hers, but it was himself that he condemned. "I was a fool not to discuss this with you before the wedding."

Her face was stricken. "What . . . do you mean?"

He opened his mouth to explain but had no words for the confusion churning in his head. Perhaps it was too soon for this, for them, given their short acquaintance and her past. But there were things she damn well needed to understand.

Physical arousal was part and parcel of the human species. He'd known it personally since adolescence and intellectually from his university studies, before the war had stolen his medical ambitions and made him a soldier. He hadn't really wanted female comfort since Becky's death, but he wasn't fool enough to believe that he never would.

"What did you think, Addie?" he asked, his voice low, his expression painfully baffled. "That I'd just ride over to Ruby's when the urge hit and pay for release?" He laughed then, a brittle and cynical sound. "How clinical and emotionless and easy. Too bad it's adultery," he added, his voice hard and flat. "I won't preach one brand of morality to my sons and practice another for myself."

He glanced briefly at her bare finger. There hadn't been an exchange of wedding bands, but that didn't negate the marriage. He searched the strain and uncertainty on her face for some hint of understanding or acceptance but found utter and complete confusion, as if she hadn't heard a thing he'd said. He raked his fingers through his hair in frustration, wondering how long it would take her to adjust, how long to forget Willis. He didn't have to love or even care for a woman to desire her, but he wouldn't use his own wife like a whore.

"It'll all work out, Addie," he said softly, but there was a bitter edge to his voice. "I don't make a habit of molesting unwilling women."

She stared back at him in stony silence, feeling betrayed. She didn't believe a word of it, but wished with all her heart that she could.

6

The wagon hit a rut as they approached the house, and Addie clutched Cole tighter to keep him from bouncing off her lap. Behind her Zeb whooped for his pa to do it again, but Josh, as usual, remained sullen. Zeke pulled to a stop at the front porch and quickly put a hand on Addie's arm to detain her.

She tugged away instinctively but his hold was light enough to follow the movement. His fingertips rested over her forearm, darkly tanned against the edges of her worn shawl. She lifted her gaze to his and found the slightest hint of amused provocation there.

His fingers stirred, neither a caress nor a command, but some sort of combination of both. Addie pulled her gaze away. "I'll help you down," he said mildly. "The boys need to learn their manners even if you don't have any use for them." His dry tone took the bite out of his words but did little to console Addie. He climbed down and rounded the wagon, then gripped her firmly by the waist.

She stiffened.

He didn't move an inch, just stood before her like

some golden hero she'd once seen in a picture book with the sunset falling all around him like vaporous fire, making no effort at all to lift her. His gaze was so blandly patient that Addie knew her resistance was fruitless, and silly besides. The only thing he was forcing upon her was common courtesy, for God's sake! She eased the baby to one side and forced herself to relax.

His hands tightened securely as he lifted, then swung her clear of the wagon. She had the exhilarating sensation of flight for the briefest second before being set lightly on her feet. "You and the boys go on in. They'll show you around while I see to the horses and chores."

Addie nodded and mounted the steps, but paused when she reached the porch. Slowly, almost surreptitiously, she turned back, inexplicably drawn to the puzzling man who was now her husband. His hands had been strong but gentle on her waist. She could still feel the imprint of his fingers. She hadn't known such simple consideration since her father's death.

The dying sun cast coppery shadows across Zeke's strong jaw and darkened the outline of his silhouette. His shoulders were broad beneath his coat, his hands powerfully competent on the reins. He was so handsome it almost stole her breath.

He was different from Willis but intimidating in ways she couldn't begin to comprehend. There was a confidence about him that wasn't brag or bluster. He always seemed in control of his emotions, unlike Willis, who had swung wild and unpredictable in his moods. She touched her lips gingerly, remembering the fleeting kiss, the gentleness.

The boys moved up the steps behind her and she shifted the sleepy baby to her shoulder, then stretched one hand down, knowing Zeb would take it and Josh would not. Funny how she could gauge the three males next to her but didn't have a clue about the one rambling away.

"I'm hungry," Zeb declared when they entered the house.

Addie knew he couldn't hold another bite after the feast they'd just shared at the Parkers', but it was a good excuse to avoid bedtime. "Let me get the baby settled first," she said. "Show me where you sleep."

Suspicion narrowed Zeb's eyes. He pointed to a door off the sitting area but stayed rooted to the floor. He wasn't about to lead her in and get himself tricked into staying there. Smiling softly at his tenacity, Addie headed in the direction he pointed. With just enough daylight left to see without a lamp, she changed the baby and settled him in a crib. She wished she could just hold him awhile, maybe rock him to sleep, but he was already snuggling down, his fist in his mouth, content to be left alone after the tiring day.

She lightly stroked his soft curls, knowing she should be grateful he was an easy baby, but as soon as she pulled her hand away she felt the lack, the empty space left in her since her family's death. She so needed the warmth of innocent human contact to fill that void or at least dull the rough edges. She bent to kiss Cole's cheek, then backed quietly out of the room.

Zeb was standing where she'd left him, a million excuses churning through his head. Addie took a breath to bolster her courage but felt like a villain. "What time does your pa put you to bed?"

Zeb screwed his face up. Time held little importance in his four-year-old mind, but sundown meant bedtime, and he didn't know how he was going to draw this out.

"Pa reads us a story." His hopeful smile melted Addie clear down to her toes.

"I can read you one."

"We want Pa," Josh said with obvious contempt. He usually helped with chores and didn't like being stuck in the house because this lady didn't know where anything was. Feeling brave with his pa out of hearing, he added, "You're not our ma."

"Is too," Zeb countered. "Pa said so."

Josh rounded on his brother, and Addie moved between them quickly to stave off further argument. She looked straight at Josh.

"I'm not your ma. I can never be her because I'm me: Addie. See? My hair is different, my eyes are different, even my voice is different. But I'm gonna help take care of you like your ma would have before she went to heaven. It's what she would want, Josh, to have her boys taken care of."

The hurt was so vivid in Josh's eyes, Addie wanted to hug him up tight and absorb it into herself. Knowing that wasn't possible didn't ease her own pain any, and watching his expression close over in defensive anger only made it worse. She braced herself to take the backlash of his hurt repeatedly in the months to come; they would be a long time settling in. She knelt down so they would be eye to eye but didn't dare touch him yet.

"I lost my ma and pa about four years ago," she said softly. "It was the most awful thing to ever happen. I wanted to die too. But I guess the good Lord had better plans for me—" She paused on the lie. She guessed the good Lord hadn't been anywhere in hearing distance four years ago or she wouldn't have ended up with Willis. "I guess He's got big plans for you, too, Josh. The hurt doesn't go away, not ever. But it gets easier after a while. You remember all the good things, and you let yourself feel happy sometimes because it's what your ma would want."

She reached out and lightly touched a button on his shirt, the first small step in many she hoped to make. "You see? When you let yourself feel happy, then your ma can feel happy too."

Not by the flicker of an eyelash did Josh let on what was churning through his head. Addie wondered if she was doing right by encouraging him to let go of the pain or only putting a worse burden on him to feel things he wasn't capable of yet.

She and Old Grief had a personal relationship she didn't wish on any child, but it was one of those nasty things life threw at you when you weren't looking. You could go forward or die with it. She wondered sometimes which one she had chosen.

One tear rolled down Josh's cheek. He smeared it away with the heel of his hand. "You won't stay," he said viciously, then turned and ran from the house.

Addie got up slowly and watched the back door slam behind him. *Oh, Josh.* She couldn't promise him that her life wouldn't be taken early, but she wanted to, wanted to tell him she'd be around to watch him grow into a man, wanted to offer him more hope than she herself had felt in four years. She turned and opened her arms for Zeb, needing his acceptance so. He flung himself at her, sensing the awful tension but not understanding it. She wrapped him up close to her and buried her face in his dark curls.

"Are too gonna be my ma," he muttered fiercely. "Pa said so."

"Yes," she whispered, so grateful he and Cole were too young for grief to get a stranglehold on them, too.

She got his face washed and nightclothes on before he started an all-out strategy to avoid bed. Oh, he was sly, talking a mile a minute to keep himself from nodding off. But Addie was sly, too, and experienced. How many times had she bathed the new baby or tended her younger brothers just to give her ma a rest? She held Zeb close and kept up a rhythmic rocking, not adding much to the conversation but an occasional hum, until he finally burned himself out.

She tucked the covers around him, then stretched and kneaded the small ache in her lower back. "Nothin' nicer than a sleepin' child," her ma used to say. At this point Addie was inclined to agree. She turned, then stopped short to see Zeke lounging in the doorway. He nodded at his sleeping son.

"Zeb give you much trouble?"

She smiled softly and shook her head. "He's tough, but I'm bigger."

His eyes made a cursory run from her head to her toes. "Not much." He stepped aside to let Josh by, his eyes never leaving hers. "I'll hear his prayers while you put your things away. They're by the bedroom door."

Addie nodded, feeling odd inside at the familiar way he'd looked her up and down. Disconcerted, she scooted past him and found several crates lined up against the wall. She picked up an armful of clothing and entered the bedroom, then stopped dead still.

It wasn't the furnishings that made her pause. A lamp burned on the bedside table, illuminating a large carved bedstead in a hazy yellow glow. Purer moonlight spilled through the windows, slanting across a matching wardrobe and commode to the polished floorboards but leaving the corners deep in shadow. It was a beautiful room, simple in its elegance, the kind of room she might once have dreamed of. But the collection of male garments and sundry tools sent a dreadful kick to her gut. The bundle of clothing fell from her nerveless fingers, and she spun around to find Zeke crossing the threshold.

"No." The word was direct and inflexible despite the rapid pounding of her heart.

Zeke didn't pretend not to understand. "We have to share this room, Addie. For one thing there's not another one, for another—" He jerked his hat from his head and tossed it onto the bedside table, then raked his fingers impatiently through his hair. "Zeb gets scared sometimes and crawls in bed with me. It's not normal for a man and wife not to be in the same bed. His memory of Becky is fading, but he'll be a man one day. I don't want him to have unnatural notions about . . . things."

His smile was derisive, a mere slant of his lips. "You know he talks. I won't have Laramie buzzing about things that are none of their concern because Zeb let everyone know his pa is sleeping in the barn or on the floor."

"I'll sleep in the barn," she said, but that wasn't the point and she knew it. "Please . . ."

"No, Addie. If you care for the boys, just let it go. I told you I'd never hurt you and I meant it. If I have to prove it right here in this room, then so be it."

Anger burned through her so hotly she thought she might swoon with it. "You knew," she said in a small, furious voice. "You knew we'd be sharing the same room and didn't tell me. You let me think—"

Zeke swore beneath his breath, tired to the bone of her unwarranted fear and his inability to deal with it. Though he didn't have her anxieties, he felt every bit as awkward and uncomfortable about the thought of sharing a bed with a stranger. He'd been up since before daylight getting as much work as possible done so he could take time to go to the church and marry her. He was so exhausted, he could have slept on the ground and not noticed.

A vein throbbed in his temple. He couldn't change their situation just because she objected to it, couldn't make this right for her, and he was too worn out to temper his words or his tone. "I didn't set out to fool you. I assumed you knew we'd share the same room."

He shut the door so their quarreling wouldn't wake the boys, then advanced two long strides toward her. She threw her hands out in warning. "Don't come any closer!"

He stopped dead in his tracks and had to bite the inside of his jaw to keep his mouth from tilting up in an irreverent smile. She looked ridiculous trying to hold him off, even worse than the day she'd done it to Jake. But unlike the sheriff's startled expression, Zeke's face was intractable, his stance just as unbending.

"I can't add a room overnight," he attempted reasonably, but his jaw was clenched, reflecting an inexcusable tendency toward humor, especially in light of his rising frustration. The lines that fanned the corners of his eyes spoke of bone-tired weariness. "It's been a long day, Addie."

She only stared back at him, stubbornly mute, clothing puddled around her feet like wreckage.

"Please, just get undressed and into bed." Her face blanched, and her lower lip began to tremble. Whatever small amusement Zeke had experienced evaporated and his frustration soared. "And don't you dare start crying, either!"

She flinched, looking ten years old in a party dress as

white as her face, her big green eyes glistening above a quivering mouth. Zeke thought if one tear fell, he'd either be on his knees begging her forgiveness for something that wasn't his fault, or tossing her out the front door. The urge to do both was so strong, he knew better than to move one tense muscle.

Suddenly, mercifully, her mouth pursed and her chin tilted up so obstinately he wanted to sigh with relief. "I'll give you some privacy if you're shy," he said, "but frankly it seems a waste of time since we've got to get used to it sooner or later."

Addie just stood and stared back at him until he sighed and turned to leave. She watched him every step of the way, angry betrayal in her eyes until the door closed behind him. Shaking all over as though she had a chill, she hurried to pour water into the bowl for washing and splashed her face over and over until she felt some of her composure return. She gripped the table's edge and just stood, bent over and breathing hard, forcing her insides to uncoil. She took deep, uneven gulps of air until her arms and knees quit trembling and a numbness finally seeped through her extremities.

She couldn't stay here, couldn't lie beside him tonight or any other night. She'd return home until the bank claimed it or winter set in. Her legs were immobile for a second, then stiffly obeyed her command to move. Glancing back over her shoulder covertly, she tiptoed to the window and raised it. A blast of cold air hit her, daunting, but she hooked one leg over the sill and was halfway through when the memory of Grady's leering face swam before her.

Oh, Lord! She paused and gripped the window frame, knowing she couldn't go home. She'd go to Beatrice's house then, take her up on the offer—

She heard the baby wail, then Zeke's long strides as he crossed to the boys' room. Her resistance dissolved until her knees felt weak. If she left now, she took all hope with her, any chance of having a family of her own. But she didn't know if she could bear the cost expected of her to mother the three little boys just yards away.

She dropped her forehead to the windowpane, feeling nothing, not the cold or the fear or the utter desolation. Zeke had sworn he wouldn't hurt her. She couldn't believe him, but she wanted to, desperately enough to try. A calm settled over her at the decision and she pulled her numb body back into the room. One night, two, whatever it took to find out if she could trust his word or if he was just another monster like Willis.

On wooden legs she stepped back and removed her gown, then hung it with utmost precision inside a large wardrobe. She unfastened her chemise in the same meticulous manner and placed it in a drawer. With detached correctness she found her night rail and pulled it on over her head, then climbed into bed and clutched the quilt to her chin.

The light rap on the door didn't even startle her. She was too far removed to hear or see anything beyond the bright, warm, safe place in her mind.

Zeke stepped cautiously into the room, half expecting some missile to come flying at him. Deafening silence greeted his arrival. He found Addie lying on her back, staring up at the ceiling with a blank-eyed look, like a punished child. But she wasn't a child. She was nineteen; she'd been married for four years. What in hell did she think he was going to do to her that could possibly be worse than what Willis had already done? It pricked his male pride that she could so loathe the idea of sleeping in his bed when she'd shared that lazy bounder's for years.

The thought struck him discordantly, off-colored and out of sync, like someone hitting the wrong key in a song. He stared down at the dead look in her eyes, then deeper. It was that underlying look that caught him, the glazed-over but still visible look of a trapped animal. He bit back an oath. She didn't fear anything worse would happen with him after all. She feared a repeat of the same. The four years behind her with Willis meant nothing when compared to a lifetime ahead of her with him.

A chill hit him and he turned to see the window wide open. Everything in him seemed to retract, then shut down at the obvious conclusion. "Change your mind?" he asked, his words as frigid as his emotions. Addie shivered slightly but didn't answer. Zeke crossed the room and closed the window, then returned to the bed. He reached down and gripped her jaw, forcing her to look at him. "Don't *ever*," he said with lethal softness, "try to sneak out of this house again. If you decide to leave, go through the front door. I'll never stop you."

He stepped back and began to undress, not bothering to hide himself. True, he wasn't modest, but she wasn't looking at him anyway. Just staring at the blamed ceiling like she might manage to float right up through it if she looked hard enough. Naked except for his undergarments, he blew out the lamp, cloaking them in blessed darkness that hid the absent look in her eyes. Rounding the foot of the bed, he crawled in, careful to keep his distance.

He heard her sharp intake of breath when the bed dipped, knew as well as if he were touching her that her heart was racing like a runaway train. He was glad he couldn't see her face. He lay back, arms behind his head, and tried to will the tension from his body.

The silence was complete, a vacuum that obliterated everything, heightening his senses. The scent of soap and sunshine bathed the air along with the musky, obscure hint of feminine flesh. The unaccustomed warmth of her nearness conjured up familiar memories, hard to take, harder still to ignore.

He resented it, both the memories and Addie for resurrecting things he'd tried to forget. He didn't want her here, this fragile wasted person who was as stubborn as his mule one minute, then afraid of her own shadow the next. He threw his forearm over his eyes, trying to bury his resentment. It wasn't her fault that circumstances had brought them together, any more than it was his, but the knowledge didn't make their situation any more palatable.

Don't come any closer!

A smile, slight and wry, curled his lips. *Don't worry, lady,* he thought, but the smile grew easier when he remembered the spark in her green eyes. Damn if she didn't challenge him with those occasional outbursts. She might have taken a beating in life but she wasn't whipped. He was thankful. He knew how quickly this land swallowed up the unwise and the weak. No matter what else he or anyone thought of Addie, she wasn't weak.

He rolled his head to look at her. There wasn't much to her but a small rounded bump, ensconced as she was in the feather mattress with the quilt pulled to her breasts. Diminutive in stature, washed out in visage, she'd made him feel anger and resentment and frustration, intruding haphazardly and completely on the deathless chill of the past nine months—that painless void so much easier to endure than the external, physical demands his body was now making, proving he was alive.

Moonlight spilled silvery ribbons through her wild curls and slanted across her face. Her eyes were closed, her lashes tawny against her pale cheeks. She looked small, defenseless, her arms wrapped around her rib cage as if holding herself intact or inviolable. But Zeke knew there was an inner strength that had seen her through the rough times, would see her through this. The grip of her arms flattened her nightgown against her breasts, modest yet firm orbs that rose and fell shallowly beneath the heavy cotton.

His gut tightened in reflex. He closed his eyes and tried to force sleep. Even tired as he was, it would be a long time coming, but he suspected it would be a lot longer for Addie.

The baby's crying woke him. Disoriented, Zeke eased up on one elbow and felt the bed shift, then a gentle bump as something rolled into him. He listened again for Cole but the sound wasn't coming from the boys' room. It was coming from his bed. Addie.

She was curled into him, one knee drawn up, her lips parting from time to time as she sighed sadly in her sleep. Her brow was troubled, but she wasn't crying, nor did she appear to be in the grip of a terrible nightmare. There was just profound sadness in each soft moan, a wrenching despair in the fingers that worried the ribbon at the neck of her nightgown.

Zeke touched her shoulder and shook her slightly. She moaned again but still didn't wake. "Shhh." He brushed the rowdy curls back from her temples, lingering in the silky strands a moment to savor the texture, then lowered his hand and wrapped his fingers around hers to stop their fretting. She sighed once more, a broken sound that faded into even, relieved breathing. Her hand tightened around his thumb and she nestled into him, finally at peace.

Desire trickled through him, unbidden and unwanted, a slow warning to get himself back to sleep before he touched her further. Her night rail was bunched up around her thighs, her bare knee pressed into his groin. He needed to move her, but touching her naked leg seemed a bit like gambling right now—a little sinful, a lot enticing.

His hand slid down and pushed her knee back a space, then traced her lower thigh lightly, so lightly she would never know. Disgusted, he pulled his hand back, feeling lecherous. He was a grown man, not some teenager sneaking his first feel. But the result was the same, a low stirring at the titillating sensation of sleek female flesh, a dangerous excitement coupled with guilt, and a low heat that began to throb with his pulse.

He retreated immediately but wouldn't lie to himself. He wanted the mind-numbing oblivion of being inside a woman, that point of sublime forgetfulness when nothing mattered but the grinding surge of his body as it pounded into female warmth, the breath-robbing point of pleasure-pain when his muscles clenched, then peaked in release. He turned gingerly away until he was flat on his back and staring up at the ceiling.

Oh, Addie. There's not a chance in hell this is going to work out the way you want it to.

Daylight wasn't supposed to be the enemy. But it felt that way when it struck Addie full force behind her closed eyelids. She murmured something hateful and turned over to bury her face into the pillow, welcoming the dark respite. It smelled vaguely like sunshine and something else. Something warm and human and . . . Zeke.

Her eyes flew open and she slid a glance sideways to see that his side of the bed was empty. Relief rushed at her for a fleeting second before she fully regained her senses.

Where were the boys? She sprang up, pushed the hair from her eyes, and swung her legs over the bed in one motion. Daunting sunlight poured through the window, piercing straight into her conscience. She hadn't slept this late since . . . since ever. She splashed water on her face to clear the sleep from her mind, then threw her clothes on.

The kitchen was a bustle of whispered voices and clanking dishes. The baby banged on his high chair for another biscuit, which Josh delivered with a loud "Shhh!" Zebulun saw Addie first and jumped up in his chair.

"Mornin', Ma!" He beamed. "Pa told us to be quiet and let you sleep, but Cole don't know how to mind yet."

Addie felt thoroughly nonplussed at Zeb's calling her "Ma" combined with Zeke's thoughtfulness. Unaccustomed warmth stole through her, soft and strange and welcome, then was dashed when Josh sent her a mean look and rose from his seat. "I gotta go help with chores."

"Wait, Josh." Addie hurried over to the table, feeling about as guilty as she'd ever felt in her entire life. It must be getting close to eight o'clock. The boys were dressed and breakfast already cooked and eaten. Zeke had taken care of her duties while she whiled away the morning like a lazy slug. She couldn't imagine what he must think of her, or what price she would pay for her dawdling. "I'm sorry, I overslept. Can you tell me what usually gets done and when?"

Josh frowned at her like she was too lame-headed for him to acknowledge. "Stuff gets done when it needs to." He turned, grabbed his lunch pail, and ran out the back door before she could grab him for sassing and hoped she wouldn't tattle to his pa.

Addie watched the door slam behind him. *So, that's the way the wind blows.* Things got done around the house whenever they found the time to do them. Well, there had been little enough to keep her occupied when she was married to Willis, but she remembered the frenzy of endless chores in her mother's house. She'd lost yesterday for Monday bread baking and would have to catch up today. If she managed that and got the washing done, she could iron on Wednesday, make butter and cheese on Thursday, then on Friday . . .

Thinking about it all wouldn't get any of it done. Addie set out immediately to find the things needed for dough, then mixed what she hoped was enough to last the week and left it to rise.

Zeb helped—talked—and kept the baby occupied while she worked. It was disconcerting to be surrounded by his chatter when her world had been mostly silent and oppressive for the past four years. But there was joy as well, a deep and profound joy, in his trusting childish exuberance. When Willis was home, he had barked orders, she had obeyed, then he had chastised her for getting things done so poorly. She didn't know if Zeke would be any different, but his son at least seemed happy just to have someone to listen to him.

Zeb's cheerfulness helped to offset the strangeness of

settling into a routine in another woman's house. Becky's presence was everywhere, in the handstitched pillows, the small porcelain figurines on the mantel, the neatly lined pantry shelves. Addie was loath to change or rearrange anything and call attention to the fact that she now resided in the home another woman had obviously decorated with love.

After clearing away the breakfast dishes and washing them—Lord be praised—at the inside pump, she gathered up the mountain of dirty clothes. Even the muscle-wrenching chore of doing the wash was a delight with Zeb splashing and the baby chortling outside at the tub. The day was balmy, more like early summer than late fall, and Addie grabbed every precious moment to bask in the sunny warmth as if she could store it away to pull out later when winter came.

The clothes were snapping on the line when they trudged back inside for lunch and a nap. Zeb was ready for the former, but used every trick known since Creation to avoid the latter. Addie ended up rocking him until her calves were just as sore as her parched, story-telling throat before he finally nodded off.

Her head dropped back against the rocker in weariness. She didn't know how Zeke had done it all these months since Becky's death. She'd relished every second of keeping busy and knowing she was doing something useful for the boys, but she was so tired she felt like collapsing. How in the world had Zeke done the laundry, the farm chores, and kept up the ranch and the house, too? Respect for him niggled at the back of her mind, but she was too exhausted to dwell on it. She pushed out of the chair, wincing at tender overexerted muscles, and laid Zeb on the bed before she could fall asleep herself, and went back to the kitchen to start supper.

Disgusted, Zeke slung the broken harness into the barn. He'd lose two hours tomorrow repairing the blasted thing. A squeal shattered the late afternoon quiet and his head whipped around in time to see Zeb dart across the backyard. Addie lumbered after him, her fingers curled into talons, the baby on her hip chortling gleefully as he bounced along.

Zeb clambered up the porch steps, laughing hard and shouting, "Base!" The "monster" slowed and dropped her head in a disgruntled fashion to stare at the ground. As soon as her eyes lowered, Zeb leaped from the porch and shouted, "Can't catch me!" which started the chase all over again.

Zeke hung back just inside the barn door as Addie swung Cole high over her head and twirled, girlish and free in the setting sun. The baby's giggles carried across the yard, mingling with Zeb's taunting refrain. She spun in a circle again, her curls swirling wildly about her face, mirroring the vibrant sunset behind her. Gold, topaz, and silver winked and shimmied in incandescent threads, a jeweled illusion that spilled over her shoulders to the bodice pulling tightly across her breasts. The outline of her hips and legs showed through her skirt.

A masculine itch shivered down Zeke's spine, and he shifted his weight to accommodate the heavy rush of blood elsewhere. He had to get that woman a petticoat.

Zeb darted close and tagged her skirt, then raced away again. Laughing, Addie fell to her back on the ground, knees raised, bare toes curling over each other in the grass. She planted the baby on her slender stomach and turned her head to call out breathlessly, "You win, Zeb. Cole and I admit defeat."

But she didn't look defeated, Zeke thought, as the baby bounced on her tummy, his plump fists planted on her plumper breasts as he rode her like a bucking bronco. Her cheeks were flushed, her eyes sparkling, as she stroked the sweaty curls back from his face. She looked alive for the first time since Zeke had met her.

Zeb tumbled to the ground beside her and notched his head into her shoulder, knees raised like hers, his feet just as bare. He pointed to a cloud overhead and she nodded then pointed to another. Their words didn't carry but the gesture was ageless and beckoning.

Zeke's fingers closed around the frayed leather strap of a halter hanging on the barn wall, and he wondered what she'd do if he walked over there right now and plopped down beside them. Probably get her fanny all twisted in a knot trying to get away. He released the halter and moved back farther into the barn to finish his chores, but the memory of her laughing and playing so carefree with his sons lingered long after he heard her call the boys back inside to wash up.

Josh called from one of the stalls, and Zeke felt the squeeze in his chest, the familiar mixture of pride and guilt that his son had so much responsibility at his young age when he should have been romping with the others. But it wouldn't be that way much longer. He'd be hiring ranch hands come spring, and Josh would be attending school instead of doing his lessons at night after chores.

They finished up in the barn and sauntered back out to the pump to wash the day's work from their faces and hands. Tantalizing aromas wafted from the open kitchen door, causing Zeke to pause and just savor the flavors. Lord, he'd almost forgotten what it was like. It had been so long since he'd been able to work straight through without the little boys underfoot, so long since a hot meal greeted him at the end of the day instead of waiting for him to prepare it. The delicious smells of frying ham and hot bread were so welcome he wanted to wallow in them, just roll around like a pig in mud.

He could tell Josh welcomed them too, though his son would never admit it. Josh's nose was turned up, inhaling, his eyes closed in ecstasy as he let the cold water run over his fingers. But memories intruded too with the familiar smells, painful recollections better left unspoken. After a short pause with neither wanting to hurt the other by confessing his thoughts, they washed up in record time and headed for the house.

"Pa!" Zeb squealed as he launched into Zeke's arms from the back porch and commenced to tell him about his day. For five minutes he chattered nonstop about how he helped with the bread baking, the baby's antics at the wash tub, and their rollicking game of chase. But near the end his voice grew gloomy and his young brow puckered in concern. "Did you get any work done wiffout me and Cole to help you, Pa?"

Zeke had gotten four times as much done as usual. "It was tough, Zeb, but we managed."

"Good, 'cause Ma says she needs us too much to . . . uh, what?" He swiveled his head around to look for Addie.

"Loan," she called from the cupboard where she was stacking dishes.

"Yeah, 'loan' us out anymore." Young hands cupped older cheeks, solemn blue eyes met amber. "Sorry, Pa."

Zeke patted his son's backside as he put him down. "That's all right, Zeb. We'll do just fine if your ma needs you here."

He searched for Addie and found her stretched on tiptoe reaching for the highest shelf. She was wearing the same dress she'd had on earlier, a faded summer-weight cotton inappropriate for this time of year. It fit her slender figure like a glove that was one season away from being too small. A flour-sack apron was tied at her waist and emphasized the gentle slope of her hips. Her hair was tamer now, tied back at the nape with a frayed ribbon, but the usual defiant tendrils curled over her forehead. With her hair pulled back and her outdated dress, she looked about as old as Gracie Parker. The thought made Zeke smile, then frown for no reason he could name.

He stepped farther into the kitchen and hung his hat on the coatrack, then stuck his hands in his back pockets and propped one shoulder against the doorframe. She was ignoring him. Gone was the young woman who had chased Zeb around the yard and twirled Cole high above her head in the rays of a setting sun. She fumbled with a plate, her shyness transmitting itself loudly with each awkward movement she made.

"Evenin', Miz Claiborne," he drawled, just to get a reaction from her.

"Evening," she mumbled back, then turned with her arms full of dishes. Her gaze bumped into his, then skittered away.

Zeke pushed off the door and strolled forward to ease her burden, but Addie rushed to the table and began setting each place with more care than the task required. The baby banged on his high chair, and Zeke watched as she smiled automatically at Cole and offered him a piece of bread. Such easy charm she bestowed on his children, to be so uncomfortable with him.

He helped settle the boys around the table, then

seated himself and waited for Addie before saying grace. After a chorus of "Amens" they began eating. The ham was slightly charred around the edges, the potatoes overcooked, the carrots a mite underdone. The food tasted like sheer heaven to the man who'd not had to prepare it.

He found the meal pleasant, if intellectually lacking in adult conversation. The boys babbled about fishing while Cole, not to be left out, added gibberish to an occasional understood word. Addie remained patient and watchful of their needs, so determined to please, she hadn't touched much of her own food. Zeke wanted to tell her to simmer down but figured that would only make her more self-conscious.

She had just started clearing the dishes when Zeb scrambled from the table, then returned with a Montgomery Ward and Company of Chicago mail-order catalog. "We gonna order now, Pa?"

Zeke took the catalog and placed it on the table. Just a few years before, Aaron Montgomery Ward and his partner, George R. Thorne, had begun a mail-order business in a livery-stable loft with a single sheet listing a few items of dry goods. Their business had grown with such speed that the company now occupied an entire floor over a stable and published a seventy-two-page catalog listing almost two thousand items. With Becky gone and no established tailor in town, Mr. Ward's mail-order business had made it easier for Zeke to get the boys clothing without having to pay exorbitant general store prices.

Zeke pulled a chair close for Zeb and opened the catalog. "We'll pick out the things we want tonight, and I'll send the order off when we go into town tomorrow."

Zeb clapped in delight and the baby mimicked him.

Even Josh's eyes brightened as he leaned closer. On the pretense of taking another dish to the sink, Addie inched up behind Zeke and peeked furtively over his shoulder to see what all the excitement was about, then jumped back guiltily when he turned around to look at her.

"Come on, Addie. You can help us pick out the winter clothes."

"No, you go ahead," she hedged. She'd never heard of ordering clothes from a book. "The dishes . . ."

He caught the tail of her apron when she tried to step away and tugged her back to his side. A battle of wills ensued instantly, fought only with their eyes, as she stiffened and swung around to stare at him. Her spine was rigid, her fists clenched on the plate, her chin stubborn enough to back down a buffalo. One brow rose over Zeke's amber eyes. "C'mon, Addie," he murmured softly, "get the starch out of your drawers and sit a minute."

Her cheeks flamed and the words flew out before she could stop them. "I don't have on drawers."

A terrible, lazy grin lifted one corner of his mouth as his thumb made a circle on her hip. "I know. Best come order some."

Her cheeks burned hotter and she looked away, but Zeb was wheedling now for her to hurry, so she stepped back far enough to get Zeke's fingers off her apron, then untied it and eased forward to sit self-consciously on the edge of the chair.

The catalog looked like the advertisements posted in the general store, and her curiosity grew with each page turned until she was leaning over to make out the writing. She jerked back suddenly.

"What foolishness!" she said, more appalled at the

shipping cost attached to the orders rather than at the cost of the goods themselves. "Who would pay such prices?"

Josh choked on a cough and his eyes widened on his father. Addie glanced back and forth between them, stricken to silence by their odd exchange. She realized thirty-five cents was a good price for seventy-two dozen shirt buttons, but who needed that many? Her abashment grew when they turned to stare at her.

She had the terrible urge to slink off and hide, but straightened her back in pique. "Why would someone pay that much to ship a pair of pants, when you can make them for little or nothing and not have to wait for them to get here?"

Zeke leaned back in his chair and said calmly, "I can't sew."

"Oh." Color suffused her cheeks. She looked at the catalog, then back at Zeke. "I can."

His eyes never left her face to travel over her worn dress. They didn't have to for Addie to realize what he was thinking. Without a word, she jumped up from her chair and rushed out of the kitchen and disappeared into the bedroom. Zeke closed his eyes briefly on a sigh, then pushed back from the table to go after her. He hadn't meant to hurt her feelings, but facts were facts.

Before he got a foot from the table, she was rushing back in, a tiny garment in her hands. She shoved it at him. "See," she said softly. "I made this."

His fingers closed around a baby gown, an airy cotton so delicate he could see his hand through the dainty folds. It was a short-sleeved christening gown, about three feet in length and elegantly decorated with embroidery and lace. Every inch was exquisitely stitched.

There was no doubt in Zeke's mind that it had been done by experienced, loving hands.

He handed the gown back to Addie, a thousand unanswered questions running through his mind. "There's a sewing machine in the barn. I can bring it back inside if you like."

A sewing machine? Oh, Lord. Addie held the infant gown tight to her chest, knowing the marvelous invention must have belonged to Becky and wondering if it would be hard for Zeke to see it in the house again. She wanted to dissemble for his sake, to gracefully decline the offer so he wouldn't be burdened by another reminder of his late wife, but a sewing machine! She couldn't even imagine how much faster and easier the work would go, how much time and energy she would save.

Mary Adaline Claiborne realized something important that she'd never known about herself. She hadn't an ounce of charity or compassion in her avaricious heart. She nodded once, trying to look as if it didn't matter, then avoided his gaze completely when she spoke the words to excuse her greed. "I know I'm not much of a cook, but I *can* sew. It will save you a passel of money."

"Good," Zeke said, though money wasn't a problem. The problem was her face. Her eyes were bright with hidden anticipation, her cheeks flushed so charmingly she looked fresh as a spring rose. His gaze dropped to her mouth. Her teeth were chewing her bottom lip expectantly, as if waiting for him to change his mind. He stared at that mouth a second longer, then cleared his throat. "I'll get whatever you need in town tomorrow. Just make a list."

7

Addie pulled her nightdress on, then bent to pack the baby gown away. Zeke had put the boys to bed while she finished the supper dishes. The house was quiet now, the only sounds coming from nocturnal animals outside and the occasional creak of settling timber. She ran her hands softly, almost reverently over the infant gown, remembering . . . remembering. The ache in her chest swelled with the familiar pang of remorse, so she carefully folded the gown and placed it in a drawer, out of sight, never far from mind. Emily had been more than her baby sister, she'd been the child of Addie's heart and newly budding fantasies.

By age fifteen she had been helping with the care of her brothers for years, but Emily's birth had stirred something bright and new inside her. She had watched her mother nurse the newest sibling and for the first time wondered what it would be like to nourish her own child, to hold an infant close and watch its small mouth suckle her. At fifteen the thoughts had embarrassed her; at nineteen they made her ache.

She crossed her arms over her breasts and held tight,

containing the dull throb in a safe circle to cherish the recollection, while trying to forget the pain. Deep within, hidden until now from her own awareness, surged an unbidden desire. She wished Cole were younger, wished she could release the buttons of her bodice and cradle him close, wished she could turn his small mouth to her and pretend—

Shame swept hot and certain through her, prickling the tips of her breasts into hurting points. She hugged herself tighter, frightened by the immoral thoughts and by how unnatural and depraved she must be to think such an indecent thing.

Zeke's hands fell lightly on her shoulders, and she straightened quickly on a gasp and spun around. Her elbows quickly folded and her hands came up, fingers twined tight and prayerlike between her breasts. He could feel the resistance in her tense shoulders and let his arms fall to his sides. He glanced down into the open drawer and at the tiny gown folded so neatly, then stared into her wary eyes. His voice was thickly laced with speculation. "Did you have a baby, Addie?"

She shook her head, flinching away from his intrusion into her memories at a moment when she felt so emotionally vulnerable. "My little sister. I had taken her gown and the one I wore at the wedding into town the day the farm was attacked. I needed thread and . . ." Her gaze drifted off to nowhere, seeing too much. Her stomach knotted and she dropped her arms to hug her middle. "She was so young, so tiny."

Her desolate, whispered words compressed Zeke's nerves and tendons, becoming part of him. He was no stranger to the feelings swamping her or the helplessness that came with them, but he rejected the urge to reach out and pull her close, making the familiarity worse. There was no tenderness he could offer that she would accept.

He tore his eyes away from the sight of her diminutive frame standing reserved and uncomfortable so close to him. "I'm sorry about your family, Addie," he said, glancing out the window at the land broken only by the jagged black silhouettes of the mountains at the perimeters and the murky blots of scrub brush and tumbleweed in the valley. Bathed in twilight, it looked peaceful and asleep, deceptively gentle. "The land takes its toll," he said grimly. "There was nothing you could have done."

She shook her head, mutely denying him. She could have been there, could have warned them, or . . . She shuddered at the awful resurrection of blame. "I know. In my mind, at least, I know." She dropped her eyes, needing to escape the thoughts and especially the man standing before her.

He was a paradox. Teasing one minute, sober the next. He showed an ease around his sons that was warming, yet even when he played with them or offered comfort, there was an air of reserve about him, as if he had lost something intrinsic deep inside and hadn't yet found a way to get it back.

And there were the memories, haunted and soulful, that never quite left his eyes. They lay there just beneath the amber surface in warning. *Don't stray too near.*

Addie wouldn't. She knew better. He was as hard and unpredictable as the land he gazed upon, quiet one moment, restless the next. She wouldn't pretend to guess what he might do if she ventured too near, delved too deeply. She lifted her eyes to find his profile sharp in the afterglow of a fallen sun, so very handsome as the shadows deepened. Stars began to twinkle, one by one, in an ebony sky. When he turned back his expression was like the night, dark and intense upon her.

His eyes touched and probed, first her hair, then her eyes and finally came to rest on her mouth. Addie felt her chest tighten, a suffocating constriction. Zeke watched her face tense, cool porcelain in the moonlight, and slid his gaze down her throat to the prim bodice of her night rail. He saw her breasts suddenly go still, then rapidly rise and fall when she remembered to breathe. It was hard to tell her shape beneath the prudish gown, but his imagination easily filled in the curves and angles beneath the thick cotton.

Addie couldn't bear his silent perusal. She felt captured and examined, like an insect under glass. She shivered slightly, unaccountably, and spared him a brief anxious glance, then squeezed past him and hurried to the bed. He watched her unnecessary flight and balled his fingers into fists, wondering how long it would take her to learn he was no threat, that she didn't have to shore up her pitiful defenses every time they were in the same room. Especially every time he got closer than two feet.

The cotton nightgown drew tight against her buttocks as she lifted one knee to the mattress and crawled into bed. His skin pulled tight everywhere in reaction. He damned Willis's memory and his own inability to erase after death whatever the man had done to her in life. Disgusted with the undeniable impulses of his male body, he moved to the bed and sat on the edge to pull his boots off, then rose again to tug his shirt from his pants. He caught the flash of uncertainty in her eyes before she quickly turned her face away. He was tempted to strip naked. He was tempted to shake her until her teeth rattled. He was tempted to roll her beneath him and prove she had every right in the world to fear him.

He didn't follow through with any of his frustrated insanity, just climbed in beside her and rested one arm behind his head.

"Addie." She jumped slightly at his deep voice and turned just her head to look at him. "What did Willis do to you?" She snapped her head back and squeezed her eyes shut.

"What did he do that makes you so afraid of me?"

She refused to answer and Zeke reached over to cup her chin, turning her toward him. She tried to shrug his hand off, but his hold only tightened. "Don't!" she cried, jerking her head away again.

Zeke opened his fingers before he might carelessly leave bruises on her pale cheeks. "I'm not him, Addie."

"I know." But it didn't matter at this point.

"I can't help you if you don't tell me what he did."

Her gaze speared straight through him, a mixture of anger and confusion. "I don't need your he—" She stumbled on the words. She was here because she couldn't survive alone and they both knew it. She flung her gaze to the ceiling. "I don't want to talk about it."

"I know, but I can't help that either." His hand dropped to her waist and she almost bolted from the bed. "See? I didn't hurt you, but you jumped like I'd just set a hot brand to your bare skin."

Addie only stared upward, feeling tortured. His thumb circled her navel through the cotton gown, and her stomach flipped. "Stop . . ."

"Why, does it hurt?"

He knew it didn't. Nothing he did in word or manner was anything like her brutal former husband. Instead, the things he did were more disturbing than truly terrorizing. Addie dropped her eyes to his hand. "Please."

His fingers spread over her rib cage, his skin deeply tanned against her white nightgown. He felt her muscles contract. "What is so terrible, Addie? It's just my hand."

Yes, she thought shakily. Strong and dark, very beautiful. A hand that would turn ugly and painful before he was done.

His fingers moved lightly, a swirling caress that sent heat fanning out to the circumference of her abdomen and made bile rise in her throat. "What did Willis do to you?"

She sent him a baleful look, then shut her eyes tight against his probing stare. Thwarted, Zeke slid his hand up her torso slowly, feeling the warmth of her body permeate the gown, the slenderness of her waist and rib cage. With every inch he trespassed, he felt her grow stiff and withdrawn. With a perverseness he couldn't seem to stop or understand, his palm rose higher until it fully covered her left breast. "Do you miss this, Addie?" he asked deeply. "Do you miss being married in this way?"

"No." She struggled with the word; she couldn't get enough air. His touch was heavy and warm, so frightening she wanted to scream, but she could barely breathe. *Now, it begins. Now, he'll get angry and insulting, brutal words that eventually turn into physical hurt.*

He watched every nuance of expression on her pale face, felt her flesh rise and hollow unevenly beneath his palm. His hand stirred lightly and her nipple pebbled, sending a hot flood of desire through him so sharp it was painful. He snatched his hand away in some belated attempt at self-preservation, but he didn't want to stop touching her, didn't want to lose the human contact that seemed inexcusably vital at this moment. Carefully, as if testing the limits of his self-control, he placed his palm back on her rib cage and felt every shallow breath she took, every uneven tremor in the warm flesh beneath his fingertips. "Tell me about him, Addie. Tell me so we can get past this."

A long pause followed, suspended between two worlds, two very different pasts.

"No."

When the word finally came it was flat, emotionless. She had distanced herself from everything he was doing, to that other place where numbness was blessedness and she couldn't see or hear or feel the pain and the humiliation that followed.

Zeke wanted to shout at her to fight back or explain, but she'd closed herself off in some internal sanctum, unreachable. He rolled toward her in frustration. "Addie, look at me."

No response. Nothing but her accelerated breathing and clenched eyelids. Zeke cursed beneath his breath. He felt at once both manipulated and cut off. If he had an ounce of self-respect, he'd leave her to her lonely frigidity until the clawing emptiness inside her was too much to endure, until the risk of letting him in was worth whatever fears held her back. But he couldn't forget the feel of her, soft and lush beneath his palm, warm despite her chilling response.

The gathered neck of her night rail was puckered, revealing the small hills of her breasts. Lamplight played over her fair skin, turning it golden in places, deepening the shadows in others. He lifted one finger and traced the top edge of the gaping neckline and felt her cringe, then dropped his hand to her hip, safer but no less stirring. She was so slender beneath his palm.

Driven by the challenge to make her respond in anger or acceptance, anything other than her vacant withdrawal, his thumb made circles on the fabric of her gown, bunching the cotton up inch by slow inch until it reached her knees.

"What would you do, Addie, if I took it off?"

Seconds ticked by like eons before she whispered, "Hate you."

He grimaced, then smiled ruefully. "Wouldn't want you to do that," he drawled. His hand slid from her hip and he pulled the quilt up over her chest, then moved to his side of the bed. " 'Night, Miz Claiborne."

Relief seeped through Addie by tentative degrees, as if leery of moving through her too fast. She peeked over at him beneath her lashes to find him contemplating the ceiling, one arm behind his head, the other lying limp across his middle. His touch had been firm, strong enough to force her to do anything he chose. But he had stopped. At a few words from her, he had stopped.

Tears stung her eyes. Regret, fear, relief? She was too confounded to wonder at her reaction or why her answer had mattered to him, and she was much too tired to dwell on it. He was about as confusing as a man could be, but she was beginning to think that maybe, just maybe, he might be trustworthy.

She spent a fretful night, afraid she would oversleep again. When Zeke stirred just at dawn, she scrambled from the bed, donned a frayed robe, and hurried to make his breakfast. Quiet as possible for the boys' sake, she stoked the fire and put coffee on, then began cutting bacon to fry and rolling out biscuits. By the time Zeke entered the kitchen, she was already out at the chicken coop hunting eggs.

The dawn air was crisp enough to make her bare toes curl, and she knew she had been foolish to rush off half-addled. She gathered the last egg, shivering as she wrapped it in her robe hem, then hurried back into the house. The kitchen had warmed up and the heat wrapped around her like a soft blanket when she stepped through the door. The aroma of fresh coffee was tantalizing. Zeke sat at the table, his hands resting on a cup, looking more handsome than a man had the right to look at the crack of daylight. His gaze swept slowly from her tousled hair to her bare feet.

"When you need eggs, I'll gather them before I do the milking. You'll freeze solid come winter if you go out like that."

Addie blushed and turned away to put the eggs in a bowl. She felt foolish for not dressing first but hadn't wanted to don her clothes with him still in the bedroom. She put the biscuits on to bake, then hurried out of the kitchen. She'd just caught the hem of her nightgown and pulled it over her head when Zeke walked through the bedroom door. She whirled around, gripping the gown in front of her for modesty, then went rigid when she saw the look in his eyes: he wasn't one bit shocked or embarrassed.

"You came in on purpose!" she accused.

He hadn't, not in the way she meant, but he didn't feel like explaining. He had to bite back a smile at the utter outrage in her expression, as if she had just come face-to-face with the town lecher. He wasn't in the habit of peeking in windows just to get a glimpse of leg or bosom, but as he gave her a slow, sweeping glance, he realized the thought had merit. Her bare feet, ankles, and calves were visible beneath the bunched-up gown, her slender arms and shoulders above. Her skin was the color of cream and just as soft looking. Inviting.

He cleared his throat and tried to offer a serious mien. "Don't go back out half-dressed again," he said. "I'll turn my back mornings if it makes you feel better." She just gritted her teeth and stared back at him, shivering from head to toe. "What if one of us gets sick?"

She shrugged, mute and embarrassed and angry, her backside and legs crawling with chill bumps.

"Are you going to tend to me with your eyes closed?" he continued in a practical tone. "I don't plan on doing for you that way. A person can lose a considerable amount of dignity when they're ill and someone else has to care for them." His eyes ran over her again. "Might be better if you weren't so modest now."

"Might be better if I don't get sick," she said, as if she were just stubborn enough to keep it from happening.

Zeke smiled wryly. "Might be," he agreed. "I'd sure like to see you accomplish that over the next forty or fifty years." With that he turned and walked to the door, leaving her and her modesty a little shredded but intact. He paused at the threshold and looked back over his shoulder. "You sure have a fine pair of ankles, Miz Claiborne."

Addie's gaze flew down to her bare feet as the door closed. Of all the hare-brained, ridiculous . . . Abashed, she held her gown to her and snatched her clothes from the wardrobe. She had thought him trustworthy the night before? Stupid, fool-headed Addie. Awkwardly, she dressed one-handed until she was sufficiently covered to fold her nightgown and put it away.

Forty or fifty years! Her fingers stilled on the last button at her collar. For the first time it occurred to her what "till death do us part" might actually mean. The other phases in her life had been short and quick and brutal. Her childhood had been saddened by Tommy's death, her adolescence by the death of her parents and remaining siblings, her young adulthood destroyed by marriage to Willis. Forty or fifty years with the same family just seemed a little too optimistic for her to believe in right now.

Zeke had Cole dressed and the other two boys managing on their own by the time Addie returned to the kitchen. She mumbled an apology at him having to do woman's work for the second day in a row, but Zeke just gave her an odd half smile. He'd been doing household chores for so long, he'd forgotten what it was like not to have the whole burden to carry.

He felt energetic this morning, revived. He'd put in a full workday yesterday, not the half-ass getting-by he was used to, trying to juggle the house, the ranch, and the boys. Getting his sons dressed and settling them around the breakfast table was nothing compared to what he had been doing.

Addie took the baby from his arms and put Cole in the high chair, then turned to find her overdone biscuits on the counter. Zeke eyed the browned edges dubiously but didn't comment. Josh rolled his eyes at her and followed his pa out the door to do chores. Zeb was even less tactful. He murmured something that sounded like "Bluck!" and stuck his tongue out.

Cole mimicked his brother, but Addie dished them up anyway, fried bacon and eggs, and plopped down in the chair nearest the baby, feeling as though her whole world was somehow settling to dust. Gathering eggs was her duty along with dressing the boys and getting breakfast. Zeke had plenty enough work of his own without having to help with her chores, too. Zeb made another face at his biscuit, and Addie propped her chin on her hand with a sigh, feeling like a failure.

"There are too many men in this family," she said, spooning eggs onto Cole's plate. He gave her a semitoothless grin and banged one of the hard lumps of burned dough on the table.

"Is not," Zeb said, affronted.

"Four boys and only one girl," Addie said, but she was smiling so he wouldn't take her words to heart.

The back door slammed, but it was Zeke's words that made her flinch. "Sounds like your ma needs to get us a baby sister to start evening things up a bit."

Addie spun around in her seat and sputtered without thinking, "Do you always have to sneak up on a body that way?"

"Guess I could knock at my own back door." He smiled lazily. "My own bedroom door too."

"That's the dumbest thing I ever heard," Zeb said.

Which was, of course, exactly why Zeke had said it. Addie swung her blazing cheeks back to the table, knowing he was goading her. He had already made it clear he didn't want any more children, so why was he poking fun? She felt the scales of her reason tip at his inconsistency. He'd been cold and insistent last night, pragmatic at daylight, and almost playful now around the boys.

The only part she understood was the last. It wouldn't do to drag the children down in the mire of this awkward marriage. Keeping things safe and secure and normal for the boys was as important to her as keeping them that way for herself.

But she didn't know what normal was in a real marriage. She had only her parents for a pattern and she couldn't picture herself ever being that easy with Zeke.

She glanced over to see him filling his plate from the stove beside Josh. Father and son stared at the biscuits, exchanged forlorn looks, and silently moved on to the bacon. She felt her heart give a little at their despondency.

She averted her eyes and mumbled to the tabletop, "I'll make a double batch in the morning." No one said a word for several seconds until Zeb couldn't stand the unnatural silence.

"That's all right, Ma. Me and Josh'll use 'um for target practice. You can knock over a lotta bottles with biscuits this hard."

A fit of coughing erupted from the two standing at the cupboard.

"Well?" Zeb said on a huff. "That's what we always do when you cook 'um, Pa."

Addie's head slunk down between her shoulder blades to suppress the humor rising in her throat. She took a bite of her eggs but had to struggle to keep them in her mouth.

"Well, we do," Zeb continued, baffled by all the averted faces. "Don't we, Josh?"

Josh wasn't saying a word. He was too busy biting the inside of his jaw.

"Stuff your mouth, son," Zeke warned as he sat down. "Your tongue needs settling down." He turned his attention to Addie but she was in no shape to look him in the eye. "Have you made up the list for town?"

She hadn't even thought of it since the night before. "I forgot," she said sheepishly.

"I'll do it. I know most of what we need anyway, but if there's anything special you want, just pick it up while we're there."

She looked up slowly, all humor vanquished. "I'm not

going." Zeb's face fell and he began whining that he and Cole wouldn't get to go if she didn't. "Suppose I could then," she murmured. But she dreaded going into town and enduring all those speculative looks almost worse than she dreaded disappointing Zeb.

Zeke understood her apprehension; he didn't look forward to facing the town either, but figured it was something best gotten out of the way. The more they appeared together, the sooner Laramie would get used to it.

As soon as the dishes were done, they loaded into the wagon and set out. Clouds of dust rose on Main Street beneath the clop of the horses' hooves and rolling wagon wheels. Harnesses and spurs jingled as they passed other shoppers; greetings were hailed and returned. Traffic moved with the choking pace of a lively and congested town.

Addie gripped Cole tighter, using him like a shield to bolster her courage. The baby squirmed at being caged and she was forced to ease up so he could twist and turn to get his eyes full of the hustle and bustle of progress.

Beatrice Parker was sweeping the sidewalk in front of the general store where she helped Sam three days a week. She paused when the wagon pulled to a stop. "Hidey, Zeke, Addie," she called, her eyes giving them a thorough once-over. "Nice day. Last good one for a spell, I reckon. Hidey, boys."

The Claiborne sons made suitable responses. Mrs. Parker had candy jars full of tempting treats, and they always got their pick if they behaved. Addie nodded hello and forced herself to sit still and wait for Zeke to help her down. It wouldn't do to cause a scene in front of a woman like Bea.

Zeke swung her down, then left his hand at the small

of her back as if they were familiar with such. Short of ramming her elbow into his middle, there was little else Addie could do except allow it for the sake of propriety. He gave her a little nudge and she stepped up onto the wooden planks that lined the business district.

The baby went all round-eyed when they stepped into the dim interior of the store. Jars of striped candy sticks and peppermint balls lined a counter along with a variety of everything imaginable. From whiskey to entertain the spirit and Bibles to assuage the soul, a whole terrain of goods lay in between. Coal oil, calico, and canned oysters packed the shelves for the body, along with McGuffey's Readers, Pike's *Arithmetic,* and Byerly's *Speller* for the mind. Ewall's *Medical Companion* provided study for good health, while candles and crepe were sold for when it was no longer necessary.

A bench was placed near the front for ladies to rest their feet and grow accustomed to the gentle gloom before loading up with vinegar, sugar, flour, and molasses. A potbellied stove sat in the middle, an island of warmth in winter. Surrounded by chairs, it stood near a cracker barrel that sported a checkerboard on top. Two of the town's oldest citizens were engaged in a game.

"Howdy, Zeke," Nathaniel Pickens said in an aside as he jumped two of Ian MacAlister's men, then cackled with a toothless grin, "Crown me, ye old coot."

Ian, garbed in the Confederate uniform he still wore every day of his life except Sundays, grumbled something around a wad of tobacco, then aimed a spew of brown juice at the brass spittoon near his chair.

Beatrice let fly with her broom when he missed and clobbered the back of Ian's chair. "Now see here, mister," she railed, "you can take it outside if that's how you're gonna do!"

Ian eyed her as if he was sighting down the barrel of his breech-loader and called her a Yankee sympathizer. Beatrice thwacked his chair again. "One more word, old man, just one more . . ."

Addie backed up a step at the woman's intimidating brashness, wishing just once in her life she could find the courage to be that bold toward a man, even if he was ninety, hard of hearing, and had one foot in the grave. She glanced over at Zeke and found him trying to steer his wide-eyed sons away from the fracas.

Addie watched him go, then nearly jumped from her skin when Beatrice slammed the broom against the counter next to her. "What can I do for you, Addie?" After a pause, the woman said brusquely, "Well, what is it? Speak up, girl. I haven't got all day."

Addie shifted the baby to her hip for something to do with her hands and looked for Zeke. "My . . . husband has the list."

Beatrice dropped her head like a bull ready to charge and gave Addie a direct look right down the blade of her nose. "Don't you know what's on it? Lord knows, I haven't got a bit of patience for a woman who won't speak her mind."

Addie decided she didn't have much patience for being browbeaten this morning, but she sure admired the woman's brass. She lifted her chin a fraction. "No, ma'am. Zeke made the list."

Beatrice sent her a snide "so that's the way it is" look, then caught Addie by the arm and hauled her toward the back of the store. Surrounded by crates of dry goods and hardware, she released her victim, then crossed her arms over her generous bosom.

"Everything all right between you two?" When Addie nodded, she continued sternly, "Good. Now, you listen to me. Zeke is a right fair man, if there is such a creature. You want something, you just tell me. We aren't claiming to be Bon Marché of Paris, but I'll see that Zeke gets whatever you want." She sent Addie another frank look. "Gotta speak up, girl, if you want to be heard."

Throat dry, Addie nodded. Zeke *was* a fair man as best she could tell, and she wasn't about to turn Mrs. Beatrice Parker loose on him. "Yes, ma'am," she said. "If I need something, I'll let you know."

"See that you do," Beatrice said, then turned and retrieved a package from the bottom shelf, rubbed the dust off with her apron, and handed it to Addie. "Just a little wedding gift I set aside when y'all got hitched. It's not much, but it's as fine as any you'd get at R. H. Macy and Company of New York City." With a nod, she spun her considerable bulk around and marched back to the front of the store.

"Thank you" fell on empty space as Addie watched Beatrice disappear. She took a deep breath, tucked the gift under her arm, and put Cole down to toddle around for a while. She let him roam at will but kept a close eye out for trouble, handing him safe things to explore and leading him away from the breakables. Most of the merchandise in Parker's General Store was in the nature of necessary goods, but there were a few frivolous items to tempt the whims of anyone with extra cash.

Zeke called from the next aisle, and Addie rounded a jumbled display of leather boots and belts to find him eyeing the counter dubiously. The musty-sweet tang of fresh fabric bolts permeated the air, overriding the aroma of plug tobacco and pickled fish an aisle away. He signaled her closer. "Pick," he said succinctly. "I haven't got a notion about any of this."

Addie fingered the fabric lightly. So much to choose from, depending on how he wanted his boys dressed. "Well," she hesitated. "What do you think?"

"I think they need to be presentable. One good outfit for Sunday and several sturdier ones for the week ought to do it. Get whatever you want for yourself." When Addie still didn't say anything, Zeke took the baby from her and started walking away. "I'll get Bea. She can help you better than I can."

Addie squeaked a protest, but he had already disappeared from sight.

Cheeks flaming, arms loaded down, Addie followed Mrs. Parker to the front counter where purchases were paid for or written down in the charge book. Zeke was going to have a conniption when he saw everything Beatrice insisted a woman needed to make up a suitable winter wardrobe for her family. Addie hadn't minded so much for the boys. It would be a joy to sew the fine cloth into pants and shirts and nightclothes. But she wasn't so sure about herself. Beatrice had bullied her into more and various fabrics than she'd seen in a lifetime, and Addie didn't know how she was going to explain it all to Zeke.

She caught sight of him at the entrance where Sam was loading the last sack of grain into the wagon. Zeke called his thanks, then turned and walked to the counter. Handing Addie the baby, he began settling his bill. She waited, eyes on the floor, for him to start ranting about the excessive amount of cloth, thread, and fancy gewgaws Beatrice had insisted she needed to complement each intended garment.

Zeke nudged her when everything was totaled. "You sure you don't need anything else?"

Addie peeked up at him beneath her lashes and shook her head. So, he wasn't going to make a scene here in the store, but what about when they got home?

Zeke turned to the store's proprietor. "Has she got everything, Bea?"

"Well . . ." Beatrice drew the word out slowly, sort of huffy and innocent at the same time, all the while eyeing Addie slyly. "I couldn't get her to pick any of that gorgeous new fabric I've got for making ladies' unmentionables. You won't find better at Marshall Field and Company of Chicago, but she says she already has one. One! As if that's all the underpinnings a body needs."

Addie closed her eyes briefly, wanting to die, then sent Beatrice a narrow-eyed warning glance, which was no threat at all to the woman who could smell money nine miles away. Addie wasn't about to let her sniff out any more of Zeke's than the woman was already getting.

"I have everything I need," she said stridently. "Thank you."

Beatrice's chin lifted a haughty notch. "Well, I must say you are frugal, Addie. I just hope you don't plan to carry it too far over into cheap. Being fancy is one thing, but being civilized is another. Zeke has *always* kept his family well dressed."

Addie knew what was coming next before Beatrice even spoke. She could feel it in the air, like the lowering pressure that precedes a storm. She had expected everyone to make silent comparisons. She should have known Beatrice would be bold enough to voice them aloud.

"Why, when Becky was alive—"

Zeke slammed his money down on the counter. "If this doesn't take care of it, put the rest on my account." He scooped Zeb up, called for Josh, then took Addie by the arm and ushered them all toward the door. "Wrap it up," he called back over his shoulder. "I'll be back for it later."

Sunlight blinded Addie when they walked through the doors. She blinked several times for her eyes to adjust but didn't dare look over at Zeke. She didn't want to see the expression on his face, whether anger or disgust or hurt.

It was only midafternoon, but tinny music floated over the dusty air from the saloon across the street. An occasional burst of raucous laughter erupted through the partial doors followed by a coarse female giggle. One voice rose above the others, and Addie clutched Cole convulsively and stepped back into the shadows of the general store as Grady stumbled through the swinging doors.

His arm was hooked over the neck of a garishly dressed woman who was smiling up at him, her painted face even more vivid against the backdrop of a colorless dirt road and the weathered boards of the saloon. She hiked her skirt indecently high when they stepped onto the street, revealing satin shoes and black stockings. *Shameful and shocking,* her mother used to cluck about such things when Addie was young.

As a child, she hadn't understood why her mother would thump her ogling brothers and snatch Addie's arm to steer her away from peeking at the brightly festooned ladies, nor why her mama's pretty mouth would go pinched when Addie asked about them. "Satan's handmaidens," she would whisper while shaking her head sadly. "Poor, misguided souls."

Addie hadn't thought so, craning her neck to stare back over her shoulder at the women as her mother hauled her along. They looked more like a brilliant sunset to her, gowned in vivid pinks or oranges or scarlets, their hair piled lusciously atop their heads and adorned with feathers.

Addie believed her mother now. Anyone who could laugh and carry on with Grady so easily must be the devil's own kin and doomed to eternal damnation.

Grady weaved around an approaching wagon and headed straight for the general store. *Oh, Lord.* Addie felt her stomach lurch and looked at Zeke. She wanted out of here, fast. Zeke caught her expression the moment she grabbed his sleeve in a frantic grip, and glanced up to see Grady and his strumpet headed straight for them.

"Miz Addie." Grady's eyes were snide when he tipped his hat with one hand and pulled the woman forward with the other. "May I present Miss Lou Ellen Mullins. Lou Ellen, this is Addie Smith . . . Claiborne."

A muscle twitched in Zeke's jaw. It was unconscionable of Grady to present a whore to a lady. Lou Ellen knew it as well and cut Grady a seething glare. She had no fuss with Addie and certainly didn't want to antagonize Zeke. She waited for the younger woman to lift her chin and sweep her skirts aside as any other self-respecting woman would and march across the street to escape breathing the tainted air.

"My pleasure, Miss Mullins," Addie murmured.

Lou Ellen blushed, something she hadn't managed since she was thirteen and spreading her legs for the first time in a New Orleans bordello. *How impossibly absurd,* she wanted to shout at the young woman. *Don't you know any better?*

Zeke felt something inside him uncoil. Addie hadn't responded at all to the disservice done her, thereby thwarting her brother-in-law most effectively, and she had Lou Ellen so uncomfortable the woman was fairly itching to get back at her escort. He sent Grady a knowing smile.

"You lose, Smith." He nodded, then tipped his hat to Lou Ellen and his smile turned masculinely gracious. "Good day, Miz Mullins."

Lou Ellen felt her heart drop to her slim white belly. Zeke Claiborne's southern drawl was so slow and lazy, she could taste the scent of honeysuckle on every word. Not for the first time, she wondered if he loved that way, hot and easy as summer. She'd been after him for as long as she could remember, but she'd never gotten him. Not before his beautiful wife died, which she accepted, nor after, which she didn't.

Like most ranchers in Laramie, Zeke came into the saloon at least once a week when in town for supplies. But unlike the others, especially the single ones, he'd never given her anything more than that blinding God-forbidden smile when she flirted.

He'd softened up over the last three months though, she was sure of it. She had seen him look a bit closer and take a little longer doing so out of whiskey-colored eyes that made her pulse rise. And at this point in her career, it took a helluva lot to make Lou Ellen Mullins's pulse do anything more than lie there. And all for what? Nothing, that's what, because she'd heard days ago that he'd taken another wife.

She slid a veiled glance at the wife in question and felt her hopes teeter indecisively. Pretty little thing, but too thin. Prim the way a man wanted a wife in public, but not the way he wanted one in bed. She shielded her eyes from the sun so she could run them suggestively over Zeke's body without anyone but him being the wiser. She sent him her most dazzling smile in case he was interested, then dug her long, sharp nails into Grady's arm. "Come on, sugar, about that new hat . . ."

Grady allowed himself to be led away but smiled as he strolled past Addie. "Been meaning to stop by and pay you a little visit."

Addie said nothing, just stared at the crown of the baby's head until her stomach settled down and she was certain Grady was out of sight.

She sat as still and straight as the wooden frame of the buckboard when they headed out of town. She hadn't wanted to go into Laramie in the first place and now her day was ruined. She tried not to think of Grady. It made her too panicky, but in forcing thoughts of him aside, she was left with the earlier part of her wretched afternoon and Beatrice's comment.

Becky *had* kept her family well clothed, not flashy like that Miss Mullins but so refined and proper. They had made a striking family on church Sunday, riding into town in their finery. Addie didn't mind the comparison so much for herself, but it must be awful hard on Zeke to be constantly reminded that he had lost a wife so lively and pretty and accomplished. She slid a glance his way, wishing she could tell him . . . what? That she was sorry for not being Becky, for being only herself? Like that would do either of them any good!

Burying her face in Cole's curls, she inhaled the sunny fragrance of fresh air and warm baby. His chubby fist reached up to grab the ribbons of her bonnet, knocking it askew. She pulled it off and let him play with it, enjoying the breeze and sunshine on her face. Zeke looked over at her, and Addie felt her cheeks heat up.

"I'm sorry about Beatrice," she said.

He turned his face back to the road. "Don't be. Her tongue has a tendency to outrun her manners. I've come to expect it. She means well most times."

Relieved that he wasn't angry, Addie picked up the package. "She got us a gift."

Zeb scrambled up from the back and leaned over between them. "Can I open it, Pa?"

Addie handed it to him. "Let Josh help," she said, enjoying his excitement more than the gift itself. She'd already received a storehouse full of pillowcases, pot holders, and recipe books from the socially correct inhabitants of the town.

Zeb tugged at the string while Josh tore at the paper, but their enthusiasm died a quick death at Zeb's disgusted "Bluck!" as soon as the wrapping fell away. Addie turned to look at the object of his disgust and her eyes went wide and appalled when he held up the flimsiest, most delicate, and thoroughly indecent night rail she had ever seen. The wind picked up the fabric and tossed it like a banner as Zeb giggled and held it aloft. Sunlight streamed through the gossamer folds and exquisite lace. Ivory satin ribbons trailed out in all directions, heralding their passage down Main Street.

Addie's cheeks throbbed with embarrassment. It took her a full ten seconds to gather enough wits to close her gaping mouth, snatch the gown from Zeb, and wad it up in Cole's lap before the whole town witnessed the sight. The baby cooed delightfully and buried himself in the soft fabric.

Addie turned her horrified gaze to Zeke. He was staring straight ahead, but a muscle flexed repeatedly in his jaw. "I'm sorry . . . about the boys seeing that," she whispered miserably. "I didn't know what was in it."

He murmured "Gitup" to keep the horses moving, then cut his eyes to Addie. His voice held a strange, hard edge when he spoke. "Remind me to do a lot more business with Beatrice Parker in the future."

8

Addie put the boys to bed, then packed away everything they had brought from town except one item—the night rail. Glancing around slyly as if someone might be spying, she picked up the transparent gown and held it to her. Her hands traveled gingerly over the weightless, gauzy fabric, fearful of touching it too roughly. She'd never seen anything more beautiful or more useless. She'd freeze to death come winter, if she were ever to wear such a thing, which she most certainly would not. It was thoroughly indecent.

Oh, but it sure was pretty! Light and delicate, it flowed before her, looking as sweet as spun sugar. She twirled once and let it billow around her, imagining how luxurious it would feel to sleep in such. Hearing the door open, she turned quickly and shoved the gown behind her.

Eyeing her curiously, Zeke dropped his Stetson on the night table as he took in the high color on her cheeks, the startled look in her eyes. He smiled slowly. "You gonna put that on, or stand there hiding it all night?"

Addie sneaked a look down to see the diaphanous layers pooled around her feet. "It's not fitting," she choked out. "It's so thin and all. I don't think—"

"Try it on," Zeke said levelly. "It's a gift, Addie. You should at least see if it's the right size."

Her teeth worried her bottom lip and her eyes traveled everywhere but back to Zeke. Hot color spread up her chest and neck. "I don't want you to see me in it."

Zeke let out an exasperated breath and shoved his hands into his pockets. "Why?"

Eyes on the floor, Addie pulled the night rail from behind her and held it up for his inspection. Lamplight danced over the airy folds, turning the trailing ivory ribbons to palest gold. Zeke could see straight through to his wife's shadowy outline behind.

"It would look real nice on you, Addie."

Her eyes snapped up to his. Many emotions warred for dominance in the deep green depths, but shock and disbelief were the most prevailing. She smiled shakily. "You're joshing me again."

"No." Zeke crossed the distance separating them and fingered one of the ribbons. "Try it on, Addie."

Her eyes grew cloudy with hurtful memories, and she turned her face away. "You wouldn't like it on me."

Zeke frowned, bewildered by her words and reticence. Modesty he could understand, but she seemed to be alluding to something else. His fingers trailed up the ribbon, brushing the back of her hand. Her fingers were cold, gripping the gown like a lifeline. Her head was turned, her curls scattering candlelight like a prism. Her chest rose once on an indrawn breath before she turned back, her eyes large and luminous green above a troubled brow.

"Try it on," he coaxed again. "I'll turn my back if you like."

She blinked and shivered slightly, as if shaking herself free of some memory. Her mouth pursed suddenly. "No."

His smile was slow, his eyes too aware for the innocence he feigned. "You don't want me to turn my back? Why, Miz Claiborne, I never."

Her cheeks grew hot, but her voice remained stubborn. "No, I won't put it on. It's not decent."

"Decent," he echoed, as if he had to mull the word over to grasp its meaning. His eyes were clear and untroubled as he regarded her. "It's just a nightgown, Addie. Some people sleep in less."

Nothing could be less than what she held in her hand, except naked. Her body jerked at the realization.

"Shocked?" he asked wryly. His fingers traced the ribbons again up to the lacy bodice. "C'mon, Addie, try it on."

"I'll freeze!"

"Not any worse than I do every night, looking at you in that suit of armor you sleep in."

Her eyes flared in hostility. "That is a perfectly proper and modest nightgown!"

He leaned forward until they were almost nose to nose. "Yeah, for some dried-up old maiden lady." He pulled his head back and smiled slowly. "You're not old, Addie, and you're no maiden lady. Try it on."

She knew better than to deny him. Hadn't she learned from Willis the awful consequences she'd pay when a man's teasing turned serious. Her stomach tightened as Zeke continued to wait, towering and silent before her. Her resistance would be nothing if he decided to use force.

She had known it would come to this. Since the night she found out she'd be sharing his room, she had known. The dread had been such a terrifying thing to carry, she would almost rather get it over with and know for certain what kind of man she had married.

But she wouldn't be that fifteen-year-old again, cringing and powerless and silently obedient. If she had to do this, she would do it by her own hands, under her own power, not by his dictate.

Her chin wavered, but the rest of her was rigid and braced. "No. I won't wear it." Unable to hold his stare, her eyes flew to the floor, and she wondered if she was two heartbeats away from being backhanded to her knees.

Zeke felt something in him retreat at the fierceness in her tone, coupled with the defeated drop of her chin. He stepped back, the physical distance only barely measuring the span between them. "Fine," he said flatly. "Put the old one on then."

But instead of leaving the room, he turned and presented his back, wondering what she'd do now. He was prepared for some sort of rebuttal and was stunned to hear the rustle of fabric, a muted huff of displeasure, then the slither of cloth softly hitting the floor. His pulse accelerated.

Time dragged forward until seconds felt like minutes, minutes like hours, and days stretched upon a torture rack toward eternity. This had been a bad idea, one of his worst. He should have taken himself and his undernourished, overactive libido off to the kitchen instead of engaging in a power struggle. By now his wife stood naked behind him, but whether trusting him or testing him he didn't know. He'd rot on the spot before he'd turn around and give her ammunition to hurl accusations. But his imagination wasn't as grounded as the rest of him.

Every soft sound painted a vivid picture of unveiled limbs, satiny hair picking up candlelight as it fell over pale shoulders, slender ankles stepping out of durable homespun. His impatience grew with the steady thump of blood pulsing in his veins. *A very bad idea.*

Addie cleared her throat, and he thought *Finally, finally I can get out of here and go stand outside in the frigid night air.* He turned around to excuse himself and went dead still.

Well, hell!

She had put on Beatrice's gift after all. Her hands were crossed loosely in front of her, the fingers laced. Her eyes were focused on some distant spot, as unreachable as if she were miles away instead of inches. Moonlight played in ghostly patterns over the sheer fabric draping her, outlining her shape beneath while illuminating her hair in silvery strands. She was thin but well formed, graceful without being full fleshed. Chilled, her breasts stood high and tight against the thin lace, the aureoles dark spheres above a small, athletic rib cage and waist. Her hips flared out over slender, long legs.

Zeke sucked in a deep angry breath. She was testing him all right, clear down to his toes, with an extra helping lumped midway between. She was more than he had expected, all delicate curves and slender ripeness. The scent of new fabric lingered in the air, as crisp and soft as the lacy bodice that hid nothing from his imagination. Feelings crept through him in uncomfortable ways. A hint of tenderness for her obvious discomfort, a measure of pride for her courage, and basic and unavoidable lust. Frustrated, he refused even to pretend to understand what had prompted her to change her mind, but he knew one thing for certain. She was completely and competently making him lunatic.

Twin spots of color heated Addie's cheeks as she waited for his rejection, for the ugly names and disgust she'd gotten from Willis for four years. The smell of stale whiskey that accompanied his words even now rolled through her mind. *God, look at you! You ain't got nothin' a man would want. Turn around, girl, before I lose the stinkin' dinner you cooked.* Then he would come at her from behind, bending her over the bed until her face was smashed into the feather mattress to muffle her cries. She never knew whether he would use his belt or his hands on her; she couldn't remember which was worse.

She imagined herself braced for Zeke's cruelty, but when he snatched the quilt from the bed suddenly and covered her, she wanted to weep at having revolted him. Debilitating rage and shame swept her. "I told you," she whispered wretchedly.

"You're cold," he said, everything in him held tight to control the desire to touch her.

Beatrice Parker must have shopped hell's own backyard to find a negligee as tempting as this one. He didn't know whether to curse the woman or reward her. His fingers tightened on the quilt but images shimmered before him still, imprinted on his memory. The cool silvery outline of her form beneath a whisper of cloth. Her face, tense with an uncertainty and shyness so much more potent than the most blatant seduction.

His voice was thick and grainy. "God, you're beautiful, Addie. I could look at you all night, but I don't want you to catch a chill."

She stared at him as if he'd gone mad, then a small,

nervous giggle bubbled up inside her and swelled until it burst. She slapped an unstable hand over her mouth but couldn't seem to stop the flow of inane titters. With a strange look, Zeke pulled her slowly against him. "You don't believe me?"

She shook her head. She wasn't much to look at, certainly not beautiful. Even at fourteen when she'd finally gotten her monthlies she'd been merely passable, flat-chested and rangy like a boy, which her younger brothers were always eager to point out despite the scolding they received. At nineteen she was a tad more filled out, but little else.

Zeke pulled her even closer. The light in her eyes dimmed to wariness. "Don't be afraid, Addie. In that gown . . . you look so pretty it makes a man crazy, but I swear, I won't do anything you don't want me to."

Her thoughts tumbled in massive confusion, like her tripping heartbeat. She had the desperate urge to ask him to say it again, the part about being pretty, but didn't dare set herself up for a fool. She didn't know if he was taunting her in the cruelest way or if his compliment was just part and parcel of his gentleman's charm. He was that way, lifting her from the wagon, pulling out chairs, helping with the boys.

Zeke felt her heart hammering against his fist and wished he had the words to ease her, knowing the truth would not. But the truth was all he had.

"I want you, Addie." His hands rose and cupped her cheeks to prevent her from turning aside. "I need to be a part of you, inside you." She recoiled immediately at his bold words and the heat in his eyes. "I know you're scared," he whispered gruffly. "You need to tell me why, so I don't frighten you worse."

The words sounded preset, like he had made his decision and there was no changing it no matter what they had agreed upon. She thought of the boys: Cole's cherub prettiness, Zeb's enthusiasm, Josh's pain. She would do almost anything to keep them. She squeezed her eyes shut, hurting. If she did what he wanted, he wouldn't want her anymore. Then the punishment and reprisals would start. *Oh, Lord.*

"I won't fight you," she said flatly.

Desire and dread sluiced through him, two opposing forces colliding. "Fight me?" he asked in a raw voice. "What the hell did Willis do to you?"

Her resolve broke and she struggled violently to get away from him then, but he only dropped the quilt and cinched his arms around her so tight her breasts were crushed against his hard chest. It was a mistake to restrain her. The contact was volatile, lush flesh melding with hard musculature, his hands tangled in the sleek fabric of the gown at the small of her back, the twist and turn of her hips against his. He could feel her everywhere, against his chest and loins, the gentle slope of her buttocks beneath his fingertips, and it shook the core of his hunger until it expanded to encompass all of him. He was no longer concerned with her fear but the resistance she showed every time he broached the subject.

"Listen to me, Addie." He tightened his grip slightly to get her attention and she ceased trying to twist out of his arms. "You can't shut me out every time his name comes up. I can't help what Willis did to you, but you've got to tell me so I won't do the same thing." His hands released her only long enough to rise and cup her face, tough and callused hands as gentle as his voice. "Did he hurt you? Was he too rough or forceful? I know a man can get carried away sometimes, but I won't do that if it makes you afraid or causes you pain."

She was burning up with shame. She could feel it on her hot cheeks and chest, the grip of it in her belly. She couldn't tell him about Willis. She'd just let him have his way, then he'd see for himself. "I said you can do what you want," she whispered furiously. "I'm not saying anything else."

Zeke let go of her immediately and stepped back. "Then I'm not *doing* anything else. When I take you to bed it'll just be the two of us. Not you and me and Willis's memory." He jerked at the buttons of his shirt, cursing when one popped off, then dragged it from his shoulders and slung it over a chair.

Addie stared at him in bewildered amazement, astonished that he'd taken his anger back with him instead of directing it at her. Her eyes widened as he undressed, but she was unable to turn away from the play of candlelight over sleek muscles, the strength and harmony in the powerful flex of his arms and chest. A weakness invaded her limbs and she reached out to steady herself against the bedpost, transfixed by his shameless lack of modesty and what it was doing to her insides. When his hands reached his belt buckle, her eyes flew to his.

"I didn't aim to make you mad," she said on a strangled breath.

He gave her a scathing look and stripped the belt from his pants, then began unbuttoning the fly. Addie wanted to dash from the room but was frozen where she stood. He sat on the edge of the bed and pulled his boots off, then peeled his pants down and slung them on top of his shirt. As he sat in only his short cotton undergarments, his legs were strong and tan with a fine sprinkling of hair covering long, fit muscles.

Addie's mouth went dry. He was so perfectly formed, lithe strength cording the musculature into perfect symmetry. His chest was wide, his hips narrow, every line and curve a solid plane that flowed together in superior equipoise. Her eyes were as riveted to Zeke's magnificent physical attributes as her feet were to the floor, but when he moved, her abashed gaze flew to his face.

Zeke's eyes pierced straight through her as he tossed the sheet back and got into bed. "If you're coming, bring the quilt."

Having her own stubborn ire flung back at her was more provoking than her fear or embarrassment. She set her chin and stared at her husband as if he were one of the boys instead of twice her size and half naked.

"I said, I didn't mean to make you mad." He gave her a narrow-eyed look, and she fought the urge to cringe back. Tilting her chin even higher, she asked shakily, "And where else would I sleep anyway?"

He flew from the bed so fast she didn't have a chance to move, much less run. In one broad sweep, he had her off her feet. In one step, he had her sailing toward the bed. She landed with a bounce and lay flat on her back, her heart lodged in her throat. Without a word, he stomped back across the room, grabbed the quilt, and climbed into bed.

While Addie was still struggling to find her breath, he gripped her shoulder and rolled her toward him. "I want a wife, Addie, not just a mother for the boys and someone to keep the house."

If she had been able to speak past the constriction in her throat, she would have called him a liar and a cheat, but her breathing was too shallow to force out any other word except "Fine."

Zeke jerked back as if she'd shot him. "Fine? You're

scared to death of being intimate with me and you say fine?" As she stared into the face of his anger and shock, Addie's cheeks went pale as parchment. The defiance in her waned to a mixture of tangled emotions. She felt sad for him, betrayed by him. Willis would have beaten her unconscious for sassing back; Zeke had called her pretty. Her bottom lip began to tremble.

Zeke's frustration soared, then plunged rapidly in messy regret. He rolled away and flung his arm over his eyes. "I'm sorry, Addie. I know you need time. I don't mean to rush you, but it's damned difficult to lie next to a wife I can't touch."

A chill moved over the surfaces of her skin, but his words stirred something deeper, warmer, way down inside. "Why?" she accused weakly. "You said you didn't want . . . that."

He shifted slightly and sighed. "I never meant what you assumed. I never meant to mislead you either, but I'm just a man, Addie. I need more from you than a cold shoulder at night." His arm lowered as he rolled to his side and his fingers reached up to touch the ribbon at her throat, searching for some feminine vanity that Willis might not have managed to destroy, but he didn't know enough about her past to even guess what would stir her. "What do you want, Addie?"

She blinked in confusion. She wanted peace and safety, freedom from fear and degradation. She wanted a houseful of children to cherish, but he had made it clear he didn't want any more babies. Her lashes fluttered down to shield the longing in her eyes, and she shook her head on the biggest fib of her life. "I don't want anything but what I've got."

"You little liar," he said softly, never realizing the full extent of his accusation. "Everyone wants something."

Their bodies were so close, he could feel the warmth of her flesh, smell the clean soapy fragrance of her hair. He should have blown out the candle before getting into bed. It cast just enough light to illuminate her shape beneath the transparent gown.

He hadn't known she would be so well formed. She wasn't shapely in the classic sense but slender and strong, lean and compact, instead of busty. Her lashes cast dark shadows on her pale cheeks, and her full bottom lip was slightly puckered. With her piquant features and pouty lower lip, she didn't look a day over fifteen.

She would have been so pretty four years ago. Even more so than now, because she would have been fresh and trusting in her innocence, instead of frightened and wrung out. With a shy smile and demurely lowered lashes, she might have accepted him then, instead of flinching in dread.

Despite his better judgment, despite any judgment at all, he lowered his head to brush her lips lightly, then again, unable to comprehend his own motivation. Her lips were soft and sweetly complaisant, tasting of her fresh scent. He felt the shiver of her indrawn breath and was surprised when she didn't cringe or turn away. Even in the darkness he could see a faint blush stain her cheeks, shyly virginal, as if she were a young girl experiencing her first kiss.

The sight struck him slowly, a dawning, then slammed into him like a blow to his solar plexus. She'd never been courted, never been innocently pursued as a teenager. She'd been thrown off on Willis at the age when she should have been coming out into society and given a chance to choose her own beau.

He should have seen it before. The world-weary wisdom in her eyes as she went about each adult task; the joyful innocence of childhood when she played with the boys. There was a wealth of lost years in between, the adolescent transition between child and woman when she should have learned the art of flirting and dissembling and coyness. The interim rite of passage when she would have felt the first blossoming and awakened to the breathless fascination of simply being female.

Regret laced with desire moved through him, along with the impulse to show her what she had missed. He rejected the emotions. He no longer had it in him to play the courtier. He didn't want to be her teacher or her tempter. He just wanted physical relief from the normal urges that plagued all men, and a wife congenial enough to allow it.

He turned to his back and stared through the darkness, knowing they would never bridge the gap easily. He should have taken her when she agreed and not let ethics intrude and override his body's needs. He could be losing himself in her right now, rocking deeper with each thrust, reaching for that shattering point of oblivion. He rolled farther away before he did something unforgivable, and heard her sigh—a repressed sound of relief—and wanted to slam his fist into the bedding.

Addie's gown of brownish-pink taffeta was simple but fit her perfectly. It had taken her over a week of careful stitching to get it just right, but her efforts were rewarded in the finished product. It was the prettiest gown she had ever owned. The tight bodice buttoned down the center, and there was a hint of ecru lace at the neck, cuffs, and hem. Her semifull skirt rustled over her petticoat when she bent to pull on her new chamois leather boots. She stared down at the soft and pliable footwear, hoping they were as strong as Zeke claimed to warrant the outrageous price he had paid for them.

She took a deep, uncertain breath and peered at herself in the mirror. Her hair was shiny clean, swept up away from her face and pinned in the back to fall in curls just below the nape of her neck. Through some trick of the light, or a faulty mirror perhaps, the girl who stared back at her was a stranger, someone younger and half-pretty, someone worthy of enjoying a gay night beside a handsome man. Addie didn't recognize the girl as herself.

She spun away from the mirror and fought the urge to rub her clammy palms down her skirt. Instead she laced her hands together and wondered what Zeke would think when he saw her. Something soft and feminine within her wanted him to find her passable; another part of her didn't want him to look at her at all.

He was an enigma, generally warm with the boys yet superficial in his dealings with her. It was that insular aloofness that bothered her, the intangible knowledge that whatever rested on the surface was not what lay beneath. She should have been pleased by the truce they seemed to have reached over the past week. He made no demands upon her, hardly touched her at all, and always treated her with utmost respect. But there were those rare and unsettling times when she would find him looking at her, just looking, his amber eyes moody and unfathomable.

She smoothed her dress down and tried to push the troubling thoughts aside. It was useless to wonder what he thought, senseless to worry whether or not he found her lacking. They were bound by wedlock and the needs of three little boys, irrevocable bonds. She smiled softly, remembering how pleased Zeb was when she finished the gown. She was pleased as well with her handiwork, proud of the way the gown fell just so over her small frame. But she didn't really want anyone else to take notice.

And there were plenty who would. In just a few short minutes, they would be on their way to town for the last social before winter set in. She didn't want to go, but Beatrice had cornered the boys at the general store and got them all excited about the prospect of a fun evening without ever consulting the adults who would have to escort them. Zeb had pleaded, Josh had murmured something almost hopeful under his breath, and Zeke had simply stared at Addie until she'd given in. She hadn't been proof against their combined efforts a week ago but was sorely regretting it now. She set her chin and took a determined step toward the door, knowing she couldn't stay locked in the bedroom all night.

The strident "C'mon, Ma!" from the kitchen made her pause then smile. Zebulun Taylor Claiborne was growing impatient. She took a deep breath and walked slowly across the room, then opened the door. Four males in various sizes and ages awaited her entrance. Her smile stretched wide at the sight.

"Oh, my," she breathed, as her palm rose to her heart. "How handsome you look!" Her words were directed at the boys dressed in their Sunday finest, but she was painfully aware of how aptly they applied to Zeke. His coat fit perfectly over his broad shoulders, his starched cotton shirt vivid against his weather-tanned skin. She had ironed that shirt herself, imagining all the while how he would look in it. Her expectations had not been amiss, and Addie's heart skipped a beat with secret pride at his masculine beauty.

Zeb beamed at her compliment and puffed his chest

out like a rooster, making her smile. Josh stared at the toes of his new boots, fighting to show no emotion, and Addie was heartened that he had to struggle to keep a cool detachment. He would take time, but she had a whole life ahead of her to win him over. Cole squirmed in Zeke's arms and held his hands out for Addie. She stepped forward to take him and planted a kiss on his fresh-scrubbed cheek, hiding her face in his baby curls to avoid her husband's assessing eyes.

"You sure do look fine, Miz Claiborne," Zeke said in a deep drawl, forcing her gaze to yield to his. "Doesn't she, boys?"

"Yes, sir," Zeb said dutifully, and began anxiously hopping from one foot to the other. "Can we go now?"

"May we," Zeke corrected, but his eyes were not on his son, they were traveling appreciatively over Addie. With one finger he touched the button at her neck, then slid down to the one below, then down one more. "Ready?"

Her heart beat crazily against his finger, and she felt her breath hitch. His eyes were dark and hot, his voice pitched low. Her stomach fluttered, but she swallowed back her trepidation and nodded. "I'm ready, but your collar . . ." She pointed at the crinkled edge.

Zeke took Cole and handed him to Josh, then leaned forward to accommodate her height. "Fix it for me?"

Addie reached up and smoothed the collar down, feeling like a nitwit for blushing at something so simple and meaningless. It was just that it seemed such a *wifely* thing to do, and it brought his face so near that she could see lighter gold flecks in his amber eyes, could smell the tantalizing aroma of his cologne. His clean-shaven jaw was firm, the slight cleft in his chin intriguing below well-shaped lips. Unbidden came the memory of those lips upon hers and the feel of his hands, hot and certain, touching her so indecently . . . so gently. He had done nothing since that night, but the feelings of anxiety and awe lingered just on the fringes of her mind.

"There." She averted her gaze and stepped back quickly to collect diapers for the baby.

With an odd glimmer in his eyes and a mysterious half smile, Zeke grabbed the boys' coats, along with blankets for the return trip.

The night air grew crisp as the sun slipped below the mountain peaks, the rhythmic clip-clop of the horses a nice backdrop for Zeb's ceaseless chatter, which temporarily diverted Addie's attention from all the doubts and insecurities of mingling among the citizens of Laramie. As they approached town, her apprehension grew. Lights twinkled in the distance like low-flung stars, then grew more distinct at the glow from lanterns strung across the front of Brann's Livery, revealing numerous horses and wagons, and their owners.

Ruddy cheeked from too much beer, Eli Brann smiled hugely, looking robust in a linsey-woolsey shirt and twilled cotton trousers as he stood out front welcoming guests.

His establishment provided the best spot in town for citizens to gather for something more lively than a sedate Sunday church service. Barn dances were held regularly in warm weather, but Addie had not been allowed to go when she was younger because her mother hadn't held with imbibing spirits in a public place, nor later because Willis wouldn't take her.

Dozens of people were already present when Zeke pulled the wagon to a stop, and most of them were staring at Addie. She retreated immediately behind a wall of indifference and pulled the baby tighter against her, wondering what they all found so fascinating.

"Show no fear," Zeke whispered. "Don't give them anything to feed on."

Her head swung toward him, a tiny spark of anger in her eyes. "I'm not afraid of them."

"Good." He smiled with a trace of pride.

Gracie Parker caught sight of the little boys and rushed over to offer help. "Evenin', Mrs. Claiborne. I like your dress." Gracie beamed when Cole stretched his hands out for her, and Addie grudgingly turned him over. "I'll take the other two, if you like," Gracie added hopefully. Addie could hardly deny her, though she would have liked to keep the boys close as a buffer.

Zeke walked around the wagon as his sons scampered off and put his hands on her waist. "Ready?"

She glanced at the horde of people standing off to the side, knowing she couldn't stay in the wagon all night. She nodded and went willingly into his arms for the first time, needing his strength to face the hours ahead. He held her against him for a moment after her feet touched the ground, and Addie gazed up at him with a look that was almost pleading.

Her face was so open, so vulnerable, Zeke had the insane urge to toss her back into the wagon and take her home where doubt and trepidation were slowly beginning to soften from her expression. Day by day she was becoming more easy and relaxed, not nearly as self-conscious about simple things as she had been. She didn't tense up anymore when he came inside for meals, and she never hesitated to question him about things concerning the boys. If she still lay stiff as a poker beside him at night, he assumed that, too, would fade with time. He gave her a brief, reassuring squeeze and stepped away but left his hand at the small of her back.

People began congregating around them, most merely curious, some after any new bit of gossip, a few jealous at losing Zeke when they had marriageable daughters at home. And some, like the Parkers, who were genuinely glad to see them. Addie stepped back into Zeke when Beatrice strolled forth and bussed her cheek.

"My, you are a pretty sight! Isn't she a pretty sight, Sam?"

Sam's skillful "Yep, near 'bout purty as you, Ma" had everyone chuckling. He just as skillfully began engaging the men around him in conversation to get their gawking eyes off Addie. Darn fools acted like they'd never seen a purty girl before.

Beatrice looked the young woman over thoroughly. "You seem fit enough. Zeke and the boys must be treating you right good."

"Just fine," Addie said cordially, but uncertainty nudged her backbone straight. She couldn't look at Beatrice without picturing the outrageous nightgown. "How about you?"

"Doing just dandy, thank you." Bea's eyes cut to Zeke. "Better keep a close eye on her tonight. There's many a cowpoke inside who're apt to forget she's a married lady."

Zeke sent Beatrice a dry grin and linked his hand through Addie's. "Not likely."

Beatrice snickered, pleased, and sent him an audacious wink. "Come on. Dancing's about to start if Jed Hawkins can git his old fiddle tuned up proper."

Zeke offered Addie his arm and escorted her into the livery. Sawdust covered the wooden platform that had been set up as a dance floor, and lanterns hung from pegs, giving the room a cheery welcome. Tables lined one wall, covered with every delicacy the gentle women of Laramie had to offer. Addie eyed the various dishes with a sinking heart. Already self-conscious, she looked up at her husband.

"I should have brought something."

He followed her gaze to the tables, realizing she hadn't known it was customary. "No one'll notice, Addie. You can bring something next time."

The minstrels tuned up and the murmur of voices died down as everyone anticipated the first dance of the night. Jed Hawkins struck a loud chord, and a foot-stomping rendition of "Skip to My Lou" had most couples heading for the floor. As soon as Zeke stepped forward, Addie's hand tightened in his and she set her heels.

"I can't dance!" she whispered.

Zeke paused and nodded. "Then we'll wait for something slower to teach you."

Addie wasn't convinced she could learn to do more than trample Zeke's toes on any type of music but didn't want to argue with him in front of a crowd. She planted a false smile on her face and prayed the fiddler didn't know any slow songs.

Irene Clarkson stopped by to chat but was thwarted by Ian MacAlister, who came hobbling after her on an arthritic leg that didn't slow him a whit when in pursuit of the widow. Nathaniel Pickens, shouting because his own hearing had gone bad, elbowed his way in next, and Addie found herself hiding a smile when the widow turned her nose up and berated them both for their coarse manners.

"Manners?" Nathaniel boomed. "I suppose you think manners is standin' in line to vote when you should be home makin' supper." He aimed a spit of tobacco that landed just short of the widow's toe. "Women votin'. Don't that beat all! Yankee subterfuge is what that is. No self-respectin' southerner would think of such, much less allow it. World's gone to hell since the war."

"Why, you narrow-minded old coot!" Irene began, and proceeded to lash into him further with both barrels.

Eyes wide, Addie glanced over at Zeke but his expression gave nothing away on either point. In a flurry of high chagrin, the widow swept her skirts aside and presented Nathaniel her back as she walked away. Nathaniel chuckled and winked at Zeke.

"She's a fine one, ain't she? Keeps my blood boilin'. Gotta go see if I can ruffle her feathers a little more." He nodded at Addie and headed off through the crowd.

Others stopped by, the less tactful offering condolences on Willis's death in the same breath they offered congratulations on her marriage to Zeke, but most kept the conversation civil before moving on in search of more gossip.

Addie scanned the room for the boys and found Gracie jiggling Cole on her hip while she watched her brother Luke show Zeb and Josh how to shoot marbles in the corner. Addie smiled softly at the boys' eager, intent faces as they hunkered down to try the next shot. Out of the corner of her eye, she caught a shadow moving and glanced over to see Grady lean against the wall next to the boys. Everything in her went cold and still. Her hands tightened into fists when he took a flask from his pocket and tipped it, his eyes never leaving the boys until they rose to meet hers.

He lifted the flask in salute, and she saw the threat hidden beneath his smile. He was watching her and waiting. Nausea churned her stomach when he reached down to ruffle Zeb's hair, and she wanted to shout at him to get his filthy hands off her child. In his innocence, Zeb looked up and smiled, his trust making Addie's head spin. She didn't know what to do, how to keep her family safe. She looked over at Zeke. He was saying something but she couldn't make out his words over the background noise and the clanging of fear in her own head.

". . . dance?"

The last word penetrated when he repeated the question and she noticed that the banjo had gentled to a lonely plucking as the fiddler called out "Down in the Valley."

Addie never noticed when Zeke took her hand and led her toward the dance floor until they reached the raised platform. "I can't. The boys—"

Zeke gave her a droll look, grabbed her at the waist, and stepped up onto the raised floor, then pulled her around to face him in the midst of other couples already moving to the haunting melody. "Just follow me," he said into her distressed eyes.

Addie looked over his shoulder, frantically searching for the boys, and found them in the same spot, hunched down beside Luke as if nothing had occurred. Grady was nowhere in sight. Not there looming over her boys or anywhere else in the room. She checked every inch. She trembled in the aftershock, then breathed a sigh of relief. Brought back to herself, she realized Zeke's arms were draped loosely around her. She felt awkward and self-conscious, but he did little more than sway in time to the music.

Zeke could feel the stiffness in Addie's shoulders and back fade a little as he continued to move slowly and made idle conversation to keep her mind occupied on him and off her feet. She listened intently, drawn by the promise of shelter in his arms when her security had just been so badly shaken.

Inch by slow inch, the surrounding world began to fade away as the notes drifted around them, dreamy and substanceless as a cloud. Addie closed her eyes, losing herself in the blending of intonation and rhythm in each chord. Music had a color she could feel. The higher notes were warm, soft reds and yellows, the lower notes cool blue, emotionally charged yet soothing, flowing with the motion of their bodies. She hadn't known one could find such pleasure in simple movement.

Zeke pulled her closer, one palm strong on her lower back, the other holding her small hand close to his chest. Her eyes startled open. "Relax, Addie," he said, his voice deep and fluid as the music. His fingers splayed wide at her lower back. "No, don't tense up, just listen to the music . . . Yes, like that."

His face was ruggedly handsome, his eyes warm amber in the lantern light, as mesmerizing as the music. The thump of his heartbeat was reassuring against her fingers. His head dipped until they were cheek to cheek, and she felt his fingers automatically flex to massage the contracted muscles in her lower back.

"Yes, that's it. Just go with it," he said, his breath whispery against her earlobe and neck. It sent shivers clear down to her toes.

She could feel his smooth sun-browned cheek against hers, a singular moment since the rough stubble of his beard grew fast and thick by day's end, leaving a heavy shadow on his jaw. A hint of sandalwood teased her nostrils, woodsy and fragrant as it mingled with her own

soap-scented curls. For some odd reason, it made her
heart skip, and another shiver raced down her spine.

"Cold?" he whispered along the sensitive shell of her
ear.

Addie jerked and shook her head, not trusting her
voice. He continued to move fluidly with the music, his
body brushing hers from breast to thigh, sending her
unsteady heart rate and temperature soaring. Flustered
by the tingling confusion in her body, she pulled back
slightly, but Zeke swept her into a turn that had her
clutching at him for support. His large hand swallowed
her smaller one as his arm tightened across her back,
and she found it both suffocating and comforting, as
oddly desirable as the erratic pace of her heart.

He moved with lean, hard grace, his motions a controlled freedom dictated by the rhythm of the music. He
was virilely beautiful in the muted room, his golden hair
absorbing light from the lanterns, but his eyes glowing
with their own inner fire, the color of whiskey and just
as intoxicating.

Though her cheeks grew flushed with her teetering
emotions, Addie thought she could stay forever in the
close circle of his arms, surrounded by his warmth and
scent, and shielded from the rest of the world. There
was no Grady, no past. No one could intrude or terror-
ize her here within the shelter of his arms. There could
have been a hundred other couples on the dance floor,
but she felt totally isolated and protected, untouchable
by the outside world.

For the first time in years, she felt at peace as the
melody wafted around them, seemed to become a part
of them. Magically and mysteriously pacifying, it cast a
wondrous spell that soothed and enchanted her. Her
entire body felt buoyant, and her imagination floated

free from earthly restraints. After so many hopeless years, she dared to dream for this moment that things were right, that she and Zeke had married by choice rather than necessity. That the three little boys were her own flesh.

The daydream faded when she was bumped by another couple, but Addie didn't care. They couldn't read her thoughts or feel her yearning. Even if she was being silly or stupid or immature, no one would know. Willis had stolen that fanciful part of her. With him she had never dared to dream. Enfolded in Zeke's arms, it seemed as natural as breathing.

As the last strains died, Zeke laced his fingers through hers and escorted her from the dance floor. She still felt dazed, floating in his embrace, but the moment was shattered when people began to converge around them again.

"Would you like something to drink?" he asked.

It took her a moment to decide, and she felt foolish for making more of it than the situation required. "No, thank you."

The Barrett sisters walked up, Annie with a perpetual cupid's smile creasing her lined face and Lucile with one of the half-dozen canes she'd owned since "The Fall" as she always termed it, adding, "One must never forgo fashion for the sake of inconvenience." Addie smiled with genuine affection. Between the two elderly women, no one else could get a word in edgewise, which suited her just fine.

There was the usual debate about politics and the role of women in their modern society, but since the sisters always took opposite sides in any discussion, all Addie had to do was smile and nod as each point was covered. As soon as the Barrett sisters moved on, there

were other less chatty citizens to contend with. The wistful moment on the dance floor faded further, and Addie's heart sank when Liz and Mark Simmons strolled
near along with several other prominent members of
their small society.

Addie felt smothered by the attention and inadequate
discussing local and national politics, so she remained
quiet unless spoken to directly. But curiosity, being inherent in most human nature, was not absent from the
townsfolk of Laramie, and the talk soon turned personal. People who normally gave her little more than a
passing glance now eyed her keenly and bombarded her
with questions and comments.

*Yes, the boys were cute; she was lucky to have them. Yes,
they were a handful and kept her busy. No, she didn't
know much about ranching but supposed she could learn.
Yes, she had made her dress . . .*

And on and on it continued. The more open her answers, the more intimate the questions became, until
she grew evasive, her tone subdued and noncommittal
as she retreated inside herself because she couldn't just
walk out leaving a husband and sons behind.

Zeke watched her withdrawal descend like dusk fading to twilight and knew she couldn't endure much more
of the civil interrogation. Her ease on the dance floor
had evaporated, leaving her pale and drawn. She had
slowly inched up beside him, each question bringing her
closer and closer, until he was afraid she was eventually
going to slip behind him and hide. His arm stole around
her waist, much as it had the day of the wedding, but
there was little else he could do but stand beside her
and try to deflect some of the attention himself by bringing up the issue of sheep versus cattle ranching, which

took everyone's attention off Addie's domestic travails. But it also drew a larger crowd.

Ben Jenkins jumped smoothly into the middle of the discussion as it heated up, but not without a few glib words to the ladies to keep their attention. He was a young upstart new to the area, self-important and backed in his ranching endeavor by his daddy's money. Zeke didn't begrudge the young man his benefaction; it was Ben's gaze and lascivious smile he took exception to. The man was surreptitiously assessing Addie with a practiced eye.

"Ben," he said coolly, "have you met my wife?"

"I don't believe I've had the pleasure," Ben returned with the requisite urbane smile before turning to Addie. "Ben Jenkins," he said, and picked up her hand and brought it to his lips. "How lovely you look tonight, Mrs. Claiborne."

"Mr. Jenkins." Addie pulled her hand back immediately. He was young and pleasant looking, with an air of smooth self-importance. His smile was genuine but his eyes were not. His insincerity reminded her of Willis and Grady and his flattery did nothing but disgust her. Her disconcerted gaze went to Zeke. "I . . . I need to check on the boys."

Zeke made their excuses, then turned her toward the door. "Let's get a breath of fresh air first. We can fetch a diaper from the wagon before we find Gracie."

Grateful, Addie walked with him out the entrance, oblivious to the sly glances from some of the townsfolk, completely unaware that a man who escorted a lady out into a moonlit night had questionable intentions, and that the lady who allowed it was asking for sweet trouble.

Zeke was well aware of their prurient thoughts, but

he had an advantage over any boy who might have tried it when Addie was fifteen. There were no hawk-eyed parents watching her every movement, no one who would take issue with a husband's right to take his wife out for a stroll. If he didn't exactly feel like a sixteen-year-old whose hormones had just kicked in, he felt close enough to it to experience a twinge of the old anticipation and danger of a stolen moment.

Blissfully unaware of anything but the strains of the next song, Addie welcomed the freedom from the stuffy room and the cool air on her heated face. Light from the lanterns didn't reach the parked wagons, and she and Zeke were cloaked in the darkness. The stars shone brilliantly overhead, but even their fiery magnitude didn't dispel the night's black cover.

Addie leaned back against the wagon, exhausted from the barrage of questions and the draining effort of trying to fit in with the same people she had avoided for four dismal years in an effort to escape their pity. Zeke noted the droop of her shoulders and damned Ben and the rest of the town for stealing her earlier pleasure.

"They meant well," he said. "You just have to give them a chance."

I did, four years ago, she thought, then felt mean and shallow for blaming the town when her own reticence and passivity had done more to isolate her than the people ever had. "I know."

She closed her eyes and tilted her head back against the wagon to ease the throbbing in her temples. Starlight spilled silvery through her curls, illuminating the fair skin of her cheeks and throat. She looked young and fragile, Zeke thought. Fragile in a way that had nothing to do with weakness but with delicacy. Fine porcelain.

He studied her in the weak light, the way her lashes lay like dark crescents on her fair cheeks. Her dress was modest but fitted, accentuating the firm mounds of her breasts and a waist so slender he could span it with one hand. He had. And the memory of that night was sharp, igniting a slow burn inside him.

Zeke moved closer, then reached over her and fumbled in the back of the wagon. His chest partially covered her, blocking the wind. Though his heat was welcome, his closeness sent nervous willies down Addie's arms. She shrank back against the buckboard to give him more room, but he only pressed closer, his jaw grazing her temple, his thigh brushing her hip.

He straightened, then pulled back and held not the diapers she thought he'd gone seeking but a thick wool blanket. Before Addie could question him, he slung it over her shoulders, then leaned back against the wagon beside her.

Warmed by his consideration, she smiled. "Thank you."

He shrugged, his shoulder bumping hers with the motion. She pulled into herself a little but remained oddly content with the night. Small and cocooned in the woolen blanket, she looked small and childlike. Everything was cast in shadow. No color existed, just images, gray, darker gray, black. She was a small blot in the hueless night, her face starlit so that it stood out like a soft beacon, the only point of reference to draw the eye.

Her mouth rounded in an oval of wonder as she suddenly pointed. "Look." Zeke followed her direction to see a meteor trail down in an arc of light. "Do you think it made it?"

"To earth? I don't know. Maybe."

Her mew of displeasure crept inside him, touching

vacant places, voids as dark as the surrounding night. Finding no foothold, the feeling evaporated as quickly as the shooting star had. Mild disappointment followed.

"I always wanted to go and see," she whispered to herself. Her brow furrowed as she peered into the darkness, as if she could pinpoint the exact location.

The wistful eloquence of her words surprised Zeke. "Why didn't you?"

She turned toward him with a wry smile. "I did. But meteors are like rainbows. The closer I got, the farther away they seemed."

Something unbearable and intangible inside him gave a fraction. He turned quickly, well aware that he was sidestepping the tug on his senses. Like her, there were parts of him that he didn't want touched or violated. He reached over and pulled her tight against him.

"Shhh," he whispered. "Someone will hear."

"Hear what?" she whispered back, her heart thumping faster at the hint of warning in the rough edge of his voice.

"Shhh!"

Addie's eyes grew round as they scanned the darkness, and she listened as if her life depended on it. The rustle of night creatures blended with the music and floated softly on the wind. A horse whinnied and snorted, another answered. Addie's senses heightened acutely as she listened for whatever danger the blackness concealed, but she could hear little more than the blood pumping in her veins.

Suddenly, the howl of a coyote broke the stillness, his eerie cry running chills up her arms. She grabbed the front of Zeke's shirt and held on tight, her eyes wide as she tilted her face up to his.

"Don't move," Zeke said roughly. "He's probably rabid. You can hear it in his cry."

Her eyes grew rounder, her fists tighter. "Rabid? What do we do?"

Without the slightest warning, Zeke's arms closed around her and his mouth lowered. "This," he said before his lips covered hers. Before she could utter more than a gasp of protest he deepened the kiss, firm but gentle, insistent and inebriating. No one had ever kissed her like this, tender and enticing, stealing the breath from her body with unyielding strength and uncompromising gentleness. She put her hands on his chest to push him away, to gain some distance, but his breath was hot as his lips moved over hers in warning. "Don't move, Addie. He'll find us."

Addie couldn't have moved if Satan himself was snapping at her heels. She was rooted to the ground, transfixed, but not by the danger at hand. Instead, she was mesmerized by the moist warmth of Zeke's mouth and the protective strength of arms that pulled her closer into the heat of his body. His heartbeat thundered against her breasts, and her own raced to match the cadence. It felt so frighteningly good to have the taste of his lips on hers, the weight of his body pressing possessively into her.

His mouth slanted across hers again, shaping her moist lips to fit his purpose. "Keep pretending," Zeke said. "It'll throw him off guard."

"Off guard," she murmured, her mind foggy with the drugging potency of his lips as they continued to play lightly over hers. Somewhere the tinkling laughter of other partygoers wafted on the breeze, unsuspecting and unafraid. Addie wanted to shout a warning to the unwary in the split second before her mind cleared.

"Oh!" she cried, and pushed against Zeke's chest.

His lips never left hers as she struggled to break free, and she could feel the laughter tighten his mouth, the vibrations of it caress her own. Something coiled tight and deep within her at his humor, and she bit down on her lower lip to keep from answering with unforgivable laughter of her own. She felt so silly and childish for falling for his trick, but another feeling kindled within her, one of unfamiliar delight and joy.

His eyes were dark with mischief as they shone into hers, and his tongue dipped out to tease the up-tilted corner of her mouth. Alarm shot through her, but it was laced heavily with other, equally powerful emotions—intrigue, fascination, and even a bit of chagrin at her own naïveté. She was awash with strange, new sensations; her world felt shaken and tilted off-balance. She inhaled an unsteady breath and let it out with a sigh. Zeke drew back only a space as his hands came up and cupped her face. She could feel the pad of his thumb stroke her cheek, softly, softly, before his expression changed completely.

An intensity entered his eyes. They sharpened, narrowed. All tenderness seemed to have evaporated, to be replaced with a predatory gleam. His head lowered, and his mouth once again captured hers with a seriousness that belied his earlier humor. Addie moaned weakly at the strange combination of panic and awe, then gasped when his tongue penetrated her mouth.

It swirled along her teeth, daring and unwavering, until they parted, then delved inside to touch her tongue. Overwhelmed with confusion, Addie retreated and pulled back, but he sought her again, carefully at first so she would grow accustomed, then with earnest intent, sweeping her inner mouth with humid heat that sent a trickle of liquid fire through other parts of her body. The heat inside her intensified with every touch of his tongue, every breath he stole, thawing the iciness that had walled off her heart and filling the emptiness. A pure, blinding heat that left her yearning and desperate for something she didn't understand. She gave a whimper of fear, of desire, and at that small sound, Zeke deepened the kiss, until the heat was inside him as well, an invisible current between and around them, both enthralling and suffocating.

Addie's hands pushed weakly against his chest, but her fingers also curled to bring him back. She could feel the strong throb of his heartbeat against her hands, but her own was much faster, rioting in her breast. Her serrated breaths were raspy and uneven. Undone by her first taste of real seduction cloaked masterfully in tenderness, Addie's head fell back limply to the wooden rail of the buckboard. "Stop."

His body flowed into hers, and she instinctively arched in shock at the intimate contact of his hard, uncompromising strength. Her head swam so fretfully, she didn't know whether to resist the pleasure or give in to it.

"Why?" Zeke said as his lips grazed her cheek and jaw, then moved down the tight cords of her throat. She didn't flinch or move away, just hung limply against the buckboard.

"I can't breathe." Her words feathered over his cheek, and his body tightened to even that mere stimulus.

"You can. You are," he said, feeling the staggered rise and fall of her breasts against his chest. He tried to hide his immediate reaction—a surge of raw lust so powerful it made him tremble—but he couldn't seem to stop himself from reaching for her. His senses were overflowing with the sensual limpness of her body, the innocence of her response. She didn't know herself very well, and the challenge set before him, to help her discover her own passionate nature, surged through him with alarming potency. His hands slid beneath the blanket and encircled her rib cage, pulling her more fully against him.

She jerked automatically at his nearness and her hands flattened against his chest, but she had no strength to push him away. "Oh, stop."

"Why? You like it, Addie. Don't deny it." Hot color bathed her cheeks, heightening her fairness. He pressed his hand over hers. "Feel my heart? It's racing away, Addie. I like it too."

If she'd been fifteen and unattached, she might have slapped his face for being so forward. But at nineteen, having lost those years and twice married, she didn't know she could. Zeke felt the power of his advantage and need flow hotly in his blood, and tried to temper it, but it was growing insistent and aggressive—a pounding in his temples, a deep throbbing lower.

They were only yards away from half the town, and he had her shoved up against a buckboard with full intentions of mauling her. But at this point he didn't care. His flesh overruled any rational thought but getting closer, deeper into the heat of her, to be whole and free from the loneliness for that moment.

His mouth grazed her temple, and he inhaled the fragrance of her hair and skin, taking it deep inside himself to a place of hunger and desire that wouldn't reject it, the only place he could still feel. He forced himself to go slowly, not wanting to frighten her, but knew he wouldn't pull away even if she protested. His breath rasped against her bare throat, and his teeth gently scraped her sensitive skin to the lacy edge of her neck-line.

"Sweet," he murmured. "So soft." He felt her hands go lax and drift down his shirt. Every muscle of his abdomen clenched and he had to grit his teeth to keep from moaning aloud. His body swayed into hers, the slightest brush calculated to titillate without threatening. But when their bodies connected fully, a growl rumbled in his throat, needy and long-suppressed desires flaring to the surface of his skin like fire.

Addie made a small answering sound against his lips, vulnerable. The access to her sweet shape was too great now for Zeke to control the urgency gripping him. He pulled her arms up and draped them over his own shoulders, then leaned heavily into her. For a few heart-breaking seconds, they stood still, their bodies fitted together so perfectly, the pleasure of their touching savored and memorized as if both assumed the goodness was fleeting. Addie's fingers curled into Zeke's collar as his chest pinned her shoulders to the wagon, and she held tightly to prolong the moment, welcoming the cool wood against her back, the brace of something solid to uphold her. Then suddenly heat covered her from breasts to thighs as Zeke pressed forward, and his lower body met bluntly with throbbing pulse points she'd never known existed.

A distressed sound escaped her and she twisted slightly, restless and confused. The motion sent fire to her toes. "Do I encourage this?" she asked, her voice lost, her mind cloudy, as his mouth worked a terrible magic on her sensitive skin.

"Just feel it," he whispered. His teeth nipped at her lips, sending tingles through other parts of her body. His left hand slid down her back in a firm unalterable path, leaving vibrant warmth in its wake. She felt everything, she felt only him. Her skin grew tight, her nerves screamed at the edges of her flesh for something soothing and comforting that would put an end to the torment that was both frightening and wondrous.

She inhaled sharply when his hand dug into the small of her back, then smoothed lower to the rounded curve of her buttocks. "Oh, please," she began, but his fingers flexed and brought her more flush against him, startling from her another cry that he absorbed into his mouth. "No, wait—"

"Yes, I'll wait," he whispered against her lips, but his right hand was sliding up her rib cage even as he said it, gliding over the taffeta to cover her breast.

Her next cry was stronger, high-pitched yet throaty with tension and uncertainty, but Zeke was past caring whether it was desire or protest and probed her tongue with his own in the same rhythm he began stroking the sleek bodice of her gown. Her nipple grew taut and achy against his palm, the small sounds in her throat more distraught.

"It's all right, Addie," he soothed. "It's just a touch, harmless, but it feels so good." And he knew the source of her next impassioned moan wasn't protest but acquiescence. Her knees went weak and her body sagged, supported only by his. Her fingers gripped his collar like a lifeline and held on. Her face slanted to the side to better accommodate the tilt of his head, the press of his lips.

Zeke was lost, lost to the bright hot sounds in her throat, the ripe wonder of her shape, the exquisite yielding in her kiss. Only when his hands began working feverishly, inching up her skirt to search beneath, did he realize what he was doing, what he was planning, how insane a direction his lust had taken. He stopped abruptly and pulled back, gripping her arms as he leaned his forehead against hers. His ragged breath was hot against her cheek, the shudder along his tall frame a counterpoint to her own.

He turned finally to lean back weakly against the slatted wooden rail of the wagon for support, pulling her around with him to lie against his chest. He breathed deeply to recapture the air that her unexpected response had sent sailing out of his lungs.

He brought himself under control by slow degrees, an inch at a time, as if one wrong or fast move would send him back over the edge. He had come outside to offer her respite from the crush of people; he had ended up trying to seduce her. But she, shy and stubborn and introverted Addie, had ended up thoroughly beguiling him.

"How quaint." The dark, mocking comment materialized out of the night into the face and form of Christian LaFleur. He held his doctor's bag up for inspection, his eyes glinting hard and strange in the moonlight. "How inopportune of me to interrupt, but an emergency calls. It seems Mrs. Whitmore has gone into labor a few weeks early." His eyes swept Addie lazily, causing her to blush and stiffen in Zeke's arms. "It appears you'll be needing my services in about nine months' time as well, Mrs. Claiborne."

Her head still hazy, her body still throbbing from Zeke's caresses, it took Addie a moment to comprehend the hateful impertinence in his voice. Zeke's arms constricted in an iron band around her and his voice was chilling as he pushed away from the wagon to stand upright.

"Stay the hell away from her, Christian."

Addie turned in Zeke's arms and anxiously looked back and forth between the two men. Their stance radiated animosity, their hostility tangible, reeking hatred and worse—abject pain. Whatever had caused such bitter malice between these two well-respected men still flowed between them, incomprehensible to Addie, who had never heard anyone speak of them except in glowing terms.

Christian's cold, detached demeanor had always made her nervous, but his ability as a physician had never been in question. Five years earlier he had set her father's arm after a bad fall; eight months later he had delivered her baby sister. Little more than a year ago, he had tended her. Through it all he had been competent, if remote, remarkably skilled, and he accepted goods for payment as readily as cash.

Addie's apprehensive face tilted up to her husband's, unaware that her eyes were yet dusky and dreamy from their lovemaking, her face still softly aglow. "We should go back in."

"Please, not on my account," Christian said smoothly. "By all means, carry on. I can use the business." He tipped his hat and made a gallant bow from the waist, which in no way was mistaken for anything but a gesture of ridicule. "I bid you good evening."

Addie felt the tension slowly ebb from Zeke's arms as the doctor collected his black gelding and seemed to fade into the night. She pulled away slightly, self-conscious and worried about what had just happened between the two men. Combined with the earth-shattering situation of only minutes ago between her and Zeke, she was lost to everything but the emotions still whirling around inside her. She had never been kissed in such a way, never been touched in even a remotely similar fashion. And she had never been so embarrassed in her life at being caught doing both.

Zeke turned and grabbed Cole's sack of diapers. Addie nervously called his name when he started for the livery without her. He paused but didn't turn, just waited for her to catch up. It was the rudest thing he had done since their acquaintance and cast a dark pall over an already confusing evening. She approached tentatively, uneasy with the rigid set of her husband's shoulders and the way he seemed to hold himself intact by sheer willpower rather than any rational or natural calm.

Horribly ill-at-ease, she thought she would simply move on past him and escape this hard, moody facet of his personality until he could put himself to rights, but as soon as she tried, he reached out and gripped her wrist.

His head turned toward her, and his eyes were cruel and fathomless. "Stay away from him, Addie," he said coldly. "Understand?"

No. She didn't understand anything, like how he had changed so quickly from warm and giving one minute to cold and remote the next. She shook her head, wincing at the pain from his hold.

Zeke's tight grip relaxed immediately and he soothed her injured wrist with light strokes of his thumb, regretting his inexcusable carelessness. Her eyes were large and bewildered, her cheeks still faintly flushed. He wanted to haul her back into his arms and forget himself in the wonder of possessing her, but the moment was lost.

"Christian is worthless. Just stay away from him."

Addie tugged her hand away and nodded at the harsh concern in her husband's voice, though she didn't understand. She considered people like Willis and Grady worthless, not the town's only and very competent doctor. She laced her fingers together and studied them, unable to look at Zeke when she spoke.

"What if one of the boys gets sick?"

"I'll take care of the boys," he answered succinctly. "We don't need Christian."

Addie glanced back up, hurting for Zeke and not knowing why. He had used the doctor's name freely, not Doc or Dr. LaFleur, as most of the town referred to the physician. She suspected the two men had known each other a good while, maybe even been friends, and she wondered what had caused such a terrible rift that they couldn't even be civil now.

She wished she had enough gumption to ask, but she wouldn't. She knew better than to pry into someone else's secrets when she had plenty enough of her own to hide.

9

Winter tested its welcome slyly, not with one grand thrust that would have had everyone settling in for the long haul, but creeping in stealthily as if to fool the frontier into relaxing its vigilance. Addie wasn't fooled one bit. She knew how unpredictable the weather was at this time of year and continued preparing for the long, isolated days ahead.

Mornings were spent doing the usual chores. Afternoons were filled with the constant whir of the sewing machine as she turned out woolen shirts and pants to keep Zeke and the boys warm, along with durable, heavy dresses for herself. Evenings fell earlier and were reserved for reading, knitting, and darning.

But the sewing machine was silent today. Dark bloated clouds covered the sky, dropping the temperature to a prevailing chill that the bleak sun couldn't dispel. The ground was already dusted with a light coat of white and the smell of new snow hovered in the air, making the animals restless and sending Addie hurrying outside to gather the rest of her wash. She pulled the last shirt from the line, then hurried back toward the house to the steady staccato beat of cracking timber.

Zeke had been cutting wood for two weeks and was now splitting and stacking the logs closer to the house. He looked up when Addie reached the back porch and called to her.

She turned, even more shy with him since the night of the dance a month ago. Things had been strained since, more awkward in some ways than their first two weeks of marriage. Zeke had kept his distance emotionally, though he was civil when daily life forced them into close contact. Addie knew she was responsible for his distracted state. She'd been so upset on the ride home after the dance, short with the boys and even more jumpy with him every time he got near.

He, in turn, had grown increasingly remote, offering her little more than his polite disregard. It was no more than she had expected of their relationship, and better even than her mildest fears, but she felt oddly let down by the internal distance that kept them strangers. She wondered if he thought of that night with regret, if he thought of it at all. She could think of little else.

She watched Zeke raise the ax handle and bring it down with a precision that sent the split log flying in two directions. He had strong hands, work toughened and baked brown by the wind and sun. Those hands had been so gentle when they touched her a month ago, but he hadn't touched her that way since. She was thankful. At least, she kept telling herself that over and over until she was quite certain she would believe it one day soon.

The cold wind tugged at her hair, and Addie shifted the clothes basket to her hip with one hand to hold down her skirt with the other, as she watched Zeke finish the chore. Seemingly immune to the cold, he wore neither coat nor vest to warm his upper body, only a shirt that pulled tightly across his shoulder and back muscles when he swung the ax.

There had been times lately when she would approach him with a question only to find him gazing off in the distance, his eyes bleak and cold as he stared at the stone marker on the hill. And she would feel a pain that went deeper than her own memories, a despair for him, because Willis's death had meant release for her, whereas Zeke had lost so much.

Deep inside, in a place she had thought long barren, she would hurt a little for herself as well, because she had realized over the past six weeks that God had intervened this time and not left her to the fickle whims of fate or chance. Zeke was so much more than she had hoped for in a husband, but she feared she could never be the wife he had lost.

Silently, she would watch him, wondering what his life with Becky had been like, if they had laughed together or ever argued, if they had discussed plans for the future. Her face grew hot and she pressed a cool hand to her cheek, wondering not for the first time what had gone on between them after the boys were put to bed and they were alone. The thought of Zeke touching another woman the way he had touched her that night made Addie's heart thump uneasily with envy and jealousy that outweighed the fear she had felt up to this point. She would slip away and save her questions for later, trying to make things better for him by not intruding.

She couldn't deny that she was still afraid of Zeke as a man, one who held the power to dominate and demean her with little effort, but she was also becoming more aware of him as a husband and a person. Not one like Willis but like her father, someone with whom to share confidences and concerns about the children, someone with whom to plan a day or a season or a future. Though he remained separate in many ways, he was still accessible to her, never belittling or berating her when she had questions about the boys or a problem around the house she couldn't solve on her own.

The sound of splitting wood echoed far into the mountains as he landed one last powerful blow with the ax, and Addie thought of the strength and determination with which he pursued each task. His ranch reflected care and organization, a penchant for details without obsession. He seemed to recognize those things that were most important while maintaining a margin of patience for human or natural error. She deeply appreciated his balance and control in the face of calamity. He was strict with the boys but never unfair. He expected a certain code of behavior but took into consideration their moods and the circumstances surrounding any infraction.

She closed her eyes briefly, thankful, so grateful that the stranger she had married never raged at her or the children. With nothing more than an intimidating look from his amber eyes, he could cower them all to silence, her included, but even when provoked he contained his anger and disciplined with a firm but gentle hand. She couldn't have tolerated had he been otherwise with his sons. And herself.

Yet for all his gentleness and strength, there was a dark unreachable place within him, a place of profound sorrow that permitted no trespass or release. The walls around his inner self were high and unbreachable. At times, Addie sensed his loneliness and the sadness that had scarred over his emotions until they were as tough as his callused hands. The battered part inside her reached out to him intuitively and without hesitation, just as she had responded physically to his passion and hunger that night outside the livery.

The reaching-out, so uncommon and repressed for the last four years, frightened Addie. Every instinct told her to step away, to preserve herself, to let things be. In opening her heart and emotions, she left herself undefended and vulnerable. She could see to his home and his children and be content. She neither wanted nor needed anything from him personally.

Why, then, in broad daylight, was she remembering the feel of his arms around her, the shocking pleasure of his lips?

Zeke stacked the last log, then brushed the wood chips from his hands on the seat of his copper-riveted blue canvas pants. He had been on the range earlier and still wore leather chaps to protect his legs from thorn thickets and a new Colt caliber .45 strapped to his hip as protection against wild animals.

Addie thought he looked a bit lawless as he strolled toward her, a combination of daring and danger with a day's growth of beard stubble on his strong cheeks. That same face had drawn close to hers a month ago with a tender aggressiveness she had never known from a man and couldn't think of now without blushing.

As they had so often lately, nervous jitters raised gooseflesh across the surface of her skin. It had nothing to do with fear or anxiety, but a restlessness she didn't understand, a discontent that had no basis in fact but seemed to be increasing day by day. She wasn't unhappy, quite the contrary, but there was a measure of dissatisfaction deep within her that wouldn't seem to abate. And it had been there since the dance. She couldn't imagine what had gotten into Zeke that night, but even worse she couldn't imagine what had gotten into *her*.

She'd let him kiss her without raising a ruckus, while feeling like she was about to faint dead away. There had been times since when that same weak-kneed breathlessness would come upon her just looking at him, and she wondered if she was going just a little mad. Instead of looking away as was probably prudent for any sensible young woman, she only stared harder, studying every facet of his physical makeup, as if that would help her decipher the emotional man within.

Unlike the surrounding landscape, his hair gathered the feeble sunlight and reflected it in a dull gold sheen as he approached, his ground-eating strides making him appear predatory. A certain pride welled up inside her at his primitive grace. It seemed a strange thing to feel, but when he was some distance away his strength made her feel protected. And lately, even when he drew close enough for physical contact, the dreadful apprehension inside her was tempered by the respect and good fortune she felt at being his wife.

It was foolish, she knew. He hadn't wanted her any more than she had wanted him, but since necessity had forced them together, she would allow a little fancy to color the situation rosier than it really was. No one would ever know that at times she embellished the ordinary things he said or did and turned them into something more personal and meaningful. Or that she fantasized about him taking her hand and walking beside her while they talked of not just the daily peculiarities of the children but also of politics or music or art, those things of which she had only rudimentary knowledge but boundless curiosity.

And at other times, rare and uncalled for and unsettling, she even imagined him kissing her again. Not on the lips, that picture was too distressing, but softly on her cheek as he whispered some endearment.

Zeke reached the porch and took the heavy clothes basket from her arms, startling her from the mental images she'd been entertaining. Addie ducked her head at the embarrassing flush on her cheeks and turned toward the house. He couldn't read her thoughts, but still they shamed her because she enjoyed them so. She was, no doubt, a silly chit to daydream about him, but he only exacerbated the situation with his thoughtfulness.

She was constantly awed by the easy way he did the simplest things for her, dumping wash water, toting her burdens, helping with the children. In her mind and heart, she wasn't deceived. She knew he did them by rote, but she couldn't seem to stop herself from feeling as though he were handing her the world each time he helped. She hadn't known such simple consideration since her father was alive.

Stupid, silly-headed Addie. This man was no father but husband; he could turn on her at any time. But when he eased her burdens or conversed with her like an equal whose opinions actually mattered, she just couldn't seem to remember that.

"There'll be heavy snow by morning," Zeke said as he held open the back door.

She moved past him, wondering why he had brought something so obvious to her attention. He wasn't a man who made idle conversation, and he knew she'd been preparing for the first big fall for days. Once in the kitchen, she took the basket and began folding clothes, while Zeke paced by the window, lost in his musings. She wondered what he was thinking on so deep but didn't dare ask. After four years of trying to dissolve into shadows, four years of moving like a wraith so as not to be noticed, she was loath to call attention to herself. It was hard to break a pattern established in terror, even when the terror seemed to be gone, even when her curiosity was eating at her something fierce.

Finally, Zeke stopped and turned. Addie's hands went still at the guarded look on his face.

"I have a sizable herd built up," he said. She nodded for him to continue but a slow dread began building in her stomach. "I've got good Durham shorthorns, Addie. They're far superior table beef than the half-wild Spanish longhorns. People said these barnyard cattle couldn't survive out here, but they have and thrived. Come spring I'll need to drive the bulk of them east. They'll fetch a good price."

The shirt fell from her numb fingers. "No, it's too dangerous. Rustlers and Indians—"

Zeke cut her off with an impatient look. "I've got problems with rustlers now. So far they've only been hauling off the mavericks."

Her eyes went wide. "I didn't know."

"It doesn't matter. It happens to us all, but if they get any more spread out, I'll start losing branded cattle as well." At her blank look, he continued in a clipped tone. "Did you think I was raising a herd this size to use at my own table?"

She hadn't thought much about it and his tone made her feel inferior. She refused to answer him, and lowered her eyes to hide her embarrassment. Zeke realized she was getting her back up, but there was little he could do. "I'm only going as far as Cheyenne. I can ship the cattle from there to the Chicago stockyards on the railroad."

Addie snatched up another shirt to busy her hands. "Spring is a long time away."

"I'll have to make trips into Cheyenne this winter to meet with the Wyoming Stock Growers Association."

"Why?" She sounded peevish, but couldn't help it. There was more meaning beneath his words than what he was saying aloud. She felt the resentment creep in and settle like a dead weight in her chest. If he was holding back or trying to hide something, so be it, but she wouldn't make it easy for him. "Why do you have to go?"

Zeke watched her mouth thin at the corners. They had gotten to the crux of the conversation, the part he had been avoiding for weeks. "The association is trying to obtain a treaty with the Sioux and Cheyenne Indians to get permission to use the vast rangeland in the north for grazing."

Addie's back stiffened with the words, the fusing of old hatreds. She gave up the useless attempt to fold the shirt and tossed it back into the basket. "Why are you doing this?"

"I joined the association when it was formed for the mutual purpose of protection against Indian raids and to look after our interests in matters of raising and marketing our cattle. We were the Laramie County Stock Association then, but more than the name was changed in '74. The members are getting greedy, Addie. The broad pasturelands they want to use are the hunting grounds of the Indian tribes. If we overrun their lands, eventually the only thing left for them to hunt will be our cattle."

Addie wouldn't look at him. She didn't care what happened to the Indians, not after what they'd done to her family. And she didn't want to be left alone. The fifty-mile trip to Cheyenne would take days, days she'd be alone and vulnerable at the ranch with only the boys for company.

Zeke found it extremely difficult to stare someone down who wouldn't look at him. "Addie." When she didn't respond, he continued curtly, "The federal and territorial governments are trying to impose restraints and regulations on the free appropriation of the rangelands, but the association is becoming powerful enough to control the territorial representatives. I'm not certain how much power they yield with the federal government yet, but they are determined to take control of the new rangeland as soon as possible."

Addie heard the concern in his voice but couldn't push her own fears and prejudices aside. "So?"

Zeke raked his fingers through his hair in frustration, knowing anything he said would sound treasonous after what she had suffered, which was why he had put off telling her until now. He planted his hands on his hips and refused to continue until she lifted her stubborn head to face him. It was then that he saw the fear and pain in her eyes. Sighing, he walked over and moved the basket out of her reach and sat down in front of her.

"There has always been an unwritten law out here. The first one to effect squatter's rights enjoys priority of his claim as long as he can protect it against any outside force. Claim jumping isn't legal, but it happens all the time to miners and homesteaders. When a ranch is involved, an attack is usually and conveniently blamed on renegade Indians." He paused, wondering how best to tell her what he had suspected for some time, what he was fairly certain of now. "I think the same thing could have happened to your family."

Her eyes flared in shock as her small hand rose to

cover her mouth, physically shrinking from him and his implication. "No." She shook her head. She'd carried her hatred for too long now to consider anything else. "The bank got the ranch, not a claim jumper," she said, as if that proved something.

"If someone wanted to take it," Zeke said carefully, "he wouldn't have known the land was entailed. Your father started out homesteading like most of us. A land grabber wouldn't have known the ranch had a mortgage against it."

Addie bit the inside of her jaw to stop her lip from quivering. Why was he bringing all this up? It had taken her years just to accept her family's death. She didn't need this now, not when she had a new family to ease the loss of the other. She pulled her gaze from his and ran her finger along the surface of the table, following the pattern of the woodgrain and wishing her life was as uncomplicated and enduring and solid as the pine beneath her fingers.

Her nails scraped along the table as the turmoil rose inside her. "They were massacred!" she cried. "Everything burned to the ground, Mama and the little ones and Daddy! How can you side with the Indians?"

Calmly, Zeke took her hands, stilling their agitation. "Because I don't think it was Indians that got your family, Addie." She tried tugging her hands back, but he wouldn't release her. "The night you showed me the infant gown, something bothered me about the fact that you had gone into town and escaped the attack. If there had been renegades in the area, they would have murdered you before you left the ranch or kidnapped you. But they wouldn't have let you go idly on your way just for the hell of it.

"I asked Jake to look into it again. He said there was

no trouble at that time, and the arrows left were a mess of Sioux, Cheyenne and Nez Percé. Claim jumpers were after your father's ranch, not Indians." He tightened his hold on hands that had gone still and lax, needing her to understand. "Addie, I think it was probably Willis. He might not have known you had gone into town or he purposefully waited until you did, then killed your family, hoping to claim the ranch through marriage to you. And I don't think he meant for it to burn."

"No." The word was flat and emotionless, as blank as the green eyes staring back at him. But she was keening inside, parts of her threatening to come apart in so many directions she'd never pull herself back together again. She wouldn't believe him, wouldn't give Willis that much destructive power. She hated him enough for what he had done to her; she couldn't bear to think she'd been so stupid as to play right into his scheming, twisted plan. "Why are you saying all this now?"

"Because I want you to understand my actions," he said. "I don't want you to think I don't have any feelings for what you went through when you lost your family."

"You don't," she accused blindly, needing to flail out at something, someone. "You don't have any feelings at all. Not for me, not for the boys—"

His eyes flared, so bitter cold it stunned her to silence. She made a tentative gesture to reach for him, but dropped her hands heavily, ashamed of directing her anger at him when it was she herself she longed to chastise. Nausea and hatred coiled in her stomach for being so stupid and naive about Willis. "I'm sorry, Zeke. I . . . didn't mean it."

His eyes were hard, his voice dispassionate. "We need laws, not just to protect the Indians but to protect the white man also. The cattlemen plan to rule by the same flexible code the frontier has established, building feudal empires and expecting their actions to be upheld by the law they themselves live beyond. There's talk of outside investors now, wealthy Europeans willing to pour money into the cattle business. With so much at stake, this could all get out of hand. The territory is ungoverned enough as it is. Without restrictions, all hell will break loose."

Her fear resurfaced and came out as stubborn resistance. She felt shallow and intolerant but couldn't seem to help herself. "Why you? Why does it have to be you?"

"I made a place here to raise my family in peace, and I don't want to leave my sons a seditious legacy. They should be allowed to grow to manhood with law and order on their side, not a corrupt and greedy form of survival."

The tension inside her wound tighter. She understood his goals and ambition. She had lived in the shadow of terror for so long she, too, wanted peace but not at the expense of his leaving. She had found more contentment in the past six weeks than she had known in four years and didn't want to lose it. The only way she knew to get through to him was to strike at the heart of his concern. "If you leave us here unprotected, anything could happen to the boys."

Frustration underscored his words. "I don't plan to leave you unprotected. Luke Parker will come over to help you with the chores."

"He's seventeen!" Addie cried. She scraped her chair back and stood up, hands on her hips, too distraught to realize what she was doing. "You're just being bull-headed! He's not much more than a boy—"

Zeke rose also, a steely note in his voice. "I was

marching down a dirt road, headed straight for battle at seventeen; you were even younger when you married Willis. Don't tell me a boy Luke's age can't handle the responsibility of an adult."

Addie clamped her mouth shut, snatched up her basket, and stormed out of the kitchen. Her legs were quivering with anger and resentment when she rushed into the bedroom. She hadn't been anything close to an adult when she married Willis. She'd still been a girl who liked playing hopscotch and teasing her little brothers. She'd been able to cook and clean and sew at fifteen, but that hadn't made her a woman, and it certainly hadn't prepared her for life with Willis.

She slammed the door closed with her hip and dumped the clothes on the bed. She began to sort through them haphazardly, her eyes and nose stinging with pent-up tears. Zeke came in quietly behind her and watched her fumble with the laundry, useless motions mirroring her inner turmoil. After she had folded and refolded the same shirt three times he walked over and put his arms around her waist.

She jerked hard to shrug him off, violence in her action but not her spirit. Deep down she felt crushed and frightened. If a storm hit while he was gone, there was no telling how long it would take him to get back, or if he would make it at all. She twisted again to no avail. His hold was secure, his chest warm and solid against her back, his arms strong at her middle—a strength that was more welcome than she ever would have realized had she not been about to lose it.

Confusion reigned within her at the fact that she was more afraid of his leaving than staying. Less than a month ago, she would have sent him off with her blessing. She had wanted nothing more than his sons and the bounty of his safe home. She certainly hadn't wanted him.

But things had changed living here, seeing his face mornings and evenings, watching him with the boys, having her ideas questioned and her suggestions taken to heart. She was in danger of losing that companionship to nothing more than an idea that something *might* happen. As far as she was concerned, he could let the lawmakers take care of it.

She twisted again to get out of his hold, hurt and worried that he could leave her and the children for something so insubstantial. But it was more than just the newfound security, and she knew it. It was something much deeper and more fervent than mere safety.

Twist, turn, twist again. Her backside plowed into Zeke's groin with each movement, the undersides of her breasts grazed his arms. His palms flattened on her lower stomach and he pulled her flush against him, knowing there was one sure-fire way to get her to stop fighting.

"Mmmm, that's nice, Addie," he whispered in her ear. "Keep it up." She went still as death. With a cross between a smile and a grimace, he loosened his grip enough to turn her around to face him.

"Go then!" she cried. "See if I care. Me and the boys will do just fine without you."

It was absurd. Zeke didn't know why he felt like smiling, except that for such a small thing, she was fairly magnificent in her anger. One look at her militant stance along with the feel of her soft, slim body against his chased away all the weeks of brooding frustration and his efforts of maintaining an emotional distance. Her cheeks were flushed, her eyes sparking with green fire, and her breasts swelled rather temptingly against her blouse every time she took a deep breath.

"I didn't aim to make you mad," he teased.

"Well, I am!" she countered, then spoiled it when her bottom lip trembled.

"No, you're not," he said softly, and pulled her closer. "You're scared. What are you afraid of, Addie?"

She shook her head to deny it, but her hostility was crumbling beneath the weight of her fears. She was afraid something would happen to him and she would be left alone to raise his children on a ranch she had no hope of caring for properly. She was afraid of being pawned off like chattel to another man when she couldn't make it on her own.

And she was afraid, in the deepest, most hidden heart of her, of the things she had never thought to fear: never again seeing him cross the fields in rays of a setting sun, or hearing his voice carry on the wind as he shouted orders to Josh, or feeling the warmth of his callused hands on her skin.

Immersed in the weight of her wretchedness, she dropped her face to his chest, unable to admit her weakness and insecurity to a man who epitomized all that was sure and strong to her. "Was Willis that evil? Could he really have done that?"

"You tell me," Zeke whispered against the top of her head.

Memories rushed at her, hateful, hurtful. A viciousness and bitterness she'd never understood in the man who'd asked her to marry him, then had turned cruel within a week. And other things, illegal and immoral and depraved. "Yes," she said, the word muffled in Zeke's shirt. "Oh, Lord." His hold tightened around her, secure and protective and bracing. He smelled like sagebrush, leather, and cold mountain air. Familiar scents that she was growing accustomed to, that she didn't want to be absent from her life. "How soon?" she asked. "How soon do you have to go?"

"There's a meeting next week."

She leaned her head back to look at him. "Why didn't you tell me sooner?"

Zeke looked into her eyes. They were bright with unshed tears and some terrible need that he couldn't quite discern. He was going to Cheyenne to help secure the future for his sons, the territory, and Addie. Why, then, did he feel such a terrible urgency to stay? He ran his hand automatically down her back, and tensed up himself when he realized she didn't. His fingers curled into a fist against her hip to keep from grabbing for her further. "I didn't tell you sooner because I knew you'd act like this."

She pulled back. "How'd you know?"

"Women always react this way," he said. "I bet Sam is having the same problem with Bea."

Addie smiled slightly. "I bet Bea wins."

Zeke gave her a squeeze, wanting to do more, knowing better than to try. The tension of keeping himself in check was wearing, grating on him more and more lately. Night after night he lay beside her, not touching, the hunger in him building to a sharp-edged point that left him feeling blind and deaf to everything but the need to take her. He didn't dare release an ounce of the aggression he was feeling, because he was very much afraid that he would pass the point where he wouldn't listen to her pleas, wouldn't care about her fears, wouldn't be able to hear her say no.

Even with Becky he'd never felt this fierceness, this insanity. He had even taken to watching Addie at night while she slept, touching the satiny perfection of her skin when she sleepily rolled toward him, listening to each soft breath that made her breasts rise and fall under his sentient gaze. Her face was even more youthful and unguarded in slumber, and night after night he stripped away that innocence with his greedy thoughts. Only under the safety of darkness and witnessed only by him, would he allow himself to feel so emotionally needy.

His hand rose and stroked the curls back from her face, but even that simple contact made him sting everywhere, hot needle-pricks of desire that seemed to be growing stronger with each week passed. His fist curled in her hair as if he could contain the craving there, in a small silken knot. He needed this trip to Cheyenne in more ways than one. He needed distance and perspective and a chance to cool off.

He watched her facial muscles tense in wariness at his sudden intensity and released her hair. With a concentrated effort, he made his voice light. "You might be right, but Bea feels the same way I do, so she just might let Sam go. The territory has lived by its own rules too long, Addie. We don't need more corruption perpetuated in the name of good, or more trouble with the Indians."

She took a shallow breath, knowing she had no power to sway him, but needing to try. "Don't go."

"Apathy is so dangerous, Addie. Anyone who turns an indifferent eye will be as responsible for the outcome as the ones who cause it. I'd never let anything happen to you and the boys." He moved back slightly and stared at her with disturbing concentration. "Why does it matter to you?"

Because she'd miss him. Because, after only six

weeks, she counted on his presence and steadiness in a life that had once been so filled with turmoil. Because if she weren't so frightened of letting her guard down, she'd be half in love with him.

"Because I can't handle all the chores around here," she said instead, "even with Luke's help. It'll be all your fault if things are a mess when you get back. I'm not taking the blame for any of it. Do you hear me? I'm not taking the blame!"

Zeke eyed her oddly, then a slow smile tipped the corner of his mouth. "Are we having our first real fight, Miz Claiborne?"

"No." But Addie realized they were. In a strange way it was invigorating to be able to fuss at him without fear of reprisal. He might narrow his eyes in chagrin or raise his voice in frustration, but he never did anything that was harmful or painful.

Zeke's eyes took on a peculiar light. "I don't think things will be a mess when I get back," he said. "I imagine you can handle just about anything that comes your way . . . except me."

She blushed and turned her face away, wondering at his meaning while feeling the stirring truth of it low in her belly. "I don't know what you're talking about."

Zeke ran his hands lightly, purposefully, up and down her arms and waited for her to pull away. When she did, he smiled wryly. "You know exactly what I mean."

"I . . . I think I hear the baby," she said, and tried to duck under his arms.

Zeke tightened his hold briefly, then let her go. It was no use trying to restrain her when she'd only get flustered and panicky. She was a strange combination of stony resistance and deep-hearted generosity, good at toughing things out from a distance but cowering easily when confronted face-to-face. She was getting better though. She'd just stood up to him without growing timid. However unintentioned, she'd even laid her head on his chest.

And it had felt good to him, good in a way that he didn't particularly want to feel but didn't seem capable of stopping. Soft and warm, whispery and soothing. Comfort that wasn't at all comfortable.

It was wholly vexing that she didn't want him going to Cheyenne, didn't trust him enough to see to her welfare, but he welcomed the fight. Her arguing was a far cry from the dismal, silent woman he had married six weeks ago. And arguing, if not the preferable outlet, gave him at least a measure of relief from his rising frustrations.

10

Addie paced by the kitchen window, watching the snow swirl and dance like lace-cloaked pixies in celebration. Nature's display would have been beautiful were it not so potentially destructive. The cattle were huddled in groups, their backs turned to the wind. The horses were secure in the barn except one. Zeke's roan gelding. He had ridden the horse to Cheyenne a week ago and still hadn't returned.

Addie spun away from the window, past worried to angry. The worry would come again when night fell and he still wasn't home. Zeb sneaked past her to climb on the cupboard in search of a cookie. Addie promptly got him down and handed him several to share with Cole and Josh. The two younger boys had asked about their pa daily. Only Josh had refrained, as if he didn't trust her answers enough to risk asking. Trying to engage him in conversation was like running into a barn wall—too hard to get through, and too painful and senseless to keep trying. Addie figured she must not have much sense, because she kept trying and kept getting rebuffed.

It had dawned on her days ago that Zeke must feel a little like that when he tried to get close to her. At nothing more than an innocent touch or the brush of their bodies, she'd get her back up like he'd threatened her. She could see now that he meant nothing by it. He was an innately demonstrative man. Touching came easily to him, showing affection as normal as breathing. She saw it time and again in the way he treated the boys.

His restraint and distance around her wasn't normal but a result of her own skittish nature. She wondered why she could see that so clearly now when he was gone. She also wondered if that's what had kept him away so long, if he was tired of the time and effort it took for no reward but her cold response.

A dark silhouette caught her eye, riding through the gloom in a straight path for the house. Her heart stirred, then began beating faster as she rushed closer to the window.

"Boys," she said, breathless with anticipation as the rider continued to draw closer. Josh looked up, then headed for the door, but she caught his arm before he could open it. "Wait. It's too cold. Let's get the fire built up, so your pa can get warm fast when he comes inside."

He shrugged her hand off, but he was smiling as he rushed to put more logs in the hearth. Zeb squealed, "Pa!" and scrambled back up on the cupboard to get a closer look, and Addie didn't have the heart to make him get down this time. The wind picked up, swirling the ground snow as well as that which was falling, and the rider disappeared behind a curtain of gray-white obscurity, then reappeared closer to the house.

The house, not the barn.

Addie's heart fell. Zeke would have stabled his gelding before coming inside. "It's not your pa," she told the boys, and felt every groan they emitted rise in her own throat. She peered closely out the window as the rider dismounted and tethered his horse, wondering who it was, hoping beyond the rising panic in her stomach that it wasn't bad news.

But she knew, with the same desperation that every other wife and mother in Laramie knew, that no man would come out in this weather to pay a social call.

Her heart a leaden weight in her chest, she crossed to the door and had it jerked open before the stranger could knock, bracing herself, refusing to give her imagination free rein. Only when the man was shouldering his way inside did she recognize him. Her muscles contracted violently and she tried to slam the door shut, but it was too late. Grady Smith forced her farther back into the room and barricaded the door himself.

Addie backed up and grabbed Cole, then ushered the two others boys behind her. "Get out," she said viciously. "You're not welcome here."

"Is that any way to greet a relative?" he asked silkily. His eyes took in her protective stance, the way she gathered the children around her like a mother hen. He smiled. "Your man at home?"

Nausea robbed her of a quick answer, not that it mattered. Addie could see by the look on his face that Grady knew she was alone and had planned it that way.

"What do you want?" she asked coldly.

His gaze narrowed and swept her body slowly, his grin intentionally leering. He needed her frightened and intimidated so she would buckle. "I want Willis's chest."

My chest, she wanted to scream. But already she could feel the familiar dread, the sickening humiliation of years of submissiveness. The air was so thick with tension she could scarce draw breath. Light-headed and weak-limbed, she knew she was floundering, but couldn't find her balance.

Cole whined and squirmed in her arms. She automatically shifted the baby to a more comfortable position and felt a surge of strength streak through her in the simple, protective motion. She glanced down at Zeb and Josh, realizing she would lose everything if she didn't act.

Like the calm before a storm, her voice was strong and controlled. She wouldn't have recognized it as her own. "I don't have your demon chest, Grady. It's gone. Willis destroyed it to get back at me."

Grady blinked at her assertiveness, then smiled in scornful triumph. "Hardly." His voice lowered, sweet and compelling and lethal. "That chest is my ticket out of this one-horse town. I've got a buyer, so hand it over or I'll need to have a little discussion with your husband."

Outwardly she didn't flinch or cower or crumple. Maybe she was too numb or stricken. Or maybe she'd had enough of being terrorized by Willis and Grady's threats. She knew he expected her to fall apart, but she wouldn't give him the satisfaction of seeing her beg. Never would she debase herself like that again. Her entire world might be threatening to fall away beneath her, but she stared back at him quite peacefully and lied with frank sincerity, "Tell my husband anything you like. It doesn't matter anymore, Grady. You can't bully me. Even if I had the chest I wouldn't give it to you."

His lip curled in a sneer and without warning he lunged forward and gripped her upper arm. "You stupid bitch," he hissed in her ear. "I'll get the sheriff so fast it'll make your head spin."

"Then you'll have nothing," she managed coldly.

A terrible look entered his eyes, so much worse than anything that had come before. He reached up and stroked Cole's head. "You've got three little boys here, Addie, so young and tender. It's mighty cold outside." He released her and stepped casually back, smiling. "Go get the chest, Addie."

She finally broke, as he had known she would. Her face lost all color and she bent down and handed the baby to Josh. "Go on to your bedroom," she whispered. "I'll come get you in a minute."

"But, Ma . . ." Zeb whined, looking crestfallen.

"Go now," Addie said evenly. "I'll have a surprise for you when you come out."

Zeb brightened and took off, but Josh clutched the baby tightly and looked back and forth between Addie and the man. His eyes full of wounded disgust and accusation, he turned his back and followed Zeb. Stricken, Addie stared at him until the door slammed, then turned away and headed for her own bedroom, not needing to look at Grady to see the gloating victory on his face.

When she returned to the kitchen, he was staring out the window assessing the weather. "If your man doesn't return, I just might need to stay the night, to . . . protect you." He turned, a leer in place, then froze.

The rifle was pointed dead center at his heart. Addie stood, steady and outwardly calm, three feet from him, her finger around the trigger. "I told you, I don't have the chest," she said flatly. "Now, get out or I'm going to send you straight to hell with Willis."

Grady smiled, an oily, mirthless tilt of his lips. He didn't think for a second she had the guts to shoot, but the damn thing could accidentally go off in her hands.

"You're not being reasonable," he coaxed, his voice

so deceptively charming. "They hang people for murder, Addie."

"Willis is buried," she said coldly, "and I'm still walking around." His eyes narrowed briefly in contemplation, then flared in acknowledgment and rage. Before he could speak, Addie added, "I don't have any compunction at all about trying it twice."

He knew she was bluffing, dammit he *knew,* but her hands were steady, her eyes dispassionate and level down the sight of the gun. He just couldn't take the chance. He smiled thinly and backed cautiously toward the door.

"You are going to regret this so badly, Addie," he whispered. He looked around the room slowly, as if measuring it. "I wonder if this house will burn as quickly as your other one."

His words hit her like an anvil to the base of her skull, but she neither moved nor even blinked, nothing that would show him he'd gotten to her. As soon as he was gone, she rushed into action. She dashed to the door and bolted it behind him, then ran to the sink before her legs collapsed and heaved up her dinner. Her knees and elbows were watery as she leaned over the basin, her breathing gaspy and unstable. Her hands trembled wildly as she propped the rifle against the wall, then dampened a cloth and pressed it to her mouth. She wasn't certain she could remain standing.

"Ma?" Zeb called tentatively from the bedroom.

On a strangled moan, she folded against the cupboard and sank to the floor, the unloaded gun falling beside her with a thud. She dropped her face into her hands. *Oh, Lord.*

Zeb called again from a slight crack in the open door. "You got our prize yet, Ma?"

The sweet words, so trusting and unaffected by the evil that had invaded her home, roused her as nothing else could. She gripped the edge of the cupboard and pulled herself up, her empty stomach roiling. "Just a minute," she said unsteadily. "I'm not quite ready."

It helped to think of other things, to set her mind to pleasing the boys, no matter how false the excuse had been. On rubbery legs she headed back into her bedroom and retrieved several things she'd been making the boys for Christmas.

"Ready," she called, a fixed bright smile on her face, a terrible, unstoppable desperation in her soul.

There was only a moment of panic when a rider approached two days later, heading through the snowstorm for the barn. But Addie recognized Zeke's roan gelding a split second before the growing blizzard swallowed horse and rider up. She swung Zeb off the cupboard where he was rummaging again for cookies, grabbed the coffeepot, and put water on to boil. After the hard ride, Zeke would be starving. She scurried around like a chicken with its head lopped off, stoking the fire in the oven to heat leftover meat and vegetables and getting the table set.

"Pa's coming!" Zeb cried, and Addie felt the joyous relief of it deep in her chest.

She unlocked the back door and smoothed her hair, then her dress, thinking she looked a mess. The door swung open, blowing gusts of snow and frigid air inside. Zeke stepped through and slammed it behind him. His hat and clothes were spangled with ice crystals, his movements slow and stiff from the cold. Suddenly the world was right again; the time of his absence—intolerable and agonizingly slow—was only a memory.

The children squealed their greetings, but it was Addie's frightful "Have mercy, you're frozen!" that caught Zeke's attention. She rushed forward to pull off his coat, then grabbed a blanket and slung it around his shoulders, all the while pushing him toward the fire.

"Oh, get your boots off," she admonished, shoving him down in a chair before he'd even had time to warm his hands up. "Of all the hare-brained, senseless . . ." She rambled on nervously as she tugged his left boot off, incoherent snatches of rebuke that spun out in diverse directions, then seemed to circle back. When his other boot hit the floor, she stood to face him, hands on her hips, green eyes blazing.

Zeke couldn't recall ever being so manhandled in his life. Her eyes sparkled with benign outrage and the flush on her cheeks was wholly becoming. He started to say something, but she was glaring at him as if he'd committed a crime.

"What were you thinking, to ride out in weather like this? You're gonna catch your death!"

Zeke only stared back at her. He was cold and hungry and tired. He'd accomplished nothing in Cheyenne but collecting a few enemies and getting himself frozen on the way home. He'd walked into his house, not to a warm welcome, but to a wife who was nagging at him like a . . . wife. He smiled slowly.

"Evenin', Miz Claiborne."

Addie huffed and spun around to get his coffee, while the boys began a barrage of questions about his trip, who and what he'd seen, and finally if he'd brought them anything. She returned to the sitting room just as the boys rushed off to rummage through Zeke's saddlebags for their treats.

"Foolish thing you did, coming back in a storm," she said, and handed him the steaming mug.

Zeke savored the heat and aroma a moment, then sipped the coffee slowly, letting it warm him from the inside out. He glanced up over the rim of the cup. "It wasn't snowing when I left Cheyenne."

"You should have taken shelter when it began," she said, feeling her inexplicable ire slip a notch. His hair was drying on the ends, curling up boyishly around his handsome face. He was safe, and he was home.

One eyebrow lifted over his amber eyes. "And here I thought I was gonna be welcomed with open arms and a loving smile."

Addie blushed to her toes, but didn't back down an inch. "If you catch a fever, I'm gonna—" Her words skidded to a halt when Zeke set his coffee on the floor and rose slowly, a spark in his eyes she'd never seen before.

Addie wisely closed her mouth and backed up a step.

Zeke took one toward her.

She backed up again, but it was the last step she took.

In one long stride, Zeke swept her completely off the floor and pulled her tight against his chest. "What are you gonna do, Miz Claiborne?" he whispered, before his mouth came crashing down on hers. He tasted of cold air and warm coffee, his arms a welcome and crushing weight around her.

Her reply was muffled against his lips, her breathing a silly, unstable flutter in her breast. Her eyes went round as saucers, then slowly lowered as the feeling of being in his arms overtook her. Zeb shrieked with delight at the sight, while Josh just stood in openmouthed astonishment. Zeke pulled back a fraction of an inch, barely breaking contact.

"That's how a wife welcomes a husband."

He relaxed his hold, and Addie slid slowly down until her toes touched the floor, the rest of her still planted firmly against him.

"That's how a wife welcomes a husband who's been gone over a week, a husband who's cold and hungry and aching for his bed."

Addie only gaped at him, confounded and embarrassed and so entranced she thought she might fall over in a swoon. Cole toddled over and tugged at his pa's pants, not to be left out. Zeke bent and scooped him up in one arm, every hard muscled inch of him brushing against every soft and startled inch of her. His hot amber eyes never left her dazed green ones. "You got anything for a hungry man?"

Addie pointed weakly at the dinner on the stove.

But it was dessert that Zeke was contemplating.

11

Addie slowly hung her dress in the wardrobe. A nest of bees swarmed in her belly, her mouth felt dry as cotton, and her limbs felt both weightless and heavy. All because Zeke had offered to hear the boys' prayers while she got ready for bed. The offer wouldn't have upset her so much except that he'd said one last thing in parting.

"Wear the nightgown Miz Parker gave you."

It had been a demand, softly spoken but direct. No chance she could have misunderstood. *Oh, Lord.* Shivering from more than the chilled room, Addie disregarded the request and pulled her old nightgown over her head, then crossed to the bed and dove beneath the covers. Her fingers were trembling as she gripped the quilt to her neck, but she wasn't exactly afraid.

She was relieved.

Grady's visit had sparked a fight in her that had yet to die down. She was tired of being bullied by men, tired of having her will stolen or manipulated, tired of having to pander to someone else's whims or wants. Everything she had feared and fretted over since marrying Zeke was about to come to pass, and she was glad. Not because it was what she wanted, but because it would be gotten out of the way.

She was blatantly disobeying her husband, and she would finally know what kind of man she had married. She had made her stand. In part rebellion, part fear, and part determination, she had put on the old cotton nightgown and made her stand.

But it was a hollow front. Her heart thudded anxiously, because she knew. With a terrible and unsettling realization, she knew she wouldn't deny him. She wasn't brave enough or strong enough. And she wouldn't risk losing the boys.

If he was brutal or cruel—

The thought gave her pause, the subconscious revival of old fears that had no basis now. Zeke was neither of those things. He had proved himself time and again to be a patient man, strong but gentle, above reproach. So what was she still so afraid of? The truth settled with a small thump in her chest. The not knowing how it would be with him, for him. The thought of intimacy had kept her edgy, jumpy at his slightest word or touch. After tonight she would know if her nervousness was warranted.

Zeke walked to his bedroom door and paused. His mind was made up but the rest of him was as unsure as a callow virgin. He was going to take Addie to bed. He reached for the doorknob and turned it. Come hell or high water, tears or fears, struggles and recriminations, he was going to have his wife. He just wasn't sure when.

The thought of taking her by force was obscene, but he wasn't certain how much longer he could last and retain his sanity.

He'd made the decision in Cheyenne. In a cold and friendless hotel room, he'd lain in bed alone and aching, knowing he need not have been by himself. Whores spilled from the saloons, ready and willing to ease a man in the cheapest, most loveless way. Temptation had even come from Arlene Johnson, wife of a cattle baron and sister of Jesse Gordon, whom Zeke had fought with during the war. Dressed in exquisite satin, her enticing perfume drifting across the space that separated them, Arlene had been worldly and beautiful and self-possessed. Nothing about him had frightened or alarmed her, nothing about him had repelled her.

The lure had been strong enough to shake him to his boots—the temptation to hold a woman again, to feel her softness and eager acceptance, to bury himself in her warmth until they were both mindless with pleasure. He had refused because of his marriage vows and because of Addie herself, but it had made him bitter for the span of seconds it took Arlene to nod gracefully and walk away, dignified even in rejection.

Jesse had joined him soon after and Zeke's bitterness had then turned to hard realization and self-contempt. Jesse had lost everything a man could value during the war, his family and land and livestock. His left arm hung awkward and lifeless from taking a bullet to the elbow outside of Chattanooga. A once handsome young soldier, his face was battle scarred. Deep lines scored his forehead and eyes and bracketed his mouth, testament to the agonizing pain he'd gone through to recover.

But Jesse had recovered. When he strolled toward Zeke, his right arm was hooked over the shoulder of an engaging brunette whom he introduced as his wife. Neither the loss of his family, nor the war, nor a crippling injury had stopped Jesse Gordon from going forward with his life. Zeke had felt something critical within him respond to the challenge of doing the same.

He had two choices. He could wallow in his old grief and self-pity until he was nothing but an empty shell or he could go forward and make a new life with Mary Adaline Claiborne.

For him there was only one choice. Having made it, Zeke realized he and Addie could no longer spend the rest of their lives as polite strangers. They shared the same house, the same children, the same bed. When he returned, they would share more. But the decision wasn't his alone. Addie, who was so afraid of him because of the memories of a dead man, would have a choice to make as well. Zeke didn't feel guilty that he had almost forsaken his marriage vows with Jesse's sister. He felt angry. Angry at Addie for being afraid of him. Angry at himself for not proving to her that she didn't have to be.

His patience was exhausted. He couldn't change her past, not with time or patience or abstinence. He couldn't ease it or wash it away as if those four years had never existed. He could only prove that with him it would be different.

Taking a deep breath, he opened the door. Entering the room, he put his hat on the table, then walked to the bed. He glanced down to see that Addie's eyes were wide and unblinking, staring up at him. The quilt was clutched to her chin. He turned away to unbutton his shirt, wondering if she knew, if she realized, that tonight might change forever the course of their marriage.

Addie's eyes flared wider when he stripped down to nothing, his buttocks as strong and muscular as the rest of him. He'd never come to bed naked. The realization sent her mind reeling. If there had been any doubts as to his intentions before, there weren't any now. The bed dipped when Zeke slid in beside her. Her breathing escalated, but she faced him, her green eyes open and dilated. Her insides rolled and ebbed until she couldn't bear the uncertainty anymore.

"What are you going to do?" she whispered.

Apparently a lot more than you want me to. "I missed you in Cheyenne," he said.

"I missed you too." There was a brief pause, then she persisted. "What are you going to do?"

Zeke sighed and touched the hair at her temples, then laid his palm along her cheek. "You know what, Addie. It's past time."

It was a statement that required no answer, but she nodded anyway to prove that he couldn't trick or fool her, that she knew what he was about and was willing to get it over with.

Zeke accepted her tacit agreement in the spirit in which it had been offered—tentatively. He folded the quilt back to her waist to see that she had donned the same old serviceable nightgown she always wore. Addie's hand rose, a telling gesture, to fret with the frayed ribbon at her neck.

"This isn't the right one," he said.

"No." The word was breathless but defiant. Her fingers gripped the ribbon tighter.

"Why?" Zeke slid his hand beneath hers and felt her heartbeat skip, then soar, felt also the tantalizing rise and fall of her flesh. He pulled her anxious fingers away from the ribbon and placed them on his chest, offering her the liberty of exploring him as he intended to explore her.

Awkward and unsure, her fingers curled into a fist against his bare skin, but his own rough-textured fingers spread wide upon her. Lightly, he ran his palm over her breasts, feeling their plump roundness through the fabric, the tight buds forming at the center. She fit perfectly, lushly, into his hand, and there was male satisfaction in that and a stirring call to do more. Yet he controlled the need because underneath his hand, he also felt the small shivers of uncertainty flowing through her.

"Are you comfortable, Addie?"

"No. Are you mad?"

"About the gown? No, disappointed. Do you want me to stop?"

No. *Yes.* "Does it matter?"

Not tonight. "Everything matters." His hand slid down over her rib cage to her slender waist, and his eyes bored into hers with an intensity that dismantled her feeble bravery.

"Wait—"

"You don't have to be afraid, Addie. I can make you want this, if you just give me a chance."

Her lashes fluttered down, shielding her thoughts. Her words were barely audible. "Why tonight?"

"Because it's long overdue. Because I can't go on like this. Cheyenne was lonely in a way it never should have been."

Shakily, she whispered, "It's Cheyenne's fault?"

Zeke smiled. "No. It's mine for not realizing I'd need more from you than a housekeeper and nanny. You need more too."

She'd never believe that, not in a million years. She had everything she wanted just the way it was—the boys, a home, a considerate husband—and it was all about to be ruined. She sighed sadly, accepting it. She hadn't really believed the goodness would last, hadn't let herself. No matter how courageous she had been when she put on the old nightgown, she was wallowing in trepidation now and a full measure of resentment. It wasn't his wrath she wasn't willing to chance, it was his disgust— the fear that she would be less than what he needed, a great disappointment, as she had always been to Willis. She closed her eyes tightly, hating the fact that she even cared what he thought, that he mattered.

Zeke recognized her passive resistance and knew with a twist of resentment and disappointment in his gut that he could have her only if he took her. There was nothing in her that wanted him, nothing that would respond. He exhaled a silent sigh and resigned himself to the fact that it wouldn't be tonight. Still, he couldn't stop himself from trying, couldn't stop himself from seeing just how far she would allow him to push the boundaries before she pushed back.

His eyes glinted golden with challenge in the candlelight as he lifted the ribbon at her neckline and tugged until the gown fell open. Addie stiffened as his fingers curled inward, dipping beneath the edge. His knuckles brushed her flesh as he slid his hand back and forth, starting small hot tremors inside her.

"I just want to touch you," he said, "nothing else." He couldn't tell if she believed him. Her expression didn't change, nor did she relax. He ran one finger up her neck to her jaw line and reverently traced the delicate bone structure.

"So soft. You have the softest skin." A bewildered frown touched her brow, as if she couldn't assemble his words into anything that made sense. "And your eyes," he continued, fascinated when she lowered her lashes. He watched her cheeks warm and was held suspended a moment by the captivating guilelessness of her response. She hadn't an ounce of seduction or sophistication in her, but her shyness charmed him completely, her artless finesse so much more damaging to a man at the end of his rope. His thumb brushed tantalizingly across her bottom lip, and her eyes flared in expectation and worry.

"What will you do?"

It came to him clearly in that moment. Willis had never done any of this. Not only had she never been courted, but she'd never been seduced, not in any meaningful or tender way.

The realization touched a chord of pity and something more complex yet elemental inside him. He shied away immediately, or tried to, but the pull on his senses was tight and insistent, dragging him away from the comfort of nothingness. Emotion was messy and unreliable and irrelevant to his need, but knowledge was infinitely important. He strove to grasp an understanding of Addie, to balance her present needs with past experiences. If she had known only the forceful invasion of a man's body, it would more than account for her fear. He cupped her cheek to keep her from turning away.

"Tell me about Willis, so you can bury him for good."

Her stomach contracted painfully. If Zeke wanted to open locked doors, so be it. "On one condition," she said, her voice airy and shallow and rebellious. "You tell me about Dr. LaFleur first."

Zeke tensed as if she'd slapped him. "No."

Addie felt his fingers grow stiff and cold on her flesh, felt him recede—so much like herself that she couldn't help but recognize the alienation.

A great sadness came over her. The chasm was unbridgeable, stretching between them in the most humanless way, their past secrets and grievances separating them as if they were miles apart instead of inches.

"Fine," she said softly, not knowing how to heal the hurt and mistrust they carried within. "Then don't ask me about Willis."

Zeke rolled back in frustration and stared at the ceiling. "It's not the same. Christian has nothing to do with this."

"Neither does Willis."

Zeke turned back to his side but didn't touch her. "He has everything to do with us. You are afraid of me because of him."

She could hardly deny it, but the charge kindled another spark of rebellion so quickly in her that she had no time to marvel at her nerve. "Maybe I'd be afraid of you anyway, even if I'd never known him! A woman has the right to be nervous—"

He rolled over quickly, pinning her beneath him, and sealed her lips with his to stop her rambling before she got too wound up. Her eyes widened, the green flecks darkening, and she twisted beneath him, then went still as stone. His weight was heavy and smothering, but also warm. She didn't know what to make of the tangled feelings running through her—fear and security all mixed up in confusion. She didn't know what to make of the wanting either, wanting his kisses and caresses as much as she feared them.

Her gown was bunched up above her knees, bulky against Zeke's belly. He wanted to remove it so there would be nothing between them, knowing all the while that the intangible barricade of her anxiety was a much stronger obstruction.

"I would never hurt you, Addie," he said, his voice so darkly appealing.

She looked away. "It's not the pain." It was the shame that she couldn't bear, his turning from her in disgust, cursing and blaming her for things she couldn't change.

"Then what?" he coaxed, sinking into her in a meager imitation of what he really wanted. "See how right this feels?"

"It feels like you're crushing me," she said tremulously.

Dark golden eyes glittered down at her with wry humor. There was frustration and gentle mockery and a deep beckoning in his eyes and smile that she didn't understand but responded to. In one smooth movement, he gathered her tight and rolled to his back, pulling her on top of him.

"Is this better?" he asked smoothly, outwardly relaxed, inwardly near madness.

Addie reared back in astonishment. She felt wholly embarrassed sitting atop him, her gown hiked up to her thighs. Her cheeks were burning, but his flesh was just as hot beneath her, and smooth, making her feel strange and jittery inside. "I . . . I need time," she begged. "Just a little more time."

Zeke gritted his teeth, his aggravation too close to the surface, his need too coarse to answer in a voice that would be anything but gruff. It was gratifyingly painful to have her straddled across his lap, her cheeks and eyes so bright. With her curls spilling over her shoulders and her slim form hidden beneath the simple gown, she was a creature of earth and moonlight, completely unaware of her own loveliness and provocation.

It wouldn't take much, a little tender yet forceful coaxing to have her bare and riding him. He ran his hands lightly down her sleek arms and felt her contract. The shift in her weight made his breath snare in his throat, then hiss out between his teeth. It was obvious she had none of the feelings plaguing him, none of the desire eating away at his nerves until they were raw with wanting, dangerous.

Feeling awkward and uncomfortable, Addie squirmed again. Zeke's hands flew to her hips to hold her still. He knew it was cruel and unfair, that trust wasn't something that couldn't be charted or planned, but he couldn't stop the demand. "How much time?"

Trapped by her own words, Addie scrambled for an answer to placate him. "A month?" she asked weakly.

"A month," he agreed, then took her face in his palms and pulled her toward him. The kiss was searing, his mouth claiming hers possessively. Their teeth scraped roughly against each other, then his tongue entered her mouth so quickly the breath left her body. He stole every gasp, every protest, every soft and distressed moan, until she felt she had no air, that every breath she took was his. His heat touched her everywhere. When he finally relented and released her, she was breathing fast.

"Day thirty," he said, a promise.

Wide-eyed and unsteady, she pretended not to hear as she gingerly crawled off him and moved to her side of the bed. She was still pretending the next morning when he kissed her hard and said, "Day twenty-nine."

Josh's scream was the first indication that something was wrong. It was loud and piercing, a wounded wail of shock and horror. Addie dropped the pan she was washing and rushed to the back door to see Josh tearing across the yard toward the house.

"Pa!" he yelled, his feet pounding the ground as his legs pumped. "Pa's hurt!"

Addie met him halfway to the house, a sickly calm in her stomach that didn't match her rapid heartbeat. Her mouth was too dry to ask questions. She just let herself be led when Josh grabbed her sleeve, pulling her so hard toward the barn she almost lost her footing. Sunlight spilled two feet into the open door, brighter for its reflection off the trampled snow. Its false warmth was vaguely reassuring until Addie stepped into the dim interior and heard the deep, suppressed moans near the back.

She froze at the sight of Zeke's horse standing untethered next to a stall. There was blood on the saddle. Josh jerked her forward. When she didn't budge, he pulled again and began crying hard, choking on his words.

"I g . . . got her, Pa!"

Zeke sat propped against the wall, his skin pallid. Sweat beaded his brow, though it was freezing in the barn. His jaw was clenched, his eyes inexplicably both dull and bright. "Good boy," he whispered through set teeth. "Get your ma's coat and some binding. Bring it back here, then go tend the boys."

Josh nodded, tears streaming down his face, then bolted from the barn. Addie just stood, her feet stuck to the hay littering the dirt floor. Zeke looked as normal as any man who'd just sat down to take a rest, except for the haggard look on his face, the whiteness around his mouth. And the holes through his shoulder and thigh seeping blood over the hands trying to stanch it.

She knelt down slowly, careful not to touch him, and began to rip the hem of her petticoat. She was so cold, her hands stiff and clumsy, betraying her will. Her numb fingers fumbled and she lifted the fabric to her mouth and bit down like an animal to shred the threads that

finally gave in a long, clean tear. Shivering uncontrollably, she slid the strip of cotton beneath his leg where the
injury appeared worse, then wrapped it tightly as many
times as it would go around before looking back into
amber eyes that were growing hazy.

Her voice was composed, unlike the panic swelling
inside her. "I need to get the doc."

Zeke shook his head and winced, then dropped it
back against the wall. "We'll handle it," he rasped out.
"I'll tell you what to do."

She wasn't about to argue with him until she got him
into the house. Josh rushed back into the barn, his face
as white as the sheet bunched in his fist. Addie took her
coat first and put it on, but it couldn't block the chill
that had seeped into her bones. She felt as if her blood
had turned to ice. She grabbed the sheet and padded
the wound on Zeke's shoulder, then said calmly, "Help
me get him up, Josh."

They got their shoulders under each of Zeke's arms
and lifted, while he took the impact on his uninjured
leg. Addie shut out his groan, knowing she would crum-
ble if she listened, and desperately hoped he wouldn't
faint before they got him into bed. His dead weight
would be impossible. The trip from the barn to the
house was the longest she had ever made, painfully slow
but unerring. She never once wavered, just kept her
eyes on the back door, saying nothing, wondering how
she would get him up on the porch.

He stumbled on the first step, then rallied out of
sheer desperation, gritting his teeth against the pain
while his head swam in dizzying waves. He couldn't lose
consciousness outside in the cold.

As if by rote, Addie helped him into the house and
onward into the bedroom. Her movements were me-

chanical, necessary. Falling apart would do neither of them any good. Flinging back the quilt, she eased him down onto the bed and helped him lie flat, then stepped back and braced herself.

"I *have* to fetch the doctor."

For a moment life flared in his feverish eyes, even if it was with hatred. All too quickly the eyes dimmed. His breathing was dangerously shallow. "No."

She gave him a blank look and took the sheet, then began ripping it into long strips for bandaging. "Get me water, Josh," she said softly, then got her scissors from the basket by the bed. She couldn't look at Zeke as she cut his pants and shirt away, couldn't bear the pain on his face. She worked as if her own hands were foreign to her, machinery to be guided, something artificial and without feeling. But her stomach heaved when she folded back the fabric to reveal his lacerated shoulder, then the ugly hole in his thigh. "What . . . happened?"

"Rustlers."

Fingers trembling, she laid the bloody scissors down and caught Josh as he came through the door. "See to the little boys," she said. "Don't let them come in."

"Pa," he whimpered.

"Go," she said softly, firmly.

His eyes were wary and frightened as he backed out of the room, but she didn't have time to soothe him. She spun back to the bed with the pan of water and began cleaning the torn flesh. Zeke's shoulder was mutilated, but his thigh was a different story. The bullet had entered, but it hadn't exited. She knew little about gunshot wounds, but she did know that if the bullet was lead, it would poison him. She worked steadily despite her trembling fingers, cleaning and binding the wounds as gently as possible.

Zeke was growing weaker. No telling how far he'd had to ride in his condition before reaching the barn. He lost consciousness before she secured the last bandage, which was just as well. When a wife disobeyed a husband, it was best he didn't know about it.

Josh was standing by the door when she left the bedroom, the younger boys still asleep. She knelt before him and took his hands. "We need the doc—"

"No," he said, shaking his head in frantic snatches. "Pa said no!"

Her fingers tightened on his, hurtful without meaning to be. Manipulation was a cruel thing, never *ever* to be perpetrated on children. But she knew with desperate wisdom that Josh would never obey her over his father's direct order. "Listen to me, Joshua," she said calmly. "Ride to Bea's house. Tell her your pa's got a bullet in his leg, then stay there. It'll be too dark for you to come back tonight. Luke can bring you tomorrow." She watched the tangle of fear and rebellion flash in his eyes. He wanted to defy her and stay by his pa but knew he had to get help. "Go!"

He broke from his stupor and ran, stumbling blindly out the back door into the frigid air. He led his father's horse out of the barn, sobbing like a baby when he mounted. Addie felt her knees go weak and pressed her hand over her mouth to hold back her own sobs. He was only eight, small and helpless; his feet didn't even reach the stirrups. She watched as he tightened his knees and gripped the saddle horn, then slapped the reins across the horse's flanks to get it moving.

Addie turned away from the sight of a vulnerable child riding out at dusk to save a father in even greater peril. Danger lurked everywhere, known and unknown, that could so easily hurt a child alone. Wild animals, deadly humans, frigid temperatures. For the first time in four years, she prayed.

It was the deeper voice that woke him. The familiar jargon he hadn't heard in years, coupled with the touch of skilled, familiar hands. *Primary hemorrhage . . . ligation may be necessary, but no resection if we're lucky.* Addie's voice came next, calm but strained, asking questions. The light behind his eyelids was soft, muted. Not sunlight. A lantern or candle that wavered, then grew brighter, then faded again. The pain was the same. A dull throb, a piercing burn, back to a throb. Who was probing the wound?

Zeke opened his eyes slowly and tried to focus. Images, foggy at first, began to congeal into shape and form. Christian's face loomed over him, expressionless, transporting him back to a crowded tent at Stones River. Rapid rounds of artillery burst, dying away into the irregular fire of distant musketry and the startling ring of quick-repeated rifle shots. Another stabbing pain, then words that seemed to echo from a distance.

Minié ball . . . bores through tissue instead of bouncing off . . . skin too elastic . . . didn't make it through the other side. Then Addie's mew of displeasure and concern.

Addie.

Not a field hospital; home. Not a skilled surgeon; a skillful, betraying enemy.

Zeke struggled to sit up, heard a muffled curse and was forced back down. Addie's gasp drew his gaze in her direction.

"Get him out of here." The words were grainy and slurred, his eyes burning with more than fever into hers. There was pain and hatred, and the knowledge that she had betrayed him. Addie cringed back but shook her head.

"You're hurt. You need his help."

Zeke cursed the weakness from blood loss as he struggled once more. The effort exhausted him and he fell back, sending a cold, furious glare at Christian. "Get the hell out."

"Sorry," Christian said without an ounce of remorse. Addie stood off to the side, her face pale and wounded, her eyes filled with concern. "The lady's paying the bill."

"My money," Zeke ground out. His chest felt heavy. He wondered if his lungs were filling up with blood but knew he hadn't been hit in the chest. "Subclavian artery?"

"Not severed. Or the larynx either, obviously. Shut up, Claiborne, and let me finish."

More poking and prodding, then Christian stepped back and spoke to Addie. "His shoulder is minor, a flesh wound. The bullet only grazed his neck and shoulder. The thigh is more serious. I need as much light as you can get in here. Tell Bea to get my kit."

Zeke reared up at the words and felt his passage blocked by strong hands. "Don't come near me with that saw, you son of a bitch—"

"Lie down or I'll tie you!" Christian commanded. "There's no profuse arterial hemorrhaging yet. The contused and lacerated arteries have retracted and shut off. Don't reopen them."

Zeke lay back, exhausted, unnerved by his feebleness. He heard Bea enter, then the clink of surgical instruments and Christian's instructions. He sent a scorching look at the doctor. "No chloroform, damn you."

Christian chuckled dryly. "Ether. I'll use the chloroform if you get stubborn and don't wake up."

Zeke growled a vicious oath and made to rise again. His only thought was not of the pain but of ramming his fist into Christian's face. When a patient didn't respond to the more common methods of waking him after surgery, the surgeon would splash chloroform on the patient's scrotum. The immediate reaction of cold did more to jolt a patient awake than every other procedure combined.

"You son of a—" Addie quickly placed her hand on his uninjured shoulder, holding him down with no more than a frightened whimper and her gentle touch.

"Your pulse is back up," Christian drawled, satisfied, then sobered and turned to Addie. "Open all the windows."

"It's too cold," she began, so afraid now that she had done the wrong thing. There was such blatant enmity between these two men, she couldn't be certain the physician would really try to save her husband or that Zeke would ever forgive her.

"The fresh air will cut the toxicity," Christian said, then folded his arms over his chest as if he had all the time in the world. He smiled wryly at the fulminating glance she gave him before she hurried to do his bidding. As soon as the task was complete, Christian leaned over Zeke and grinned. "Good night, Claiborne."

Once Zeke was surgically asleep, Christian worked swiftly and efficiently. Needing the degree of touch that was lost with a probe and reducing the chances of other anatomical damage, he located the bullet with his finger. Once confident of its location, he used Moses forceps to reduce the trauma to the surrounding tissue and withdrew a deformed lead projectile. He then switched to pincher-type forceps and meticulously removed pieces of clothing and shrapnel.

Addie wrapped her arms around her and watched while he worked, amazed at his dexterity and calm. His hands never once shook, his attention never wavered. She supposed a man who had performed the same procedure a hundred times during the height of battle found it quite unchallenging to do so in a tranquil bedroom. She found it remarkable and fixed her eyes on the skills of his profession rather than his patient. She could hardly bear to see Zeke—so vital and strong—lying wounded and unconscious. The pallor of his skin was ashen, his breathing shallow. Tears clouded her vision, but she blinked them away to watch and wait in case she were needed.

Competent and efficient, Christian set the leg, sutured the major blood vessels, then closed and bandaged the wound. The whole operation took less than thirty minutes. Addie would have sworn it was hours.

Stepping back, the doctor glanced at Bea. "Fan him to purge his lungs of the anesthetic, while I get the liquor of ammonia. One quick smell and he'll regain consciousness." He turned to Addie, his voice toneless, an odd mixture of scrutiny and appreciation in his eyes.

"You did real well, Mrs. Claiborne, but I don't imagine he'll thank you for it."

12

Addie poured Dr. LaFleur a cup of coffee and set it before him at the kitchen table. Her hands trembled slightly; she could still smell the sickly sweet odors of ether and blood. The knot in her stomach had eased up somewhat, but the rest of her felt like it had been put together with frayed twine that was slowly shredding. Mechanically, she placed sugar and cream on the table also.

Bea had fed the boys, then brought them in to see their pa for a few minutes to reassure their minds before putting them to bed. Zeke was sound asleep, the effects of trauma and anesthetic, the doctor had said. The house was ominously quiet.

Addie sat down at the table and clutched her hands in her lap, trying to stifle the tearful, shaky feelings now that the worst was over. "Thank you for coming."

"There'll be hell to pay."

"Yes." Her eyes probed the doctor's for a long moment before she added, "Why?"

Christian shook his head, then raked back a lock of

coal-black hair, his onyx eyes taking on a faraway look. "Don't ask, Mrs. Claiborne."

Less than two months ago she would have been cowered to silence by such a cold command. Two months ago she wouldn't even have sat at a table with a man if she could have helped it, much less looked him straight in the eye. Now she rallied under a need greater than her fear or intimidation. Planting her palms on the table, she half rose to her feet to face him.

"If it had been one of the boys hurt instead of Zeke, he wouldn't have sent for you," she bit out desperately. "That scares me something powerful! Don't tell me not to ask."

Christian smiled humorlessly. "If it had been one of the boys, he wouldn't have needed my help. He's as skilled as I am, Mrs. Claiborne. Not as trained or experienced maybe, but just as competent with minor emergencies."

Addie's expression revealed her shock and confusion. "Didn't he tell you?" he continued, a subtle bitterness beneath his tone. "We studied medicine together in Philadelphia. The war cut short his education and took full advantage of mine. Zeke trained with me in the field but never went back to finish when the war was over. It wasn't possible with no money and a new wife to provide for." His black brows arched over cruel eyes. "A terrible waste, wouldn't you say?"

Addie didn't know what to say to the indifferent man seated before her. It almost felt as if he was testing her. His voice had held little concern, but there was disquiet in his spirit. After performing surgery as delicately as a woman embroiders silk, his hands gripped his coffee cup like he would crush it. For some inexplicable reason, it gave Addie courage.

"What happened between you?"

Christian's expression hardened, then closed over tight. He shoved back from the table and strolled to the window, looking restless and caged. "The leg is broken, whether from the bullet or a fall from his horse, I don't know. It's splinted but I don't want to set it with plaster until the stitches are removed. You'll need to check the bandages regularly. If infection sets in—"

"What happened?" she demanded, following him with a fortitude she hadn't known she possessed, driven by the need to understand the man lying helpless in the other room. It wasn't just concern for the children, as she had told Christian. It was concern for Zeke, for whatever had put the glimmer of loneliness in his eyes, for that part of him he kept locked away. For the first time in a lifetime, it seemed, she cared for something beyond just getting through the day.

She touched Christian's sleeve, and he cut her a damning stare, but she wasn't intimidated after watching him work so hard to save a life he supposedly despised. "Why do you hate him?"

"Hate him?" He chuckled then, the sound little more than a cold and mirthless rasp from deep in his throat. His lips curled at one corner in a sneer, but something abjectly painful was reflected in the narrowing of his eyes. "I don't hate him, Mrs. Claiborne."

Her eyes closed briefly. No, he'd have to feel something to be capable of hate. She gripped his sleeve tighter. "What happened to make you enemies?"

With the precise, detached manner of a man picking lint from his coat, he removed her fingers and stepped back. "Ask him." He collected his hat and surgical bag, then walked to the door. "I'll return in a few days to check on him. He won't welcome it, so it would be best not to forewarn him. Keep him quiet and the wounds clean until then."

"Wait!" she called, but he was gone, departing into a frigid, moonless night. "Oh, please wait," she whispered, and slumped back against the door, engulfed with guilt that she had driven him out when she should have performed the most basic courtesy and prepared him a meal and a bed by the fire. She wrapped her arms around her and held tight, but she couldn't get warm, couldn't stop the chills wracking her body.

"Lord, girl, you're exhausted!" Bea crossed the room, clucking like a mother hen. "Come on. Let's get you some sleep before you keel over."

Using the last of her physical and emotional strength, Addie stood upright, smiled gratefully at the older woman for coming to help, then burst into tears. "Oh, Bea," she cried, and crumpled back against the wall.

"Oh, good Lord!" Bea snapped, and hurried to put her arm around Addie's shoulder. "There, there," she crooned, patting Addie's back until the worst had subsided before leading her over to the table and easing her down in a chair. "Have you eaten?"

Addie shook her head, her face in her hands. "I can't."

"I s'pect not, but you've got to keep your strength up anyway." Ever practical, Bea poured coffee, then placed a few biscuits on the table. "Eat. It'll help."

The first bite sat like a stone in her belly. Addie pushed it away. "Sorry—"

"Don't apologize. With eight kids, we've had our share of trouble. I know just how you feel."

"Thank you for coming, Bea. I don't know what I would have done—"

"You'd have done just fine," Bea said abruptly. "Now,

let's settle a few things, then you can take yourself off to bed. Sam's already sent for the sheriff. I s'pect he'll be out tonight or in the morning. Either way I'll answer his questions so you can rest. I'll sleep with the boys for a day or so until you're feeling more yourself, and Luke will come over mornings and evenings to do chores until Zeke gits back on his feet."

Addie felt a rush of panic at the words and tried to ward it off. She'd been so worried about Zeke's health, she hadn't even thought of the ranch. There was no way she could handle Zeke's chores and hers as well. She didn't even know anything about raising cattle. The enormity of her situation overwhelmed her and she dropped her face back to her hands.

"Oh, Bea," she whispered. "What am I going to do? How am I going to keep everything going?"

There were no pat answers, so Bea didn't pretend. "Women have lost their men before. Some survive it, some don't. I believe those who make it, make the decision to do so. At least Zeke will recover. You just have to hold things together until then. We'll help out any way we can; so will the rest of the town."

Addie didn't feel like she could hold herself together, much less the ranch, at this point, but she nodded. For the boys' sake and Zeke's and her own, she'd have to make it, be a survivor not a failure. She just couldn't see how it was possible.

Bea watched determination settle on the frightened young woman's face. There would be rough times ahead, but she didn't think they would do Addie in. "Sam'll have the sheriff out here tomorrow, but it's not likely Jake'll find out anything." She shook her head, scorn and disgust in her voice. "It ain't fitting for good, God-fearing folks to need hired guns on their own property just to keep out the riffraff, but it might come to that." She rose from her seat, discussion over. "Now, try to git some rest."

"Bea." Addie stood and waited for the older woman to turn back. Bea obliged her but was slow about it, sensing what was to come and dreading it. "What happened between Zeke and Dr. LaFleur?"

Bea's brow creased as she shook her head. "It's not my way to meddle. I don't mess in other people's business when I can help it. I've never asked, and Zeke's never offered."

For someone reputed to be the town gossip, Bea certainly could clam up when it suited her. "Fine," Addie said stubbornly. "Tell me what you heard, then. I know you've heard something."

"It doesn't bear repeating," Bea said curtly. "Leave it at that."

Addie's neck ached from dozing in the rocking chair beside the bed. Deep sleep had been impossible, but she'd napped fitfully off and on through the rest of the night. Every cough or soft moan had jolted her awake and her body was feeling the ravages of a harrowing night as the sun crept weakly toward dawn.

Zeke's face was drawn and pale, the skin beneath his eyes a deep gray. Addie's heart contracted painfully. He looked aged and worn out, like a man who had started a race young and hearty but had simply run too long. She pressed the heels of her palms to her eyes. They burned from watching him through the long night, from trying not to cry.

She wanted to shake him and rail at him for getting himself shot. She wanted to scream until her throat hurt and cry until there were no tears left in her. She pulled her knees to her chest and huddled in the rocker, willing him to recover.

His chest rose and fell shallowly beneath the quilt, the bandages stark white against his bronze skin. Mostly, she wanted to crawl in bed beside him and put her ear on his chest, just to hear the reassuring beat of his heart. What were she and the boys going to do if something happened to Zeke?

A terrible dread settled in her chest, and memories jostled her mind. He was strong and handsome, a good provider. He cared for his sons with a fierce protectiveness gentled by concern, patient even when they were irascible and out of sorts. A little over three weeks ago, she'd seen him clench his fists to keep from shouting at Zeb, using his intellect instead of anger to win the argument. And Zeb, so precious and precocious with his big blue eyes, had stated his own case clearly and concisely, as he had learned to do by example. Zeke had listened, a long-suffering look on his face, then finally nodded.

The bunny, its life hanging in the balance, was sent back into the wild, instead of into the stew pot. Addie smiled softly, remembering Zeb's triumphant grin and Zeke's hidden one. She only realized later what that smile meant. Zeke had thought Zeb would push to keep the rabbit for a pet.

She closed her eyes and sighed. One lonesome tear escaped her thick lashes and rolled down her cheek. With Willis she'd never dared to hope for anything but a way out. But with Zeke . . . what was she going to do if anything happened to him?

The truth came softly, like a fresh spring wind ruffling sweetly through the wheat grass, a whisper in her heart. She loved him. She'd known it from the moment she found him injured in the barn, and later while she watched Christian work to save his life. Her hand rose to cover her mouth as the reality sank deeper still. Love? She had never thought to feel the emotion for any man after Willis, had not thought it possible to open her heart and leave it so vulnerable. She squeezed her eyes shut to hold back a rush of hot, insipid tears. *Stupid, ignorant Addie. How could you be so foolish?*

His words rolled through her mind like torpid water. *If I lived closer to town, I'd hire you to come out and care for the boys on a daily basis.* They had an arrangement, nothing more. Zeke wouldn't appreciate her getting all sentimental. *I need more from you than a cold shoulder at night.* Yes, he wanted more, wanted her in the way she feared a good woman would shun. He had no more care or concern for her feelings than Willis had. Zeke was just a better man. The thought made her unwell and she dropped her head to her knees and rocked, hurting.

A murmured oath from the bed sent her lunging from the chair. She rested her palm on Zeke's forehead and found it only slightly warm. He moved restlessly and growled another obscenity before his eyes opened, disoriented at first, then seemed to focus.

"He gone?"

"Yes," she whispered. "Be still, you'll pull the stitches."

He seemed to settle for a moment, then stirred again. "The chores—"

"Luke's coming to help. The doctor left morphine for the pain," she added, "and a Wood's endodermal syringe he said you knew how to use."

Zeke nodded wearily, then carefully rotated his shoulder to determine the extent of damage. His neck and shoulder hurt like hellfire but there was no violent pain shooting down toward his fingers, no injury to the brachial plexus of the nerves. His leg was a different matter. He flexed it gingerly and had to grit his teeth against the pain.

"Stop that!" Addie demanded, flinching herself at the agony on his face.

Zeke sent her a baleful glare, then rested his head back on the pillow. "I ought to tan your hide for bringing him here."

"As if you could, the state you're in," she argued tremulously. "He saved your life!" She froze, remembering the accusation and betrayal on his face, and her own hurt.

Zeke smiled weakly at her spunk, and she realized with shock that he wasn't truly angry. "The boys all right?" he asked.

"They're concerned but fine."

"You?"

She was falling apart inside. "I'm fine."

"Good," he sighed. "Day twenty-eight."

A second of bewilderment entered her eyes, then Addie blushed scarlet, spun around, and dashed for the kitchen.

Zeke closed his eyes and smiled. With just a few words, he'd managed to knock a century's worth of worry from her expression.

He was a monster! A tyrant! A bully! Addie was awakened the next five mornings by a rush of swear words followed by a groan of frustration and pain. The leg wasn't healing as quickly as Zeke wanted, and he had refused to take the morphine. He simply, utterly, vociferously, didn't adapt well to inactivity. By the third day he was irritable and restless, by the fifth he was scorning her help.

Addie entered the bedroom and found Zeke trying to stand. Sweat beaded his brow and white lines etched around his grim mouth. By the time he slumped back on the bed in pain and exhaustion, they were both angry.

She gripped the breakfast tray she carried tighter but couldn't seem to get a grip on her tongue. "Dang-fool man, your leg is broken! You're not supposed to be on it. If you bust those stitches open—"

"What day is it, Addie?" he gritted out, his eyes bright with the fever that had never fully left him.

Turning beet red, Addie slammed the tray down on the bedside table and hurried out of the room, but Zeke's "Day twenty-four!" echoed loudly through the slammed door.

Beatrice looked up from the eggs she was dishing out for the boys. "Twenty-four?" she asked.

Addie skirted the question and began taking biscuits out of the oven. "You shouldn't have come in this weather. It could get nasty today."

Beatrice just shrugged, her eyes shrewd. "It'll blow over by noon. Figured you could use a rest. Thought I'd take the boys back with me for a few days as soon as Luke finishes chores."

Whoops of delight from the table had Addie smiling, but she declined. "We're doing just fine, but I appreciate the offer."

Zeb whined and turned pleading eyes her way. "C'mon, Ma, please!"

Josh wouldn't beg, she knew, but the eager look he tried to hide had Addie reconsidering. Zeke's infirmity had been hard on the boys. She'd kept them quiet so he could rest, but so much inactivity wasn't normal. They were getting more restless without a physical outlet for their energy, and their childish squabbles were growing more frequent with less provocation. "Maybe just a day or so?"

Zeb whooped again and jumped up from his seat. Addie caught him halfway to the bedroom and steered him back toward the table. "I'll pack your things. You finish breakfast."

Addie continued to wave long after the Parkers' wagon faded from sight. The wind had a wicked bite, but she ignored the sting on her cheeks and nose. She'd never been in the house without one or more of the boys and was loath to return to its tomblike quiet. Her empty arms were already hungry for the plump warm heaviness of Cole, her heart lonely for Zeb's smile. Even Josh had been more approachable since the accident, if hesitant about it.

She hugged herself against the cold and loneliness and breathed deeply, filling her lungs with the crisp, clean air. The ground was covered in a blanket of white, unmarred except for wagon tracks as far as the eye could see. Evergreens stood boldly against the azure sky, their branches heavy-laden. It was beauty in its purest, most untouched state. She studied the perspective, the lines and angles and depth, then the blend of hues. Bolder colors stained the foreground, muted shades in the distance. To capture the dimensions wouldn't be difficult, but the exact blurring of pigment would provide a much greater challenge.

A doe slipped shyly from the edge of the woods, bringing motion to the landscape. It sniffed the air, wary, ready to dash for cover. Addie knew the protective instincts that governed the animal. Stay quiet, move carefully, watch for danger in hidden places.

She was startled to realize she didn't feel that way

anymore. She felt concern for Zeke and the boys, but for herself she felt nothing but a driving desire to hold on to the contentment she had learned since coming here. Something startled the doe and she quivered, immobile for a split second, then sprang for the cover of the woods.

The moment was lost and Addie hurried back into the house to escape the cold. Zeke, wrapped only in a sheet, was braced against the bedroom doorframe, supporting his weight on his uninjured leg.

"The boys gone?"

She nodded. "I miss them already."

"It's just for a few days," he said. "The change will do them good."

She nodded again and diverted her gaze from his broad shoulders. They went on forever, golden and muscular and dusted with hair that tapered off in a line down his trim belly. Although he was a mite thinner than before, it was his eyes that had really changed. They were vibrant, more vital, as if his brush with death had somehow livened him. The sheet rode low on his hips, vivid white against his darker skin.

The perfection and balance of just such anatomy must have been the spark that ignited the Renaissance masters into deepening the imaginary space in their paintings, pulling to the forefront more solid-looking portraitures and distinctive characteristics.

He ran his hand idly over his chest and Addie's throat suddenly went dry as dust. The Sistine Chapel's frescoes had nothing on Zeke Claiborne.

She tried to swallow. "You should be in bed."

"Come with me."

Addie blinked, puzzled. She'd taken to sleeping beside him at night because he had insisted, but the idea of her returning to bed midday was ludicrous. "It's barely noon."

"So it is," he said lazily.

"But . . ." She tilted her head to the side, at a loss.

Zeke thought the gesture eloquent of her diverse nature. She had been married for years, yet didn't seem to have a clue about what he wanted. He knew she was afraid of him because of Willis, but there was no anger or fear in her eyes now, just a beguiling sort of innocence that made no sense at all.

Layered in complexity, at times she appeared as naive as a virgin, at others she panicked at the mere thought of kissing him. Her temperance was frustrating, stemming not just from shyness, but more from a mistrust he didn't personally deserve. He couldn't fault her for it, but he wanted, needed, to find a way around it. He was restless, too confined by his wounds to exercise the energy building in him with hard work as he had been doing for the past two months.

Realistically, he didn't expect her to jump naked into his bed with a jaunty smile on her face, but he would be satisfied at this point with a demure nod of agreement. He ran his fingers through his hair, mildly disgusted with himself for his wayward thoughts, but he couldn't help that either. For days she had been tending him with a care and gentleness as seductive as her naïveté. Her hands touched and soothed, her voice refreshed, her scent drifted through his senses constantly, pulling the latent fires of desire back to the forefront of his thoughts and keeping him on the restless edge of comfort. He was bored and aroused, a dangerous combination. That his thoughts would turn to a more intimate form of exercise was normal, he supposed, but that didn't make the situation any easier to endure.

Standing against the doorframe trying to figure her out exhausted him more than he had anticipated. His leg was throbbing, his limbs heavy and tired. Lying in the bed earlier he'd been randy as a stallion after a mare, but physical exertion had stolen the eagerness from him in the worst way—a lingering arousal without the energy to do anything about it now. *Some stud, Claiborne. If you had managed to get her into bed, you probably would have collapsed before the lovemaking started.*

Addie, her head still tilted guilelessly, began to grow concerned about the pallor of his skin. "You shouldn't be up," she admonished, then crossed the room and took his arm to help him.

Irritated by his weakness, Zeke let himself be led back to the edge of the bed, though he refused to lie down. He rubbed the bristles on his jaw and gave Addie a dubious look. "I could use a bath and a shave." He could see right off the suggestion got her good and flustered, but ever dutiful, she nodded and left to get the tub.

When she returned dragging a hip bath, her cheeks were warm pink. Zeke figured she was running through every excuse imaginable to get out of helping him. He immediately, and without one ounce of guilt, became the consummate invalid.

She held out a towel and soap. "I'll just go on back to the kitchen . . ."

Zeke hung his head. "I don't think I can do it on my own."

Dang man, he'd made it to the kitchen on his own. But Addie could see it had tired him in the worst way. The words he'd once spoken to her seemed prophetic now. A person *could* lose a considerable amount of dignity when ill and needing care. She just wasn't sure whose dignity was in question here, since her husband didn't appear one bit self-conscious or concerned.

Taking a deep breath for support, she crossed to the bed. Bracing her shoulder under his arm, she helped him rise. His weight was heavy leaning into her, his forearm sluggish over her shoulder. With every step she took, his limp hand brushed over her breast, sending sharp prickles to her middle and an indelicate moistness elsewhere. She stifled a confused gasp and bit the inside of her mouth. Hunching her shoulders, she helped him hobble over to the bath.

Zeke grimaced at the small stool she had placed beside the tub but knew better than to risk getting his stitches wet. He cut her a glance as he tugged on the sheet at his waist. "Close your eyes before you faint." That got her back up and she looked straight at him.

"I've seen a naked man before." *But not one quite so well formed or strong looking,* she thought when he gave her a glittering look and boldly dropped the sheet to the floor. Her eyes flew to her feet to keep from staring at him with unabashed and indecent curiosity.

She heard him groan when he eased down to sit on the stool, keeping his injured leg straight, and the sound went straight to her heart. She swallowed back a generous amount of trepidation and leaned over to dip the washcloth in the water. She soaped it vigorously then stopped. She didn't have the slightest clue where to begin.

Zeke reached for a towel and draped it over his lap before she fell unconscious. "Just pretend I'm Zeb or Cole," he said.

Fat chance she was going to be able to liken him to one of his sons, but she tried anyway as she knelt down behind him and found it wasn't so bad since she didn't

have to look at his face while scrubbing his back and
sides. A funny feeling took up residence in her stomach
and intensified as she smoothed the damp cloth over his
tanned flesh.

His muscles were ridged, rising and sloping in marvelous angles that defined tensile strength and beauty. As
she was absorbed in the wonder of examining him, the
cloth slipped unnoticed from her hand, leaving only the
heightened sensitivity of bare fingers on soapy flesh.
Her hands sculpted his back, feeling the texture and
formation of contours as a potter would study clay, and
traced the glistening broad planes and hollows. With
fascination, her hands bathed him from neck to hips,
but her eyes devoured. He had the most beautiful skin.

Zeke felt the bath cloth slide down his spine, then
Addie's bare hands. Her touch startled him. It was neither a caress nor an exploration, but seemed a combination of both. Lines and circles formed, bisecting each
other in intricate patterns on his skin, creating mild
chaos inside him. *What are you doing, Addie? Playing,
teasing, seducing?* There was blatant interest in her
touch, but whether clinical or sensuous, he couldn't tell.
The only thing he was certain about was the mélange of
emotions and sensations assaulting his very control. His
spine tingled as the pads of her fingers delicately explored and discovered every inch, warm on cool places,
stirring in him a heat and an uncomfortable awareness
of how far apart they were in their desires.

With an effort, he remained still under her questing
hands, allowing her the freedom of touching without
consequences, though he would suffer plenty for insti-
gating this. The rinse water was warm as it flowed over
his back, the palms of Addie's hands even warmer as
they slicked away the soap. Zeke tipped his head for-

ward, both relaxed and aroused by the unaccustomed intimacy.

On the excuse of pouring the last of the water from the pitcher, Addie rose to her feet and sneaked another peek at the cleft of his buttocks. The sight caused a strange flutter in her belly and a sharpness of breath she couldn't govern. Her eyes traveled back up the virile curve of his spine to the slightly darker skin of his back and powerful arms. Then, with the most indecent display of curiosity she'd ever felt, she leaned forward and sneaked a look over his shoulder.

His chest muscles were well defined, sloping down to a tight narrow waist. She bit her lip on an inhaled breath and craned her neck to look even farther down. Her cheeks were throbbing with color when she found a towel, so white against his dark legs, draped over his lap. There was heat inside her now, fiery in places once cold and empty. A tingle of expectation surged along her limbs, as if her skin were too new and tight on her body to fit properly. Bright and bell-like, it felt as if one touch would send it clanging. She pulled back quickly and took a moment to compose herself, knowing she couldn't stay behind him forever.

With more determination than nerve, she eased around to his front and reached for the soap. Flustered, she realized her hands were empty. Her brow puckered in confusion as she stared at her open palms, then looked around until she found the cloth on the floor.

"Your hands feel better," Zeke said, entranced by the mixture of confusion and embarrassment in her eyes. Steamy tendrils of hair stuck to her flushed cheeks. He reached up and smoothed them back.

The flutter in Addie's belly became a sharp twist. Looking anywhere but where she needed to, she resoaped her hands and began scrubbing a good portion of his upper body without an ounce of the finesse with which she had explored his back. The hair on his chest was smooth and curly, but not so thick that she couldn't feel the sleek skin beneath. She liked the diversity in texture but didn't linger there, not with him steadily staring her in the face.

Skipping his whole midsection, she moved lower and began bathing the ankle of his uninjured leg, then eased up his calf and shin and finally made it to his knee when something happened. The towel on his lap moved. Her gaze shot to his, confused at first, then her cheeks flooded with color.

Zeke choked on a burst of painful laughter and gripped the edge of the tub when the motion jarred his leg. His wife's cheeks were on fire, her eyes practically bugging out of her pretty head. He wanted to tell her it was something he couldn't control, a perfectly normal reaction to having her hands all over him, but she'd probably run for the hills.

Addie heard plenty of vitality in his laugh and not one ounce of shame. She sent him a glare that would split wood, snatched up the bath cloth from the floor, and shoved it at him. "If you've got that much energy, you can do it yourself."

Zeke grabbed her wrist before she could get away and tugged her back. "Addie, wait." Chagrin did wonderful things to her cheeks and eyes. "What's got you so riled?"

Her gaze inadvertently dropped to his lap, then flew back up. "I . . ." Her hands twisted the cloth, wringing a cascade of water down her skirt.

Zeke gently tugged it from her hands. "It's a normal

reaction, Addie. I couldn't help myself." He smiled wryly. "I'm injured, but I'm not dead."

Her gaze shied off and he tugged on her wrist, placing her fingers back on his chest. His hand covered hers and began rotating it in a swirling design on the soapy residue she'd forgotten to rinse away. Dizziness invaded her throat and knees. He had the nicest skin, so dark against her fairness, so warm and smooth against the cool tremors inside her. His fingers stroked the back of her hand, then the delicate underside of her wrist, making her breath catch in little furies in her breasts, and finally on the small erratic pulse there, pressing on it with erotic deliberation.

Zeke watched her face grow absorbed, misty and dreamlike; her lashes fluttered, then stilled to rest on her cheeks. Hunger made a clawing mess of his insides. "Come on and finish," he said evenly. "You missed a few spots."

Green-flecked eyes flew open, and she snatched her hand from his grasp. "I think you can manage," she said airlessly, then spun on her heel and rushed from the room.

Which was just as well, Zeke reasoned, after suppressing the urge to go after her. The parts of him at painful attention couldn't take much more of her tender ministrations. If she'd come any nearer with her gentle touch and blushing cheeks, he might have lost whatever sanity he claimed.

Finishing the bath on his own was awkward and painful. Once done, he hobbled back to the bed, so truly exhausted now he ached with it. He eased down on the mattress, pulled his injured leg up, then collapsed against the headboard. Addie must have been waiting by the door, because she came in as soon as the bed squeaked.

She had a pitcher in one hand, a towel in the other, and a contrite look on her face. "Thought I'd wash your hair and help you shave," she murmured, feeling guilty for abandoning him, even if he wasn't completely incapacitated. Hiding in the kitchen, she'd heard his struggles to finish, his lumbering steps to get back to the bed, and her heart had hurt for the childish way she'd stormed out on him.

Wading through her confusion to face herself hadn't been easy, but she had done it. The truth was buried deep in her heart, a bit unstable for its newness, but there nonetheless. Though he might never love her, he was everything she needed in a husband, strong and capable and gentle. And she wanted to be whatever he needed in a wife also, so he'd never have a reason to regret marrying her.

"I'm sorry I stormed out on you."

Zeke couldn't begin to fathom the reasons behind her mood change, but at her apology a hint of remorse nudged his conscience at the way he had provoked her. "I didn't mean to embarrass you."

She dismissed his words with a shake of her head. "I'm too sensitive, I know. Even as a child. I can't seem to correct it."

He wondered when sensitivity had become a crime. He watched her fingers clench and unclench on the towel. "Tell me how it was for you, how you were sensitive."

She gave him a bemused look, then smiled softly in remembrance. "Little things mostly. My brothers were great teasers and they outnumbered me. They were always playing pranks or leaping out from behind doors to startle me. I would jump a mile high, which set them laughing." She shrugged, undisturbed. "I never thought it was very funny, though.

"There were a lot of us. Four brothers and a baby sister. There wasn't much quiet around our house. It seemed I never had enough time for myself." Her eyes clouded. "Funny how things change. I miss that now, the noise and teasing. I'd give anything to have them back."

There was no self-pity in her words, just honesty, a thing she'd come to realize too late. A thickness clogged Zeke's throat and limbs. Her words brought him intimately into the girl she had been, and he regretted the fact that he had coaxed her to elaborate. He didn't want to know her that way, as a person apart from the woman who cared for his children, the woman who would one day share his bed. There was security for him in the strangers they were, no obligation to feel things he was unable or unwilling to feel.

In the silence her gaze had wandered, touching him, studying him, artless in her scrutiny. Arousing. She had no defenses at all beyond her fear. He wondered if that was why she clung to it so tenaciously . . . and why he was so determined to breach it.

His eyes swept her, drawn to the fullness of her small breasts, the slenderness of her hips. "There will be other times," he said, "other . . . embarrassments. In a marriage there's no way around it, Addie."

She nodded jerkily. "I know."

He glanced at the pitcher and towel she held. "Have your way with me then."

She did, and her way was a luxury he hadn't anticipated. She dragged the hip bath next to the bed and had him lie sideways across the mattress and lean his head back over the edge. She wet and lathered his hair, then began to scrub. Her hands were firm and gentle, massaging his scalp in a continuous rhythm that almost put him to sleep.

But he didn't close his eyes just yet. The view from this angle was too intriguing. An apron protected her dress but did nothing to hide her shape. If anything, it intensified the dips and curves of her slender frame. She'd gained weight over the past two months. Not much, but enough to round out the unnaturally sunken places. She'd never be lush, but she had enough fullness in all the right places to make his nerves spring to the surface of his skin, tight and edgy and hungry.

He closed his eyes to block out the sight, but memories weren't like dreams that fade with the morning, especially ones so fresh. They needed little prodding to remain vivid images behind his shut lids. He forced himself to concentrate on the rhythm of her fingers, the soothing stroke and flow of her touch.

In this, she seemed confident and uninhibited, as if she had done it countless times and it held no bad recollections. Maybe even pleasant ones, for her fingers were tireless, and she seemed to drift into her own world with the motion of her hands, humming as she worked.

"You enjoy this," he commented.

"I did it for my mother. She liked it."

"Me too," he sighed. It meant something; he wasn't sure what. Maybe that they could find common ground in the things she had known before marrying Willis.

He should have seen it sooner, how she was natural with the boys because she had cared for younger siblings, how she could cook and care for the house because she had helped her mother. All the discomfort she felt with him came from the four years after her family's death. It wasn't possible to erase those years, but he wondered if he could help soften them to the degree that they no longer intruded on the present. He could see the things she needed in a family—stability, companionship, nurturing, a place to be needed. She gave all of that to the boys. But what did she need in a husband?

Hell, Claiborne. What you really mean is what do you have to do to get her into bed?

Yes.

He was becoming obsessed. He should be concentrating on a way to hold the ranch together instead of conniving a way to hold her. He sighed deeply. He could ask her what she wanted from him, but he knew her well enough by now to know she would only look at him strangely and say she had everything she needed. Which wouldn't be at all true, not for a healthy young woman, but he was fairly certain she didn't realize that. He damned Willis for destroying the desire inside her, when nature had so graciously sculpted the outside of her to tempt him.

He shifted to ease the ever-present ache of being deprived. It was a conspiracy, nature against man, and man was losing. His fist tightened on the sheet. He had thought he was getting a woman who would take care of his house and his children and make no undue demands on him—not on his life or his emotions or his libido. But time had wrought changes. She looked healthier, smiled readily at the children and sometimes at him, and she was driving him utterly insane with her chaste disposition.

He stared up into her earnest face. "Did Willis like this as well?"

He felt her hands tense, then relax slowly as if by sheer dint of will. "I don't know."

"You didn't do it for him?"

"No."

She was scrubbing harder now, taking bits of his scalp. Zeke bit back an oath and grabbed her hand. "Was there anything about him you liked?"

"No."

He pulled his head up and smiled up into her angry eyes. "Is there anything about *me* you like?"

"Yes," she said, but her gaze shied away. She pulled her hand from beneath his and began scrubbing more gently. "I like everything about you . . . except when you ask questions about him."

Smiling, he rested his head back in her palm and murmured, "You don't like it when I touch you."

A pause. "No. Don't ask why." She picked up a pitcher of water and began rinsing the soap from his hair.

"I can't read your mind, Addie. How am I supposed to know what frightens you and what doesn't?"

He made too much sense for her to ignore the question, but she could skirt the answer. "You said I could have time."

End of discussion. He could sense it in the perfunctory way she hurried to finish. She towel-dried his hair, then helped him sit up. She wasn't adept with the razor but soaped his face and held the mirror while he scraped the stubble from his cheeks and chin. She was comfortable with the silence, so Zeke knew she wasn't nervous, but she wasn't opening up the conversation again either.

She had him move to a chair while she changed the bed linens, and he found himself less exhausted watching the sway of her hips as she moved around the bed, the rounded curve of her bottom when she bent over to tuck in the sheet. *Hell.*

He gripped the arms of the chair. If he reached out just the shortest distance he could touch . . . nothing. She was already moving around to the other side. He rested back in the rocker, fed up with himself, trapped in an ill body that was healing too slowly in some places, but was still too all-fire healthy in others.

Addie took a deep breath to steady herself and opened the door when the knock sounded. She had recognized the doctor from a distance and was glad for his presence, yet dismayed by the fact that Zeke was going to be furious. He'd already warned her not to let Christian back in. She nodded a greeting and led the doctor to the bedroom door, then hung back, loath to enter with him. He carried the same old cracked leather bag he had brought before and another hinged wooden box marked SURGEON'S COMPANION. She looked at the box, then at him.

"Isinglass plaster for securing splints."

She nodded and stepped back like a coward, then had to endure his mocking smile as he walked past her into the room.

Zeke spared Christian little more than a burning glance before he snapped, "Get out. I'll remove the stitches this afternoon myself."

"Like hell." Christian nonchalantly lowered himself into the rocker and faced the bed. "I'll stop coming by when you're strong enough to throw me out."

"How do you know I'm not now?"

"Your lady's still got that worried look. You're weak as a lamb, Claiborne."

Zeke's tone grew caustic. "Enjoying yourself? The great hero coming to the rescue."

"I saved your life," Christian drawled with immense satisfaction. "Show some gratitude, you bastard."

"I'll see you in hell first."

The doctor laughed sharply. "You probably will. You and me and Jake giving the devil his due." He rose from the chair and nodded at the door. "Don't upset her, it's not worth it."

Zeke despised hearing the truth, but said nothing as Christian examined the wounds, removed the stitches, then resplinted the leg. He could endure the man's presence one last time out of regard for Addie.

But when Christian was finished he sat down again and set the rocking chair in motion. Eyeing Zeke levelly, he said, "You bedded her yet?"

Zeke slammed his fist into the bedding. "Get the hell out!"

Christian's brows lifted over knowing black eyes. "I didn't think so."

Zeke rolled as if coming out of the bed, sending excruciating pain tearing through his leg. Christian launched from the chair and loomed over him.

"Lie down or I'll sedate you," he hissed through his teeth. "There are some things I think you should know. Listen to me first, then you can toss me out."

Hatred burned from Zeke's eyes, but the weakness consuming him could not be ignored. He slumped back against the pillow, enraged but too incapacitated to vent it.

Christian turned away and walked to the window. Bracing his hand on the sill, he stared out at the pasture, barn, and corral, seeing the evidence of Zeke's hard work turning slowly into prosperity. It had taken

Zeke years to achieve the success that lay just beyond spring round up, but Becky hadn't been able to wait that long, hadn't wanted to. She hadn't, Christian knew, been capable of it. He wondered if Zeke had ever accepted that.

But he hadn't come for a rehashing of old hatreds and turned the thoughts aside to speak his peace before Zeke killed himself trying to get rid of him.

"Addie came to me little over a year ago, half dead from infection," he began. "She wouldn't explain her problem, wouldn't let me examine her, just begged for medicine. If she hadn't fainted in the office from walking to town with a raging fever, I think she would have left without treatment."

He turned and looked at Zeke, revulsion on his face. "When I examined her, I found hideous bruises on her buttocks and thighs and abdomen."

Zeke gripped the sheet. It was nothing more than he had expected, but hearing it made it far worse. "What else?"

"She was still a virgin."

Zeke's eyes flared then narrowed. It made perfect sense; it made no sense at all. "It's not possible."

"It's possible. That perverted bastard she married wasn't capable of performing and was apparently taking it out on her. He was known to frequent Ruby's, so I asked the girls and they verified my assumption. He would blame them for his impotence and slap them around. It was the only way he could get satisfaction. He paid in gold, so Ruby wouldn't toss him out, but the experienced women wouldn't have anything to do with him anymore, only the newer ones who needed the money."

Zeke shut his eyes against the horror. "You lousy son

of a bitch," he said, his voice tinged with bitterness and old hatred. "Why didn't you get her away from Willis when you found out?" His eyes opened and blazed into Christian's. The poison of the old betrayal, the loss of a man he had once thought his best friend was there now, revealed also in the terrible tone of his voice. "You didn't think twice about cuckolding me and trying to run off with Becky. Why couldn't you have been so magnanimous with Addie?"

Christian lurched back as if he'd been slugged. His words hissed out in a ghostly whisper. "Are you insane? I never touched Becky."

They had never confronted the issue openly, just let their hatred build over the months since Becky's death. Zeke felt at a disadvantage lying flat on his back, but couldn't stop the words. "Liar. You were with her when she died. She was going off with you, leaving three defenseless sons to fend for themselves until I got in from the fields. Damn you, Christian, Cole was barely two months old."

Christian looked away, shielding himself from the vengeful hurt in Zeke's eyes, the pain of his own memories and guilt. Damn Becky and her shattered dreams. With excruciating clarity, he remembered her that day, her eyes too bright and determined as she tied a portmanteau to the saddle and mounted, never looking back at the house that held her three sons. Josh had run after her, begging her not to go. The horse had reared up when she screamed at him to return to the house.

He swung his attention back to Zeke. "Yes, I was willing to take her away, but as a friend, not a lover. She was dying here, couldn't you see that? She wasn't raised this way. The life was too hard."

"It's hard on all of us," Zeke growled. "What the hell

else was I supposed to do? Take her back to Natchez? There was nothing there. Everything was gone. She knew that, so did you!"

Christian paced by the window, seeing Becky's lovely tearful face, her desperate pleading. "I couldn't convince her of that any more than you could, and I couldn't leave her here to waste away. For God's sake, we grew up together. She was Hope's best friend! I couldn't let Becky die too."

"You had no right," Zeke grated out painfully. "You lost Hope to a fever. You had no right to take my wife in her place."

Christian rounded on him in fury, too much anger and guilt and recrimination rushing at him for him to contain it. "No, but you did. It was your duty to try to help her. You know what this land does to its women. You've watched them grow old and withered before their time as often as I have. Why didn't you get Becky out? How could you just get her pregnant year after year and expect her to hold up under the strain? For every child she brought to term, she lost one in between," he said acridly. "You rutting bastard, how could you do that to her?"

Zeke's fists tightened on the sheets. They'd tried everything he knew to avoid conception. Nothing had worked with Becky, and neither of them had been capable of abstinence.

"She was raised in a house where slaves did everything," Christian continued ruthlessly. "I doubt she'd ever lifted anything heavier than a silver teaspoon."

He turned back to the window, unable to look at Zeke any longer. His voice, drained of wrath, was tired and old, filled with derision for himself and Zeke. "She was too pampered for this kind of life. You weren't willing to save her; I was."

"By taking her from me?" Zeke whispered hollowly. "You killed her."

"No." Christian's voice was deadly quiet when he turned back, his eyes black as hell. "Although I was willing to take her to Natchez, I had come that day to try to stop her, to talk some sense into her. She killed herself, Zeke. Just lay there with Josh screaming while the horse trampled her. I don't think she could feel anything at that point but her own internal suffering."

Hot, ragged breaths rasped through Zeke's throat as he fought not to cry like a baby or murder Christian in cold blood. Josh's pain sliced through him, crippling him. He finally understood his son's resentment and withdrawal and his complete resistance to accepting Addie. "I got the herd built up and ready for market," he said thickly. "Just one more year and she would have had all the help she needed, gone anywhere she wanted. I told her that time and again. Just one more year."

Christian stared at Zeke but saw only the young men they had once been. Arrogant and privileged and indescribably happy. "One year or one month," he said dully. "Your prosperity meant nothing to Becky but a stronger trap. She couldn't see an end to it. She never got over leaving Natchez and the life she had known, kept holding on to the dream that things would return to the way they were before the war. She never stopped thinking that the past would right itself and you would take her back home where she would be the princess again and wife of the prominent doctor."

His voice was grainy but his eyes held no accusation, placed no blame. "But you had given up your medical career, and the more successful you became at ranching, the more her chances of returning slipped away."

Zeke wanted to deny it all, but the truth settled blackly in his soul, suffocating him. "I asked for one more year. She promised me one more year."

Christian glanced away, not as immune to Zeke's agony as he had imagined. "I think she meant it at the time." He shrugged, weary to death of carrying the bitterness. "A week before the accident, she came to my office half-crazed. She suspected she was pregnant again and wanted me to do something about it. When I refused to help her, she threatened to go off on her own, claimed she knew a woman outside of New Orleans who performed abortions."

Zeke stared back at Christian in silence, dead inside to everything but the excruciating pain. "Why didn't you tell me?"

Christian raised his hand in a helpless gesture. "I thought it would blow over. She was nursing a newborn, for God's sake, I didn't think she could possibly be pregnant so soon. I knew she was distraught, not thinking rationally, but I didn't know how far she would take it. When I realized she was serious about going off alone, I tried to stop her."

"You had no right to keep it from me," Zeke whispered roughly. "You were supposed to be my friend."

"I was her friend too, and her doctor," Christian said coldly. "I'll never forgive myself for what happened to Becky, but I'll never forgive you either for not seeing what she needed, for planting your seed year after year and not realizing what it was doing to her."

"She wanted children—"

The words fell off into hollow silence. There was no way to excuse himself, not his uncontrolled passion or his inability or unwillingness to see what was happening to his wife. He had courted Becky before the war, then had married her in a fever of patriotic fervor before the tide had turned in the North's favor. Young and idealistic, they had thought their love would conquer all.

She had claimed to want children from the beginning. But what she really wanted was what other women of her social rank had, offspring they could cherish and take pride in while a wet nurse and mammy took care of raising them.

Christian picked up his medical bag. "Until the end she kept trying, waiting for it to change. When she realized it wouldn't, she couldn't accept it."

Zeke closed his eyes, hurting worse than he thought humanly possible, betrayed all over again by Becky's mental weakness and defection, powerless to change what he hadn't known was wrong or had refused to see, stripped even of the ability to completely blame Christian. "Go," he whispered. "You've had your say, now go."

Christian turned to leave, but paused when he reached the door. "Addie's not like her."

Zeke just shook his head. No, Addie was strong. She had endured far worse than Becky, yet kept going, kept surviving. Addie who loved and cared for three children whose own mother had abandoned them. "Just go. Please."

Submerged under guilt and bitterness, Zeke lay in the silence after Christian's departure, hurting for Becky, hating her because he hadn't been good enough. He had promised to return her to Natchez after the herd was sold, for a visit—or a lifetime if she couldn't reconcile returning west. For almost seven years they had endured the hardship of starting over, trying to put the war behind them in order to build a future for their children. Why had it been so impossible for her to wait one more year? Her whispered words reverberated in his mind, memories once sweet now turned stale.

You love it here, Zeke. The work, the challenge, the reward. You love it all.

His gut clenched. Her words hadn't been an observation but an accusation. He wanted to shout back at her with all the fury of his betrayed feelings. Yes, he loved every bit of it but not more than he had loved her. A terrible tremor seized him and he gripped the sheet in a feverish fist. He had known she was unsuited for life out west, but with nothing back home to return to, he had thought Becky would adjust, had needed for her to. Perhaps she had sensed it, his desperation for her to love the new life they had built as much as he did.

There was no turning back. Becky was gone and he could never make amends. He could only go forward with Addie. The thought of Addie sent another tremor through him. Becky had never been able to handle the strain of ranch life when he was hale; how would Addie even hope to hold up with him confined to the bed? Even if she was capable of handling the work, he couldn't allow her to ride the range and put herself at risk. He knew Luke had been helping with the chores, but there was much more to running the ranch than putting out feed in the evenings.

He gripped the headboard behind him and shifted. His leg throbbed miserably, but it was nothing compared to his internal anguish. He glanced at the morphine on the bedside table and gritted his teeth to keep from reaching for its mind-numbing euphoria.

Damn the unfair world to hell and back.

13

Addie stared out the window at the approaching riders. There were three of them, bulky looking in winter garb, their faces obscured by distance. She clutched a loaded rifle by her side. If they meant trouble, she was pretty sure she could fire it. She didn't know if she could hit anything, but the gun's presence might be enough to scare them off. She hoped.

She glanced at the bedroom door and fought the urge to wake Zeke, knowing there was little he could do in his condition if the riders proved enemy rather than friend. She was loath to bother him anyway. He'd been strangely withdrawn after the doctor's visit, his eyes remote but haunted, as if he fought some inner torture.

Everything she had been conditioned to feel over the past four years had been suddenly turned inside out, and she didn't know how to assimilate it. She had expected him to be angry at her for defying his orders to keep Christian away, but he had said nothing at all when the doctor left, and his reticence frightened her as his anger never had. The hard, vacant look on his face had been alarming.

Addie braced herself when the riders dismounted, tethered their horses, then walked up the steps and knocked. She opened the door a crack.

"Miz Claiborne?"

She nodded and stared suspiciously at the rough-looking characters. They were dressed in canvas pants, high-heeled boots, and coats made of wool or buckskin or fur. Two were bearded to the extent that not much more than their eyes and patches of weather-toughened skin showed beneath their hats. The other was fresh-cheeked as a boy, but his eyes defied any association with youth. They were hard eyes, gutter-wise and aloof, disdaining beforehand any preconceived notion one might have of his youthfulness.

Addie had never seen the boy in her life, but her heart went out immediately to this person she knew intimately. As she had with Josh, she sensed a kindred soul, one who had been battered by life and was forced to fight back with only an inborn instinct for survival to guide him. She pulled her eyes away and glanced back at the other two and their trappings.

All had rifles strapped to their saddles, gun belts at their hips, and wicked-looking knives encased in leather scabbards. Unclean and unshaven, the men had a mangy, cur-dog appearance that she found impossible to warm up to. The horses tethered behind them looked better cared for than the men themselves.

She gripped the rifle tighter. "How can I help you?"

"Sheriff Holdman sent us," the tallest one said. He was huge, bearlike in size and appearance. Even the deep timbre of his voice was grizzly. "I'm Granger, this here's Afton, and over there's Scrapper." The other two touched their hat brims and nodded.

Addie's fingers relaxed slightly on the gun at the mention of Jake. "What do you want?"

"Sheriff said your man was laid up, a problem with rustlers. Thought you could use some help. We sure could use the work."

Addie's eyes narrowed. These three looked as disreputable as any outlaw rustler she could imagine. "You hired guns?"

The one called Granger smiled, showing tobacco-stained teeth. "We like to think of ourselves as keepers of the peace."

She didn't think much of men who lived by their weapons. "What else are you good at?"

"Well now, we can do most anything from trapping to mining, but we're best with cattle." He grinned again, half-patronizing, half-flirtatious, but mostly friendly. Addie noted that smiling came easy to his lips but never to his eyes. "I hail from Texas, Afton's from Montana. Scrapper ain't exactly sure where he comes from, but he's no tenderfoot, been driving beeves since he was sixteen."

Addie glanced over at the thin young man and refrained from calling him on his age. If he was a day past sixteen, she was a hundred and five. With a disgruntled snort, he tugged his hat brim farther over his eyes, escaping or rejecting her conclusion. She turned her attention back to the one called Granger. She didn't like his looks or his gruff demeanor, but her family needed protection and help.

"We don't have a bunkhouse yet. How are you at carpentry?"

"We're pretty good with a hammer and saw too."

She nodded slowly, but her mind was spinning faster than Cole's painted top. She hadn't yet figured out a way to make it through winter with Zeke hurt, and these three just might be the answer. "You can sleep in the barn until you get one built," she said, her voice sure, her back broom-handle straight, as if she had everything figured out when in reality she didn't have a clue. "I'll cook your meals, but you can't eat in the house unless you clean up. I've got three curious sons who are likely to be underfoot as often as they can get by with it, so keep your language clean too."

Granger grinned wider. He liked a bossy woman. Give him a filly full of spit and vinegar any day over a prissy wilting violet. "Scrapper can cook for us once the bunkhouse is built and he can handle a chuck wagon on the range come spring, but we'll be much obliged to you for a hot meal until then. We'd also like to take turns having Sundays off until branding." Addie felt the beginnings of her own smile until the big man added bluntly, "What's the pay?"

Oh, Lord! "I'll have to check." She left them standing on the porch while she slipped quietly into the bedroom to consult Zeke's ledgers. It cost him four dollars and fifty cents to raise and market a three-year-old steer that would bring thirty or forty dollars when sold. He already had lumber stockpiled in the barn for the bunkhouse along with an old cookstove, so those things wouldn't have to be purchased.

Her heart sank at the next dilemma. The money he had saved was allotted for hiring men when it came time for roundup and branding. He had estimated that he would need a wrangler to see to the horses, a cook for the chuck wagon, and several hands to hunt strays, patrol the range, clear brush, break horses, and mend gear —men he would apparently keep on the ranch permanently.

But not yet, not this winter.

Addie felt her heart sink further beneath the weight of impotent rage. She couldn't wait until spring, couldn't wait until the cattle were sold at market. If she didn't do something now, all Zeke's time, hard work, and investment would be wasted. There might not be any cattle—

She felt a spark of optimism as an alternative dawned. Her emotions swung wildly from insecurity to anticipation as she did some quick calculations, then returned to the men waiting outside.

"Room and board plus pay," she said carefully. Granger nodded expectantly for her to continue. "But there's a problem." His face fell, and she fought the urge to take a nervous step back at the stormy look in his eyes. Despite her desperation, her voice was firm when she spoke. "The only way I can pay you through the winter is if you take some of the cows into town and find a buyer. Your pay is whatever you can get for them until roundup."

Addie's heart was in her throat as Granger glanced at the other two and murmured something she couldn't hear, but when he turned back his smile was in place again. "You got yourself a deal, boss lady."

Taken aback by the address, she took a deep breath and nodded. Granger stuck out his bear-sized paw. With no small amount of hesitation, Addie accepted it and they sealed the bargain with a quick handshake.

"Guess we'll collect our stuff from town and get started tomorrow?" he offered nicely. He could use one more shindig at Ruby's before settling in for a three-week stretch.

Addie nodded. "Tomorrow is fine."

She closed the door when they rode off and went

back to the kitchen, feeling tremulous inside—tremulous and good. So good, in fact, she was fairly floating with it. With the added help, the cattle would be protected and the things Zeke had planned would still be accomplished. She had done the best she could think to do. She just hoped her best would be good enough.

And hope, being a new concept for Addie, felt so wonderful she nearly danced with it.

A distant pounding woke Zeke, the repeated echo of someone striking wood. What the . . . ? He sat up in bed and called Addie, but Josh came running in, his eyes brighter than Zeke had seen them in a long while.

"Guess what, Pa? We've got cowhands, our very own! The sheriff sent them, and they're out building a bunkhouse right now. Ma hired them yesterday and says we can go watch as soon as we finish eating."

Zeke's eyebrows rose. "That so? Tell your ma I need to see her, please."

"She's putting out feed. Luke Parker's got a fever, so he couldn't come. Ma told Mr. Sam she could handle things just fine and to go on back to his own chores." Josh's voice lowered and he shook his head on a grieved expression. "She don't know much about pitching hay, Pa, fell right out of the loft onto her rump. She's gonna be sore as a—" Josh stopped short at the look on his father's face. "She's all right, Pa, honest. I helped her up and dusted her off right good. I'll help her clean up the mess, too, don't worry."

Zeke suppressed a pained smile. "Thanks, Josh. I'd be in a bad fix if I didn't have you."

His chest swelled a bit. "Yep. I gotta go tend Cole till Ma gets back in. She's countin' on me. You need anything?"

"I'm fine for now." Zeke watched his firstborn scamper back into the kitchen and closed his eyes, a heaviness in his chest. He'd spoken to Josh about his mother's death, tried to console and assure him that it had not been his fault. Zeke didn't think the truth had gotten through until today. He'd never heard Josh refer to Addie as anything but a derogatory *her.* His injury had forced his wife and son into closer contact, communication by necessity. He was grateful that Josh seemed to be coming to terms with Addie, but Christian's words ran sour through his mind.

You know what this land does to its women.

Becky had never had the responsibility that was now forced upon Addie—caring for the boys, the house and his chores, not to mention the ranch. With Addie's introverted nature, she'd never be able to handle everything, especially a bunch of rough cowpokes. He couldn't believe she had talked to them, much less hired them. And with what? Come pay day, there were going to be some mighty angry cowpokes beating down his door.

Zeke found there would be a lot of things he couldn't believe over the next few weeks.

Addie had on pants.

Zeke almost choked on his breakfast when she came sashaying into the bedroom in a pair of tight-fitting jeans. His fork halfway to his mouth, he just stared at her a moment before he gained his composure. She'd told him—rather succinctly he recalled, as if she'd had to amass a load of courage to do so—that she had hired three men, then had dashed out of the room before he could answer. She hadn't told him she was going to start dressing like them.

He swallowed the eggs lodged in his throat. "Where'd you get those?"

Addie looked up to see him staring at her lower half. "Sam brought them. They were Luke's," she answered, self-conscious. "I know they look ridiculous, but I was ruining my new dresses." She turned back to collect his ledgers and the view from her backside was daunting. The pants hugged her slender bottom like a glove and streamlined down to mold her thighs, sending a kick to Zeke's gut. *Ridiculous hell.*

She dropped a stack of papers and bent down to retrieve them. There was no room for speculation in the pants. The way they covered every inch, she might as well have been naked. "What are you doing?" he asked, tight-throated.

"Looking for a receipt."

She didn't seem inclined to elaborate, so he prodded, "To what?"

She gave him an impatient look over her shoulder that said she didn't have time for this. "The fence wire. Scrapper says it didn't come in on the train yesterday."

Scrapper? "What wire are you talking about?"

"The new stuff I ordered." She sounded distracted and disgruntled as she sorted through the pages. "Granger says it's the best thing since the invention of gunpowder. It didn't come in, and we can't fence until it does."

Granger? Zeke felt as if life were somehow spinning on without him, out of reach and out of control. After a very deep breath, he tried again. "Fence what?"

She glanced back over her shoulder, and her look said his lame-headedness was to be pitied. "The ravine, what else? We lost another yearling in it yesterday." She went back to rifling through the papers, then emitted a sigh of delight. "Found it!" She smiled on her way out, leaving Zeke with the strange sensation of treading water in a swiftly moving river.

"Addie, wait!" She peeked back around the door, looking harried. "Don't you think we should have discussed ordering fence wire before you did it?"

"There wasn't time," she answered. "Mark Simmons came by, wanting that bull, the big one. He made the suggestion about the wire, but you were asleep. I had to make a decision fast, or I couldn't get the order off in time for it to come in before the worst of winter."

His eyes flared briefly, then narrowed. "You sold my bull?"

Her expression went from baffled, to harassed, to nervous. "Just one. We have plenty more."

That said, she was gone, taking his ledgers and whatever other plans she was making to ruin his livestock with her. "Addie!"

She didn't answer him, neither did the boys. Zeke ignored the pain in his leg and eased to the side of the bed. The plaster splint was cumbersome and heavy but gave support against jarring the injured leg. He rose gingerly and reached for the crutches by the door. Mark Simmons had more money than he could spend. The expense of fence wire wouldn't mean a damn thing to a man like Simmons. Mark had been after him to sell that bull for a year and knew Zeke wouldn't consider it.

Hobbling out into the sitting room, Zeke found the house deserted. He made his way to the kitchen window and looked out at an empty yard.

Seething and trying not to, feeling as if he'd lost all control over his life, he stayed there as long as his energy and tolerance for the pain held out, then moved to a rocker by the fire. Easing down, he propped his heel on a footstool. And waited.

Josh and Zeb rushed in two hours later, Addie on their heels carrying Cole. Their cheeks were flushed from the cold, their eyes bright with accomplishment.

"Pa!" Zeb squealed. "You should see what Afton can do with a rope!"

Afton? Zeke endured Zeb's enthusiasm and demonstrations with constraint. He even endured Addie's scolding him about being out of bed with a tight-lipped smile. But when Josh related an off-color joke without knowing its meaning, Zeke leveled his wife with a warning glare. "I need to speak with you. Alone."

She swallowed, hard. "All right." She didn't know what lay beneath Zeke's tone, but his eyes weren't friendly. She ushered the boys to the table for milk and cookies to keep them occupied, then followed Zeke's slow progress into the bedroom.

Disdaining Addie's offer of help, Zeke sat on the edge of the bed, then pulled his leg up so he could rest back against the headboard. Once the throbbing in his thigh eased, he looked at her.

"What is going on around here? There are three men out there I've never met. You're waiting for a shipment of wire I never ordered, and my son comes in telling a joke that's not fit for his tender ears or yours."

Addie's cheeks were growing hot from embarrassment and defensiveness. She hadn't known the joke was nasty either. When she and the boys had walked up behind the men, Scrapper was saying that the Widow Aims was keeping her valuables locked up tighter than a nun's knees every time he came around. The other men were laughing their heads off about it until they turned to see her and the boys. No wonder Granger's and

Afton's cheeks had turned cherry red and Scrapper had rolled his eyes and changed the subject.

"It's not Josh's fault," she said, shrugging with discomfort. "I didn't realize . . ."

Zeke realized plenty. Like how good she looked in those tight-fitting pants, how pretty with her cheeks all rosy—how terrified he suddenly was. Instead of buckling under the added pressure imposed entirely by his injury, she seemed to be thriving, as if she had somehow needed the challenge. He was so fiercely proud of the way she had risen to task, he could hardly bear to feel the extent of the emotion. But for how long? How long before the burden of responsibility got to her.

He patted the bed beside him. "Come here."

Addie eyed his dark hand on the white linen and moved forward cautiously, then sat on the edge. He didn't look angry, but she didn't know what to make of the strange, concerned glint in his eyes.

"Tell me about the men you hired."

She related the story, explaining her reasons but adding little detail. She was worried that he was going to take exception to the amount of money she was spending, but she hadn't seen any way around it if the ranch was going to continue to prosper.

Zeke picked up one of her hands and frowned as he turned the palm over. "You've got calluses. You've been working too hard."

She gave him a bemused smile. "Just doing what needs to be done." He stroked each of her fingers idly, making her feel funny inside.

"Don't work too hard, Addie," he said with a fierceness that renewed her nervousness. "Hire as many men as you need or let the whole place go to hell, but don't bury yourself trying to do everything."

She gave him a startled look. Let the place go to hell? Not likely! Not while there was breath in her body. She'd never known such security or abundance, and she wasn't about to let it all go to waste. She put a palm to his head to see if he had a fever.

Zeke took her hand back in his. "You're doing a fine job, just don't wear yourself out. And I'd rather you discuss it with me before you sell off any more of my livestock."

Her chin dropped. "You're mad about the bull. I could tell this morning."

"No, not at you. But Mark knew I wasn't willing to sell."

Her face brightened a little. "He said you could buy it back come spring."

Zeke chuckled in spite of his chagrin. "Yeah, after he's impregnated half his herd with the best shorthorn I own." He stroked the rough skin on her palm, his finger trailing over each ridge. "Mark took advantage of you."

She smiled then, her eyes lighting up like sweet green fire that sent a streak of heat straight through Zeke. "Nope. I wanted the fence wire and I'll get it. Mark took advantage of *you*."

Zeke chuckled outright for the first time since his accident. "You're pretty smart, Miz Claiborne, and you've gotten just a bit sassy too. I didn't know I had married a businesswoman."

She shrugged, embarrassed yet elated by his praise. She felt so good, good about herself and her decisions, good about how well things were going in a situation that could have been devastating.

She didn't know when the change had come, when the decision had been made. But somewhere between Zeke's surgery and the day the cowhands arrived, she had decided that life wasn't going to get her anymore, troubles weren't going to destroy her. For the first time in a long time, she had too much to lose, and she wasn't giving anything up gracefully.

"I'll bring the men in so you can meet them," she said, "and I'll ask you first before I make any other decisions." She started to rise from the bed, but Zeke detained her with a tug on her hand. He didn't want her to go. He'd never seen her look so healthy, so contented, or so optimistic. His fingers tightened on her hand. "Stay a while longer. The chores will wait."

Her heart slammed in one mighty thud against her breast at the intensity in his eyes. "The boys . . ."

"They'll keep too." He tugged again, and she eased one hip back down on the edge of the bed. His hand slid to her waist and just rested there, his thumb hooked in the waistband of her tight pants. He eased his head back against the headboard and closed his eyes.

Something inside her, feminine and soft, hurt at the exhaustion on his face, and she lowered her eyes to stare at the tanned hand resting possessively on her waist. "I'm sorry about the bull."

"No, you did the right thing." His thumb made a circle on her hip and he felt her wince. "Josh said you fell out of the loft."

She emitted a soft, self-deprecating laugh. "I feel like such a fool."

His thumb made another circle, and his voice was as lazy as the motion of his hand. "I've got liniment I can rub on you. It'll help the soreness." She made an embarrassed sound and tensed beneath his hand but he didn't care. It felt good to touch her, too good. Energy hummed throughout him, invigorating his senses to a keen-edged awareness. He wanted to strip her bare, peel the pants right down to her ankles and . . . what?

There wasn't a damn thing he could do in his condition, even if she'd let him. Which she wouldn't. It didn't matter anyway. The last thing either of them needed right now was for her to get pregnant. His hand slid from her waist and dropped limply to the bed as he feigned sleep.

Scrapper had been shot.

He lay on Addie's kitchen table, bleeding everywhere and whining and cursing like a gutter rat. With a look on her face that would frighten back a wildcat, she put an immediate stop to his bad language, but couldn't seem to halt the blood seeping through the bandage pressed to his upper arm. With determination, she pressed harder. Though he wasn't badly hurt, he needed more medical attention than she could give him. "Go get the sheriff and the doc," she said to Granger. "Afton, you stay and help me."

"But they're makin' off—" Granger began.

"I don't care how many cattle they make off with," she bit out. "It's not worth a man's life."

Granger gave her a mean look, and slammed his fist down on the table, which made Scrapper whine louder.

Addie's gaze shot down to the injured man. "Stop crying!" she commanded. "If you wake up my boys with that caterwauling, I'm gonna shoot you myself." Scrapper gave her a hurt look and she relented a bit until Granger spoke.

"You hired us to do a job, Miz Claiborne, and we're doin' it." He held himself stiffly, head lowered like a bull ready to charge. "It ain't gonna be said that me and my men can't do a job—"

She rounded on him like a termagant. "Now, you listen to me, Jonathan Granger, there's already two men hurt. I'll not have another!"

"No, you listen to me, boss lady—"

"Addie's right."

All eyes swung to the bedroom door where Zeke stood, half-dressed and leaning on his crutches. He couldn't believe his wife was standing up to one of the largest, roughest men he had ever seen. He'd met all three cowhands earlier in the week and had approved Addie's choice, but he still couldn't get over the fact that she was so easy around them.

And in her nightgown! God knew, it covered every sweet inch of her better than the pants she'd been wearing, but it was thoroughly shocking to see her so unconcerned about her attire in front of three men, and all of them twice her size. Roused in the dead of night, she was a breathtaking sight of disorder and sweetness. Her hair hung in shimmering, tousled coils to her shoulders and there was a sleepy look in her eyes. Bands of color ribbed her cheek where the pillow had creased it. If her lips had been the slightest bit puffy, she would have looked like a woman who had just been thoroughly bedded.

"I agree with Addie," Zeke said with forced calm. "One man can't fight them off, so there's no need for Afton to put himself in danger."

His slow progress into the kitchen made Addie want to weep, but she had too much else to worry about. "Rustlers again," she whispered. Her distressed expression turned cautious. "We . . . need the doc."

Zeke made his way to the table and pulled back the bandage to see that the bullet had gone straight through the fleshy part of the young man's upper arm. "He'll be all right," he said. "There's a box under the bed. Get it for me." Addie didn't argue because she didn't want her husband on his feet any longer than necessary and hurried to do his bidding. Zeke turned to Granger. "Were any other shots fired?"

"Yes, sir, Mr. Claiborne. Scrapper thinks he hit at least one of 'um. He's not sure about the others."

"They've probably taken off by now," Zeke said. "It's not likely they would linger if one of them is injured. There's no need to wake the sheriff tonight, but at first light ride out and warn him that you think one of them is hurt, so he can be on the lookout."

Granger nodded and stepped back when Addie returned with a medical kit. Zeke leaned against the table for support and tended the wound. Addie was amazed by his dexterity and control. His leg must have been hurting something fierce, but he never showed it as he cleaned the injured area.

Scrapper yowled when Zeke brought out a wicked-looking syringe and injected morphine under the skin of his shoulder. Addie bit the inside of her jaw and flinched, but within five minutes, Scrapper was as calm as a kitten with its belly full. Zeke stitched and bandaged the wound, then turned to Granger. "You and Afton take him back to the bunkhouse. He'll be sore for a few days, but he'll recover."

As soon as they carried Scrapper out the back door, Addie went to Zeke. She put his arm around her shoulder and supported him all the way back to the bed. He was pale when he sat down, the lines at the corners of his eyes and mouth deeper.

"You should have let me get the doc," she fussed before she thought.

Zeke just shook his head and eased back against the

headboard. "The wound was minor. Christian would have laughed me out of the house."

The easiness with which he said Christian's name brought her head up, and she wondered just what had transpired the day she had left them alone for so long. She tried to smile, grateful he wasn't angry, but he looked so tired and drawn she couldn't do anything but turn her face away to hide her gathering tears. Zeke reached up and touched her chin until she turned back. Her eyes were glassy, her teeth digging into her bottom lip to keep it from quivering.

"Come here," he whispered.

He pulled her down beside him before she could protest and cradled her close, tucking her head into his shoulder.

"I'll hurt you," she murmured, so close to breaking down her voice sounded garbled.

"No." Zeke caressed her back in long, soothing strokes. "Go ahead and cry, Addie. I won't shoot you."

She let out a watery giggle. "I know it was mean of me to say that to Scrapper. But all I could think at that moment was that I couldn't handle him, the boys, and Granger all at the same time."

Zeke pressed his lips to her temple and sighed. "You did fine, Addie." Fiercely proud of her, he felt even more worthless in his infirmity. "I didn't know you could be so tough."

She tipped her face up to his, feeling weak as a new foal lying next to him. "What are we going to do, Zeke? How can we stop these scavengers from stealing everything we own?"

A year ago, he would have given her the ageless answer—as he would have Becky—and told her not to worry her pretty little head about it. But he found that sentiment so patronizing in reference to Addie, he refrained. She had been managing the ranch, the boys, and him. She had never once bemoaned the added work, just dug in and did what was necessary to keep things going.

"I don't know," he admitted, "but we'll find a way." His hand swept lightly over her hip. "Been thrown by any more lofts lately?"

She ducked her head in his shoulder, hiding a smile. "No."

"Why aren't you afraid of them?"

The words seemingly came out of nowhere, but Addie knew he meant the hired hands, knew also what he implied. She plucked fretfully at the sheet. "I don't know."

"Yes, you do. It's because you don't have to share a bed with them."

She looked back up, a sadness and deep regret in her eyes. "I'm not scared of you either, not anymore."

Great, when he was nearly as helpless as a babe. His voice was rough with warning and need. "I won't have this bum leg forever."

She rose up beside him on her elbow and looked solemnly into his eyes. "I know, Zeke. Day nine."

14

"The hell you say," he growled, and rolled her over on top of him so fast she didn't have time to protest.

Addie squealed in shock and pulled her legs up quickly to keep the pressure off his thigh, bringing them into intimate contact. Completely disconcerted by the collision of their bodies and the scorching look in his eyes, she planted her hands on his chest. "Your injury . . ."

"Hurts," he said through clenched teeth, arching slightly to fight the jarring pain. He sighed when it subsided and smiled grimly into her flushed face. "I know how you could make it feel better."

At her utterly guileless look, Zeke suppressed a groan. He was in no physical shape to take her innocence—*like hell*. Technically he had all the physical shape he would ever need and found it growing increasingly painful. He wondered if she couldn't feel it as well with her knees drawn up on either side of his hips and her slender bottom pressed against the ridge of his pants. His eyes were keen and aware, as he lifted his hand and stroked her hot cheeks with his knuckles.

"You're blushing, Addie. What are you thinking?"

She turned redder and dropped her chin, her hair spilling forward to capture candlelight, muted radiance that flowed in warm rippling spirals to her breasts. Zeke's fingers threaded through the gilded strands at her temples, then drifted downward past her cheeks, her chin, her neck, then farther still until they paused at the crazy beat of her heart.

He wondered what was going through her mind as he searched her flushed face. The backs of his fingers worked slowly and achingly lower to brush the peaks of her breasts. Her eyes grew rounder, her face tense with waiting, her breath held on what? A moan, a denial? His fingers opened and released her hair, then cupped the gentle roundness of her breasts, sculpting their shape and fullness. She fit perfectly in his hands.

Her tongue darted out to wet her lips, and her chest swelled when she remembered to breathe, filling his hands further, filling him everywhere with sweet heavy wanting.

"What are you thinking, Addie?" he asked. "What does this feel like to you?"

She tried to find her voice. "Scary . . ." She couldn't collect her thoughts, couldn't put the feelings into words. Her hand went to her cheek and her eyes were distressed. "I'm so hot."

His hand lifted to curl around her fingers, and he pulled her palm to his own cheek. "I'm hot, too," he whispered. "It's normal, Addie, when two people want each other."

He knew she didn't understand, not after the obscenity of being with Willis. If he could get her to open up and divulge the awful secrets of her past, he could explain the reality of how a healthy man and woman come together.

"Did you and Willis do this?"

Her expression darkened instantly and she turned her face away, her body stiffening, making ready to scramble off out of reach. But even in her determination to flee, she was careful not to hurt him. Zeke's hands gripped her waist and held her against him, torturing himself with her nearness.

"You didn't, Addie. You didn't do anything with Willis that made you all hot inside, did you?" She looked everywhere but at him, her breathing coming fast. Her breasts rose and fell erratically beneath the cotton gown. He wanted to touch her there, where her heartbeat pounded, wanted to touch her elsewhere as well. He tightened his grip on her waist. "I know how it feels," he said in a low, compelling voice, drawing her gaze despite her discomfort.

His thumbs stroked her lower belly. "It feels like something's trapped inside, just begging to get out. Your knees get weak and your stomach feels like it's light as a feather one minute and full of lead the next."

Addie made a small, mewing sound in her throat.

"Everything gets so twisted up, you think you'll scream with it, but it only gets tangled tighter. Your nerves get edgy and raw, and the least little thing makes you want to take someone's head off."

Her eyes had gone round with the awareness of his words. The keening inside her expanded until she shuddered.

"Tell me what things Willis did that make you so afraid of me. Tell me how he hurt you."

She shook her head. Never. Never would she share her shame and degradation with the man she respected above all others. She wouldn't let him see, even through words, how weak she had been, how she had lowered herself to escape Willis's wrath and protect herself.

"Addie, I know about the bruises," he whispered painfully. "Christian told me."

Her eyes flashed in shame and shock. "He had no right!" Her bottom lip trembled and she squeezed her eyes shut to hold back a rush of tears. She struggled to move away, but Zeke's hands only dug into her waist. She hung her head and wrapped her arms around her middle, insulating herself, gaining distance from words that hurled her back into the horrible past. "He had no right."

Zeke's hands rose and pushed the hair back from her face. "Don't hide," he said fiercely. "Never hide from me." His thumb stroked her cheek, his hands touched every inch of her face. Like a blind man he studied her, his touch soft and consoling and calling forth confidences she wouldn't allow. "It was more than just beatings. Tell me the rest, Addie."

No, no, no. Her glorious curls bounced with each silent denial. Tears sparkled on her lashes.

He traced her lower lip with his thumb. "I want you so bad, I ache with it. But I can't get to you. Willis stands between us as surely as if he were still alive."

Zeke cupped her cheeks to stop the renewed tossing of her head. "What he did, that's not how it would be between us. I would never"—he paused, remembering her innocence—"I would never willfully hurt you." He searched her face, fighting down the urge to both shake her and comfort her. "Addie, I know you're still a virgin."

Her eyes narrowed, confused and embarrassed and agitated. "No." She pushed his hands away but he only grabbed her wrists and held on, forcing her to meet his gaze.

"Willis was sick, perverted." Zeke closed his eyes briefly. "You weren't the only one, Addie. He hurt other women too."

Her face blanched on a wounded cry, agony and horror in her expression. "Oh, no," she whispered wretchedly. It was too much to know that someone else had suffered like she had, that someone else had had to bear the pain and abuse of Willis's deranged mind. She crumpled then, sobbing softly onto his chest. "I hate him!"

Zeke's hands went to her back and he caressed her, absorbing the small tremors wracking her body as she tried to hold the tears back. Her sorrow sliced straight into his heart, and for every cry she uttered, he echoed in silent pain. She felt so fragile under his hands, her voice faint and constricted when she moaned.

"I didn't want you to know."

"Oh, Addie, I don't blame you for what he did. I want to help you."

It seemed an eternity before she spoke, and when she did her voice was eerie and hollow, as if she spoke from a long way off. "No one can help me now." She blinked as she sat back up and looked straight at him, disconsolate and certain. "You can't change the past."

There was something in her tone, something in the lost look on her face. Zeke knew with a sickening realization that there was more, things even Christian didn't know about. He swallowed hard, fighting the useless anger and violence he felt toward a dead man. He touched one of her curls, wondering how much depravity she had suffered, wondering if he could handle it when she revealed it. Wondered if he could heal her.

Something cold and bitter shifted within him. He was

pushing her to open up, to lay her heart and body bare, but what was he offering in return? He shied away from the question and the accompanying guilt, his neediness stronger than his ethics, stronger than anything but the desire to have her and end the indomitable ache that tormented him. To assuage his conscience, he told himself he could pleasure her too, give her something good to replace the pain of the past.

"When you're ready, Addie, tell me about Willis. I won't condemn you. I'll hold you while you cry, and I'll curse him for a depraved lunatic."

Addie only looked at him, locked in her desperation to preserve herself. Willis had kept her a virtual prisoner for the first year and a half, until his laziness had gotten the better of him. After that, she'd been allowed to go to town to purchase food and supplies. He must have known she was too ashamed to expose him. Just as she was too ashamed now.

"I . . . was just so weak, so foolish," she whispered. She didn't realize she'd spoken aloud until Zeke's eyes narrowed.

"You were just a child. How could it have been your fault?"

She was so undeserving of his concern, she laughed self-derisively. "Even a child should have the sense enough to get away, to not allow herself to be trapped." Her voice was brittle and sharp-edged, her eyes sightless. "I tried to sneak away from Willis one night when he was gone. After that, he wouldn't even leave a lantern or candle in the house. I had never been afraid of the dark, but I would sit there and hear every creak, every sound, hating him beyond human capacity." She shut her eyes and drew a ragged breath. "But I hated myself worse because, as badly as I despised him, I wished he'd come back home so I wouldn't have to sit in the dark alone." Tears leaked from her eyes; angry hands tried to wipe them away. Her jaw was clenched, the words forced out. "He didn't care. I tried—"

Zeke put his fingers to her lips, his eyes fierce and protective. "Hush," he said roughly. "I know you well enough to know you tried, but he wasn't worth one second of it."

"I know." She buried her face in her hands, pressing hard to stop the tears. His tender concern was too much. She couldn't bear his compassion when she knew what she was, knew everything she had done to escape Willis's wrath, especially at the end. She looked back up, her eyes grave. "You don't understand," she said. "I really did kill him, Zeke, and I don't regret it. Don't you know what that makes me?"

He pulled her hands from her face. "Addie, you're not a murderer. You just don't have it in you. The bastard deserved to hang for his crimes. I hope it was a painful end."

She just shook her head. "Sometimes I wish I could do it again."

He caught a tear that trembled on her lower lash. "I wish I could do it for you."

She smiled sadly, diminished by the memories, unable to accept his protection. "You just don't understand."

Zeke swept the wondrous curls back from her cheek, inhaling the scent of rose water until it became the air he breathed. "Make me understand. Tell me what happened and get it behind you, Addie. I'll be your confessor, judge, and jury."

He had little idea until this moment how much it meant to him to hear the truth from her, and he returned her stare with a level, calm gaze. For a moment, he thought she would refuse, then his balance went off kilter as she nodded slowly. There was some measure of trust and yielding in that single gesture, and perhaps one day she would trust him enough to tell him all of it.

"I was up in the barn hiding from him that day. He'd come home drunk, and I knew better than to get near him. He found me . . . he always did." She took a deep breath and continued. "By that time I was so numb with fear and crazy with hatred, I think I was going to throw myself out of the loft. He wanted something . . . I refused. I was just so tired. So damned tired—" Her voice broke slightly, then she rushed on as if she needed to finish it. "He came at me with his fists, saying terrible things. I shoved him." She tilted her head to the side, her look so bewildered, as if she still couldn't piece together the puzzle. "The distance to the ground wasn't that far but he hit his head on a large stone."

"It was an accident, Addie."

She shook her head, her voice void of all emotion. "No. I wanted him dead so badly, I would have done it sooner if I'd known it would work."

Zeke felt something inside him give at her fierce, uncompromising tone. "No, you wouldn't. You could have taken a gun to his head anytime while he slept."

"I thought about it often enough."

"Thinking and doing are two different things, Addie." If he had done to her all the things he'd been thinking about lately, he wouldn't have a raging arousal and she wouldn't have one ounce of innocence left.

She closed her eyes briefly, wondering how he could be so forgiving, so unconcerned. "On the nights he didn't come home, I even used to pray that he was dead. I don't imagine God was real thrilled with that, but since I was living with the devil, I didn't think He could hear me anyway."

Zeke laughed softly. The back of his knuckles brushed with aching tenderness across her cheeks, then floated down her neck. His eyes were as questing as his fingers.

"There's more," he said; somehow he could feel it. "Tell me the rest of it."

She flinched and shook her head. "I can't . . . not yet."

Zeke nodded and pulled her to him and closed his eyes, well aware that she hadn't said, "Not ever."

Addie felt the safety of his strong arms enfold her and relaxed in the comfort of his patient compassion. He was warm and solid and she would have given anything in that moment to have been his only wife, his only love. In her heart she was.

Grady cursed a blue streak as Lou Ellen bandaged the small wound at his side. "There you go, sugar," she said, patting it for sheer deviltry and taking a secret gloating delight in watching him recoil against the pain.

"Bitch," he hissed between his teeth. "Get me some more whiskey."

"Sure thing," she cooed sweetly, and backed away from the bed. Her eyes flickered over him briefly before she turned. She despised Grady, and others like him, but he paid good money for an easy poke, and she knew better than to alienate him. The men she'd have to take to replace him with were far worse. He was clean, fairly handsome, and never tried to short her. He also didn't have unnatural tastes like some, like his perverted brother. Grady was straightforward in his demands, nothing too strenuous or unusual. No doubt about it, she could do worse and knew it from hard experience.

"Here you go." She held out the glass, taking silent satisfaction when he gulped it down and asked for another. He had paid for the whole night, but she wouldn't have to perform. Tonight he was paying for secrecy and a place to lay low. "What happened?" she asked, her voice innocent and unconcerned, as she tipped the bottle. He would recognize sly; his kind always did.

"Just a disagreement," he said, backing her down with a hostile stare. But the whiskey was beginning to mellow him, coating his anger and pain in queasy euphoria. He didn't want to antagonize her. He wanted to be mollycoddled and fussed over, even if he was paying for it. "Come here, baby."

She smiled and sat beside him, her carmine lips the only thing he could focus on now that his vision was blurring. "Bad cards?" she asked compassionately, searching for the truth before he passed out. She ran her fingernail gently down his cheek. She was very good at the more subtle forms of blackmail. She never threatened to go to a wife or a sweetheart or the sheriff, she knew better, but she was a master at picking a conscience or finding a weakness. Get them to spill their guts and they would quickly spill their pockets.

"Someone accuse you of cheatin', darlin'?"

Grady took a long pull on the whiskey. His tongue was numb, the pain in his side fading. "Rustlers," he murmured. "Me and Jimmy and Coolie."

Lou Ellen's eyes narrowed. She knew Little Jim and that Coolie fellow, no-goods both of them. Town vagrants always down on their luck and looking for a fast buck. "No, really? How'd you tangle up with rustlers, sugar? You haven't got any cattle."

"No?" Grady smiled sleepily, and reached up to fondle her breast.

Lou Ellen waited for more, but his fingers fell limp to her lap and he began snoring. *Stupid bastard.* She picked his hand up as if it were dirty laundry and dropped it by his side. Men were nothing but weak, overgrown babies. They strutted and postured and boasted, prouder of what lay between their legs than what lay between their ears. She gave Grady a disgusted look and eased carefully off the bed. She scooped up the bloody rags she had used to clean his wound and stuffed them in a pillowcase, then erased all other evidence that an injured man had been in her room. In a cloud of lacy lingerie, she glided across the frayed carpet and sat before her vanity to preen.

A paid night off was rare. She could make extra by slipping downstairs and picking up a few quick tumbles while lover boy snored. Della's room was available. The twit had died after a botched abortion two days ago. Lou Ellen frowned, risks of the trade, but didn't dwell on it. Frowns would wrinkle her flawless skin.

Anyway, Della was stupid. She should have been more careful or at least found a doctor or midwife in Cheyenne who got rid of mistakes on the side, not the inept kitchen help.

Lou Ellen slid her hands down over her breasts to her own flat stomach. She'd never had more than a twenty-two-inch waist and was careful to keep it that way. At thirty-one, she was still the most sought-after whore in Laramie.

She glanced over at Grady and rejected a sneer as useless exertion. She loved men almost as much as she hated them. Their constant flattery fell on deaf ears, she knew how pretty she was, but their money stirred her heart completely. She would have made a good mistress to some fancy New Orleans gent but always rejected the semipermanence of such relationships.

She loved the rough-and-ready men of a cowtown because they were so damned easy. Cowboys stayed on the range for days or weeks before getting back to town and were always faster than they should be, which was slower than she liked it. And then there were the locals. A little more attention was required but the payoff worth it. Get them a little tipsy, get them real hot, and she had them by the balls. Literally. From the head of the town council to the traveling preacher's brother-in-law, once she got them talking, she made as much in guilt money as she did for lying on her back.

They'd leave, happy and self-important and feeling like they'd gotten away with something. And they had. She'd never tell; she knew better.

She picked up a crystal atomizer and sprayed just a touch of perfume between her breasts. It would be wasted this night, but she didn't mind. There was plenty of money for more, especially now that she had a new customer, a regular. After only one night, he had reserved her for every third Saturday.

She squirmed and felt her nipples pucker just thinking about him. He was big as a bear—everywhere—and too slow and careful by her way of thinking, but she'd change that soon enough. She'd find out what made his clock tick faster or start charging him double for the extra time.

She glanced over her shoulder to check on Grady. His clothes were scattered across her floor, typically messy man. She felt an inkling of greed flutter her belly and tamped the urge down. Uncontrolled greed was too dangerous and she'd learned to temper it. But boredom was something she'd never learned to endure, and right now she felt about as dull as dishwater. She could search his pockets, maybe pilfer a little extra. She'd done it often in the early days, but she didn't need that now. A man who gave freely was a happier man and more likely to return.

But her curiosity was harder to smother than her avarice, and a little search never hurt anyone. At times it gave her more insight into her patrons. At times more ammunition.

She turned on her velvet-tufted stool and gingerly picked up Grady's trousers with the tip of one long nail. There was nothing useful in his pants pockets but the rustle of paper in his jacket pocket caught her attention. A search revealed an opening in the lining. She slipped her fingers inside and withdrew a packet wrapped in brown paper.

"My, my," she drawled, as she stared at the package. "What have we here?" She glanced back up to make sure Grady was still sleeping, a sly and intrigued grin on her face. "Oh, sugar, what do we have here?"

Zeke's progress toward the barn was slow. His leg hurt like hellfire, but the exercise made him feel good everywhere else. The world was winter white, blinding and invigorating. Icicles hung from the eaves, just waiting for the boys to grab them in gloved hands to lick like candy. The air was still and cold, but it felt less frigid with the sun glaring off the snow.

The interior of the barn was gloomy. He had to blink and wait for his eyes to adjust. The scent of hay, manure, and horse flesh permeated the air, along with the dust motes dancing in the sunbeams streaming through the open door.

Addie stood leaning over a pile of hay, rubbing her backside gingerly. "Tarnation," she murmured, and scooped up a handful and dumped it in the trough, then limped over to the milking stool. After settling herself carefully, she began the morning chore. Hunched on a stool, her head resting against the cow's belly, she rhythmically squeezed milk into a pail. She talked to the animal from time to time, silly bits of conversation that Zeke had uttered a thousand times himself in the chill of early morning while feeling the comfort of warm teats beneath his fingers.

Becky had hated the chore. Always ill in the mornings with each pregnancy, she'd had a difficult time with any work before noon, so he'd taken over the task. It hurt to think of Becky now in ways different than before. Before there had been anger and betrayal and longing. Now there was only profound guilt to hollow out his gut. He deeply regretted that she had not been strong enough to handle life out west, and that he had not known how to help her, but he was realistic. It was too late to go back and change things for Becky, and he was determined not to make the same mistakes with Addie.

Humming softly, she aimed milk into the pail. A skinny barn cat leaped from the loft and began rubbing against her leg, circling, begging for a taste. "Not yet, Tabby," she admonished. "When I'm done." The cat plopped down as if it understood and began bathing herself with a disgraceful lack of modesty.

Zeke leaned against the stall and watched Addie work, but his thoughts weren't on the business at hand. They were on the day, the number to be exact. Day one. A sense of urgency tightened his nerves, but he dreaded to think what could happen if Addie conceived now when she had so much extra to do. He knew the steps to prevent it—precautions that would be embarrassing for her when he tried to explain them without the intimacy of a longer, more comfortable relationship to ease the way. He wished it were possible to leave things as they were, the way she preferred them.

But he was no martyr or monk to spend the rest of his life celibate. Her hair bounced against her shoulders in rhythm to her motions, her backside round and sculpted in the boys' pants. No, nothing about what he was feeling at this moment would qualify him for sainthood.

Zeke cleared his throat so as not to startle her and watched as she roused from her dreamy pose against the cow. She turned to him, smiling, then frowned.

"What were you thinking to walk all the way out here?"

"I needed to work the leg." Christian had stopped by the day before to remove the bandaging and splints. Talking anything but medicine was still too painful, but the silence between them had been placid instead of fraught with strife. Zeke flexed his leg, eager to test his limits, then limped forward and leaned against the stall. "Let me finish for you. I need to feel useful."

"You need to—"

Her words halted abruptly when he caught her behind the head, leaned down and planted his lips firmly against hers. "You need to obey your husband," he murmured against her mouth. He felt the vibration of her giggle and saw that her eyes were dancing with what she perceived as silliness on his part instead of seriousness.

The astonishing lightheartedness of her reaction so startled him, he kissed her in earnest, molding her mouth to fit his, and felt her sweet and stunned acceptance sigh out in a hot breath. His fingers tightened on her hair and he tilted her head back and up to meet the full fervor of his mouth. He nipped at her lower lip until she gasped and opened for the penetration of his tongue. Through half-lowered lids he watched her eyes flutter as he continued to kiss her, then close completely as her cheeks warmed to peach. Her arms fell lax at her sides, the milking forgotten, her body so malleable he was tempted to tumble her in the hay before she regained her senses. But she deserved better than that her first time, and it would be dangerous without precautions.

He gentled the kiss lazily, a very slow inch at a time, until their lips barely touched and the condensation of their breaths mingled in the chilled air.

"Go back into the house and warm up," he whispered. "I'll finish here."

Addie rose, her legs like jelly, and stumbled blindly from the barn, feeling so warm already that she could only stand outside in the freezing air and let it cool her hot cheeks. Gathering her faulty composure, she took a deep breath and headed for the house, only realizing when she reached the back door that she'd just been manipulated into doing exactly what Zeke wanted.

Of all the sneaky, conniving, underhanded . . .

She paused and smiled, shylike, as if someone might be watching. She'd just been well and truly kissed and it hadn't frightened her, not one bit. It had been exhilarating and breath-robbing and exciting. But it hadn't been scary. She pressed her fingers to her lips in wonder.

She couldn't think what it meant, something wonderful maybe, like finding the first flower of spring peeking up through the snow. She knew she was growing fanciful and hurried her shivering body inside the house, knowing all the while she'd left her heart back at the barn.

After milking, Zeke cleaned up the barn with more vigor than his injury allowed to keep his mind off the day that stretched before him, or rather the long hours until night. When he was done, he realized he was finished in more ways than one. His leg was throbbing in excruciating agony. The cold had seeped clear down to the bone, and he had to grit his teeth to fight the pain as he made his way back to the house. His limbs felt heavy and useless, weighted down by extreme exhaustion.

Addie took one look at his face when he entered the back door and scolded nonstop as she helped settle him back in bed. When she tried to stuff another pillow behind his head, he grabbed her wrist none too gently.

"Stop fussing! You're not my mother."

Her eyes held wounded surprise as she let go of the pillow and tried to jerk her arm back but Zeke wouldn't let her go. He closed his eyes on a sigh and brought her wrist to his lips.

"Sorry, Addie." Fatigue and pain underscored each word. "I'm aggravated at myself, not you. I should have known better than to do too much my first day out." His lashes slid open and he regarded her with a strange, intense look. "Know what today is?"

She thought about dissembling but nodded jerkily instead. "Day one."

"I'm sorry, Addie."

She nodded again, uncertain how she felt herself. A little disappointed, a little relieved, a lot of both maybe. She tried to think of something comforting to say but nothing came to mind that wasn't completely embarrassing. "Can I get you anything?"

For all that he hurt like he hadn't hurt since getting

shot, Zeke could still enjoy the soft blush on her cheeks, the uncertain innocence in her eyes. "The liniment?"

She nodded and left to retrieve it from the kitchen. When she returned, he had a sheet draped across his lower half and his chest was bare. His shoulder had healed nicely, only a slash of fading red marred the hollow at his neck and shoulder, but his leg might be a different matter. She hadn't seen it since the day Christian performed surgery. She swallowed and handed the ointment to Zeke, but he didn't take it.

"Would you do it for me?"

Her hand trembled and she gripped the bottle tighter. Something in her throat forbade her from answering, so she merely nodded stupidly.

"You have to get a little closer," Zeke said gently, the pain in his leg easing a little at the humor of her predicament.

"Oh, of course." Addie moved forward briskly as if jabbed from behind, and glanced down at the sheet, her cheeks flaming. An all-too-hesitant hand reached out and pinched just the edge, then folded it back nearly six whole inches.

"How daring, Miz Claiborne," he drawled dramatically.

Addie jumped, glowered at him so fiercely he expected her to hurl the bottle at his face, then without one hint of warning, flipped the sheet completely off the bed. It was hard to say who blushed redder. Addie, who realized her husband was completely naked beneath the cover, or Zeke, who was thoroughly unprepared for the move. It was definitely Zeke who choked on a laugh first and draped an arm over his lap because something about her huge green eyes made him feel exposed to the world.

Addie only lifted her chin at a haughty angle and held up the liniment. "Where does it hurt?"

Every muscle in Zeke's body tightened. "You don't want to know," he laughed beneath his breath, and snatched the bottle from her hand.

15

Spring was only a wish in the most optimistic mind, but the Claiborne family loaded into the wagon as if its promise lay just over the next hill. The sky was an impossible blue, so rich it went on forever, its deep clarity reaching even to the horizon. Addie turned her face up to the sun and savored the heat and freshness of the outdoors. Snow still covered the landscape and made thick clumps on the branches of evergreens, no less beautiful, but wearing for its lengthiness, like a visitor overstaying his welcome.

Christmas had come and gone, the sweetest thing Addie could remember since childhood. Zeke had ordered from his catalog after all, the sneaky man, and there had been loads of gifts for her and the boys. She should have known something was up the day John White from the train station stopped by. With secret smiles, he and Zeke had gone off to the barn. The exquisite fur muff keeping her hands warm was only one of her surprises Christmas morning. There had been others, but her real joy had come from the boys' jubilant smiles and bright-eyed squeals in the wee hours just before dawn.

It had been harder for her to conceal her own gifts with Zeke confined to the house most of the time. She'd made woolen scarves for the hired men and managed to make Zeke a shirt on the sly when he thought she was sewing for his sons. She made each of the boys a jacket with matching pants, along with books she had hand-lettered and illustrated. It hadn't seemed much next to Zeke's gifts, but the boys had been pleased. As she had feared, Zeke had been astounded by her talent, but Addie had managed to sidestep his praise. If it hadn't been for the fact that she had nothing else to offer the boys, she wouldn't have done the books. Her art was something she had kept secret since Willis.

But for the first time in a long time it had meant something to her. The pleasure had been so sweet she could hardly contain it, but there had been a hunger too, a driving force inside her to do each one perfectly, as if it might be her last chance.

By the middle of January, the boys were tired of being cooped up inside the house, as was Zeke. Addie was tired of delayed wash days and frozen water troughs. Trips to the barn had taken on the same anticipation as the idea of being bludgeoned.

She was so delighted to be paying a visit to the Parkers, she could feel the joy of it clear down to her bones. The wagon had hardly come to a stop in Sam and Beatrice's yard before Josh and Zeb were tumbling over the side, shrieking and running for the house.

Cole squirmed on Addie's lap, not to be left out, and it was all she could do to hang on to him until Zeke rounded the wagon to help her down. Beatrice greeted them from the door, dusting flour from her hands onto her apron.

"Well, aren't you a welcome sight!"

Addie kept her pace slow for Zeke's sake. It was his first outing away from the ranch since the accident. He was managing well enough, but still limped badly, and she hated to think how disastrous a fall on slippery ice could be for him.

Beatrice put on coffee and sent for Sam, while the children hurried off to play with Gracie and the other kids. Precious time away from work to visit wasn't taken for granted, but enjoyed fully for its rare worth. After lunch, Zeke went out to the barn with Sam to inspect some new equipment, and Addie put the boys down for a nap.

When she returned to the sitting room, Beatrice handed her a fresh cup of coffee and motioned to a rocker. They sat before the fire, savoring the coffee and the warmth and solitude of a quiet house.

"You seem to be getting on fine with the boys," Beatrice commented.

Addie smiled and rested her head back against the rocking chair. "They're good boys, but I wish I could borrow Gracie about three days a week."

Beatrice chuckled. "I know they keep you busy." She glanced over at the younger woman, her gaze keen. "And Zeke?"

The rhythm of Addie's rocking chair paused, then continued. "He's such a good man, Bea. I nearly died when he got hurt."

It wasn't the answer Beatrice was seeking but she let it pass. "Heard tell you've become quite a business-woman. Hired some cowhands and took over running the ranch while Zeke was down." At Addie's startled look, she chuckled again. "Not much goes on that we don't know about around here. Guess you should know those men you hired are praising you far and wide as having a smart head on your shoulders for such a purty little thing and a bad temper when necessary."

"I do not!" Addie said, affronted and pleased at the same time. "Oh, Bea," she added softly, "you should have seen Zeke's face when I finally got brave enough to wear the pants Luke sent over. Those britches made things a lot easier for me but they nearly made my husband strangle on his breakfast."

Beatrice laughed with her, but her eyes probed as she set the rocking chair in motion. "You and Zeke getting on all right?"

Addie nodded. "Fine."

"We gonna be stitching blankets and bibs for any new Claiborne babies this summer?"

Addie looked up, confused at first, then blushed. "I don't reckon."

Never one to mince words, Beatrice snapped, "Why not?"

Addie shrugged, uncomfortable. "It's not that way between us." Not only had day one come and gone but so had all subsequent days since. Zeke had healed slowly but steadily. The stronger he grew, the more anxious Addie had become. She had even spent the better part of the last few evenings in nerve-riddled anxiety, tilting like a seesaw between nausea, panic, and acceptance—and all for nothing. It darn-near made her mad. "Zeke doesn't want any more children."

"So I heard," Beatrice said dryly. "How do you feel about that?"

Addie smiled nervously. "There's days when the three I've got are about three too many."

Beatrice chuckled; how well she knew. "And other days?"

Addie just shrugged and stared into the fire as if she

could lose herself there. "I don't know. I'm not too anxious, I guess."

Beatrice recognized the words for what they were, not a lie but an unknowing, a misunderstanding of the deepest nature of the female body. To love and be loved was bred into every cell, muscle, and bone, unless the woman had been cruelly or unnaturally stripped of her most basic desires.

"Marrying without courting is hard," Beatrice said. "There's nothing to get two people ready to be together. You know that Sam wasn't my first husband?" Addie looked up, startled. "No indeed, my first man got thrown by a horse on our way out here, leaving me with two kids to support. Sam had lost his wife to a fever and was struggling to raise his own kids when I pulled into town. Being a smart woman and not of a mind to starve, I married him almost faster than he could get the proposal out."

She paused to make certain Addie was listening to every word. "Nights were the worst at first. I felt like a whore lying beneath a man I hadn't known more than a week, much less loved. I reckon Sam felt a bit guilty too at first, because he was always sort of cautious and hesitant, like he was afraid I was gonna box his ears or something. But I knew my duty and didn't want to risk getting booted out on the next train with two hungry babies."

Addie's cheeks had grown hotter than the flames in the hearth, but her hostess wasn't backing down from what needed to be said. "Now, Sam is a man who minds his responsibility, and he wouldn't have done such a thing, but I didn't know that at the time. Anyway, it paid off later. Me and Sam got right cozy through that first winter and by the second I had a lot more to offer him than duty in the way of respect and love."

Addie wasn't about to ask where this was leading. She was afraid she knew. "It's up to Zeke."

"Figured you'd say that. Most women would," Beatrice scoffed. "Now, you don't have to tell me nothing about Willis. I know he was hard on you by the way you carried yourself those four years, always looking beat and avoiding people. You've got a different look now, Addie, happier, brighter. Why, you've fairly blossomed."

Addie gave the older woman a bemused smile. She didn't know about the blossoming part but she definitely felt different—safer, happier, more content. And yet, with the peace of the past months had also come a restlessness she didn't understand, an itchiness, like spring fever had come upon her and everything inside her was just bursting to shed winter and bloom. "I do feel . . . different," she admitted.

"Like I said, you look different too." Bea grinned and gave Addie a direct look. "If I didn't know better, I'd say you had the look of a woman in love."

Addie's face went pale. When she brought her coffee cup to her lips, her hands were trembling. "Zeke wouldn't care for that much. We have an arrangement—"

"Hogwash!" Bea snorted. "Ain't a person alive that doesn't want to be loved. It's human nature." Bea's voice grew softer but no less direct. "I know Zeke's not so anxious to give up his heart again or make another baby, but—"

"Why?" The word burst from Addie, more demanding than curious. Although her cheeks burned with a touch of embarrassment, her eyes never once wavered from Bea's. "Tell me about his first wife. Help me understand how it was for them, so I can try to understand him now."

Bea took a deep breath, nodded, and began in unusually subdued tones. "His Becky was a pretty thing and about as friendly as a woman could be. I reckon she loved Zeke something fierce and he loved her back the same way. But Becky wasn't . . . suited. I know she cared for Zeke, but she'd come out here from one of those fancy plantations that got burned during the war. She talked about it a lot at first, then acted like it didn't exist anymore." Bea shook her head. "But there was something . . . I don't know. Sometimes you'd just see her eyes go all sad, like maybe she was thinking back but didn't want anyone to know.

"Anyway, as you can imagine, it was tough on Zeke after she died. Cole was just a wee thing. I offered to care for him here, but Zeke wouldn't hear of it. He toted Cole on his back like an Indian baby while he did chores, with Zeb trailing behind and Josh helping.

"Cole didn't take well to goat's milk either and spent a good part of those first few months bringing back up whatever went down and fretting something awful. Some days, I imagine the hardship of missing Becky and caring for the boys alone near 'bout killed Zeke. I don't figure he's worked through the memory of it yet."

Addie stared at her hands, wondering if Zeke still loved his first wife as he had when Becky was alive or if he had accepted her passing. Picturing Zeke's struggle with the children hurt so badly it made her throat ache. "Can't blame him for that."

"Not placing blame," Beatrice said frankly. "Just wanted you to know the reason behind his reluctance." She paused, then offered carefully, "Men and women got needs that go beyond just being a helpmate to each other, Addie. Take my word for it. Men git right fractious without a woman's love, and women git the same way, though not half of them would admit it." Addie might have been married before, but Bea could tell the young woman didn't have a clue about anything she was saying. "There's things you could do to change Zeke's mind about a baby."

Addie shook her head adamantly. "It wouldn't be right."

"Maybe," Bea said. "But those things would also make life a lot easier for both of you, baby or not."

Addie's hands were laced tightly around her cup, the knuckles growing white. Her voice was breathless when she spoke. "What things?"

Beatrice hid a self-satisfied smile. Joshua Ezekiel Claiborne didn't have a chance. "Some of this might sound downright shocking, Addie. Just pick and choose what seems right for you, and let Zeke take care of the rest."

Zeke pulled a packet out from under his coat as soon as he and Sam reached the barn. Without preliminary, he handed the books Addie had illustrated to the older man.

"Well now," Sam drawled, "that's real nice of you, Zeke. I don't recollect I've been given such a gift since I was in knee britches."

Zeke chuckled at the droll sarcasm. "I'm glad you like them, but they're not for you." At Sam's mock-wounded look, he continued, "Addie drew them."

Sam's eyebrows rose in astonishment. "No foolin'?" He turned back the cloth-covered backs and thumbed through the pages in serious observation, seeing the portrayal of several well-known children's fables. He looked up and handed the homemade books back to Zeke. "I'm no expert, but it appears to me she's a right good hand at this sort of thing."

"I think so too," Zeke said. "I'm not an expert either, but I've seen art. My mother was a minor collector before the war." He flipped through the pages for the hundredth time since Christmas morning, vacillating between confused and appreciative and stunned. The style was decidedly Rubens. Strong, full-bodied lines and violent, swirling action made the animals so lifelike they appeared ready to leap right off the pages. "We had plenty that didn't look half this good."

Sam shook his head in bemusement. "Her family moved here when she was still a young thing, no more than ten or twelve, I'd guess. She wasn't old enough to have already studied at some fancy school, but I do remember her pa ordering her books every chance he got. Guess she learned that way."

"I guess," he echoed in a bewildered tone. "Her talent is purely natural, but she shuns praise like it's a curse. Wouldn't even discuss it with me."

Sam was as perplexed as Zeke. "What you reckon that means?"

"I haven't the faintest idea," he said.

Zeke stared at the embers glowing in the hearth and massaged the ache in his thigh absently. There were other parts of him in far worse agony. He was sufficiently healed enough to ease the ache with Addie, but he was loath to approach her. He knew they had to take precautions to avoid getting her pregnant and wondered how he could explain that and the fact that their first time would most likely be painful, when he had promised to never hurt her. He was either a hero or a coward, he wasn't sure which, but he had no desire to see the fear enter her eyes.

She deserved more than his lust her first time, but that was all he had to offer. Sweet words and false devotion wouldn't come easily to his lips, which was why he had avoided trying to seduce her. He knew he could tempt and titillate her body if she allowed it, but he doubted either of them could get far enough past her inhibitions the first time for it to be anything but awkward. It just didn't seem right anymore to think about laying her down and appeasing his hunger without the tenderness and caring she needed.

He had grown to respect her over the past few months, more than he thought possible, enough to feel that she deserved so much more than his lechery. He wished he'd taken her the first few weeks of marriage, when nothing mattered but his carnal desires, when her blushing and stammering and fearfulness wouldn't have meant much.

But he felt things for her now. Esteem and honor and even a bit of reverence. Those things might count when voting for a politician or choosing a new pastor or teacher, but they were little consolation in wooing a virgin. He knew his body well, knew how long it had been and how difficult, how damn near impossible, it would be to take things slowly.

Thoughts of Becky were intrusive and unwanted at this point, but true wisdom was always gained by experience, and Zeke remembered their first time with regret and sad longing. They'd been so eager for each other before the wedding, unfettered by youth, driven by love. Her parents had been so glad to see him during the middle of the war that their minds had been taken up with politics rather than chaperoning their engaged daughter and her nineteen-year-old beau.

They'd allowed Becky to walk out with him in the graying shadows of evening. Full up with thoughts of the conflict, her parents had retired inside the house to hopelessly glory in the impending triumph of the South. Left alone with their youth and eagerness and love, Zeke had led Becky down to the banks of the Mississippi River and let his fervor take him. She'd been ardent and willing in his arms, but she'd also been innocent. Buttons and laces and inhibitions had dissolved beneath their fingers, until they were both writhing on the fecund grass, unwilling to stop with the stolen kisses and improper petting that had halfway satisfied them until then.

Caught up in a storm of passion without the experience to temper it, Zeke had taken her wildly. She had cried out when he entered her and wept until he was done. Inconsolable, she had gathered her clothes around her, thinking herself ruined in his eyes, because she'd always been told that good girls waited and gentlemen respected them for it. Half ashamed himself by what they had done, he had soothed her the best he could, with words of love and promises easily fulfilled because they had come from the heart.

But he couldn't offer that to Addie. Whatever the war had not managed to strip away, Becky's death had. Something in him had closed the day he buried her, something vital and alive and necessary. There was so little of that idealistic young man left inside him, that any true or worthy emotions he could still feel were reserved for the boys.

Zeke smiled bittersweetly, glad that at least he was capable of thinking about Becky now with a clear head and no tightening in his gut. Addie had enabled him to see beyond the pain and reconcile himself to let the past be, because it was what she had learned to do for herself. He hurt for Becky still, for the life she had lost, the joy he'd not been able to give her. But he could at least put it all in perspective now. Until the last, she had tried to love him and be what he needed, keeping her ever-increasing dark demons from him.

He'd never known how close she was to the edge, but he understood now that even if they had returned to Natchez, he couldn't have replaced for her the dreams and illusions of the world she had once known. Life's disappointments had been too great for her and had finally broken her. They had broken him as well. But a broken man had no place in the future. He had his sons and a new wife to consider; merely surviving wasn't enough, and he would have to put the past aside and go on.

He turned from the fire, reconciled by the memories to wait, at least as long as he was capable of it. He had no desire to go to his grave a frustrated, dried-up old man, but also didn't want to push Addie so hard that she reverted to the way she had been when he met her. She had softened toward him over the past months, and he hoped it would be enough, that she would one day be as ready for him as he was for her, enough that any pain or shyness would only be a memory compared to the pleasure.

The glow from the lantern was the only warm spot in the bedroom. Addie stared at it with an obsessive intensity to keep the panic at bay. She wasn't scared, she *wasn't,* she told herself over and over until it had become a litany in her mind. Her palms grew clammy and she brushed them down the transparent nightgown Beatrice had given her. The bed was there, not two feet away. She could dive beneath the covers and burrow like a chipmunk seeking safety, but no. That wasn't what Beatrice had suggested.

So her feet remained planted, her legs trembling, her resolve crumbling beneath the weight of her timid wretchedness. She shuddered when the door creaked open, but didn't move.

Zeke took one step into the room, then paused, frozen in his tracks by the sight before him. He opened his mouth to say something, but whatever he intended was lost as time came to a screeching halt and everything outside receded to a blur. Everything but this room and his wife. Addie stood in the gossamer nightgown, looking pensive but determined, and so alluring his heart stopped beating completely before it began to race.

She was substance and shadow, healthy curves outlined by candlelight, her face an ethereal porcelain mask. Her long, slender limbs were gracefully poised and still as an indrawn breath, but her eyes flickered once with uncertainty.

Zeke retreated instantly from the emotions rushing at him, but it wasn't as easy as it had been in the past, and it was impossible to retreat physically. He slowly raked his fingers through his hair, commanding caution from an eager, too-long-deprived body.

He took a careful step toward her, afraid it was all an illusion, and let his gaze roam where his hands wanted to until he finally met her eyes. Her face was rapt, tense with uncertainty and a determination that made her unnaturally still and pale.

"You sure, Addie?"

She nodded, not trusting her voice.

His hand rose and he touched a curl at her temple, reining in the sweet desire to bury himself within her generosity. "You don't look sure." He leaned forward and brushed her lips to test her commitment to the course she'd just laid, half wondering if she'd bolt, fully knowing she wouldn't. He touched her nowhere but her lips, the distance between their bodies akin to miles if measured by his desire.

She felt his mouth move over hers, the faintest brush of warmth against cool. Her head felt light. Dizziness assailed her stomach and legs, setting off a weakness that made her tremble.

"I would like to do this right," she said. It was not a statement but a whispered plea that sent a sensual sting to all parts of Zeke's body.

So, it would be tonight. He wondered why, what she hoped to gain. He wasn't sure if it mattered, or if he was even glad that the waiting was over. He knew for certain he stunned. And grateful. From that heady relief came the awareness of what she was yielding to him, willingly and trustingly. The sweet wholeness of her gift tempered his hunger and brought a rush of unexpected completion to his soul.

His mouth continued to move gently over hers, a caress rather than a kiss, a promise rather than a demand. The fragrance of her hair wafted on the still air and mingled with the mild tang of heat from the burning candlewick. She filled his senses until he overflowed with the taste and aroma of rose water. His hands rose and very lightly, almost adoringly, gripped her upper arms. Her skin was smooth and cool, pearlescent in the moonlight. He drew her closer and felt the beat of her heart struggling to find a safe rhythm, and his own answering in rampant passion.

His fingers flexed on her arms. Uncontrolled, he would hurt her. He might not be able to avoid it anyway. The thought settled darkly in his heart, and he pulled back slightly. Lacing their fingers together, he tugged her over to the bed.

He turned back the quilt in invitation, because he wanted her there, but knew they needed to talk first, to sort through this night so there would be no regrets or recriminations later. While there was an ounce of willpower left in him, she would lose her innocence willingly or not lose it at all.

Addie climbed into the deep comfort of the feather bed, glad to seek its concealing cover and support. Her quivering legs wouldn't have held her much longer. Zeke began unbuttoning his shirt. She watched each familiar movement that tonight took on a new and indelible reality until his hands reached his pants, then turned her face away. She had started this; she wondered if she could finish it.

Zeke climbed into bed and rolled toward her, keeping a margin of distance necessary for his sanity and her virtue. He strove for lightheartedness to alleviate the tension.

"You sure look pretty tonight, Miz Claiborne. What did you have in mind?"

Addie's entire body blushed. If he didn't know, she wouldn't tell him, and she was wholly embarrassed that he'd asked the question. With all her sage suggestions, Beatrice hadn't led her to believe that Zeke wouldn't realize what she was offering. "Just thought I'd try this nightgown on," she hedged, her cheeks flaming.

Zeke touched her face, urging her with gentle pressure to look at him. "Oh, thought maybe you had something else in mind."

"No," she murmured, so embarrassed she was drowning in it, "unless you do."

And in that instant he found the way. Reprehensible maybe for its sneakiness, but necessary because of her past. Become as innocent and uncertain as she. "No, I don't have anything in mind except sleep. But—" He shook his head so sadly, so convincingly, the theater would have snatched him up in a heartbeat. "It's just, I'd like to kiss you." His voice deepened, growing mysterious. "Just a good-night kiss. We've never really done that, you know."

She'd never heard him so humble. "All right," she murmured, relaxing.

His lips were dry and hot on hers, so light her breath held on a pause. She stood just at the edge of some high mountaintop, a place of perilous excitement. She wanted to pull him closer and hold tight, so as not to plunge headlong into the waiting cavern. She curled her fists into the bedding and waited for what he would do next.

He only continued the tender, weightless meeting of their mouths for seconds that seemed to span eternity. There was no time, no existence, beyond the hazy anxiety of the moment. She waited and waited for the sharp twist of aggression, the panicky suffocation when his body covered hers. The moment never came. He did nothing but set his mouth over hers in reverent softness, substanceless as a wish, beguiling as a caress.

Addie grew restless inside. She could not put a name to the feeling. It was nothing so simple as hysteria, but a complex reaction of yearning and striving that felt nearly like the grip of apprehension but without the fear. She felt a subtle shift in his body, barely discernible, then his tongue probe her lips. And all she could think was *finally* something more. On a sigh, she opened for him, welcomed him, but he did little more than increase the pressure of their lips.

She began to feel squirmy and restive, needing more substance, not knowing how to get it. She moved restlessly, brushing against him and felt his tongue suddenly sweep along the edges of her teeth once, swift and hot. Then his lips were gone, evaporating from hers as if they had never been. She cried out softly in disappointment.

Her confusion was so dear to Zeke, he knew he had chosen his path wisely. There was no fear at all in her eyes, but there was untold hunger. "What's wrong, Addie?"

Everything was wrong. Everything! Beatrice had said the sheer nightgown would be enough, but it hadn't been. Tears of frustration burned behind her eyelids, but they were only an overflow of the discontent deeper within her. When he reached out to cradle her cheek, she turned her face into his palm, soothed by the tenderness. Her tongue darted out to wet her dry lips when she tried to speak, but the effort was so hard. His eyes followed the course of her pink tongue with sudden intensity.

"You . . . you said you wanted more than a mother for the boys and a housekeeper," she whispered.

"I still do."

Her gaze shot to his, the tiniest spark of challenge in the green depths. "Well, why don't you do something?"

Every soft, distressed word made the blood thicken in Zeke's veins. "Because I don't want you to be afraid."

"I'm not." But she was, for a lot of reasons that had nothing to do with him. She was afraid she would be incompetent. She was afraid she would disappoint him or so disgust him that he would turn angry and mean like Willis had. *You ain't got nothin' a man would want. Turn around, girl . . . turn around . . . turn around . . .*

She sighed, so close to tears the sound came out as a disgruntled moan. "Well, Beatrice said men had needs and things would go a lot easier if . . . and, well . . . you said . . . but now . . . you don't." She stopped, then blurted out in a heated rush. "And I don't blame you, but I wish you hadn't changed your mind." Her voice had risen until it was trembling. "And you don't want any more babies!"

Zeke put a finger to her lips, calming her, quieting his own raging emotions. "No, but I want you, Addie, so badly I hurt with it."

Her eyes widened and everything in her grew quiet and poised on the edge of enchantment. "You do?"

"More than I've ever wanted anyone."

"You don't have—"

"Yes, I do. Please listen." He ran a finger down her cheek, sketching the outline of her beautiful face, but feeling the more worthwhile qualities inside her, the strength and endurance of her commitment, the openness of her giving. He felt crass and unworthy of her, of everything she was offering, when he could give so little in return. "Becky and I were young when we married. We had the world. Nothing could harm us, nothing could get in our way.

"But Becky wasn't . . . strong, though I think she tried to be. I knew things were difficult for her, but I was too busy fighting the war, then fighting the land to be what she needed. Our love wasn't enough to fight her loneliness and longing for the life she had left behind. She lived in a dream world; she only existed in the real one. The day she died, she was leaving me and the boys and returning to Natchez."

"No," Addie whispered, stricken, unable to believe any woman would want to leave this man. "No," she denied again, but saw the heart-wrenching truth in his eyes. "Oh, I'm so sorry."

"So am I," he admitted, "but not for the reasons you might think. Becky was pretty and smart and vivacious, but she was displaced out here where life is so hard. She tried desperately to fit in, but deep inside I think she always felt above the simple folks in town. She was never meant to leave the luxury of her plantation home and her privileged upbringing."

He drew Addie closer, but kept a margin of space between them to finish what needed to be said. "You are so much like her, Addie, smart and pretty and full of life when you let yourself feel it. But you are also much more. You're a survivor, with an indomitable spirit. You face life's darkest moments and find the strength and courage somehow to rise above it. I know that if anything happened to me, you'd be here to raise the boys. You'd do what needed to be done and never falter in your love and care for them."

He pulled her deeper into him, and his eyes burned with the powerful hunger in his body. "You are everything I need in a wife, and I want you more than I've ever wanted any other woman." His voice grew deeper, rougher, as his hands tightened on her. "But I don't have anything to give you in return. I saw too much terror during the war to believe in the basic goodness of man. I lost too many dreams to believe that any kind of innocence lasts. I'll support you financially and I'll love you physically, but I can never be what you deserve otherwise."

His thumb stroked the corner of her mouth as his fingers caressed her cheek, but for all his tenderness his eyes were fierce. "You deserve so much, Addie. I wish I could be that man, a young idealist who could offer you sweet romantic words and bright hopes for the future. But he no longer exists inside me. Can you accept that?"

She swallowed and nodded, but her heart was breaking into sharp little fragments. He would never love her, never be the man of her dreams. She wanted to lash out at him for the unfairness of it all, but turned it inward instead, blocking and isolating the pain because, no matter how she wanted him to feel otherwise, she understood his reasons so well.

His thumb caressed the underside of her jaw, then drifted down her neck. "I want to do this right," he said gruffly, "but I don't know how much longer I can hold out."

The strength of his words overwhelmed her, filling her with both fear and wonder until she couldn't contain herself. She buried her face in his chest, not wanting him to see the tears gathering in her eyes.

"I'm sorry, I didn't mean to frighten you."

She shook her head, fiercely suppressing the need to cry. Her throat worked spasmodically to hold back the tears, but it seemed as if years and years of them were built up inside her, screaming to be let out.

Zeke sighed and tucked her chin under his head, knowing he had hurt her. He wanted her physically with a gripping severity, but he had too much respect for her to take her in that manner. "Have you changed your mind?"

She shook her head, and Zeke tensed at the commitment. There was no turning back now. He let himself feel what he'd been trying to ignore for the last few minutes—the flow of silky fabric over his abdomen and chest, the feel of her bare legs pressed against his. He suppressed a groan rising deep in his throat and brushed the curls back from her face as he lifted it up to his.

"Addie," he began carefully. "I said I would never hurt you and I meant it, but—" How to go about this, how to explain something she should already know? "If you're still a virgin—" He felt her stiffen and inwardly retreat.

"I'm not," she mumbled, stubborn and mortified. Her face dove back into his chest.

"How do you know?"

Because Willis had rubbed his hot, sweaty body against her too many times, then beat her because she hadn't pleased him.

"I was married for four wretched years, and even if I hadn't been, I've been around animals all my life," she said, so embarrassed she couldn't look at him. "Don't you think I'd know?"

"Willis wasn't . . . normal," Zeke began as gently as he could and still make her understand. "Unless things changed between you after you went to Christian . . ."

Her eyes widened and she pulled away from him, then scrambled up until she was sitting against the headboard. Her legs were drawn up to her chest, her face buried on her knees. "I can't talk about this."

Zeke eased up beside her. "I'm not trying to shame you, Addie. I need to know, so I don't hurt you. The first time can be painful."

"*Every* time with Willis was painful," she said in a disgusted voice.

If she hadn't looked so vulnerable hugging her knees,

he might have smiled at her fierce tone. Instead he gently pulled her back down until they were both lying on their sides, facing each other.

"Animals and people are the same in some ways, but different too. What Willis did was neither animal nor human. He might have imitated the act but that was all."

Her eyes had grown wide as saucers, beautiful green pools of bewilderment and embarrassment and curiosity. He could tell she wanted to hear more, but was too ashamed or modest to ask.

"He didn't do it," he repeated in a gentler tone, "couldn't do it. He took his own inadequacies out on you, but you weren't to blame. He was physically impotent." Her prim little backbone stiffened as she, for the first time in too long, recognized just what he was saying. "He need not have hurt you," Zeke continued, "but I think he took his hatred for himself out on you." He touched her shoulder then began to soothe her tense body with tender sweeps of his hand. "I can prove it to you, if you'll let me."

16

"Prove it how?" she asked, wary now.

"Touch you—" He felt her violent shiver and didn't finish the answer that would send her flying from the bed. Instead, he lowered his mouth to hers, plotting how he would go about this without losing the tenderness she deserved or creating even more embarrassment. Her lips were firm against his in resistance, her body pulling back in retreat, but he only slipped one arm beneath her head and draped the other around her back to hold her against him. "Where are you going, Addie?"

She quit squirming immediately. "Nowhere."

He smiled against her sweet lips and marveled at her self-control and sacrifice. "We don't have to," he said, wondering what he'd do if she actually agreed.

Color flooded her face. She gazed thoughtfully up at him and said with studied deliberation, "Beatrice said—"

"To hell with Bea," he said gently. "It's just you and me, Addie. No one else can dictate our lives." His lips played lightly over hers, the vibrations of his voice sending shivers down her extremities. "I'm going to touch you now . . . no, don't get tense. You can tell me to stop at any time."

But she couldn't say anything because his mouth had covered hers again and she was lost beneath the warmth and tenderness of his kiss. His heat was a comfort, surrounding her, protecting her from the harsh and cold reality of an outside world. Her lips trembled and she grew soft and receptive, yielding to Zeke so sweetly he was lost to the pleasure as well. He pressed more fully, slanting his mouth across hers while his body sought its own comfortable closeness. The curves and hollows of her slight frame were filled with his larger one, warmth against cool, the natural coming together of puzzle pieces too long separate. She didn't resist but neither did she respond, just seemed to wait for whatever he would do next.

His hand slid down her spine to the small of her back and held her just there, with gentle force, while his lips continued to engage hers with tender aggression. He wanted to touch her further, every inch, but he could feel a deeper assertiveness taking hold of him. His pulse thudded faster as his mouth molded and shaped hers to find the way they fit, masculine and feminine, wind-roughened cheeks against smooth. Her lips parted on a sigh that whispered through him and his breathing grew jagged and unstable. His approach was critical. If he left it untempered, he would lose control.

His leg moved lightly over hers, a barely discernible motion, as the rest of him gently rocked against her, applying pressure to her lower back to teach her the rhythm. Malleable, she flowed with him, but when his tongue touched her lips, she made a small sound and opened fully under his questing mouth, needing more of him than the external warmth and heaviness of his body.

She needed him inside her as well, a part of her. Her tongue caressed his, uninhibited, and hot chills raced across Zeke's skin, sharp pinpricks of desire that covered every inch. He absorbed her small gasp with his own deep moan, drinking in the scent and feel of her until it filled him.

Rolling, he pressed her to her back, needing greater access. Her gown had risen above her knees, escalating his heart rate and his hunger. Consumed by the sight of her slender legs bathed in nothing but candlelight, he ran his palm over her ankle and calf, reveling in the feel of sleek skin over lithe sinews. Her flesh was cool to the touch, but her eyes were hot from both wariness and anticipation. He felt the brush of her nightgown against the back of his hand as he finally slipped beneath the hem to touch her silken thigh. He felt her quiver, and rushed his lips back to hers.

"I've always thought you had the most beautiful legs," he whispered against her lips, letting his fingers wander aimlessly so she would grow accustomed to the feel. "I used to watch the wind plaster your skirts to you, outlining every inch. I wanted to be that close." With exquisite gentleness he stroked her thigh as his mouth moved to the satin skin of her neck. "And here, you're so beautiful here," he said, brushing his lips over her throat to her shoulder, then down to the hills of her breasts. "And here."

His mouth opened over one taut nipple, and he felt her jerk delicately. His tongue laved her through the lacy nightgown, wetting the fabric until it was so thin and transparent he could see the rosiness of her areole and the tight bud at its center. He heard her breath skip and felt her arch tensely against him, but the motion was nothing compared to his own lurching heartbeat, the hot intensity of blood rushing through his veins. The muscles of her thigh contracted beneath his fingers but he transmitted none of the aggression inside him and continued to smooth her skin in gentle unerring sweeps until she relaxed.

His hand rose in a gliding motion that touched her everywhere yet nowhere like a warm zephyr that billowed just on the fringes of her gown. He loosened the ribbon at her breasts, then parted the edges wide until she was fully revealed. Her hands fluttered instinctively, then gripped the sheet to keep from covering herself.

Her voice was tight and breathless. "What will you do now?"

"Taste you." The notion was so foreign she had to consider it, and he waited until she had gained her composure before lowering his head to the ripe wonder of her flesh. With reverence he trailed his lips over the slopes of her fragrant skin, then with care his mouth closed lightly over one tight, achy nipple. Her gasp was song, a cry of wanting constrained deep in her throat. Her chest went utterly still.

"Breathe, Addie," he whispered, before bathing her with his tongue. She cried out then and rose high, aiding him well. He moved to her other breast and repeated the words and the seduction, finding himself drawing too close to the edge for comfort or reason. His hand slid back to her thigh, but she hardly noticed with his tongue working a feverish magic at her breasts.

His fingers searched out the hot, moist center of her and he felt her cringe, but only slightly, for the motion of his mouth changed quickly, purposefully, to a tender adhesion as he began to suckle her, providing a wondrous deterrent for whatever thoughts she might have had of stopping him. His mouth worked its mystery and she was lost beneath the passion of his lips and tongue, the slight scraping of his teeth. Her small gasps burned through him in waves of liquid fire. As her hands clasped and unclasped on the sheet in a state of sensual panic, his fingers sought the entrance to her body.

"Hold on to me, Addie," he whispered, and her hands flew to his shoulders as if she'd but waited for permission. He pressed inside to find her humid and heavy with desire.

She retreated then on a cry, embarrassed and confused. Her nails bit into his skin, but he followed her withdrawal and soothed her with words, while pressing deeper. "It's all right, Addie. Relax and let me."

His exploration was clinical, separate in his mind from the intimacy he wanted but necessary to keep him from ravishing her. Yet he could not completely divorce himself from the sensations, the moist tightness of her body surrounding him, allowing him to become a part of her. With iron restraint, he took a deep breath and withdrew. He had found what he had been seeking, the restrictive band of her innocence, and knew why Willis had never been able to breach her. Even if the man had been capable, she was wary and tight, every tiny muscle a constricted barrier. He groaned inwardly and wrapped her up in his arms, wondering how much prodding and pain it would take to enter her.

He tried for lightness but his throat was tight. "Addie, you are definitely still a virgin."

She blushed and turned her face away, embarrassed by her own ignorance and the intimacy of his touch. Zeke turned her face back and brought his lips to hers. Reining in his desire, he kissed her with care and concern and without an ounce of the terrible passion gripping him.

"I'm so damn glad Willis didn't touch you that way." His arms contracted to iron bands around her, and his voice was thick. "I don't want to hurt you, Addie, but I want to get deep inside where I can be a part of you. The first time can be . . . difficult."

After everything he had done for her, everything he had been to her, she didn't believe him. "I want you to, no matter what."

A thousand fiery darts shot down his spine, tightening the muscles of his buttocks. "Let's take your gown off." He didn't wait for agreement. The stiffening of her body was either from shock or fright, or both. In one quick movement, he lifted the hem of her gown over her hips, arms, and head, then tossed it to the floor.

He didn't linger to look at her; it was too dangerous. Instead, he held her pressed against him, feeling every contour of her naked flesh along every hungry inch of his. "I need you, Addie," he said as he rolled and positioned himself between her legs. "Remember," he implored as he moved forward, an inch at a time, until he met moist resistance. He kept his weight on his arms as he gazed down into her wide, deep green eyes. Bands of hot color spread over her cheeks, but her lips were bloodless, her thighs locked against his hips. "Do you want me to stop? I can stop now, Addie. I don't know about later."

"I want you to kiss me again," she pleaded.

He did, chasing her fears so far away there was no hindrance, no barrier strong enough to separate them. His kiss was hungry and aggressive, but so gentle it swept Addie up into its center. Her body yielded, the muscles of her legs relaxed completely as she lost herself to the wonder of his mouth, the rightness of his hands on her body. But when he pressed to fully enter her, she went rigid, her body instinctively contracting to fight his penetration. Her hands came up to push against his chest and she twisted to get away, searing his sensitized flesh with the motion.

"Addie, don't—" He gripped her hips to stop her, but she panicked and bucked to throw him off, deepening their contact and her own agony. Zeke sucked in a breath but there was no turning back. Her body began to tear and he thrust once, fast and hard, to finish it. Addie arched at the pain, her eyes dilated with wounded surprise.

"I'm sorry . . . sorry," he repeated over and over, holding himself still as death. Sweat beaded his brow and his fingers bit into her hips as he fought for control.

"I can't," she cried, her hands locked against his chest, her eyes glazed over with confusion. Beyond that Addie couldn't speak, couldn't breathe. She felt suffocated and torn, stretched beyond her body's capacity, and so frightened by the fierce and tortured expression on Zeke's face.

"No more pain, I promise," he said, his voice oddly constricted. He did nothing but hold himself immobile, but it took all his control and strength not to plunge within the molten heat clasping him.

"But I can't breathe," she said a little wildly, her chest rising and falling rapidly to belie the statement.

"You're just panicked," he said gently, and took her face in his hands and stroked her cheek with his thumbs in a consoling, repetitive motion until the wildness left her eyes. He kissed her then, consoling and penitent, hungry and passionate, as if he could breathe life into her with each kiss he took.

She welcomed his onslaught, her mouth joining his in mute acceptance of his possession. It was the hardest thing Zeke had ever done, to lie still and quiet while buried in her tight warmth. His muscles trembled from the strain, and he didn't know how much longer he could hold out. He dropped his head to the hollow of her neck and ran his tongue over the corded tendons. "Are you all right now?"

She nodded but couldn't speak. The terrible sting was a slow throbbing now, uncomfortable and foreign but fading. "Zeke?"

He lifted his head to look at her.

She swallowed at the agony in his eyes. "You all right?"

He chuckled slightly, painfully. He hurt like hell, burning up with a desire he couldn't release in her tender body. Her flesh tightened around him, and he gritted his teeth to stop the groan rising in his throat. "I'm fine. Never better."

She reached up and touched his face hesitantly, her eyes huge and alarmed. "Willis never . . . I don't know how to do this right. Please . . ."

"God, Addie," he rasped out. Everything in him co-alesced into the needy obsession to possess her further, to strip away every memory of Willis until there was nothing left but an awareness of him for the rest of her life, for all of eternity. "You're doing everything right. I just don't want to hurt you further," he said raggedly. She inadvertently shifted and the desires of his body betrayed him, overriding everything but the desperate need to reach completion.

He rocked gently against her, testing, but the motion was too much for his deprived body. Savage tension curled within his body and he began to move faster, escalating the tempo until the thunder of his heartbeat matched the cadence of his body. He searched her face for signs of strain or hurt, but the gripping passion of filling her took over and he couldn't see or hear or feel anything but the joining of their bodies, the perfect completion, the primitive rightness and violent necessity of becoming one with her as deeply as possible.

He might have had more restraint if she had fought him or at least berated him for his callousness, but holding back was impossible when she accepted him, uncertain of the ways but mutely flowing with the motion of his body, her arms clinging to his shoulders, her nails digging into his back.

Tension stabbed like needles down his spine, and he thrust faster, consumed, his hips grinding into hers until the months of wanting came together in one blinding rush and his body went taut. He gave a gritty cry as he reached the pinnacle and buried himself fully, then poured himself into her in throbbing pulses of fulfillment that faded into drained contentment. Then eventually, inevitably, into regret. His harsh breathing slowed, his heartbeat quieted, and he finally dropped his gaze back to hers. His arms trembled as he searched her face.

"Addie," he whispered, and rolled gently to his side, keeping her pressed against him. "Addie, look at me."

She turned her head to face him, feeling shaky and disquieted. There wasn't much to it, she decided, certainly nothing she should have been afraid of. But there wasn't much to recommend it either. She didn't understand what compelled men to want to do it. It had been generally uncomfortable and embarrassing, but if it was so important to Zeke, she thought she could do it again.

"I'm sorry." He reached out and touched a damp curl by her face and watched it wind tightly around his finger, entrapping him. "I should have been more considerate of you. The first few times . . . a man needs to be considerate." His eyes closed briefly. "But I wanted you so badly!"

Lamplight loved his hair. It caught in every damp strand and scattered golden brilliance like a mesmerizing prism. His skin shone bronze, slick with sweat, his face still taut with tension and sharp with arousal. She swallowed the lump in her throat. "I'm glad."

His eyes flew open at the words to see one tear roll down her cheek. His heart contracted and he pulled her deeper into him. "Don't cry, Addie, please don't cry."

"I can't help it," she sniffled, her voice angry and resentful. "Willis told me no one could ever want me. But you did."

He still did, with a terrible, renewed urgency that didn't bode well for her tender state. "He was sick, Addie, insane." He brushed the tear from her cheek. "I want you again, right now. I can't help it."

She grimaced. She didn't particularly find that thought appealing, but said softly, "You can, if you want."

He smiled over the painful stirring of his body and eased back to break contact. "No, it's too soon for you. You need a little time to heal." He didn't know whether to laugh or cry at her unconscious sigh of relief. "It will be better next time, I promise."

She nodded, uncomfortable with the intimate conversation even as she reveled in it. She guessed it was different for a man. For herself, she felt sticky and sore and didn't know what she was supposed to do. An unsettled feeling lingered in her middle and her skin felt strange and impermeable. She took a deep breath but there was no calm within her, just a restless tolling that couldn't seem to escape the confines of her flesh.

Shivering, she tugged up the quilt to cover herself, then blushed when she caught Zeke's stare. Without a word, he rolled to the side of the bed and stood.

It seemed indecent to watch him cross the room in nothing but the magnificent form God had given him, but Addie watched anyway, her lids half lowered, as if that made it only half as lewd. When he returned with the washbowl and cloth, her eyes widened and she blushed crimson.

He placed the bowl on the nightstand, then wet the cloth. When he held it up and looked back at her he found Addie clutching the quilt to her nose, her eyes stricken. He'd forgotten his nakedness and glanced down to find blood smeared on himself. He suddenly felt exposed and awkward when there shouldn't have been anything but relief and contentment, the quiet basking in the aftermath.

He felt something in him recoil and shut off, even as he cursed his thoughtlessness. She needed more than one quick coupling to grow accustomed to him prancing around the room naked, but it was too late now, and he didn't have much patience for modest games.

"Hold on to the quilt," he said, as he reached under and stripped away the top sheet. He wrapped it around his waist, then disappeared out the door.

Addie eased up against the headboard and rested her chin on her knees, feeling disoriented. She had displeased him somehow. Her teeth chewed her bottom lip, then a small spark of anger burst within her. Her legs were trembling, other parts of her hurting, though not badly. He wasn't the only one displeased. She heard water running and roused quickly to bathe herself before Zeke returned.

Her knees went weak when she stood and glanced

down at herself. There was blood on the sheets and on her. Her flesh stung when she bathed it away. Her hands trembling, she rinsed the cloth and wrung it out. The water ran pink into the bowl, somehow obscene, and everything seemed to rush at her all at once.

She dropped the cloth, then clutched convulsively at the bed sheet and tried to strip it away, but the corners were caught. By the time Zeke walked back in, she was sitting crumpled on the floor, naked and crying, the soiled sheets clutched to her. He paused and closed his eyes briefly, then made the bed with the fresh linens he had collected. Once done, he crouched before her and gently pulled the sheet from her clutched fists, then picked her up and laid her beneath the covers.

He held her close while she cried, his emotions shut tight against the sound and the impulse to comfort her with words that would be meaningless at this point. Yet something in him ached and yearned to give her peace, to find it for himself. When she finally eased, he pushed the soft curls back from her face. "Did I molest you, Addie? Did I violate you tonight?"

"No."

"Then why are you so upset?"

She didn't know. She could no more explain it to him than she could understand it herself. "There was so much blood and I couldn't get the sheets off and—"

He kissed her lips then her eyes, tasting the salt of her tears. "It's normal the first time, Addie. Don't let it distress you." He studied her face. Her lashes were still wet, shining like polished mahogany. "What else is troubling you?"

She shrugged, feeling tired and achy and unsettled. "It was on you too. Did—"

"No, it wasn't mine." Part of him was astonished by

her naïveté, another part accepted it as typical of her. Willis had kept her isolated and ignorant, but was he himself any better? He had spent little effort wooing or courting her. She had accepted his penetration as a wifely duty, wanting to please him, but had found no pleasure in it herself. He wondered if she even knew the pleasure existed for her?

Her shoulders were bare above the quilt, slender and pale. He knew how her breasts fit in his palms, how they tasted in his mouth. He knew how the flesh of her buttocks was satiny against his callused fingers. He wanted her again badly, wanted to bring her to the same release he had found, but he knew better than to attempt it tonight. "I won't hurt you again, Addie. You'll be tender for a while, but it won't be like that again."

"Willis never . . ." There was confusion in her voice, then hatred. "Was it my fault?"

"No," he said calmly, though he was furious inside at the worthless bastard and what she must have suffered. His arms tightened around her. "I certainly didn't have any trouble. I've wanted you for so long, I thought I would go crazy with it."

"Why did you wait?"

"You were too scared. I was afraid too. I was worried I'd get carried away and end up raping you. I almost did anyway."

"No." Her cheeks grew pink but she continued, "You could have."

He tensed as renewed heat flooded him. "I'll make up for it."

She cringed slightly. "Tonight?"

A muscle in his jaw twitched and his fist clenched to keep from rolling her beneath him again. He tried to smile. "No. It would be uncomfortable for you."

She relaxed, then murmured sleepily, "Tomorrow?"

She was going to be the death of him. "We'll see how you feel in the morning."

Addie was gone the next morning when Zeke awoke. He wasn't surprised, but he still felt confounded about how to deal with her. The kitchen was dark and cold when he entered. He could hear the boys stirring in their bedroom. He got a fire going to take the chill out of the air, then went looking for his errant wife.

He found her in the barn, supposedly milking, but her hands were idle on the cow's teats and there was little milk in the pail. As soon as his hands fell on her shoulders, she stiffened and spun around.

"Don't," he said quietly. "Don't be embarrassed, Addie."

She rose from the stool, feeling disadvantaged. It had been disconcerting to wake beside him, naked and sore, the memory of their joined bodies still fresh in her mind. She had stared openly at his long, lean body, seeing nothing different, wondering how that could be when she was completely changed herself. "I don't mean to be."

"How do you feel this morning?"

She felt raw and nervous. "Fine."

"You don't look fine. You look shy and uncomfortable." He tipped her chin up. "Do you regret last night?"

"No, but . . ." She pulled her chin back and dropped her eyes. Hay littered the barn floor, a warm honey color in the muted light. "What if I get a baby?"

Zeke recoiled inwardly. Not once, not one single time had he thought to use caution. He'd been so caught up in possessing her, his reason had flown straight out the window. He swallowed and tried to make his voice light. "One time probably won't matter. We'll have to be more careful from now on though."

Addie's heart sank, but she nodded and kept her eyes averted. "How . . . ?"

"I'll show you later." He reached for a curl by her face, then dropped his hand. He couldn't seem to stop the need to touch her. "I'll finish the milking. The boys are awake. They'll be looking for breakfast."

Addie was out of sorts all day. The boys sensed her agitation and were as testy as she, demanding and irritable when they didn't get their way. She finally bundled them up after lunch, and they all trekked out to the range to see if the men were working close enough to catch a glimpse.

The fresh air was invigorating and cleansing after the stuffiness of the house. Snow lay in thick clumps in the shaded areas but the ever-present wind kept huge patches of ground clear. The men were nowhere in sight, but the boys found plenty to occupy them and romped and played as boys should. Addie sat on a fallen log and watched them with a wistfulness that was gratifying and soothing to her troubled spirit.

She found herself smiling impishly when Zeb crept up on Josh and dumped a handful of snow down his back, then took off running. *You better run fast, Zebulun Taylor Claiborne,* she thought, as the images turned to past ones. A Tennessee mountain at dusk when everything caught a purplish haze beneath the setting sun. Childish squeals as Tommy, scratching and whooping, came after their other brother, Ben, for the leaves he'd dropped down Tommy's neck. Their ma, a baby on her hip, calling everyone to supper.

Cole toddled along behind Josh and Zeb, trying to keep up, and took a spill that tumbled him end over end and left him on his bottom, squalling loudly.

Addie scooped him up and soothed him as she dusted snow from his hair and cheeks. He stuck his fist in his mouth and snuggled into the crook of her neck.

" 'Tory," he said sleepily.

"Yes, I'll read you a story when we get back," she said. He snuggled deeper and her breasts tightened unexpectedly. Addie bit back a startled gasp and dropped her cheek to his head. She loved him as if she'd given birth to him, but it wasn't the same. She'd never felt her belly swell as she carried him in her womb; she'd never nursed him at her breast.

She stroked his hair softly, taking comfort from the soft texture and his perfect acceptance. She knew she could never feel any greater affection for a child of her own body than she did for the children surrounding her. Which was good, she supposed, since she'd never have a chance to find out.

The range took on motion and Addie shielded her eyes against the glare of sunshine and snow. Afton appeared, riding hell bent for leather. He barely reined in as he approached and shouted, "Gotta git the sheriff!"

Addie hoisted her skirts in one hand and held on to Cole with the other as she began to run toward him, panic quickening her heartbeat. "Zeke?"

"Ain't nobody hurt," Afton called, pulling back on the reins so sharply, the horse sidestepped and tried to shake the bit from its mouth. "Easy," he soothed, and patted the beast's neck until it had calmed. "Some of the cattle were slaughtered last night. The rustlers didn't even bother to haul them off, just left the carcasses for the buzzards." He shook his head in disgust.

"It's crazy, Miz Claiborne. Don't make no sense at all. Guess it's some kind of gang, cause they left this behind like a token or warning." He pulled a silk scarf from his belt and held it up. "It was just pure meanness what they did to those beeves. No other explanation for it, downright pure meanness."

Pure meanness. Addie had known it firsthand. Her face went white as she watched the scarf snap in the breeze. The colors blurred before her eyes, crimson and sapphire and forest green, looking obscene against the pristine snow. She gripped Cole tighter as Afton turned his horse and rode off toward town. In silence, she watched him go, seething and afraid, remembering Grady's warning so clearly. *You're going to regret this so badly, Addie.*

She called the boys and returned to the house, her passage jerky and mechanical. She put the two youngest down for a nap, while Josh worked on his lessons at the kitchen table. She answered his questions as she prepared supper, keeping things excruciatingly normal. But nothing was normal and she knew it. She hadn't turned over the chest at Grady's demand and she would pay. He was going to destroy her, and he would do it through Zeke.

The evening meal was nothing short of torment. The sheriff had been invited to supper, and Addie was forced to listen to the men's distaste and speculation over and over as they tried to figure out what was happening and why.

"Makes no sense," Jake had repeated time and again. "They were slaughtered, pure and simple." Zeke had nodded agreement, his face lined with anger and worry. "Mark Simmons had some trouble with rustlers a while back, but nothing like this." Jake rubbed his hands over his eyes and shook his head. "I could understand if they had taken the cattle, but this just doesn't make sense." He picked up the scarf and ran his hands over the silk threads. "Somebody got a grievance against you, Zeke?"

Addie moved silently about her duties as the discussion continued in the same vein. Guilt twisted her insides as she put the boys to bed, wondering if she were putting them in danger as well. She returned to the kitchen, numb yet hurting, panic threatening her with each nervous heartbeat. She didn't know what to do, how to stop the past that was rolling closer and closer. Her hands trembled on the coffeepot when she placed it on the table. She didn't dare pour for the men.

She went back to the cupboard and cut them another helping of pie to keep her hands busy, only realizing when she turned around that Zeke hadn't touched his first piece. A sob rose in her throat and she dropped the plates back onto the counter, then rushed from the kitchen before she disgraced herself.

Zeke found her gazing out the bedroom window, her face pale as the moonlight. She didn't flinch when his hands fell on her shoulders, and that more than anything told him how far removed she was from everything going on around them.

"Addie."

"What?" she asked dully, her eyes fixed on the land outside the window.

"Don't distress yourself over this. We'll find out who it is."

She glanced over her shoulder only briefly, then returned her sightless gaze to the mountains. "It's Grady."

"What?" He turned her around. "How do you know?"

"The scarf." She took a shuddering breath. "He gave it to me one Christmas. I . . . left it behind."

Confusion turned to suspicion in his amber eyes, as she knew it would. "Why didn't you tell Jake?"

Addie's trembling fingers rose to cover her mouth and she tried to turn away. Zeke's fingers tightened on her upper arms and held her in place. "Please," she whispered.

"What does Grady have to do with this?" he asked.

The confusion in his voice she could bear, but the mistrust tore at her like talons. "Please," she whispered again. It was all coming apart, thread by thread her life was unraveling and she couldn't stop it. She had known all along she couldn't escape her past. No matter how she had pretended that life was normal over the past few months, she had known the dark secrets would catch up with her. She closed her eyes and turned her face away.

Zeke shook her lightly, his voice gruff and demanding. "Two men have been shot, Addie, and I've got dead cattle rotting on the range. Open your eyes, dammit, and tell me what's going on."

One tear slid down her cheek when she blinked and a sob rattled in her throat. "I . . . can't." She twisted violently to escape his hold and he hauled her up tightly against him.

"No more secrets, Addie. If you know what's going on, you have to tell me."

17

Addie wouldn't answer. She lay in silent misery beside Zeke, feeling his seething anger with each nervous heartbeat. There was panic in her now, chipping away at her reserve, her ability to deal rationally. One word, one sudden move, would shatter her like glass or send her screaming out into the night. She felt fragile, her skin too thin, as if a simple touch would bruise her grotesquely. The air was thick and bright, she had to close her eyes against the pain piercing her temples. Zeke hadn't been able to force the truth from her, though he had tried to frighten and intimidate the truth from her with words that had little effect after her four years with Willis.

There were no words now, nothing to intrude upon the vacant withdrawal of two people who never thought to feel enough to hurt each other.

The morning dawned pinkish orange, the sun a fiery ball spreading color through the dark and ominous clouds that tried to shield it. Gray and brooding, they hung over the mountain peaks, threatening another heavy snowfall to strip away the hope that warmer days were just over the horizon. Zeke stirred and rolled toward Addie, his heavy arm an impaling weight across her rib cage. She lay still, her breathing arrested for a second at his nearness and comfort. Her eyes, gritty from lack of sleep, focused on the window where she could watch the sunrise through the parted curtains.

It wasn't the first time they had drifted into wakefulness like this, intertwined like lovers while the haze of sleep still clouded their minds. But it was the first time Addie lay still to cherish it. Zeke's breath was warm against her neck, his golden hair tickling a spot beneath her ear. His leg was drawn up over her thighs, the blunt weight of his arousal stabbing against her hip. She wanted to turn into him and bury her face against his solid chest, to feel his arms wrap around her and hold her close and safe.

A shuddering sigh escaped her. He'd been so angry last night, so coldly furious he had frightened her. But not with physical harm. Her fear came from the knowledge that she was losing him to the murky secrets of her past. Willis would win, as he always had, and even in death he would destroy her. A sob tightened her throat and she gritted her teeth to suppress the sound. She didn't want to wake Zeke. She wanted this small moment in time to treasure being held by him before the anger and betrayal of the night past again entered his eyes.

She felt him move against her in his sleep, a slow erotic thrust that made her heartbeat an unstable flutter in her breast. She closed her eyes tight, wishing he would roll her beneath him and join their bodies, wanting him to want her. She didn't care how awkward or uncomfortable it would be, she just wanted him to be a part of her, to infuse her with his strength so that she

could face what lay ahead with more than her own pitiful cowardice. His hand swept boldly up her side, sending her heart skittering away in a fast-paced rhythm that
threatened to leave her breathless.

He was awake.

The knowledge made her blood purl faster through
her veins. He was awake and wanting her. Her nipples
ruched to hard points, unbearably sensitive against her
cotton nightgown, and heat pooled out in ripples to settle heavy in her lower belly. She didn't look at him,
afraid of what she might see in his eyes, but she gasped
when his hand rose farther and covered her, kneading
the small mounds. She bit her lip to suppress the deeper
moan rising in her throat and turned her hot face into
his shoulder.

He slipped lower to caress her rib cage and waist, firm
and confident and aware of every inch he explored as he
boldly moved down over her hip. She could feel his fingers curl around to her buttock and dig into the flesh,
pulling her toward him. She shivered as her belly met
the source of his passion and she found no fear to cause
her to turn away, just a desperate wish for him to pull
her tighter into him. The heat was constant now. Outside it caressed her, chasing away the chill of early
morning, but inside it coursed through her in burning
waves of discontent and hunger. Her hands went to his
broad shoulders and she clung tight, desperate, as if it
were the last time she would be allowed to do so.

His hand was under her gown now, lifting the hem
over her calves and knees. He snarled an oath when it
caught, then jerked it roughly up over her hips and belly
and breasts. Startled, Addie stiffened, realizing he was
not only fully awake but still angry. Chilled air prickled
her skin, but her heart beat faster, generating heat from

within to dispel the external temperature. And his heat was there as well, covering her, surrounding her as she was rolled and pushed deeper into the mattress by his heavy weight.

Not like this, she pleaded silently, *not in anger.* She didn't think she could bear it when his knee wedged roughly between her thighs and parted them. "No!" Her fingers fisted in his hair, and she pulled his head back sharply. "No, Zeke—" She felt his flesh, hot and smooth and insistent, prodding her, and she twisted to prevent his penetration. "No, not in anger!" she cried.

His eyes blazed into hers and she saw not the anger of the night before but tortured confusion battling a more primitive desire. On a muted gasp, she opened for him, her legs locking around his hips as her arms clutched convulsively at his shoulders. He entered her with a quick, deft rotation of his hips, wrenching a soft cry from her lips.

She heard him groan and the sting of tender flesh gave way to desperate need. He was pressing into her, hard and hot and thick. She was slight and very small, but there was rending, no force, only exquisite softness of her acceptance as her flesh accommodated him. His mouth found her breast and suckled vigorously, and in seconds she was drenched in her own passion, easing the way for the forceful thrust of his hips. Her muscles clenched around him, at first tentative and innocently curious, then drawing him, demanding more of him.

He groaned and pushed deep, almost mindless in the ecstasy of her, then withdrew only to thrust forward. Plunge and retreat and plunge again, the rhythm increased to a point of pleasure-pain, drowning her into a realm of pure neediness, that had her muscles tightening around him everywhere their bodies touched. She dug her fingers into his shoulders and kissed him where she could reach, his shoulders, his neck, his chest.

The power of him, the strength within him, seemed to flow into her with each thrust and she cried out, swept beyond anything in her experience. It felt as if she were both flying and falling, caught up in a whirlwind. She grabbed his head and brought his mouth down to hers and lost herself in his kiss. Her teeth captured his lower lip and she bit down gently, then devoured him, her tongue twining madly about his, her hands wild and clawing on his back and shoulders.

There were no words to mar the moment, no mistrustful past or uncertain future, just two staggered heartbeats thundering in counter tempo and two voices —one deep, the other breathless—filling the air with the sounds of their desire. She felt his body tense suddenly, as if fighting off some inner struggle, then heard a gruff cry of anguish as he snatched his body from hers, leaving her bereft. Her own cry followed, a wounded wail that was swallowed up in his lips as they crashed down upon hers.

"Too fast," he rasped out. "Too soon." His hands were ravenous, stripping the nightgown over her arms and head, then returning to ravage her naked, throbbing body. His mouth devoured her neck and shoulders, trailing down until it fastened on her breasts. Her back arched at the contact, and the world spun out from under her. She was falling, falling, spiraling down toward a hot, dark abyss that waited just below. But he was with her, his mouth hot and certain on her everywhere as his hands shifted and maneuvered her body until he was once again thrusting into her heated flesh. On a cry, she rose against him, into him, swept up in the rocking cadence. She felt her extremities recede until there was nothing but the blinding point of heat in the center of her body.

Her head arched back as her heels dug into the bedding and she surged against him with a terrible urgency she had never known or felt before, a driving force that obliterated everything but the need to be filled, to be consumed by him. And he drove into her with the same need, the same striving necessity to reach that point of supreme oblivion where everything was reduced to one exquisite moment.

Zeke felt her body contract around him and heard her sobbing little cries intensify. He thrust long and deep within her tightness, wild with the sheer bliss of their joining. She arched high on a strangled cry and he plunged deep and held her there, poised and unraveling as he filled her. Then he came down over her, impaling and crushing her, a moan rumbling in his heaving chest. Dark gold eyes, still wild and savage, stared at her with vague astonishment and intense satisfaction.

Her own eyes stared back, her own chest heaved. With a small cry, she burrowed closer into him, their bodies still mated, and wrapped her arms fiercely around him. Heartbeats slowed, ragged breaths resumed a normal rhythm, but the minds and souls of the bodies still entwined could feel only the terrible reality of daylight hastening toward them.

They could not go back now to the months of frustration and caution, but they could not go forward with the terrible barrier of secrets separating them.

Awareness lit the dark amber eyes, but when he would have moved away from her, her slight movement of protest stilled his reluctant effort. He gazed steadily at her, his expression unreadable, and Addie felt herself grow pink and warm in response. His voice came rough and constricted.

"Did I hurt you?"

She shook her head and lowered her lashes from his searching gaze. His chest was covered in a fine sheen of sweat, the hair glistening from exertion. The muscles of his chest wall and arms bulged from supporting his weight on his hands. The chest hair tapered off into a thinner darker line down his abdomen to his groin where it meshed with her own lighter curls.

His body stirred deep within her from the effects of her perusal, and her eyes flew back to his. His amber gaze, so unreadable only a moment ago, was hot now as it bore into hers. He no more wanted to meet the day than she did, not now while there was something to make him forget. On an oath, his body began the rhythm again, stealing the breath from her lungs. His voice was grainy when he spoke, as rough-edged as his passion.

"Now?" he rasped. "Am I hurting you now?"

"No," she breathed, caught up in renewed passion.

"Then take me, Addie," he grated out. He gripped her buttocks in strong, callused hands and lifted her. "Take all of me."

She flung her head back as she rode the storm, waves of utter pleasure cresting one upon the other until there was no beginning, no end, just a point that swelled and expanded with each thrust, a hot crest that rolled higher and brighter with each plunge until she was writhing with him, against him, taking everything he offered and demanding more. The need to reach the end overpowered everything else, coming at them even stronger and faster than before. They were lost to the art and finesse of seduction and were left with only the thrashing need for each other. She felt powerful and whole; he felt complete.

A growling cry strained the tendons in Zeke's throat as he threw his head back, and Addie's own ragged cries mingled with his, as did the gasping breaths that followed in the aftermath.

He dropped his head to the crook of her shoulder, his heartbeat pounding into her breasts. Damp tendrils of hair grazed her cheek and she lifted a trembling hand to brush them back.

Zeke raised his head a fraction and rolled weakly to his back, one arm flung over his eyes. His chest still rose and fell heavily, as if he couldn't draw enough air. Limp and sated, Addie tugged listlessly at the sheet and managed to get it up high enough to cover her breasts. He made no move to touch her and she lay where she was. Only inches separated them but the space was filled with an emptiness so cold and unbearable it could have been miles. The musky fragrance of their lovemaking still lingered in the air and on the bedclothes, a scent as tousled and uncivilized as the two had been. A wild taste also lingered on Addie's swollen lips, the taste of Zeke's kisses, his passion.

Her knuckles were white where she gripped the embroidered edge of the sheet. She swallowed the knot in her throat but didn't speak. Words would come soon enough for both of them, hurtful accusations if there were any left from the night before. She heard Zeke clear his throat and tensed inwardly, though her extremities were too weak to do more than lie limply beside him.

"Was I too rough?"

"No, I . . . no." Tears burned in her throat. She wanted him to hold her again, to wrap her up and make her forget that there was a world outside the frosted windowpanes. But he was already withdrawing, taking all tenderness with him.

He eased up slowly against the headboard and draped his arm over one updrawn knee. He raked his fingers through his sweat-dampened hair, his eyes taking on a cold, faraway look. "You'll be tender. Tell me if you need something for it."

Her cheeks caught fire at the suggestion, though there was nothing more intimate than what they had just done. A rush of anger caught her and held her fast in its talons. "Thank you, *Doctor*."

His eyes seared her as he looked down at her flushed face. Her eyes were greener than he had ever seen them, seductively slumberous, but they were also stubborn. His voice was cool and wry. "Regrets?"

"No!" The word burst fast and harsh through her lips. She gripped the sheet tight and sat up to face him. "No, I don't have regrets," she said in trembling defiance. "Do you?"

His eyes narrowed lazily, but there was a tenseness around his mouth. "I should have used more caution." He shrugged. "But no, I don't have any regrets."

He reached over and tugged the sheet from her fingers. It fluttered down to pool at her waist. Pink stained her chest and neck as his tanned palm flattened on her breastbone and drifted over her burning skin to her belly, then much farther down. She jumped, her heart in her throat, and a slow, languid heat flowed through her as he cupped her there, possessively and proudly. His eyes flickered up to hers, and the look there, hot and almost sly, sent warning bells peeling along Addie's nerves.

Stifling a groan, she snatched the sheet back to her

chest, though it was poor protection with his hand still touching her so intimately, knowingly. "I won't tell you about Willis or Grady."

Zeke caught her behind the head and brought his mouth crashing down on hers, marauding her tender, swollen lips with insistence. His hand stroked and teased and opened her until her breathing became unsteady. Her resistance alternately gave and rebelled, but she was weakening with each nip of his teeth, each swirling plunge of his tongue, each brush of his skillful fingers.

A desperate moan trembled in her throat as she felt herself pulled to her knees and pressed flush against him.

"I won't tell you—" The words were cut off by the feel of strong hands running voraciously over her back and buttocks.

"Yes, you will," he growled. And then she was toppled forward and sprawled across him like a wanton as he fell back. The sheet fell away, the dying candlelight bathing her slim, lush body in secretive shadows and valleys. He wanted to search each place, every hidden curve. Her eyes held mystery as well. They were wide with wonder and just a hint of fearful excitement, as if she wasn't certain she should feel the madness gripping both of them.

And it was madness, this wanting, this insatiable craving. Sweet, sweet madness. He caught her beneath the thighs and lifted and spread them until she straddled him, the heat of his arousal burning into her tender flesh.

She flinched when he entered her, but already her raw flesh was drenching them both in renewed passion to make the way slick and welcome, to keep the rest of the world at bay for a while longer. His hands on her hips, he set the pace at a slow consuming rhythm that soon obliterated everything, and they were rocking together, straining toward the peak that remained just out of Addie's grasp.

Zeke saw her face tense with the struggle to overcome the abrasion of his repeated thrusts and knew he should pull back, but he was too far gone in the velvet grip of her body to do more than ensure her pleasure in the ride. His mouth found her breasts and suckled while his hands sought her hot center. She stiffened, then her eyes half closed in a look that was part seduction, part discovery, then beyond both. Her lips parted on a cry and she ground her hips urgently upon him. He stroked her flesh once and felt her quick gasp give way to shattering convulsions that triggered his own release. With quick deft strokes, he took them to the edge, then hurled them over into beyond.

Addie felt savaged when it was over, her flesh throbbing painfully after the last pulses of pleasure died away. "No more," she whispered into his shoulder, limp as a ragdoll. She was too exhausted to move or even blush at her sprawled position.

His hand stroked her back in slow, soothing sweeps, but frustration colored his words. "Addie—"

"No," she said in weak defiance. "I won't tell you about Willis even if you do it a hundred more times." She felt a chuckle rumble in his chest, but it emerged brittle and self-derisive.

"I wouldn't advise wearing the boys' pants for a few days."

A faint blush found enough initiative to stain her cheeks, but that was all she could manage in the way of indignation. She was too depleted to do anything but try to roll to her side. She didn't even have the energy to pull the quilt up to preserve her modesty and sagged sleepily against him.

Zeke did it for her. The sight of her naked flesh might yield no immediate reaction in his body, but it wouldn't take long for him to be ready again if the past hour was any indication. She was like an insanity in his blood, a constant yearning since the first night he'd lain beside her. But it was worse now that he'd had her.

Instead of depleting his desire, having her had only made it keener, sharper. He had only entertained notions of what it would be like before. Now he knew. And the knowledge was hot and heavy inside him again.

He flinched slightly when his sex swelled, but the sharper edges of desire were blunted by his own rawness. If he felt a tenth of what Addie was feeling, she must be ready to take a frying pan to his head . . . or elsewhere. Guilt trickled through him but it had little real chastising force when the pleasure had been so fulfilling.

He turned his head to look at her. Dawn filtered rosy fingers through the wild mass of hair scattered across the pillow. Her arm lay limply on the quilt; the small palm turned up. Her features were soft and delicate in repose.

He hadn't known she would be like this, giving her all and taking in return. He had expected . . . what? A quiet, inhibited romp. Acceptance without involvement.

She had been anything but uninvolved.

Things were changed now and he knew it. The nights need no longer be spent in unfulfilled frustration for either of them. But the daylight wasn't altered at all. His fingers curled into a fist as rage and confusion curled in his gut. What was she hiding? What was so terrible that she wouldn't share it with him, even to save the ranch?

He could hear the boys stirring and slung his legs over the bed and rose. On a muted curse, he walked toward the basin and washed quickly before one of them came searching for breakfast.

Beneath lowered lashes, Addie watched Zeke cross the room. His mouth was grim, his eyes cold and shadowed. There was no hatred or loathing in the look, but a darker kind of pain, the kind that bespoke betrayal. She turned her face away, but the action didn't stop her own hurt or despair, or the terrible feeling of desperation— the absolute knowing that she would have to do something fast to stop Grady.

Zeke dressed and left the room. As soon as the door shut behind him, Addie made up her mind to do something she had sworn she would never do. She slowly got up from the bed, aching in places she didn't know she could ache, and walked to the wardrobe.

Her fingers trembled when she pulled her clothing on. They continued to shake when she washed dishes and tidied up the house. By the time she loaded the boys into the wagon, her stomach was churning so badly she thought she would lose her breakfast.

Business was slow enough for everyone to stare when she rolled down Main Street. She had left the boys with Gracie and knew she should stop at the General Store and make a purchase to validate her excuse for being in town, but she didn't care. Her mission was more important than satisfying the curiosity of the town folk.

She imagined eyes boring into her back as she headed out of town in the opposite direction from which she entered. She knew Zeke would hear of it, but that didn't matter either. She would tell him herself when she returned to the ranch.

Her palms were clammy on the reins. She shouldn't have forgotten her gloves, but her mind hadn't been on such normal, mundane things as protecting her hands when there was so much else to worry about. The noise of town faded behind her and she forced herself to continue on, each quarter mile more threatening than the last. When she slowed the horses to turn down the rutted lane to her old shanty, her heart began a frantic, unsteady beat.

She felt feverish and light-headed. She knew it would soon be hard to breathe. It was impossible to will the panic away but she managed to control it by sucking air deep into her lungs then letting it out slowly while ignoring the churning in her stomach.

The old stone and dirt-packed house loomed before her, looking like a forgotten part of the land. The yard was overgrown, thick unseemly tumbleweeds encroaching on the front door. The shed sagged even farther toward total decay. She stopped the wagon and looped the reins around the brake handle, then just sat and stared warily at the old house, as if it had the power to leap out and swallow her.

An inch at a time, she forced her muscles to respond and finally managed to stand. She even succeeded in climbing over the edge of the wagon to the ground. But it was impossible to walk forward, to approach the shanty and the memories it held.

Clouds were brewing in the distance, ugly and portentous, casting the rough walls in an eerie light that made it look even more ominous. Shadows cast by spiney branches stretched and spread across the colorless outer walls like gray gnarled fingers. Then slowly the shadows wavered and began to disappear into the encroaching darkness. Startled, Addie glanced around her at the falling gloom. The wind was rising, bitter cold and heavy with the smell of snow. The sun was completely hidden behind a blanket of gray doom. She had to hurry or she'd be caught here, her only protection from the elements a house that had been her purgatory for four years.

She raced for the door, the wind so strong at her back that it plastered her woolen cloak and skirt against her buttocks and legs and whipped her hair across her eyes. She grabbed for the door handle and tugged against the force of the wind. It gave a fraction, then slammed shut. She tried again, pulling with all her strength until she was able to squeeze her body through the opening, and brace her back against the door to keep it from slamming her to the ground. She closed her eyes to adjust to the dark interior, and tried to ignore the suffocating smell of dust and neglect.

But it was impossible to ignore the fear. It hit her full force, buffeting her emotions and rattling her nerves to the snapping point. She blinked and tried to focus but the murky interior gave up only the outlines of shapes, nothing so substantial as a specific chair or a bed. She groped along the wall for the lantern that had hung there but found only an empty peg.

The hiss of a striking match and a sudden yellow-orange glow dispelled the darkness. "Looking for this?"

Addie felt herself waver on her feet and clung to the wall for support as Grady's face appeared behind the glow of the match. He held the lantern up casually, evil satisfaction in his eyes. "I knew you'd come, Addie. I've been waiting for you."

Crumbling mortar scraped against her shoulder

blades. She didn't realize she was falling until she was
halfway down. She caught herself, digging her nails into
the wall, clawing to keep her sanity as much as her footing. Her breaths were staggered now, coming fast and
erratic. She didn't want to faint. Please, God, don't let
her lose consciousness.

Grady touched the match to the wick, illuminating
the room in a dusty orange light. Addie turned her face
away sharply and inched back flush against the wall so it
would support her weight. She was cornered and she
knew it. There was no use trying to run. It would change
nothing, solve nothing. Cowering never had. Grady
strolled forward and hooked the lantern on a peg, then
smiled evilly.

"Where's the chest, Addie?"

She pointed weakly at the cot on the opposite wall,
despising the tremble in her fingers. Grady backed
toward it, his eyes never leaving hers, and flipped back
the moth-eaten quilt. He didn't bother to look beneath
the bed. He had already searched the room too many
times to know the chest wasn't in plain sight.

"Get it."

"I'll need a shovel," she said, and his eyes glittered in
triumph.

"By the door." He jerked his head in the direction
just to the left of her, grinning with such brittle, unholy
gloating it made Addie queasy. He pulled the bed aside
to reveal nothing beneath but smooth earth. "Sly little
bitch," he crooned. "I've already dug up half the yard.
Leave it to you to hide it right under my nose." His eyes
swept her body slowly, intimately, as he strolled forward. But she didn't move; she could hardly breathe.
When he was inches away, his hand reached out and
touched her cheek.

"I should have known. You hated that bed, didn't you, sweetheart? Hated having old Willis grind against you without satisfaction. I bet Claiborne has shown you plenty of what Willis couldn't." His hand slid down to her bodice and she flinched away from his words and his touch. Grady ground his palm against the plumpness of her breast and laughed cruelly. "Yeah, your husband's got three boys to prove he's a man, while old Willie rots in a grave, his pecker harder in death than it ever was in life."

Addie shut her eyes briefly, struggling desperately to keep her composure. "Don't do this, Grady."

"Why not? I've tried for years to give you what Willis couldn't, but you wanted no part of me."

She had never understood, not his words or the leering looks or the reasons behind his sporadic attempts to touch her when Willis wasn't looking. But she had felt exposed and soiled each time he visited. He leaned into her and ran his tongue along her neck, his breath hot and wet. Her stomach revolted and she had to grit her teeth to keep from gagging.

"Don't do this, Grady." The whine in her voice sickened her along with the panicky catch in her throat that made it impossible for her to scream out her revulsion. His fingers bit into the tender flesh of her breast and she felt his other hand fumbling beneath her skirt. When he touched her thigh, she cringed deeper into the wall. "Don't!" she cried, and grabbed his wrist, her nail breaking the skin.

His body tensed, then his voice changed instantly to a cold, feral command as he moved back, grabbed the shovel, and pushed it into her hands. "You get the chest now, Addie." He held his wrist up so she could see the bloody marks she had left there, then flattened his palm over her breast and pinned her momentarily to the wall. "I'll get you later."

Addie's fingers wrapped around the smooth wood, and she used the handle and blade as leverage to push herself upright as soon as he stepped away. She was so cold she could hardly move, her legs heavy wooden appendages as she forced herself to put one foot in front of the other, her gaze fixed only on the spot beneath the bed that held just the slightest bit of heaven within its damnation.

The dirt wasn't hardpacked, just smoothed over to cover any trace of digging. It gave easily as she braced her foot on the shovel and lunged. Numb and woodenly, she dug. Small mounds of dirt piled up before she finally hit something solid. The scrape of metal against metal rasped loudly in the silence. She could almost smell Grady's anticipation, the noxious lust and greed of his black soul. He rushed forward and pushed her aside when she had the chest half unearthed and clawed away the rest of the dirt around the small trunk with his hands. With a grunt of satisfaction he pulled it from the shallow grave and carried it toward the light.

Setting it beneath the lantern, he knelt and pried away the dirt from the latch. He was so intent upon his treasure, he never saw Addie's hands lift, never saw the violent swing of the shovel heading straight for the back of his head.

With the baby under one arm while she tried to work the reins, Addie couldn't afford to push the horses any faster. Josh and Zeb were already bouncing around like rubber balls in the back of the buckboard, but their whooping delight at the hair-raising ride had already begun to pale. The storm was bearing down on them, gaining leverage with each passing minute. Snow swirled and floated around them, like the teasing lace of a daring woman's petticoat. But soon, too soon, it would become a blinding and suffocating cloak of frigid white death.

The instinct for survival rose within her, stronger than the gusts of freezing air, and Addie hollered louder than the keening wind for the boys to hold tight as she slapped the reins over the horses' backs to increase their already reckless gait. Landscape whizzed by, cast into obscurity by the dangerous pace. She could still make out the road but the perimeters were rapidly dissolving into gray-white gloominess. Her hands were growing numb; she could barely feel her fingers curled rigidly on the leather straps. Ice crystals frosted her hair, and puffs of cloudy condensation pooled out with each laborous breath she took.

Her arm tightened on Cole. She heard Zeb whine as the terror of their predicament began to invade his innocent mind. Josh shouted an encouragement that was torn away on the wind, leaving only the heartwrenching echo of the fear in his voice. Addie sobbed once then held it, knowing there was nothing she could do but try to outrun the storm that was already enfolding them.

The chest bumped in the back as they hit a shallow hole, and she groaned in agonizing anguish for the three lives entrusted into her safekeeping. Her foolishness, her vanity, her self-preservation, had brought her to this. She accepted the fact that it would be her destruction, but she wouldn't accept the annihilation of her three children as well. She slapped the reins harder and yelled at the horses struggling to outdistance the blizzard.

Fatally, her vision narrowed further as the blanket of

white began to enclose them and the tracks of the road disappeared completely. She wanted to sleep, to curl up in a ball, her back to the wind. She thought she heard the baby whimper, but the roaring of the wind swallowed the sound. Ice spangles coated her lashes. She could see nothing, feel nothing but a cold cheerless death descending on the lane that would have taken them home.

18

Like giant black vultures, the shadows swept up alongside the wagon. One separated, its muted orange eye glowing out of the pale darkness to swoop down at Addie's side. She cringed away and Josh's scream had her lashing out blindly.

"Pa! Pa!" he screamed again, and Addie felt an echoing cry rise in her own throat. Her hands fumbled on the reins as relief flooded her, and she gripped them harder by instinct rather than feel, because there was no longer anything but acute numbness in her fingers. Zeke's shout was stripped away on the wind, but his wildly swinging lantern gave her a focal point to concentrate on, a place to keep her sanity and hope alive. Afton and Granger were there too, just ahead to help light the way, while Scrapper pulled around to the rear.

Safely encircled, she felt her heart give in shattering relief and her tears began to spill and make frozen tracks on her cheeks. The house glowed like a beacon in the distance, brighter with each yard traveled. Zeke grabbed the horse's halter to slow the pace as they neared the gate, then led them through and across the expansive yard to the front steps.

He grabbed the boys first, and handed each to a waiting cowhand, who took off immediately for the warmth of the house. Zeke then reached for Addie. Her body was rigid and huddled. He had to pry her fingers loose from the reins before he could pull her into his arms and carry her inside.

The heat was searing, striking her frigid cheeks with stinging needles of pain. She moaned and turned her face into Zeke's shoulder briefly but he was already pushing her away to strip the outer layer of clothing from her body.

"The boys—" She struggled to get out of his arms and go to them, but he held her still as he flung her cloak aside and pushed her closer toward the fire.

"They're fine," he said, chafing her hands to bring back some color and warmth. A chill seized her, convulsing her entire body, and Zeke's hands moved up to briskly rub her arms. Anger burned in his eyes, hotter than the hearth or the friction of his solicitations, and was reflected in his voice.

"The boys were bundled well for the cold, thank God, but you . . ." His breath hissed out in a snarl of hot wrath. "What in hell were you doing, Addie? How could you take them out in this weather?"

Addie couldn't answer. Her body was tortured with shivers, her teeth chattering uncontrollably as heat seeped back into her paralyzed limbs. Zeke's voice blasted her again, but this time concern and fear seeped in to mingle with his outrage.

"If you don't suffer frostbite, it'll be a miracle," he ground between his teeth. "Dammit, Addie, how could you?"

She made a small sound in her throat, a choking whine garbled by tears. "S . . . sorry. I—" She shuddered again and would have fallen into a boneless heap had Zeke's arms not supported her.

"Here, boss."

Zeke caught the blanket thrown by Granger and didn't miss the barely veiled warning in the cowpoke's eyes. They had all been so worried, almost crazed with it, when they returned from the range to find Addie and the boys gone. Scrapper had offered what comfort he knew best and prepared a pot of beef stew. Granger and Afton had paced, careful speculation in their conversation to keep Zeke's growing rage and fear in check. But when the storm had moved in, they no longer tried to find excuses for why Addie was gone. They had just gone to find Addie.

"You should'a seen her, Pa," Zeb said around a mouthful of stew. "Ma drove the wagon like a wild woman."

Granger and Afton forced a chuckle, because it was best to indulge Zeb and keep the boys occupied when things were so serious near the fireplace. They all knew the danger of a white-out, they'd all found bodies frozen where they'd fallen in a blizzard.

Scrapper exchanged looks with Granger from the corner of his eye and ladled out another helping of stew for Josh, then went back to feeding the baby. By his reckoning, Miz Addie was in a heap of trouble. And though he didn't argue that she deserved a good tongue lashing, he hoped the boss wasn't bent on worse when he got his wife warmed up. Scrapper didn't hold much with hurting women, not after what he'd watched his ma suffer at the hands of the drunken men who'd come and gone from her room like flies after honey. He couldn't rightly say what Mr. Zeke thought as the boss rubbed life back into his wife's arms, but the man's eyes were as forbidding and threatening as Hell.

Scrapper shivered and turned back to the baby. He couldn't afford to interfere in the boss's business, but he couldn't help but feel sorry for Miz Addie. She was one tough lady to be so small, but her husband was tougher . . . and angrier than a man had the right to be after rescuing his family from certain death.

The baby was done, potatoes and carrots spread from one end of his face to the other. Uncomfortable with the chore of tending such a small fellow, Scrapper awkwardly wiped the baby's mouth and lifted him from the highchair. The squish of a sodden bottom had him flinching, then sighing. He'd fixed broken harnesses, stitched saddle leather, and brought down wild cats at twenty paces. He guessed with a little trial and patience, he could manage to pin on a dry diaper.

Granger, feeling grizzly as a crossed bear, gave Zeke another hard look. Miz Addie was huddled beneath a blanket by the fire, her feet in a pan of warm water, the bowl of stew in her lap forgotten. She looked about as lost as a foundling child, and Granger wanted to know the reason for it. It wasn't solely exhaustion lining her face, or even the aftermath of danger—that kind of receding fear that turns a man's bowels liquid. It was more than any of that and a whole lot more than he could figure out.

Afton jabbed his arm, and Granger turned away from the sight of Zeke looming over his wife like he wanted to take her head off and kiss her at the same time.

"Boss looks purt-near mean about this."

"Scared is all," Granger said, but his words were less than convincing. The storm howled around them, fitfully looking for chinks in the wooden walls. The windows rattled as sheets of ice pummeled them with stunning force. "Don't reckon we can return to the bunkhouse tonight," he added, loudly enough to wake the dead.

"Naw," Afton agreed, his eyes fixed on Zeke's severe countenance. "No chance of it tonight, not with the storm and all."

Zeke sent them a fulminating glare, along with a brittle smile. "Blankets are in the linen press, boys."

Afton felt a chill move up his spine and wondered if he'd be forced to collect his pay when the storm blew over.

Addie stood at the bedroom door, her heart throwing up barriers that were cracked and useless. She reached for the doorknob but didn't seem capable of turning it. The brass was cold beneath her fingers, inhospitable. She wondered if the man inside would be the same.

The boys were asleep, no worse for wear after her insanity. She had held them a long, long time before tucking the covers close and safe about them. She hadn't been able to let go, not even with Zeb squirming and mumbling *bluck* and Cole already asleep on her shoulder. Josh had held her back for the first time, his arms a heavy welcome weight around her neck. She had wished desperately that she could stay like that all night, warm and loved within the circle of their arms. But there was another she had to face.

She leaned her forehead against the doorframe, trying to gather the strength to step inside, but her legs were useless things, with jelly for knees. She had bade goodnight to the men bedded down in the sitting room and thanked them for their help. But the words had been so simple and mundane, like a child's composition. They didn't begin to describe the gratitude she felt.

The polished wood was cool and smooth against her forehead, maybe the only thing holding her up. She took a deep fortifying breath, but her chest still felt hollow, as if all the air had seeped out. She wondered what had happened to her heart? Her fist tightened on the door-knob, she knew she couldn't put this off any longer.

The chest, looking vile and obscene, sat in the middle of the bedroom floor. Addie felt her stomach recoil but knew she couldn't back away or ignore it. One never escaped the past. It always lay there in moldy memories just waiting to resurface and slay the one who tried to outrun it.

Zeke was standing just behind the chest, his legs spread in an unyielding stance, his arms crossed over his chest. The gun belt was still strapped to his hips, looking ominous, but not nearly so dangerous as the hard, seething look on his face. Addie dared only a brief glance at his implacable expression and walked toward the trunk. The vision of Grady lying facedown in the dirt of the shanty passed through her mind but had no hold. There was no feeling in her, not guilt or fear or even numbness. She was so far removed from what she must do, there was nothing left but acceptance.

She knelt and almost reverently brushed snow from the latch, then pried it loose with fingers that trembled only once. The metal gave with groaning resistance, offensively loud in the silence, then fell open to thunk against the chest as if giving up the struggle. Addie lifted the lid slowly, protecting the contents from the run-off of snow melting on the top and sides.

Zeke held himself immobile by sheer willpower, but

he wanted to rip back the lid and expose whatever lay inside, whatever was so precious that Addie would risk herself and the children to protect it. Nothing appeared but a length of blood-red velvet packed tightly around the top and sides of whatever lay beneath. He watched Addie's hands caress the fabric for a brief second before she plucked at a tucked corner and began easing it up. Air burned in Zeke's tight chest, and he realized he was holding his breath. He let it out in a silent hiss as she lifted the velvet, carefully folded it and laid it on the floor.

Framed canvases in different sizes lay stacked beneath, and she began to lift the paintings and place them around the trunk, propping each as if making a display. Rubens, Botticelli, El Greco, Rembrandt—one by one they appeared, and a coldness unlike any Wyoming winter storm began to seep into Zeke's entire body. The last few were unrecognizable in content but not in style. They mirrored the flavors of the others before them. Whether *académisme* or naturalistic, they were museum quality and shouted the names of their masters.

Zeke's mouth went dry. He thought his heart had stopped until it plunged heavily into his gut when the last painting was withdrawn. Addie didn't place this one with the others, but held it to her chest as if she would shield it.

Zeke tore his eyes from the hollow-backed wooden frame and stared at his wife. Her eyes were lowered, staring sightlessly down at something she could only see in her mind, her curls drying shiny gold around her troubled face. "She was so young," she whispered, as if saying the words loudly would only make it worse.

Zeke curled his fingers into a tight fist to keep from

jerking her up and shaking her until she explained the insanity scattered at his feet. "Where . . . where did you get these?" he asked roughly.

Addie only stared up at him, her eyes lost and hurting.

His heart was pounding too hard, putting a clinch in his gut. He knew the implications of what he was seeing but his mind refused to admit the hideous facts. Art theft. Damn her, what reprisal did art theft carry? He had the insane urge to laugh or cry as a vision of the sheriff swam before his burning eyes. *Sorry, Zeke. Gotta take her in, and you too, harboring a criminal and all that* . . .

Zeke sucked in a breath. Pain shot up his arm and he unclinched his fists. His voice was soft but stricken as his hand slashed through the air. "Tell me it was Willis or Grady. Tell me that you had no part in this."

She blinked once, and her lower lip trembled as she shook her head. Guilt flamed green and treacherous from her eyes.

Zeke moved. Lightning-quick and soundless, he lunged forward and snatched her up from the floor, his hand an iron band around her arm. The painting clutched to her chest clattered to the floor, and she made a small sound of distress as she stared down at it. "Tell me, dammit!" he said as he shook her. "Tell me you had no part in this!"

She lifted her head. A tear caught in the tangle of her lashes, then rolled down her cheek. "I can't."

He flung her away, sick and frightened, confused and betrayed, as if his entire world had just caved in and he hadn't seen it coming. His chest heaved as he struggled to find the rhyme or reason behind anything so despicable, but he could make sense of nothing. "What did you hope to gain?"

Her tongue darted out to wet her lips. "Money. Willis wanted money." Her head tilted guilelessly, as if she couldn't believe her own words. "Grady has a buyer."

Zeke raked his fingers through his hair, then gripped his fist at his side as if he didn't trust himself not to smash it into something. His voice was painfully hollow. "They hang horse thieves, Addie. Do you think they are any less merciful with art?"

She blinked again, her eyes desolate and bewildered. Her thoughts were disordered, caught in the past, in doubts and hatreds and mistrust. But the present confused her even more. "Horse thieves?"

His hand slashed again, cutting the air like a blade. But his voice was more lethal, because it was filled with an agonizing pain that pierced her heart. "Art theft, embezzling, selling stolen goods. What else would you call it?"

Her eyes cleared. She finally understood. "Forgery. It's called forgery."

His face went blank for the second it took him to assimilate her words. "Whose forgery?"

"Mine."

The word rang like a death knell between them.

Her legs buckled. She didn't even realize it until pain sliced through her knees as they hit floor amid the rubble of her life. She flinched but didn't cry out, and reached to gather the painting that had fallen earlier from her hands.

Zeke reached it before she did and snatched it up. It was like none of the others. There was no style or specific use of color to give it reference to the paintings propped against the trunk. Addie's fingers grappled for it, but he lifted it higher out of reach.

A woman in homespun gazed down at the infant she held. Colors flowed warmly like honey and sunshine across the canvas to soften her expression and the glow of love on her face. The child was like any other, innocent-eyed and pink-cheeked above a rosebud mouth. But the gown she wore, edged in lace and flowing over the woman's arm, was one he recognized. The boys' picture books flooded his mind.

"You painted these?" Zeke asked, his voice tight and hoarse.

Her eyes bleak and anguished, Addie nodded. "I'm so sorry." She shut her eyes then against his bewildered stare and dropped her head to her knees. Her voice was muffled in her skirts. "I didn't want to . . . they made me."

Her head jerked up and her eyes were fierce and tortured. "Willis found me sketching one day. The next week he brought home paints and brushes and books . . . such beautiful books—" Her hands fisted in her skirt and her voice hardened in bitter self-disgust. "I thought he was being kind. He set them all before me and smiled. 'For you, Addie, all for you.' Then he laid his belt over the top of it all, and I knew . . ." Her voice trembled and her hand rose to cover her mouth. "I wanted to destroy the paintings after Willis died, but . . . I couldn't. It was such a sin, but I couldn't do it." Tears clogged her throat and pooled in her eyes. Her voice was a deafening whisper. "I was so proud of them, you see, so vain."

A terrible, constricted laugh grated in Zeke's throat. "Vain?" His pained expression softened and he gently

placed the painting beside the others and knelt in front
of her. "Addie . . . God."

He pulled her into his arms as her sobs broke and
rocked her back and forth, his whispered words soothing and consoling, while her own apologies choked out.

"I never wanted to hurt you . . . never wanted you
to know. I thought I could keep them hidden, but
Grady—"

"Shhh," he breathed against her hair, rocking and
rocking while she continued, trying to infuse strength
into a body that had been so defenseless for four years.
Her words were strangled and pleading against his
chest, each syllable forced between sobs as if she had to
make him see, make him understand—*when I p . . .
painted, they left me alone*—but he understood already
how helpless she must have been at the hands of those
two grown men. He pulled her tighter against him, feeling her agony like a knife in his own heart. He had to
think, had to find some way to protect her, to make this
right.

It seemed hours before she was spent. When the last
tear fell, the last sob sighed away, Zeke tilted her head
back over his arm and touched her lips softly with his
own, then pulled her crumpled form around to sit beside him. He stared at the magnificent works propped
against the old trunk. "They are extraordinary."

Drained, she laid her head against his shoulder and
felt his fingers begin to stroke through her curls. "They
were my only comfort."

The words were few and simple but they carried a
wealth of painful understanding straight into Zeke's
heart. His arms tightened around her, shielding, but he
wasn't sure he could save her. "Have any been sold?"

"No." She trembled and Zeke drew her closer. "But Grady has a buyer."

"Are any missing?"

She nodded and a weak, belated sob whined in her throat. "A Pieter de Hooch. *The Music Party.*" She tilted her face up, a sad smile thinning her lips. "He took it over a year ago. It wasn't even very good. I had trouble with the contrast." She looked so confused and forlorn. "I don't know why he chose that one."

The implications were staggering, but the situation was solvable. It had to be. Zeke's arm tightened further in fearful protectiveness. He couldn't lose her, not to this, not to some greedy mongrel's manipulation.

It would be criminal to destroy the paintings, an utter defilement of beauty and talent, but it would be much too dangerous to keep them. "Addie, you have to destroy them."

She went rigid for a brief second, then nodded, but her heart felt as if it were collapsing in her chest. "I know. That's why I brought them here."

"I'm sorry."

She put her fingers to his lips to stop the words. She couldn't bear them. She could take the guilt and the blame for what she had done; she could take him lashing out in anger and accusation. But she couldn't take his concern. She had endangered their children, she might yet be bringing her husband to public disgrace. One more word absolving her of guilt would send her straight over the screaming edge.

Zeke saw panic filter through the lost look in her eyes. He took her hand in his and held tight. "We have to contact Jake," he said.

Her nerves twisted violently. "No, please . . ."

"We have to," he continued tersely. "We don't have

any choice. We've got to tell him about the painting that's missing and see what can be done to protect you."

A small, terrible cry rattled in her throat and she slumped against him. She was going to need protection for more than just the crime of forgery.

19

"I think I killed Grady."

Addie's face was so blank and colorless when she said the words that it took Zeke a moment to digest them.

"You what?"

"He was there when I got to the house. I think I killed him." Fresh tears rushed to her eyes. "I hit him with a shovel."

Zeke ran his hand over his face and fought for calm. "Are you sure?"

"He fell facedown and didn't move. I didn't stay to see . . ." Her voice broke in terrible anguish. "I had to get away!"

Zeke's arms tightened around her. "Shhh . . . You did the right thing."

"I didn't want you to know about the paintings. I thought I could destroy them and you would never find out, but Grady was there—"

"Shhh," he soothed again. "I know, hush. We'll figure this out." His words were calming but dread sluiced through him in icy sheets. "Was there a fire in the hearth?" When she shook her head, his dread intensified. If her blow hadn't gotten Grady, the storm would. Zeke might personally want to wrap his fingers around the man's neck and strangle him, but he didn't want Addie carrying the burden for Grady's death.

"I'm sending Granger for the sheriff." He could feel the renewed tremors rack her body. "Addie, you've got to trust me. We need Jake in our confidence in case we need his help."

Little more than a pink-gold blush stained the sky behind the towering mountains. The heart of Laramie still lay in darkness, sheltered in the quiet gloom of pre-dawn as Grady made his way through the alley. The back of his head was throbbing, his hair matted with dried blood and bits of dirt. He gripped the handrail of the outside staircase leading to Lou Ellen's room and fought the dizziness that robbed him of momentum. Renewed anger stabbed like a hot poker in his skull with each excruciating step he took up to the small, narrow landing.

The back entrance was nothing more than a tall window, conveniently located to ensure private entry or a quick getaway for her married patrons. Grady leaned against the cold panes of glass and waited for his head to stop reeling. Murmured voices greeted his arrival, one gruff and masculine, the other softly trilling. He ignored the pounding in his head and listened.

"I haven't seen him, sugar. Sure you can't stay awhile?"

"Another time," the deeper voice answered. "You give me a holler if you see him."

"I'll give you a holler, all right," she replied with practiced seduction. "I'll holler good and loud."

Her voice set Grady's teeth on edge and he waited

while Lou Ellen tried her wiles on the man one last time before booted footsteps and the click of the door latch told him her charms had failed. He reached up and rattled the glass.

Lou Ellen parted the curtains and jerked back in fright at the sight of Grady's filth-streaked face smashed against the window pane.

Throwing a look over her shoulder, she turned back and threw the window open. "Lord, you gave me a scare!"

Grady ignored her breathless affectation and made his way painfully into the room and over to her bed. Wincing, he nodded at the door. "He looking for me?"

"Maybe," she replied cattily. She gave Grady a sweeping glance. "You tangle up with a rock slide?"

Grady sent her a spiteful glare. "Get me some water for washing."

As soon as she brought the basin over, he grabbed her wrist in a crushing warning. "Careful, now," he said softly between his teeth. "You wash it real careful like, then forget you saw me here."

Frost entered Lou Ellen's eyes. "Sure thing, darlin'."

Seething, she gently bathed away blood and dirt from a lump on the back of his head, then poured him a glass of whiskey. "You gonna tell me what's going on?"

Grady fished in his pocket and tossed a wad of bills at her feet. "One whole day. Shut up."

Lou Ellen scooped up the money and placed it in a carved wooden box on her vanity. Rubbing her abused wrist gingerly, she said nicely, "Whatever you say, Grady."

Jake Holdman blushed three shades of red when the prettiest and most expensive whore in Laramie walked right into his office, planted her hands on his desk, leaned over so that her bosom almost spilled out of her gown, and smiled.

"Mornin', Sheriff."

"Miss Lou Ellen." He bit back a reprimand for the young deputy clearing his throat by the file cabinet. Zeke's foreman had come banging on his door before dawn with the wildest tale he'd heard in years and he was not in the mood to banter banalities with Laramie's best soiled dove. He knew Lou Ellen just about every way a man could know a woman and found it exceedingly uncomfortable to have her waltz in his office in broad daylight and smile at him like he was a candy stick ready for licking. "What can I do for you?"

The deputy's cough intensified and Jake sent the young man a look that would light kindling. "You got something to do, Billy?"

The deputy grinned like a Cheshire cat. "No, sir." Billy's job didn't pay enough for him to personally enjoy Miss Lou Ellen's lily-white thighs but he wasn't above enjoying a vicarious thrill at the sheriff's expense.

Jake leaned his palms on the top of his scarred wooden desk and rose to his feet. "You sure?"

Billy swallowed at the look on the sheriff's face. "Yes, sir. I mean, no, sir." He grabbed his hat and gunbelt on the way out.

As soon as the door closed, Jake sat back down. "You need something, Lou Ellen?"

She resisted the obvious sexual response. The sheriff didn't look like he was in the mood for teasing. "You looking for Grady Smith?"

"You know where he is?"

"That depends," she said coyly. "Is there a reward for him?"

Anger narrowed Jake's eyes but he kept his voice level. "No bounty, if that's what you mean."

Lou Ellen let her irritation show for one small second, then became businesslike again. "What's he done?"

"Nothing I can pin on him. Yet."

A string of filth flitted through her mind but never reached her mouth. The sheriff might like a little nasty talk in the bedroom, but she didn't think he'd appreciate it in his office. She tugged at the cuff of the most proper dress she owned and smoothed a scrap of lace over her bruised wrist. She was done with Grady Smith and had hoped to turn him over for a reward, but she couldn't afford to confide his whereabouts if nothing legal could be done.

"If I know where he is—and I'm not saying I do— what's in it for me?"

"Dammit, Lou Ellen—"

"Now, Sheriff," she cajoled sweetly. "A girl's gotta eat." She ran her tongue deliciously over her top lip. "Know what I mean?"

Jake knew and it made him squirm. "I can't afford you anymore, Lou Ellen."

Her eyes flashed with bawdy humor. "Not much since your sister-in-law moved in with you." She ignored the warning flush on his face. "What a burden."

Jake lunged to his feet. "You leave Sarah out of this. Do you know where Grady is or don't you?"

Lou Ellen's eyes blazed right back at his. "If you don't have anything on him, what difference does it make? A girl's got to protect herself, Sheriff. She can't be spewing the whereabouts of innocent men."

"He's about as innocent as a sidewinder and you know it." When she only cocked her pretty head and smiled again, Jake slammed back into his chair. "I need to know where he is. That's all I can tell you."

Lou Ellen strolled casually around his office, then stopped at the window and stared out at the busy, mud-rutted street. "Zeke Claiborne's foreman came knocking on my door at the crack of dawn looking for Grady." She looked back over her shoulder, arching a delicate eyebrow in inquiry. "Now, seeing as Zeke's new wife is Grady's former sister-in-law, I'd say we have a nice mystery here."

Jake felt his irritation recede to intelligent caution. "This has nothing to do with Addie," he lied evenly. "Zeke thinks Grady might be behind some cattle rustling. You know anything about that?"

Lou Ellen pressed a slender, gloved hand to her temple. The paper she'd found in Grady's pocket had turned out to be the name and address of a man in New Orleans, powerful in the sale of contraband. She couldn't see what he had to do with cattle rustling. Antagonizing the law wasn't something she could afford to do in any circumstance, but especially Jake. He was easy on the eyes and amiable in bed, but that didn't mean she could afford to give up Grady's money just to stay in Jake's good graces.

"I'm sorry, Sheriff." Her eyes lifted in genuine regret. "When you've got something more concrete, let me know."

Jake narrowed his eyes at the front door and said tiredly, "Good day, Miz Mullins. I've got work to do."

A fire blazed, sending sparks and heat shooting high to mingle with the ashes floating up with the breeze. Zeke tossed another painting onto the bonfire and heard the telltale catch in Addie's throat.

"Don't look," he said gently, hurting for her, for the years of time and energy and talent she had invested in each illegal canvas. It was nothing less than a desecration to demolish the artwork, an abomination. His fist tightened on another frame. With each toss, he felt as if he were throwing Addie herself into the fire. But they both knew it had to be done. "Go back inside. I'll take care of this."

"No, I need to stay," she said with fierce determination. But she couldn't watch as Zeke raised the Rubens and flung it into the heap. It was her favorite. The violent brush strokes had been a catharsis for the rage smoldering inside her two years ago, her only escape from an unbearable life. She forced herself to look back as the flames took hold, melting the painting in upon itself until there was nothing left but a charred frame and cinders that billowed high to stain the crisp morning sky.

One by one, they followed and she watched, hollow-eyed, her face tense with the strain. By the time the last painting met its fate, she didn't even flinch. She was dead inside, the pain gone, the regrets nothing but a memory. She turned to walk back to the house, but Zeke grabbed her arm. Dull-eyed, she looked up at him and found no accomplishment in his expression. Instead, remorse lined his face.

"You can do more," he said roughly. "Only the work was destroyed, not the talent."

A tiny spark flickered within her, the first stirring of life, an infinitesimal gathering that grew and expanded and finally burst through her in hot waves. Like the flames dying to ash, her soul felt seared, burned down to nothing, but purged.

Free. She was finally free. Her hand went to her

mouth to keep from crying out as tears spilled down her cheeks, cleansing, renewing. She felt reborn.

Stricken, Zeke pulled her to his chest, his arms a comforting crush around her. He couldn't bear the pain in her eyes, the agony she held inside. "Please, go back inside!"

She shook her head and held him as hard as he held her. "I'm free," she wept joyfully into his shirt. "Don't you see? I'm finally free."

Zeke stared at the dying flames. *Not yet, Addie. Not yet.*

"We didn't find him, boss," Granger said, stomping his feet at the back door to rid them of melting snow.

Sunlight poured in, as warm as the relief flooding Addie at his words. But after a brief moment the fear took hold again. She clutched Zeke's hand when the sheriff followed Granger inside.

"You're one dangerous woman to be around," Jake said with a shake of his head. He shrugged out of his coat and pulled the gloves from his hands. His eyes went to Zeke and all rough teasing left his voice. "He's not dead, at least not at the Smith house. The storm blew over as fast as it hit, so it's not likely he's frozen solid somewhere, just lying low until he gets his strength back." He looked at Addie. "We can't get him for attempting to sell forgeries without implicating you, so that's out. We can't get him for cattle rustling either without proof."

Addie closed her eyes. "What should we do?"

"The question is, what will Grady do next?"

Her eyes flew open; her voice was unequivocal. "Try to get back at me, make me pay."

Her words shot through Zeke like gunfire. "Like

hell," he said lowly, dangerously. His arm slid around her shoulder, but he faced the sheriff. "What next?"

Jake shrugged. "Can't arrest him for something I can't prove. If we're lucky, he's high-tailed it out of town."

"No." Addie's voice was flat and so very certain. She looked at each of the men in her kitchen, and saw not their rough exteriors and unsmiling faces, but their inner strength and intelligence. She could hardly believe the goodness the Lord had bestowed upon her. Despite everything she had done, they were standing by her. She swallowed painfully and looked up at Zeke. "Even if Grady is gone, he'll be back."

She wasn't left alone for one second. As welcome as the protection was, Addie felt stifled by the constant restriction. By the end of the first month, she and the boys had cabin fever from being cooped up inside. Nearing the end of the second her nerves were jangled and edgy.

She didn't trust Grady not to steal into her home during the night, so she and Zeke put the boys to bed in their own room. Though she took comfort in knowing the children were protected, there wasn't the relief of losing herself in Zeke. Under the cloak of darkness and the quilt covering their bed, he would touch her and she could feel the wanting in his hands. The neediness would grip her as well but there was nothing they could do with the boys so close.

Sometimes he made her laugh to ease the tension. Like a thief, his hands would steal over her in the most daring places until she was giggling and grabbing at him to make him stop. But at other times, her breath would catch and there would be no laughter strong enough to cover the hungry wanting.

Addie knew they couldn't go on like this. The boys were fractious, feeling punished for things they didn't do or understand. The weather had warmed up and would have been a perfect foil for their restlessness, but it was too dangerous for them to be outside for any extended period of time. Spring roundup was only weeks away and Zeke prowled the house like a caged beast, feeling powerless and overstrung with pent up energy.

They had left the pile of charred canvas in the yard, so Grady would know the paintings were destroyed, but Addie had little hope that he wouldn't find a way to get back at her. Through the boys, through Zeke, Grady would find some way to make her pay for ruining his scheme.

"Outside!"

The baby's pleas had grown demanding. Addie looked over at Zeke but he only shook his head and scooped up Cole to occupy him while she finished the breakfast dishes. Leaning against the sink, she swirled the cloth listlessly over the last plate.

"We can't go on like this, Zeke."

He ignored the comment. He felt it all too well in the strain and worry of wondering when Grady would strike and at whom. Granger and his men patrolled the range by day and bedded down near the cattle at night to protect the ranch, while he stayed inside with Addie and his sons. The inactivity grated on his frayed nerves and he had to fight the lassitude that came with extended waiting. It was too easy to think that nothing would occur, just because nothing had. Easy and dangerous.

Addie finished the dishes and dried her hands on her apron. "We're out of flour."

"I'll send Scrapper—" At her pleading look, Zeke relented. "Get your coat. We'll be safe enough in town."

Parker's General Store was crowded when the Claiborne family filed out of the wagon. For once Addie was grateful for the numerous questions and comments of the townfolk. She didn't think Grady would attempt anything with a horde of people present. She stood with the boys and watched the ongoing battle between Ian and Nathaniel at the checkerboard. When their language turned ribald, she steered her sons off toward other amusements.

"I'll get the flour," Zeke said. Cole stretched his arms out and Zeke took him. "Let the boys pick out something new to occupy them."

Addie nodded. "We'll be by the school books," she said, and motioned the boys toward the next aisle. She handed a set of painted blocks to Zeb, and smiled when he plopped right down in the aisle to play with them. Picking up a McGuffey's Reader, she thumbed through the pages, then turned to show it to Josh.

"See? You're ready for this—" She steeled the sudden panic at his disappearance and forced herself to walk calmly to the end of the aisle where Josh was hunched over several crates, admiring the new boots that hadn't been put on display yet. Renewed hatred for Grady burned through her at the constant fear and anxiety of waiting and wondering when he would strike. She forced a cheerful smile and held up the reader. "See, Josh?"

When Josh lifted his head to look at her, she knew the waiting had come to an end. "Ma," he whimpered.

Strangely, she saw the gun first, the cold metallic gleam of a barrel pressed to the base of Josh's skull. Grady was crouched behind another crate and had him by the back of his coat.

"Let him go," Addie said calmly, while panic rolled through her in debilitating waves. "You don't want him, you want me," she added. "He's just a child. Let him go."

Grady's smile flashed wickedly. "C'mon, Addie. We're gonna take a little ride."

She couldn't afford to rile him but neither could she docilely meet his demands. "Let him go first, Grady. You won't shoot with a whole store full of people to hear you."

"No?" Grady gripped Josh's coat tighter and pulled back, cutting off the child's air. "You're right." Josh made a mewing sound and clawed at his throat, his eyes flaring in alarm as he arched his head back instinctively, trying to breathe.

Addie stepped forward, rising hysteria in her voice. "Stop it!" she rasped. "For God's sake, Grady—"

His hand twisted cruelly, then relaxed enough for Josh to take a shallow breath. "Let's go out back, Addie."

Frantic, she glanced behind her. Zeb still sat in the middle of the aisle, stacking blocks. Zeke was nowhere in sight. She turned back to Grady, her voice pleading. "What good will it do you? The paintings are gone—"

"You'll do more," he said viciously, and for the first time Addie saw the undiluted terror in his eyes.

Her trembling hand rose to her throat. "Oh, Lord, Grady. What have you done?"

He smiled grimly as he rose to his feet, hauling Josh up with him. "I've already accepted money, a down payment." He inched toward the back entrance, dragging Josh with him. "They are very powerful men, Addie. If I don't deliver—"

He didn't need to finish the statement. Addie could see by the fear on his face that there was no question of him defaulting on the illegal agreement.

Anger rose with the bile in her throat at his unthinkable ignorance. "You fool!" she gasped, almost stalking him step for step out the back entrance. "It took me years to do those paintings! Do you think I can just turn them out again in a matter of days?"

His eyes narrowed as he backed into the sunlight and scanned the alley. "Just one at a time. I'll turn them in one at a time. It'll keep them satisfied."

He was sweating profusely as he edged toward his horse, his movements jerky, telling. Calm swept through Addie and was reflected in the tone of her voice. "You can't take both of us," she said, pointing to his lone gelding. "Let Josh go, or I'll stand here until Zeke comes looking for us."

With a vile curse, he flung Josh aside and pointed the gun at the child's face. "You move and I'll blow your skull open." He grabbed Addie's arm and shoved her roughly toward the horse. "Get up." Addie caught the saddle to steady herself but made no effort to mount. The gun barrel jabbed into the small of her back, as his words hissed out. "Get up!"

She could hear Josh whimpering behind her and stalled for time, her mind spinning frantically over options. As long as the gun was pointed at her, as long as she kept Grady's full attention, Josh was safe. The weapon stabbed into her back again and she sagged against the horse. "I can't."

Grady's voice screeched in her ear. "You stupid, bitch. Get up!"

Four years sped through her mind with clarity, the sum total of them collected for just this moment. She turned slowly then, smiling into his panic-stricken face. "Are you afraid, Grady? Is your stomach tied in knots so you feel like you could retch? Do your knees feel like they've turned to jelly?" She never once took her eyes off Grady's explosive face, even when she detected Josh's movement in her peripheral vision. The horse shifted restlessly behind her, but she remained stalwart. "How does it feel, Grady, to be manipulated by someone stronger, someone more powerful?" Her eyes narrowed, the resentment of four years blazing from the emerald depths. "How does it feel to have your will and self-worth stolen?"

He brought the gun to her face and laid the barrel along her cheek, but his hands were shaking. "Shut up and mount the horse or I'll blow your stinkin' face off."

Her smile was soft and sweetly victorious. "Then you lose. Who'll do your dirty work then, Grady? If you murder me, you have nothing."

His face blackened with rage for a brief second, then with a demented smile, he lifted the butt of the gun and slammed it against her skull.

20

The first shot caught Grady in the upper arm. With a roar of pain he spun around to find the second shot aimed at his chest.

"Drop your gun," Jake said softly. "Real slow and easy."

Lou Ellen stood just behind the sheriff, a satisfied grin on her face. She just loved the look of a lawman with a gun.

Blood seeped through Grady's fingers as he pressed his left hand over the wound. "I need the doc," he said, rage blurring his vision as he stared back at the sheriff. "You gonna let me bleed to death?"

"Yep," Jake said. "Drop the gun."

Grady's eyes lit with cunning as he slowly relaxed his arm as if he might obey and lowered the pistol.

Zeke's breath snared in his throat when he stepped from Parker's General Store and caught sight of Addie crumpled on the ground, blood oozing from a gash in her temple. Grady had a gun pointed straight at her head.

"Ma!" Josh cried out, and lunged forward.

Zeke caught him around the waist and pushed him back inside the store, then stepped slowly forward.

Grady's head whipped around. "That's close enough, Claiborne!" He had a trapped rasp to his voice and a panicky look in his eyes, but his revolver remained steady and aimed at his hostage.

Zeke stopped dead still and let his arms hang loosely, nonthreateningly, by his thighs. His eyes were cool and unreadable. Nothing in his face or manner showed how crazed he felt inside, how deranged at seeing Addie on the ground. She was so small and unprotected, one side of her face pressed into the dirt, the other bleeding. The stench of slops and manure drifted on the breeze. Zeke's stomach coiled into a hard knot of rage but he managed to keep his voice even. "You need medical attention, Grady, and so does Addie."

Grady cut his eyes warily in all directions. He had to think, had to plan. It should have been a simple abduction but everything was going wrong. His arm throbbed, and the blood between his fingers was growing sticky. "Someone get the doc!" When no one moved, he sent his frantic gaze to Lou Ellen. "Go find him, Lou."

"Sure thing, Grady," she said calmly, wondering what the sheriff wanted her to do. Jake gave her a clipped nod, but Christian had already heard the gunfire from his office two doors down and had grabbed his medical bag and headed cautiously into the alley. The sound of gunshots was common in Laramie and he knew better than to risk being caught in the crossfire.

Taking in the situation, Christian stopped well behind Grady Smith, who was pointing a gun at a small, inert form on the ground. Jake was on the other side, his pistol raised. Zeke was off to the right. Christian searched the sheriff's eyes, then caught Zeke's warning stare and realized the woman on the ground was Addie. He nodded slowly at Zeke, then at Jake and pulled a derringer from his pocket. They had Grady surrounded.

The dust beneath their feet wasn't the rich dark delta soil of a cotton field. Their clothes weren't standard Confederate gray. The enemy they faced was only one man. But the three had been in similar situations a dozen times, it seemed, in as many different battles. Though Zeke and Christian had only carried firearms for personal protection during the war, they had faced many injured men, demented with pain or hatred. They knew the routine.

His derringer pointing at Grady's chest, Christian said in a raised voice, "Somebody call for a doctor?"

The second Grady's head swiveled around, Zeke dropped to his knee and drew his own gun. Lou Ellen dove for the ground. Grady sensed the subtle shift in the air a half second before he saw—not the doctor's compassionate face—but Christian's derringer leveled at his chest. His own gun lifted automatically, one second too soon to anticipate the trap. He heard the deadly click of a pistol hammer to his left. With a bellow of rage, he swung his own weapon around at Zeke and fired.

Only Zeke's aim was true.

Grady's body was thrown back against the horse, a look of disbelief frozen on his face. His gaze dropped to his chest to find a wet stain spreading. He tried to touch it, to stop the lifeblood from flowing out of his body, but he couldn't raise his arm. His fingers twitched on the pistol still gripped in his right hand, but numbness was spreading down through his extremities and he couldn't seem to feel anything but a faint buzzing in his head and mild annoyance. He looked down at Addie, blaming her, needing to make her pay. His hand flexed, his determination greater than his physical limitations. Time was captured for one eerie second in a tight fist as he lifted his gun, then released it slowly as he buckled to his knees and toppled forward.

The air left Zeke's body and he lunged forward and rolled the dead man off Addie, then pulled her into his arms. She was limp and pale, the side of her face smeared with fresh blood. Josh crept to his father's side, his eyes stark and revealing. "Pa?"

"She'll be all right," Zeke said, but uncertainty lay heavy in his tone and even heavier inside him. Her color was bad, her breathing shallow. His hand trembled as he pushed the matted hair from her temple to find the gash swelling grotesquely and still seeping blood. He lifted his eyes to find Jake dragging Grady's body away and Christian looming beside him.

"She needs a few stitches." Zeke winced at his own words. They sounded far away and much too prosaic, like declaring he was out of milk or the eggs needed gathering.

Christian nodded once. "Get her over to the office."

Zeke lifted Addie gently, and just stood, feeling like he'd stepped into a fog. Fear, he discovered, had texture and substance. Its thickness surrounded and suffocated him, he couldn't find his bearings. There was something he must do but he couldn't think what. It came to him suddenly, and he looked around frantically for his sons.

"I've got the boys," Beatrice called from the back of the store. "Go on."

The steps to Christian's office were the longest of Zeke's life. He felt each one like an uphill battle that tore strips of his heart away in payment for the next footfall. Addie lay like a ragdoll in his arms, her face blood-streaked and ashen. He didn't know how long she had been on the ground before Josh hauled him into the alley.

He crossed the threshold into the doctor's office and paused, hurting for Addie, not knowing what he would do if Christian couldn't help her. His thoughts were messy and disoriented, completely unacceptable for the profession he had once sought, but he couldn't think what he was supposed to do for his wife except hold her. Christian lit the lamps and pulled back the draperies to add more light to the room, then nodded at the examining table. Zeke carefully placed Addie there, and smoothed her hair back from her face, but his hands were shaking so badly.

Christian put a pan of water at the head of the table and handed Zeke a cloth. "You've done this a hundred times," he said levelly, then leaned over to lift each of Addie's eyelids in turn. "Out cold. Let's get this over with before she wakes up."

Addie moaned at the hands poking and prodding the various places on her body. "Bruises, nothing broken . . . doesn't appear to have fallen far . . ." The words filtered through the pounding in her head, becoming a painful countertempo to the steady throbbing. Nausea roiled in her stomach and made a bitter taste in her mouth. The effort to open her eyes sent agony stabbing through her skull and she groaned and tossed fretfully.

Cool hands touched her cheeks and soothing words drifted just above her consciousness. She desperately wanted to sleep but couldn't reconcile the pain in her head and tried to focus on the reason for it. Images swam through her mind, but they were swift and jumpy, like thumbing too hurriedly through a picture book. A picture book . . . a picture book . . .

"Josh!" she cried suddenly, and a thousand hammers pounded in her head.

"He's fine. Don't try to talk."

Zeke's voice. She was so grateful she calmed a bit. She wanted to cry but she didn't know where Grady was and she needed to warn Zeke to be careful. She moved restlessly, fighting the terrible darkness encasing her. "Grady . . ."

"He can't hurt you anymore, Addie."

Zeke's voice soothed her again, but she couldn't collect her thoughts enough to make him understand. Her mind was fuzzy, her head hurting so badly she only wanted to drift back into the unconscious. She could feel his warm hand in hers, stroking, comforting, but she needed to help, to protect her family. She forced her eyes open and the room spun in sickening whirls. Moaning, she rolled to her side, but her way was blocked by strong hands.

"Lie still."

"I feel sick."

"Concussion," Christian stated, and shoved a pan into Zeke's hands just in case. He leaned over and lifted her eyelids again. "Looks better. She'll pull through."

The two men exchanged knowing glances, and Zeke mouthed silently, "The baby?"

Christian shrugged. "There are no absolutes. You'll know in about seven months."

Addie sat in the steaming bath, her head tilted back on the edge. The murmur of the children's voices as they bade Zeke good night was like a balm to her soul. She touched her cheek where Josh had kissed her every night since the ordeal with Grady and shyly murmured, " 'Night, Ma." The words might be few but they were sweet and poignant, so meaningful coming from Josh she could hardly contain the fullness of them. She ran the bath cloth gingerly over her face. Her head was still bruised and tender, but Zeke had removed the stitches this morning and already she felt stronger. Less than a week had passed since the incident with Grady, but she felt like a lifetime had slipped away in five short days. Her old life, so ill spent in fear and degradation, had passed on.

So would she. Never again would she go back or willingly allow the tortured memories to intrude on her new life. If at times they caught her unaware, she had only to remember the look on Zeke's face as he held her through the first painful night, while her head throbbed and her stomach acted up unbearably.

She smiled softly, secretly. He had a look about him these days. She wasn't sure what yet, not certain enough to call it love. But there was hope within her, deep and abiding and unshakable. If he didn't recognize the emotion within him yet, there was time. A whole future awaited them for Zeke to realize that he couldn't go back either.

She shivered as the water cooled and gooseflesh prickled her skin. She rose from the bath and reached for a towel only to find it missing. Pink tinted her cheeks as she looked up to see Zeke, his eyes hot amber in the lantern light, holding it up for her. She dropped her gaze, self-conscious but smiling. "How long have you been standing there?"

He said nothing as he enfolded her in the towel and helped her step over the rim of the tub, then began drying her with a brisk efficiency that changed slowly to lingering strokes. Once done, he dropped the towel to the floor and pulled her into his arms.

"How do you feel?" he asked against her hair.

"New," she whispered. "Alive."

He knew the word intimately and all its variations. Alive, awake, aware. His callused fingers swept her back, then curled around to spread over her abdomen, startling a small gasp from her. "When were you going to tell me about the baby?"

She looked up at him with a silly, confused expression that slowly faded to shock. The color left her face as she whispered, "I wasn't certain."

Zeke's eyebrow lifted in wonder. "You didn't know." At her grave look, he smiled. "I thought you were keeping it from me."

"No." She swallowed, wanting to weep and rejoice at the same time. "I'm sorry . . ." Her eyes suddenly grew fierce. "No, I'm not! I'm not sorry at all. I want this baby, Zeke. I just feel bad that you—"

"Hush, Addie," he said before he kissed her once, hard.

Her arms flew around his shoulders and she clung to him with all the joy and misgivings in her heart. Safe within the circle of his arms, she wouldn't have to see the disappointment on his face, nor burden him with the undiluted gladness on her own. But he tipped her chin up, his eyes languorous and unrevealing. His mouth lowered and devoured her, bold and reckless kisses that made her melt from tip to toe until her legs were nothing and she was flowing into him. He swept her up, then crossed to the bed, following her down onto the mattress.

"Zeke, wait," she said, breathless beneath his searching lips and hands.

"I don't want to wait." He covered her, fitting his

body to hers with such perfection she wondered how they had ever shared this bed yet remained separate.

She took his face in her hands, her eyes pleading and demanding. "You can't ignore this—"

"Addie," he said, smiling down into her warm emerald eyes. "I'm not going to ignore one single inch." His lips touched hers lightly. "It's the right thing to do. When two people make love, they make life." His body flowed into hers and she arched against him on an indrawn breath, her whole being flooded with marvel and enchantment. "I love you, Addie," he whispered gruffly. "Love me back."

She cried out and unraveled around him, her being rent by the force of his words, the utter wonderment. "I do, I will," she gasped, then begged, "Say it again."

"I love you," he repeated, and joined with her deeper, closer, until he couldn't tell their flesh apart. He spoke the words again and again, making up for all the days and nights in his lonely life that he'd not been able to. And she spoke the words back for the same reason. They moved as one, graceful and blessed by the one emotion they had run so hard and fast from that they had finally come full circle and caught each other.

Epilogue

It was talked about for years. About how the doc, a man who was supposed to heal the sick and patch up the injured, had taken part in a shooting. Even if he hadn't pulled the trigger himself, he'd stood by and watched Zeke do it, and so had the sheriff. Of course, that no-good Smith fellow had knocked Miz Addie out—no one ever did find out why—and was pointing a gun right at her head. Everyone agreed you just couldn't have such goings on in a decent, God-fearing town.

Funny thing about Miz Addie, how she seemed to perk up after that terrible day. She carried herself like a woman who knew her mind and could state her piece at a town meeting with the best of them. And hadn't she done some pretty pictures! One hung right in the town hall. Of course, everyone knew Miz Addie had talent. They didn't need the say-so of that fancy-dressed gent from Chicago who had come out on the train to talk to her about an exhibition at his museum.

There were those who still thought Miz Addie peculiar. The men didn't quite understand how her husband put up with all the woman's suffrage meetings she held right there in their home, but of course, that was Zeke's business. Theirs was making sure they kept things well stocked for the Claibornes' growing family.

Addie had given Zeke three baby girls in twice as many years, and folks thought it dandy the way Zeke had built that big house to accommodate all those young 'uns. Seeing the Claibornes file into church on Sundays, smiling, each of the boys holding the hand of a baby sister, well, it was enough to make a man want to forgive Miz Addie for stirring up the womenfolk from time to time, so a man never knew if he was getting a hot supper or a cold shoulder when he got home.

Some said Miz Addie sure had changed, but others claimed she'd only emerged. Like a butterfly in a cocoon, she'd just been waiting for her chance to come forth. The whole town seemed to be struck with the same sort of metamorphosis. Sarah Holdman up and married her brother-in-law Jake, claiming she only did it so she wouldn't have to change her name again, but no one believed her. They could see the way she smiled at him. Doc Lafleur hadn't lost much of his bitterness, but at least he and Zeke were on speaking terms again. Beatrice Parker asked Zeke about it one day, but he just gave her a bland smile, then turned to Addie and notched his hand tightly around her thickening waist. When the couple walked away, Zeke was heard to whisper the strangest thing.

"We've got to be more careful after this one."

To which Miz Addie only smiled and answered, "You say that every time."

Folks agreed they liked hearing Zeke laugh again.

Experience the Passion and the Ecstasy

Meagan McKinney

☐ 16412-5 No Choice But Surrender $4.99

☐ 20301-5 My Wicked Enchantress $4.99

☐ 20521-2 When Angels Fall $4.99

☐ 20870-X Till Dawn Tames the Night $4.99

☐ 21230-8 Lions and Lace $4.99

At your local bookstore or use this handy page for ordering:

DELL READERS SERVICE, DEPT. DFH
2451 S. Wolf Rd., Des Plaines, IL . 60018

Please send me the above title(s). I am enclosing $_____.
(Please add $2.50 per order to cover shipping and handling.) Send check or money order—no cash or C.O.D.s please.

Ms./Mrs./Mr._____

Address _____

City/State _____ Zip _____

DFH - 1/93

Prices and availability subject to change without notice. Please allow four to six weeks for delivery.

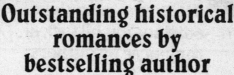